DESIRE'S PROMISE

"I'm asking you to marry me," Corbin blurted, surprised by his own statement.

"I—I can't leave Wade. Not yet."

"I see."

"No, you don't see. You can't possibly understand."

"Yes, I do. You're young, Jessie, and you want your freedom. While you enjoy having me for a lover, you're not too anxious to have me for a husband."

"Corbin, I just need time. We'll be together by spring. Everything should be settled by then."

"Maybe, but I'm holding you to that promise." He reached out for her. "Come here, you little minx." He kissed her long and hard, his lips exploring the sweetness of her mouth.

She was breathless when at last she pulled away and ran her hands across his broad, muscular chest. How could she ever let this man go? How would she ever survive until spring without him? She would have to, she thought as she pulled him to her, wanting to kiss him once more, for the memory of it would have to last her a long, long time. . . .

ENDLESS ECSTASY

Kathryn Hockett

ZEBRA BOOKS
KENSINGTON PUBLISHING CORP.

ZEBRA BOOKS

are published by

Kensington Publishing Corp.
475 Park Avenue South
New York, NY 10016

First printing: November, 1989

Printed in the United States of America

To my two children, who have been an inspiration to me and made my life so beautiful.

And, again, to Lydia Paglio, who is much more than an editor. She is a good friend who takes time to listen and to care — a teacher guiding me in my craft. A very special lady.

Author's Note

During the days of the "Wild West," outlaws were often glorified by newspapers, pamphlets, Wild West shows or dime novels. They were feared, yet idolized. In folklore, America bandits were likened to Robin Hood. America offered a tremendous wilderness for escape and hiding—the most famous being the "Outlaw Trail" stretching from Canada, through Montana, Wyoming, Colorado, Utah, Arizona, New Mexico and finally into Mexico. "Butch" Cassidy and the Sundance Kid were leaders of the "Wild Bunch," the biggest, most colorful and last of the western gangs. Their story is of particular interest to me, having lived for a time in Utah and Wyoming.

There was a human side to the outlaws. Indeed, Butch Cassidy made it a lifelong point to avoid needless violence. He shot at the horses, never at the riders, when being pursued by a posse. He once said quite truthfully that he had never killed a man. He and his gang were in fact very democratic in the way they asked members' advice on projects. Even the wanted posters described Cassidy as cheery and affable.

Pinkerton men were always on the gang's trail, for it was a constant thorn in the side of many lawmen, bankers, and railroad moguls. As a matter of fact, the Union Pacific considered a businesslike approach to the problem of the gang's venture into train robberies by offering to buy Cassidy with a pardon and a position as an express guard at a good salary. He chose to go to South America instead.

The Wild Bunch was started after a series of devastating calamaties shook Wyoming. A terrible drought struck the territory, killing entire herds. Companies that had once employed hundreds of cowboys now sent them packing and those who were jobless turned to cattle rustling. The rustlers built cabins and corrals and established strongholds along the Outlaw Trail. Three of the hideouts were "Hole-in-the-Wall" in Wyoming, Brown's Park just over the Colorado line in Utah, and "Robbers Roost" further south in Utah.

It was to Brown's Park that a young, parentless girl was taken to be raised among the outlaws. Fearless, feisty, she must face the greatest test of all when she falls in love with a man out to avenge his brother's death — a man who takes a job as deputy and is dedicated to ridding the West of outlaws.

Part One:
Flower In A Weed Patch

Brown's Park, Utah
1896

A weed is no more than a flower in disguise,
Which is seen through at once, if love give a man eyes.
— J.R. Lowell, *A Fable for Critics*

Chapter One

The mid-morning sun cast the old wooden wagon's shadow across the dirt-packed road as Jessica Watson guided the horses toward Rye Grass Station. It would be a rough journey through Brown's Park Valley surrounded by the Diamond Mountain, Douglas Mountain and Owi-ya-kuts Plateau. The road was flat and wide but nonetheless rocky and bumpy, an area where the Green River flowed down through a valley with ranches scattered hither and yon. Brown's Park Valley was in Utah and Colorado and just down a bit from the Wyoming line, giving good access to all three states. There were two other outlaw hide-aways — Robbers Roost further south in Utah and Hole-in-the-Wall just over the Wyoming line — but for now, Jessica called the Brown's Park area home.

Glancing up at the vivid blue sky, she whipped the horses into a faster gallop. She was determined to hurry with her errands so that she could return to camp at the head of Crouse Canyon before it got any hotter. Though September was usually a time when the weather made the transition between the fading glow of summer and the severe cold of winter, today it seemed unseasonably hot. Scorching. The shrubs and other foliage were shrouded in muted tones of brown and graying yellows. Bluish gray- and beige-colored mountain peaks rose majestically above the skyline, but only a few were still snow-capped.

"Dag nam it. She swore aloud, echoing a phrase often used by her friends. "Why am I always the one who has to ride in for supplies?" There were times when being a female could be a definite disadvantage, all right. Even so, she was proud to be a member of the infamous "Wild Bunch." Butch Cassidy was her hero, and if he wanted her to bring back the bacon, grits, and coffee she supposed it was the least she could do for him in return. It was just that she wanted to spend her time in more exciting ways, to have the whole town talking about her the way they did the other gang members.

One day soon she would convince the "boys" to take her seriously, and then she would be right beside them when they rode to intercept the trains. Someday, that was, when she proved to them that she wasn't still the orphan "kid" they'd taken in. Orphan, she thought grimly to herself. Well, not any more she wasn't.

Jessica had lost her parents in a tornado, out along Kansas way. At first her Aunt Agatha had given her a home, had fed and clothed her. Everything might have gone smoothly, she might even have grown to admire the elaborately dressed and coiffeured woman, if George Emming had not come upon the scene. Wooing her aunt, he had nonetheless expounded his loathing for children and made it a prerequisite to their wedding that other arrangements be made for nine-year-old Jessica. George, of course, got his way. Jessica's suitcases had been packed and she had been put aboard a train headed for Salt Lake City. There, she was to make her home with a distant cousin. Instead, she had wandered the streets of an unfamiliar city when it was learned her cousin was nowhere to be found. Jessica often wondered if Aunt Agatha had even checked it out.

After sleeping in doorways and grubbing for food for several days, Jessica was certain that the end of the world was in sight. Just as she was at wits' end, she had met Wade Slatter walking the board sidewalks, seemingly as lost and lonely as she. Wade, a one-time cowboy, had lost his wife and son to scarlet fever and taken up a life of cattle rustling to sustain his whiskey habit. Jessica gave him another purpose in life, as an adoptive "father." Their relationship became a perfect one of give-and-take, mutual respect and a true closeness. As she had grown older, she discovered his need to be needed and Wade found that he could give Jesse the caring affection that had so long been missing from her life.

Jessica supposed that clouds did have a silver lining when all was said and done. Certainly the cloud that enveloped her new-made family did. Though genuinely guilty of taking a few cattle, Wade was accused of killing a man, a crime he most definitely was innocent of. He was sentenced to hang by a biased jury and would have, if not for Butch Cassidy. Hearing of the cowboy's plight, he and Kid Curry had braved the town's wrath to save her foster father, then taken both of them to his hideaway. Now Wade Slatter was a member of the Wild Bunch and Jessie their adopted mascot. She was jokingly referred to as a "flower in a weed patch," but Jessie was determined to prove herself just as strong and capable as any of the men.

Now that she was nearly eighteen, she did her share and carried her own weight. She rustled and branded nearby cattle, broke and fed horses, but couldn't go on raids yet because she was still just a horse wrangler.

Wade told her that when she was just a child, she used to chatter away like a chipmunk, ask a lot of questions, and more or less just get in the way. But after the gang took in another orphan, Billy Morris, just a year older than Jessie, the two put their heads together to figure out how to be useful. Soon they were helping with branding, riding after cattle, cutting hay and trailing along over the "Outlaw Trail" after Butch Cassidy and the Wild Bunch.

A few years back during the winter months, when things were slow, she and Billy used to ride down Sears Canyon together to attend a small, one-room school. It was there that Jessie had furthered the schooling begun by her mother before she had died. Always one to want to be the "best," Jessie had proven herself to be the top reader in the class. She'd surpassed all the other children in that skill, giving up the simple stories for those of the kind into which she could really sink her teeth. The classics, the teacher had called them. Hell, she'd even taught some of Butch's boys to read, when she could manage the patience, that was.

Jessie smiled to herself as she thought of how the other kids had been so astonished at her daredevil ways. She could jump off a horse's rear and then on again while riding bareback, or spin a rope while standing on the horse's back and galloping at full speed. She remembered how she had often grumbled when Wade insisted that she finish her homework, even if it be by kerosene lamplight. He'd wanted her to have some learning, at least. Though Jessie loved reading, she was nonetheless relieved when she no longer had to attend school. Somehow she just hadn't fit in. Besides, now she could spend all of her time out of doors doing the things she enjoyed doing and dressing the way she chose to dress. That, most often than not, was in a baggy shirt, boots, and breeches.

She enjoyed watching the painted sky at evening sunset or sitting around campfires watching the curling smoke rise. Usually the cowboys were in a jovial mood. Once in awhile there were a few troublemakers or someone would drink too much and lose his head. But all in all, it had been a good life out in the open most of the time.

Oh, there had been a time when she was about fifteen when she had gussied up and gone into town with Butch and a few gang members. Some of them would go to the dance at the old schoolhouse while others frequented saloons, gambling halls and such. She had curled her hair

14

with a curling iron heated inside the kerosene lamp shade and put on one of her prettiest dresses, all because she had a crush on a young, handsome cowboy from Montana. They danced every dance together and she couldn't wait to see him again. After a while Jeff and she got more serious and would go outside for a drink of hooch, a little kissing and, eventually, passionate love-making. Then one day he had just upped and left town, and she hadn't heard hide nor hair of him since. Her young, girlish heart had thought he loved her. So much for dreams! From then on, her disappointment led her to hide her femininity and her heart as well. Ridin' with the gang was what she wanted most out of life now. She had no time for romance.

Why, hell, she thought, I can outshoot Wade already and I'm nigh on to becoming as keen a sharpshooter as Kid Curry. She always did some target practice when she had the spare time. Indeed, the "rowdies," as Wade called them, had taught her well. It was said that she could outride, outshoot and outswear many of the men in the combined states of Utah, Wyoming and Colorado. It was a truthful boast, although it afforded many a horrified look of reproach from some of the town's ladies. Jessie didn't care. She didn't want their camaraderie anyway. It was what Butch, Kid and Wade thought of her that mattered. They were the ones she wanted to emulate, not some prissy females. Having been raised in a man's world for the last ten years, Jessica had no use for the calico and laces the shop proprietresses, ranch wives and saloon girls wore. She was more comfortable in men's breeches, cotton or wool shirts, boots, and a large, wide-brimmed hat. Beneath that hat were thick-shorn tresses of deepest auburn, thick hair cut just below the ear.

Even dressed in male attire, however, she was a striking sight. Her large green eyes were framed by thick, sooty black lashes. Her facial contours were nearly perfect, her cheekbones high and well-defined, her mouth full and soft.

The cropped red-brown curls framed a pretty face. Not that Jessica realized that fact. She was unaware of her beauty, which only added to her charm. Nor would she have flaunted her desirability even if she'd known. She hadn't time for such things now. In fact, most of the time Jessie mimicked the "boys' " rough way of talking and their mannerisms. There were those in town who really did think her to be a lad and she didn't tell them otherwise. To Jessie's mind, "pulling the wool over their eyes" was an amusing game.

Well, there it was, just up ahead—Rye Grass Station. It was about time. No more time for reflecting on her earlier years, although such mental activity had kept her occupied during the long trip.

Reining the horses into a slower pace, Jessica maneuvered the wagon through the dirtpacked streets of the town. Wooden buildings with false fronts lined the narrow street with a brick or stone building here or there. It was a hodgepodge of styles and sizes, flattened roofs and pointed gables. It had grown some. In the last few years more people had come in to homestead. There were a lot of wagons, buggies and horses on the road. It was a bustling town for its size, providing a main trading center for the surrounding ranchers, the only place of any size along the old stage route. The main street was crowded, perhaps more so because it was the end of the week and people always stocked up towards week's end.

Like any other rural town, Rye Grass Station had its fair share of stores and shops, each with its name and type of business boldly displayed in large painted letters across the front of the building or hanging from a sign by the door. She saw a boots, shoes and saddle store; several billiard halls; saloons, one of which Butch owned, called the Arrowhead; a sheriff's office; jail; a newspaper; two pharmacists; a barber shop; a variety store called the Emporium; a dressmaker's shop; a blacksmith's and several liquor stores;

16

a livery stable and feed store; and, of course, the grocery store which also handled tools and other various items. The town had its share of boarding houses and hotels as well. One town was much like another, she supposed, but far apart in this ranch country. At least this town had a doctor and dentist, which was more than she could say for Hole-in-the-Wall, in Wyoming. There the nearest doctor was in Green River, fifty miles away.

The boardwalks on each side of the wide street were as active as a honey hive. Most of the people were men, but there were some women and children. Ladies didn't come to town very often. For now cowboys, ranchers, lawmen, and gamblers rubbed elbows as they strode down the boardwalk. Here and there was a prospector pulling his mule behind him, all loaded up with supplies for a day's excursion, or perhaps headed Colorado way to the gold mines there. A few of the men on the boardwalk chewed plug tobacco; others smoked their carefully hand-rolled cigarettes. One old codger, leaning against a post, whistled as he whittled on an old stick of wood. He waved as Jessica bounded from the wagon and she waved back, tied the horses to the hitching post, then joined the throng.

The planks of the boardwalk creaked in rhythm to her stride as Jessie hurried along Main Street. Clutching tightly to the leather pouch of bank notes, she made a mental list of all the things Wade said were needed.

"Bull Durham Tobacco," she said aloud, reminding herself of that necessity as a burly cowboy walked by, obviously enjoying his cigarette. "Bacon, beans, flour, and coffee." She mustn't forget the coffee or she'd have to ride all the way back. The cowboys could never get along without coffee nor, for that matter, could she. "And the grits." Beauregard Anderson, known as Coyote Bo, was Virginia-born and bred and wouldn't eat anything else for breakfast. She smiled as she recalled how he hated the name Beauregard. She guessed that was his real name, for nobody

17

would accept a name like that unless it was given to him. Most of the men had taken on names not their own, such as Peg Leg Elliot or Bub Meeks. Coyote Bo was as good as any other moniker, she supposed; but, oh, how she loved to tease him by calling him Beauregard!

She was so engrossed in reiterating the list as she turned the corner, she didn't see the obstacle in her path until she had walked right into him. Almost toppling to the ground from the force of the collision, Jessica maintained her balance only by the greatest effort.

"Hey, you young punk, watch where you're goin'." Towering over her by more than a foot, the tall, curly-haired blonde youth glowered down at her.

"Sorry. Guess I wasn't payin' careful attention to where I was walkin'." Side-stepping the young man, Jessica nodded politely, thinking it to be the end of the matter.

"Say, 'excuse me' agin. . . ." With a leering grin the string-bean tall lad blocked her way. He took off his wide-brimmed hat and fanned it in front of her. It was obvious that he intended to cause trouble. Even so, Jessie held her temper in check. Wouldn't do to create a stir. Besides, she had better things to do than fisticuff with some bully.

"Excuse me . . . !" Taking off her hat, she was the picture of polite contriteness. "Now, if you'll let me be on my way."

"And just where is that?" Clearly this tomcat was spoiling for a fight. Biting her tongue, Jessie sized him up and down, wondering if it was worth the bother to tangle with him.

"I'm going to the general store for supplies, if that's any concern of yours. Care to accompany me and load the wagon?" She answered his scowl with a grin. "No, I don't suppose you would." He was all bone and sinew with little evidence of muscular strength about him. Hardly one to instill fear within her breast. This time when he blocked her way, she boldly reached out to push him aside. She was losing her patience.

"Look, I'm tired of this game you're playing. I don't know who you are or what you're up to, but I can tell you right now that I ain't gonna stand for no nonsense. Got work to do." Oh, how she wished she could tell him that it was Butch Cassidy she answered to! That would send him running. But Butch was in hiding. He was wanted for cattle rustling, bank robbing, and for shooting up a town a while back.

"Work? Ha!" Sticking his thumbs in the belt-loops of his pants, he guffawed. "I seen you the last time you came into town. You were with that broken-down old cowboy. The one that tangled with my pa. You nearly broke his head."

Now Jessie remembered that scuffle. Wade had been close to losing until Jessie had broken an empty whiskey bottle over his opponent's head. They had run before there was any retribution for the ruckus. Butch had given them a severe tongue-lashing when he'd heard. He warned them not to draw attention to themselves for fear of the law stepping in and stumbling on their hideout. Their being discovered was unlikely unless they were followed. The canyon was long and the hideout well hidden. Most lawmen wouldn't enter that canyon for any reason.

It wasn't a fair fight. Wade was a mean fighter in his day but he wasn't any match for two men. The image of the fight danced before her eyes. Wade had been playing a hand of poker, had caught this bully's father cheating. When he'd called him on it the man and his companion had closed in on him from both sides. He'd sent one man flying but had met his match in the younger man. Jessie had struck out on a blind impulse to protect her adoptive pa.

Before she could argue further the young boy lashed out, giving her a sound push that sent her sprawling. Grumbling and sputtering, Jessica pushed herself up from the hard ground, her fists clenched. She was fully prepared to make him answer for his gesture.

"Come on! Come on! I'll give you a battle if that's what

you want." She was cocky, sure of herself. Measuring herself against this young smart aleck, she figured herself the winner. The Sundance Kid had taught her boxing so she was well prepared. Besides, she'd tangled with a couple of the town's youths before.

"It is!" He guffawed again, a wicked sound. "I told my pa the next time I saw you come into town I'd make you pay." Puckering up his lips he whistled long and loud. Answering the summons were three other youths about his same age. Like four hounds hoping to corner a hare, they circled Jessie.

Chapter Two

Rye Grass Station was a pretty good-sized town. Even at this early hour, there was a waiting line at the barber shop. Regardless of how long he had to wait. Corbin MacQuarie knew that he could not do anything else until he had a shave. The long, narrow mirror right by the hatrack gave him a detailed look of himself. What a grubby sight he was! Was that beard-covered face right below the flat-crowned Stetson really he? His unshaven jaw gave him a bold, aggressive appearance, like a gunslinger or outlaw. Oh, well, there were others here who looked just as bad, if not worse, than he did. Nevertheless, he was very glad when the barber motioned him forward. As he moved toward the chair, he could smell the odor of bay rum. It was a welcome change from the smells of the range, he thought.

"Haircut and shave sir?" the bald-headed barber asked.

"Just a shave." His thick blonde hair was his vanity. Taking off his hat he exposed his tousled waves to the barber's scrutiny.

"You sure? Sideburns could use a trim."

"A trim, then." Knocking his hat against his thigh to dislodge the road dust, he sat down on the thickly padded, brown leather chair and leaned back. The arm rest doubled as a hatrack.

"You look as if you've come from a long ways off," the

barber said.

"Been living over Colorado way on a ranch north of Denver." He smiled, showing pearl white teeth. "My brother is running it now. I thought it was about time he settled down." Before he got himself killed, Corbin thought to himself.

When Warren had been a Pinkerton agent, he was always chasing around after some outlaw or other. It was an unsettled way of life that held many dangers. Then Corbin had introduced him to Henrietta Smitz and the rest read like a dime novel. Oh, there was more to Henrietta than a pretty face, but Warren had fallen so much in love with her that he did not seem to mind her demands. Now that they were married, Henrietta would see to it that Warren went to church, did not drink too much or smoke those horrid cigars, and would spend plenty of time with her in her cultural pursuits.

Corbin hoped with all his heart that Warren would not come to resent Henrietta as he himself had. Warren was a man of action who could not bear to be idle for too long a time. And as for Henrietta, would she remain true to Warren, or always be giving someone else the eye the way she had him? Only time would tell. He hoped his brother had not made a big mistake in marrying Henrietta Smitz.

The foam was soft, warm, and soothing as he sat there with his eyes closed, the razor gliding gently over his face. The barber and he had not talked much while the shaving was going on, but now that it was over, Corbin opened his eyes.

"Any good land for sale or homestead?" he thought he might just as well ask.

A chuckle was his answer. "Nothing but land here. For miles and miles and miles. If it's vast plains you want, we've got 'em here. Just waitin' to be settled."

"Looks like good ranch land."

"Land hereabouts can be made into just about anything

you want it to be." Wetting a towel, the barber dabbed at a few spots of lather and wiped them from Corbin's face.

" 'Course now, I've gotta be truthful with you. After the drought in '83, beef prices dropped sharply. When so many cattle perished in the harsh winter of '87, some of the larger outfits had to dismiss a lot of cowboys. Some of the unemployed men turned to rustling since cattle was all they knew. There's rustlin' going on here all the time."

"I've heard about the rustling. It happens in Colorado, too."

"But that ain't all, young fella. Now that the Homestead Act has passed, the ranchers don't like the homesteaders either. They don't want a bunch of farmers homesteading all the good grassland to raise crops. They don't want the farmers replacing the ranchers."

"I can see the rancher's point of view. I'm not the kind to give up what I consider mine either. I'd feel the same way." Smiling, Corbin nodded his head "yes" as the barber moistened his hands with bay rum. "I prefer the odor of bay rum any day. It's not like some of those other scents. I leave those flowery smells to the petunias and the ladies."

Now that he looked presentable, he paid the barber twenty-five cents and walked through the archway connecting the barbershop to the saloon and gaming hall. The honky-tonk piano tunes drew him closer to the only place a man could find camaraderie in any new town. Here was a refuge for horse thieves, bootleggers and other misfits, as well as for businessmen. Much trading went on inside saloons. Indeed, many men spent more time in saloons than they did at home. It was a meeting place for cowboys and cowboys were clannish. Most cowboys had no fixed home but went from camp to camp.

It was a good-sized saloon. Behind the imposing mahogany bar was a huge mirror and shelves of spirits — wine and all kinds of alcoholic beverages in beautiful bottles of various sizes. On the far wall was a large painting of John L.

Sullivan, the world-champion boxer.

Slowly Corbin walked over to the bar. The two bartenders with slicked-down hair parted in the middle were ringing the cash register and pouring drinks just as fast as they could. Each wore a white apron and elastic sleeve guards.

The ten men, each standing with his foot resting on the copper bar rail, turned to look his way as he entered. The men at the game tables where gambling was going on paid little heed to anything other than their cards.

Corbin took a pickled hard-boiled egg out of the jar on top of the bar and ordered a five-cent beer. "Drinks all around," he announced. It wasn't long before Corbin and several others standing at the bar were indulging in friendly conversation.

Bartenders were known to be sympathetic listeners and knew many things. They stayed clear of religion, the merits of hanging, and the politics of Eugene V. Debs. The bartender, whose name was Hank, had a wealth of information and stories about the area.

He talked of the early gold rush, the weather, the women. The name "Wild Bunch" kept cropping up in the conversation. He told stories about them with a touch of awe, as if he admired the hooligans. A strange attitude, Corbin thought. As for himself, he'd heard too many stories from his brother to have any liking for those who broke the law.

After a time, he paid for the drinks and strode toward the door. The shrieking and hollering outside nearly broke his eardrums.

What the devil? Such a fracas — swinging fists, kicking feet, curses being shouted. It appeared that four boys were trying to subdue a fifth. Corbin stepped outside the swinging doors, viewing the scene from a closer position. The rowdies seemed to be trying to make the smallest of the group cry "uncle." Even so, the auburn-haired boy was

24

putting up quite a fight.

Corbin could not help but admire his grit. He was skillfully maneuvering his feet and fists, only to be subdued as two youths grabbed him from behind. Corbin didn't like the odds. Four against one? Perhaps because of that or because he admired the boy's spunk, he slammed out the doors, clenching his fists while swearing at the bullies. "You want a fight? I'll give you one!" He stopped, drew his six-shooter and fired twice into the air. Like the cowards they were, the four took to their heels and scattered in all directions. Reaching down, he grasped the smaller boy's hand.

Jessica felt a large, firm hand grab hers and shivered at the man's touch as he helped her to her feet. If not for him, she would have been a goner—that much she knew. She was tough and she was wiry, but no one could fight against such odds.

"Are you all right?" The voice was low and very, very masculine. Glancing up, she was mesmerized by the blue eyes that appraised her. She was suddenly tongue-tied. "You're covered with dirt. Your face, your clothes," the owner of the blue eyes said gently. Taking off his neckerchief he dipped it in a horse trough, then handed it to her. "I expect you have some bruises. Nothing broken, is there?"

"Naw!" Her auburn hair whipped her face as she shook her head emphatically. "Takes more than a few bullies to get the best of me!" Jesse affected her boyish strut, as was her habit when feeling the need to soothe wounded pride.

Corbin appraised the boy. He was small, and from what he could see of his frame beneath the loose-fitting shirt and pants, slender. In girth and strength he had been overpowered, and yet he had done quite well for himself. "You handled yourself quite skillfully," he complimented.

Jessie smiled, basking in the warmth of his praise. "You bet, and I'd soon've flattened 'em if I hadn't been so drastically outnumbered. I'm a fighter. I can hold my own."

25

Rubbing the neckerchief over herself she was surprised to feel herself flushing. Strange . . . she couldn't take her eyes away from him. Her eyes swept from the thick golden hair under the Stetson to the toes of his fancy brown boots and silver spurs. There was a strength of character in his face that drew her gaze. She liked the slant of his eyebrows, the cleft in his chin, the shape of his nose. He was not perfectly handsome but nigh on to being so. He was at least six-feet-two, and it appeared with his strength, he'd be a fearsome man to reckon with.

"I don't doubt that you could have held them at bay. As it was, you were doing quite well. I admire your bravery. Someone taught you to defend yourself." His mouth softened from the hard-chiseled line as he smiled at her. At that moment Jessica thought she'd never again see such a handsome cowboy. Not even Butch Cassidy could touch this one for comeliness. He was oh-so- pleasant to the eyes.

"Sundan—" She caught herself before saying the name. "Sundays, my pa and I spar a little. Boxing is what he calls it. I guess it's one of them eastern sports."

"Comes in just as handy in the West, I'm sure. Ya know, I saw John L. Sullivan himself once in Denver. Now there is someone quick with his fists. . . ." He quirked a brow. "Something wrong?"

Jessica suddenly realized that she was staring a hole right through him. "Naw! Just didn't know if I'd seen you before, that's all." Hastily she looked away, changing the direction of her eyes to the toes of her boots.

"You haven't. I've just arrived. Rode in from Meeker, Colorado early this morning." He laughed. "Corbin MacQuarie is my name." He held out his hand, taking hers in a firm handshake.

The touch of his hand caused an odd tingle, a jolt she felt from fingers to toes. "Corbin MacQuarie" Her mouth relaxed into a smile. "I like that name."

"It's Scottish. The MacQuarie part, that is. Corbin was

my grandfather's name. From him I also got my yellow hair. The others in my family are redheads."

"I like the color of your hair much better." As his eyes met hers she blushed a shade of red again, but this time didn't look away. "My name is Jessie. Jessie Watson."

"Jesse." Remembering Jesse James he frowned, irritated at how so many families venerated that outlaw by bestowing his name on their children. This handsome, brave lad deserved better. Strange, but the boy had the damndest eyes. Haunting. Hell, he was a pretty boy. Good thing he'd learned to use his fists. A small lad like that would be the prey of bullies all his life.

"Jessie." As he said her name a strange feeling swept over her. She was fidgety all of a sudden. She had never cared about her appearance much before, and yet, like a dad-blamed fool, she was peering into the water of the trough. She looked a sight! Instead of cleaning away the dirt, the neckerchief had merely smeared it. Frantically she dabbed at the brown spots, then turned her attention to her hair. It was in wild disarray. Unruly curls stuck up here and there. Combing her fingers through her tresses she tried to smooth them before she put her hat on again.

"You certain you're all right?" He was relieved when she shook her head "yes" again. "Then I guess I'll be on my way."

"No. . . !" The word was out before she even thought. Somehow she didn't want him to leave. Not yet. "At least let me buy you a drink, mister. . . ."

"I just came from the saloon over there."

Jessie snorted with disdain. "Saloon, you call it? Ha! That ain't no saloon. I'll take you to the best saloon in these parts. The Arrowhead." Standing with her hands on her hips she waited expectantly. "Well. . . . ?"

Once again Corbin appraised the boy. "You hardly look old enough." Hard to tell about age sometimes, but Jesse's voice sounded as if he was just at that age where the high voice of boyhood would soon change to a huskier timbre.

"I ain't no kid! Come on! I'll play you a game of billiards." The sparkle in her eyes gave him a challenge. For the moment the supplies were forgotten.

He couldn't refuse. He laughed as he thought how soon he'd show this youngster a thing or two.

Chapter Three

Jessie led the way. Corbin followed, dodging the horses, wagons, carriages and the debris scattered over the roadway, to a long, two-storied building down the street. They passed by a door marked "Wine Entrance" and Jessie wrinkled up her nose. "Special entrance way for ladies," she said, "so's they don't disturb the boys. They ain't allowed in the main saloon but have a small room of their own. Personally I don't think they should be allowed anywheres near."

Thinking of Henrietta and her ways, Corbin laughed. "I don't suppose they should." He headed for the front of the saloon but Jessie gave him a push in another direction.

"I don't use the swinging doors. Hell, I'm a special customer!" She threw her chest out proudly. Butch owned the saloon and every employee was in his pay. They were loyal to him and truly thought of him as a Robin Hood of the West. Even the bawds in the upstairs rooms were employed by Butch.

"A special customer, huh?" Corbin laughed again.

"I've got my own entrance!" A saloon usually had at least one back door and several side doors for the use of special customers, hasty escapes, and for access to the cribs out behind the main structure where "fallen doves" took their customers. "This will take us right into the billiard hall," Jessie said, opening a red-painted door.

"Hi, Jess!"

"Hello, little mite!"

Two men bent over at the large, green felt-covered tables, engaged in a game, but not so much so as to not greet her enthusiastically as she entered. Generously buying drinks not only for Corbin and herself but for them as well, Jessie prepared herself for the game, removing her cue stick from the wall rack. All cues were not alike in weight or length. Jessie's had been fashioned especially for her. It was shorter and lighter than most of the others.

Although Corbin couldn't see it from where he stood, there was a photograph of Butch on the wall in the office right off the pool room. He seemed to smile at Jessie from his place on the wall. His fair hair was cut short, his clear blue eyes looked somber and even the small scar under his left eye showed in the picture. It was the only picture of him anyone had. That picture had been taken at the Wyoming State Prison, the only place where Butch had ever been incarcerated.

He really never should have been in prison in the first place, Jessie thought loyally. There was no violence in Butch's makeup. He never killed a man during a holdup as some others had. Considering that he was the leader of the largest band of outlaws in the West, engaged in all forms of banditry from rustling to train robbery, that was really something to crow about. Oh, he could have killed, all right. He was an excellent shot. He just never wanted to.

"Picture really doesn't do him justice," she mumbled. 'Course, most wanted posters didn't. The number 432B in the lower left-hand corner sort of spoiled it. Oh, how she wanted to boast to this Corbin MacQuarie that she knew Butch, but prudence silenced her. Until she knew if he could be trusted, she'd hold her tongue.

"What did you say?"

"Nothin' . . . . pick your stick."

Corbin selected a cue suitable to his liking, rubbed the end with chalk, then tossed a copper short beer check. "We'll toss this like a coin to see who goes first."

Jessie chose the obverse side with the establishment's name on it, he chose the reverse side. It landed on the table with the words "good for 12 1/2 cents in trade" face up. Thus Corbin won the first shot. He racked the fifteen various colored and numbered balls in a triangle at one end of the table, then carefully took aim, driving his cue ball into the others, scattering them and sending one ball into each of the end pockets. As he maneuvered his body around the end rails of the long table, trying to get into a favorable position, he unbuttoned the top three buttons of his cotton shirt. It opened to show a thick covering of dark gold hair across his chest. If there was anything Jessie found irresistible, it was hair on a man's chest, she thought. It was an indication of strength and virility. As he rolled up the sleeves of his shirt, exposing his bulging biceps, she was all eyes. He was some man, all right!

"I'll try not to skin you too bad!" he said confidently. Slipping the cue stick back and forth several times between the fingers of his left hand, he tried to get the feel for the shot.

"Skin me? We'll see. But be sure to keep at least one foot on the floor," she teased as he leaned over the table attempting to get the hidden nine ball near one of the middle pockets. It came within a half inch of the hole then rolled away. The cue ball, however, rolled down into the net pocket, leaving the nine ball where it was. It was a foul called a scratch.

"Goddamn! How did I miss that one?"

Trying to hide her smile, Jessie answered reassuringly, "Happens to the best of us, I guess." Truth was she knew a secret she wasn't about to reveal just yet. "You forfeit your play and take one point off your score for that scratch, though. Tough luck! Now it's my turn again. You go and enjoy your beer while I try a shot or two. I'm gonna win this one." Her air of confidence was reinforced as she put the balls into the pocket one by one without repeating Corbin's mistake.

"Well, I'll be!" Corbin was amazed. "You're just lucky."

"Luck has nothin' to do with it. Just skill!"

The game went on for nearly an hour, the two of them laughing and truly enjoying the camaraderie. Jessie didn't know when she'd enjoyed a man's company as much. She was amazed at how strong and smart he was. He had a whole heap of stories to tell about his travelings. He was slim without any fat, but broad-shouldered and very appealing. She was around men all of the time. Why did he attract her so? She wouldn't analyze the reasons now but she knew for sure that he was more than just a passing fancy.

"How do you like Brown's Park Valley so far?" Jessie found herself hoping he'd stay.

"I haven't had time to tell. It's partly in Colorado, but the Utah side seems like more rugged terrain."

"Rugged and beautiful. I think you'll like it once you've had the chance to settle down a spell. You got a family?" Secretly she was hoping he wasn't married.

"Brother and sister-in-law. Your turn! Damn that cue ball!" Squeezing the cue stick so tightly that his knuckles turned white, he watched as she once more wiped the board clean of balls.

"New game. I got all the balls in that time."

"Yeh, and I scratched again!"

Corbin couldn't figure out how that small lad could make some of the difficult shots when *he* missed them. Jessie was really a dynamite pool player, he thought, though a bit perturbed at his own poor showing.

The truth of the matter was that there was a slight warp in the table they were playing on, though Jessie would never tell. A while back the roof had sprung a leak during a severe rain storm, right over the table. Jessie knew just how to avoid the slight rise in the middle of the pool table and had adjusted her shots to compensate. Although she felt a little guilty for not sharing the secret with Corbin, she was not so filled with guilt that she failed to bask in the lavish praise he threw her way.

"I know when I'm licked. Might as well admit it."

"I whupped your ass!"

"Yes, you did! You're the damned finest pool player I've met in quite a while and I've played a lot of pool in my days."

He showed himself to be a good sport after all, a person with a sense of humor. Certainly a truly caring man to have saved her from those bullies, she thought. Did she dare further this relationship? She was just about to find out more about him when Tillie May came in, bringing drinks to the other table. Jessie knew then that it was getting late. Tillie May didn't come to work until around four in the afternoon.

"Bull wart! I still haven't gotten my supplies," Jessie suddenly exclaimed. She had been having such a good time that she really didn't want to leave, but she knew at that moment that she had to hurry. Wade would be worried if she came back too late. "Want to help me, Corbin?"

"Sure. Least I can do for such a crack pool shot!" It gave Jessie satisfaction that even though Tillie May flirted outrageously, Corbin didn't take notice. Instead, he followed her out the door and down the street to the general store.

"Shouldn't take me long." Stepping inside she quickly scanned the large room for the provisions she needed. It was a small store. The provisions were heaped in bundles, making use of every inch of space. From food stuffs to tobacco, cracker barrels to canned food tins, hardly an inch of space was wasted. The store smelled of fresh-ground coffee and tobacco, the two most necessary items. Jessica picked up two brightly painted tins, balancing them under her arm, then she put a goodly number of Bull Durham sacks in an open gunny sack along with some cigarette papers. The beans and flour were next and she tugged at the large sacks.

"Here, I'll take those." Corbin hefted the large flour sacks. The boy must have a big family, he thought wryly. The lad was buying enough to feed an army. It was a good thing Corbin had agreed to help.

"Thanks!" Oh, how she did hope he would stay. His handsome face would sure beautify the town and make it interesting. Reaching in her leather pouch she pulled out the bank notes and paid the man behind the counter. Averting the man's eye, she hoped he wouldn't realize the signatures were forged. Butch and Wade had acquired them in a bank robbery. "Well, guess we'll be on our way." She was relieved when the man smiled and bid her good day. He hadn't noticed, but then, they rarely did. Corbin lifted the heavy sacks, balanced them on his shoulder and followed her out of the store.

Jessica watched in fascination as he helped her load the wagon, noticing again just how strong he was. Why, he lifted those sacks as if they didn't weigh a thing! Oh, how the muscles rippled across his back as he bent and strained. Made her heart nigh on to stop beating. He was a welcome addition to Rye Grass Station, all right.

"You take care. Don't let those bullies catch you alone. . . ." Corbin showed his concern as he watched her climb aboard the wagon and take hold of the reins.

She smiled her gratitude and goodbye. "Hope to see you again . . ." she said.

"Perhaps you will." He waved as she started the horses into a trot. "Take care of yourself, lad."

Lad? The word stung her. Here all the time they'd been together he'd thought she was a boy. It was unsettling and disappointing, yet it was an easy mistake to make dressed as she was. She had been mistaken for a boy several times, hadn't she? Yes, and it had never bothered her before. In fact, that's the way she wanted it more times than not. Still, for the first time in a long while, she hankered for that special look in a man's eye. Perhaps she might have won his heart if . . .

Bull wart! Get that stupid thought out of your head right now! she scolded to herself. Hadn't she learned her lesson once before? She'd been all dressed up in skirts and petticoats, had even worn perfume and what had it gotten her? A broken heart! Kisses and moonlight faded like fog when the morning came. All she'd gotten for her efforts was a lot of lovin' but empty arms when the notion to travel had come over her man. She wouldn't ever let that happen again. No sir! She'd never gussie up just for some man again. She was what she was. And yet. . . . It was more difficult than she could ever have believed to push Corbin MacQuarie from her thoughts.

Chapter Four

The shadowy outline of the mountains was a deep purple against the dark pink of the sky as Jessie neared the hideout on Diamond Mountain. She loved this time of evening when it was cooler. Little did she care it was too late to set the corner posts down by the corral. She could do that tomorrow. She wouldn't trade today for anything in the world.

Somehow she could still feel Corbin's presence. His good-natured pearly white smile flashed before her eyes and she thought what good company he had been. Downright pleasing! The corners of her mouth curled up a bit as she thought to herself of how she had whipped him at pool. He had been such a good sport about it, however. Perhaps she should feel a little twinge of guilt at how she had managed to win, but she didn't. Her method had worked to keep them together for awhile at least.

Jessica didn't meet strangers often or make friends easily. Being in the business made a body wary. Thus, most of her friends were workers at the saloon, the outlaws in her own camp or those from other camps that dropped in from time to time. She and Corbin had hit it off right from the start, from the moment she'd looked into his eyes.

For the first time, in a long time, someone outside her own circle had accepted her as she was, personality-wise, and seemed to understand her. There were few people with whom she felt really comfortable. That was not so surprising, when one considered her aunt's rejection of her when she was a child and then her first love at fifteen leaving her without even so much as a goodbye. Although she had never cared much for Rye Grass Station before, maybe all of that would change now that she had met Corbin MacQuarie.

Living in this Utah valley country meant hard work, and Jessie was not one to fall short on her chores. The area was often sun-baked in summer and freezing cold in winter, so a body had to be able to deal with the elements. She had ridden long distances looking after cattle, she'd wrangled stray horses and done just about anything that was asked of her. She had even pitched tons of hay for winter feeding. If the "boys" were in a dither because she was late in bringing their Bull Durham and coffee . . .well, they'd just have to learn to understand her the way Corbin MacQuarie seemed to. He was good for her, had renewed her self-confidence. "But Corbin MacQuarie wouldn't look twice at me in a romantic way," she said aloud. A pal, that's what he wanted. Hell, he'd thought her to be a boy and perhaps that was best for now.

"Bull wart!" Listen to her mooning, she thought.

Men could sometimes turn a seemingly intelligent woman's brains to pudding, that much was apparent. Why look at how Laura Bullion followed Ben Kilpatrick around like a fawning sheep dog, Tillie May down at the saloon had nearly spilled all the drinks on the floor while making "goo-goo eyes" at Corbin. Jessica had vowed she would never fall for a man so hard again as she had when she was fifteen, but at the first sight of Corbin's wavy golden hair and wide smile she'd come nigh on to totally losing her head.

It was smart of her to regain her senses and not tell him she was a female. If things went well, he'd find out soon enough. In the meantime she had found a good friend. She couldn't help chuckling to herself as she remembered thinking that if he wore his pants any lower down on his hips, he would have lost them. He was just the kind that could set a woman's heart to pounding at a furious pace. Hers was racing now just thinking of him.

She was nearing the home stretch. Some people called it Cassidy Point, the most lawless place in the entire West, but that was a falsehood. Cassidy had formed a systematic, harsh social order that worked for the gang. They had probably a lot stricter discipline than in some of the towns, she thought with pride. First and foremost, any member of the hideout had to pull his weight and treat the others fairly.

Fairly, she thought in frustration. When she got back she was going to complain. She didn't mind helping out, what with things being a little heated and all, but she'd be damned if she'd let herself be used for a fool.

Jessie wanted to be more than just the gang's errand girl. Her bottom ached, her legs felt cramped and her hands were sore from pulling at the reins. She was an expert horsewoman but driving a wagon irritated her. It was about time someone else took a turn at fetching supplies. She had better things to do.

At last after a long sweep through the canyon and a steady uphill climb with the wagon wheels groaning beneath the weight, she reached the hideout at Cassidy Point. Several of the boys rode out to meet her. She was not at all surprised that they had seen her coming. Butch had cleverly constructed a cabin up on the Point, beneath an overhanging ledge of rock and situated well out of sight. It commanded a view of the area for miles in all directions.

"Did ya get the tobacco?" Their voices echoed one another as they asked the same question. "The coffee?"

" 'Course I did! Wouldn't want to be banished forever." Jessie flashed them a grin, she was back in a good mood. "I

38

got everything you wanted and then some. Including sugar for your coffee, Bill." She addressed the youngest of the outlaws fondly. After all, they'd both been brought into the gang at about the same time, had been playmates of sorts.

"Good girl!" Bill showed his appreciation by unhitching the horses.

"Anyone talkin' about me?" Bob Meeks's grin was villainous. He was the only one of the outlaws Jessie could not warm up to. There was something different about him, a cruelty the others did not exhibit. Jessie knew he had joined up only when he found out that Butch Cassidy's name was becoming known in the big eastern cities. Whereas the others showed restraint, he seemed to enjoy shedding blood. She'd heard Wade say that Meeks had recently been charged with the murder of two prospectors in Dry Forks, Utah.

"Didn't hear a word," Jessie said evenly. "Guess your escapade has already been forgotten." Bob was one of the boys who enjoyed riding to town on a Saturday night, whooping it up along the main street, carousing in the saloons and the cribs. The others got liquored up and shot up the town but their greatest harm was in leaving bullet holes in the walls and ceilings. Bob had wounded a man and would probably have killed him if the other gang members had not intervened. It was for that reason that Butch was being cautious about frequenting the town, at least until the furor died down. Yep, Meeks had caused a whole lot of trouble and probably would again, if Jessie didn't miss her guess.

"Guess I'll have to give 'em somethin' else to talk about," he was saying now, brushing his fingers against the handle of his gun as if just itching to draw. Oh, he was a mean one all right. Jessie always stayed clear of him, particularly now that she had grown to womanhood. Though her shirt and pants hid her curves from sight, he seemed to be always looking at her backside and chest as if imagining what lay

39

beneath the cotton and denim. His attentions made her flesh crawl.

"Well, I wouldn't do anything rash. Remember, they are still looking for you in Utah. A necktie party is what they have in mind," was all she said, flinging that warning over her shoulder as she mounted one of the wagon's horses to ride bareback the rest of the way to the bunkhouse and cabins. The road to the ridge was a narrow strip, accessible only on foot or horseback. Wagons could not pass this way but had to take the long way around. She hurried along after the others, not wanting to be in Bob's company. She heard him swear a string of oaths. He was as mad as hell at being left to drive the wagon to its hiding place near the corral and with only one horse. Well, it served him right, she thought.

Jessie had traveled this same route more times than she could count, but even so she still cringed as she looked over the side where the hill dropped off sharply to the boulders below. At last she came near the clearing, pulled off the roadway and headed to her cabin. Wade had come over from the bunkhouse and met her at the door, evidence of worry marked on his brow.

"What took you so long, Jess?" Wade didn't like her going into Rye Grass Station alone. It was a long way from camp, several hours' ride. Some people might be a little quick on the trigger since Bob had rattled the town. Perhaps Wade would have gone with her but Butch had other chores for him to do. Besides, Butch had no doubt that Jessie could handle it alone, she thought with a measure of pride.

"Ran into a little trouble, that's all. Couple of the town's bullies wanted to tussle." She tried to make light of it.

"You been fightin'?" His piercing hazel eyes peered put under thick graying brows to look searchingly at her. "You didn't start it again, did you?"

"Naw . . . !" Pushing through the door she took off her

40

hat and flung it on the narrow cot. "But I can tell you right now that I would have, if I'd known what was gonna happen." She sighed dreamily, reliving the details of her rescue as she told him the story. "He ain't like most of the cowboys around here, that's for certain. No sir! He's a man any gal would be right proud to claim."

"Oh, he was, was *he?*" He snorted his surprise. "Never thought I'd hear you talk that way again, Jessie. He must have made quite an impression on you. Care to tell me just why *he's* so special?"

"He looked just like one of them men right out of a western novel. Handsome enough to be the talk of most of the town women and a few of the ranchers' wives as well, I'll wager. Corbin MacQuarie was his name. Even his name I like. It has a fine ring to it. Won't be long before someone snatches him up." Somehow that thought hurt, but she wouldn't let it show.

"Good looker, huh? He eyed her quizzically. "Maybe I better go with you the next time. Don't want you getting into any trouble."

"Hell, Wade, I can take care of myself! I'm eighteen ya know." He just didn't realize she wasn't the same little girl he'd found and raised as his own. Or maybe he didn't want to. Jessie looked at him closely, remembering how kind he'd always been. Perhaps he was afraid of losing her. She would just let the matter drop. They'd been through thick and thin together. She had felt much the same on occasion when it had appeared he'd found a lady friend. Yep, they'd been through thick and thin together the last ten years, and she supposed they'd be together at least another ten. There were times when she worried about him, though.

The years had not been kind to Wade. His face was leathery from endless days spent riding in the sun, lined thickly around the eyes. He was much thinner than he used to be and she missed his jovial girth. Even so, he still had the kindest face she'd ever seen. To her he was not the grizzled old cowboy she'd heard the others call him. To Jessie, he was a real hero. Who else would have bothered with a nine-year-old kid?

"Eighteen!" He ran his hands through his thinning gray hair, shaking his head in disbelief. "You're blossoming into a real woman, Jess. Yes, sir. I've got to watch over you more carefully from now on. Especially where that Corbin MacQuarie is concerned."

"Corbin MacQuarie is the least of your worries." She put a hand on his shoulder. "I wouldn't leave your side even for the likes of him. We're family, Wade, and that's the way it's gonna stay. Besides, he doesn't even *know* I'm a female!"

"Well, imagine that . . . ! Despite what you're wearing, he must have been blind. . . ."

They just stood there in silence for awhile but she was thinking, *I could have told him I was a female. I had plenty of opportunity. I guess that I just realized that being one of the boys to him wasn't such a bad idea after all. We did have a good time and that is at least a start. I could be dressin' in dresses if I wanted to. Dressin' in shirt and breeches was my idea. It was by my own hand that my auburn tresses were shorn. Perhaps now I will let them grow if only a tad.*

After a few minutes Wade said, "Don't look so glum, Jess. You're the prettiest boy I've ever seen so just wipe that frown off your face. Besides, I'll bet my last ace he wasn't good enough for you. You know it can be just plain loco to give your heart if it isn't to the right one." His eyes stared ahead for just a moment and she knew he was thinking about his wife. Wade had tried to care about other women but somehow not a one of the ladies he met could measure up to LaVerne. Her ghost had always hovered between him and any woman he had taken to his bed, until he met Agnes. Maybe something more would come of that if they ever got back to Hole-in-the Wall again.

Jessie headed for the cooking area of the cabin. "Well,

we won't talk about it any more. Hell, I can't rightly remember what he looked like." That was a lie. She remembered every curve and angle of his handsome face, but it was no use talking about it if it disturbed Wade. "The way your stomach is growlin', it's obvious you didn't eat down at the bunkhouse. It's late. You must be half-starved by now. I'll rustle up some grub."

"Sounds like a good idea!" A large wood-burning stove stood in the center of the cabin, used for heat as well as cooking. Wade hurried to light it, striking a match on the sole of his boot. He fed the fire with wood from the woodpile just outside the front door, then stood watching as the flickering flames danced about. "I'm so hungry I could eat my gun. What's it gonna be?"

She laughed. "With all the beef you boys bring in you can take a guess. How about hash? I've got a whole bag of potatoes in the crawl space under the cabin. Wash up and sit down. Don't think it'll take me long." Taking a long-handled iron frying pan down from the wall, she greased it with lard from a tin can near the stove, then set about grinding the meat and potatoes in the hand grinder affixed to the table top. It wasn't fancy cookery, but it would do for tonight.

There was little suppertime conversation. Both ate quickly and hungrily. Certainly Jessie had enough thoughts stampeding through her mind. So much had happened today. Perhaps that was why she didn't notice the knock on the door until Wade nudged her under the table.

"Probably Bill. He can smell good cookin' a mile away. Did you save any, hon?"

Bill had a special feeling for her. Jessie could tell by the way he looked at her now that she had grown up. He often came by around suppertime, "No, there was only enough for the two of us," Jessie sighed. Wiping her greasy hands on her pants leg, she opened the door, expecting to find the young man grinning on the other side. Instead, it was the blue eyes of Butch Cassidy which met hers. A most illustrious guest, Jessie thought, always awed by the square-jawed, congenial outlaw.

Unlike some of the men who rode with him, there was no strain of violence running through Butch Cassidy's makeup. He had never killed a man during a hold-up, an unprecedented record for the leader of the largest band of outlaws the West had ever known.

"I can see that you're eating, so I won't stay. Just wanted to give you some news, Jess." The corners of his mouth dipped up in a smile, his blue eyes danced at her. "Gonna pull off the biggest, most spectacular train robbery you ever dreamed of . . . and . . . *this* time I'm gonna let you join us. We'll test you, Kid, see what you're made of. See if you're as daring as you say." He winked at Wade as if they had a secret and Jessie made the assumption that being included was Wade's doing. "Soon as you're finished eating, come on up to my cabin and I'll let you in on the details; I'm gonna have to go some to beat Kid Curry."

Butch and Kid Curry had both ridden with the McCarty gang, pulling off jobs in Colorado, Utah and Wyoming. Butch had formulated an organization called the Train Robbers Syndicate and had invited over two hundred outlaws from the territory to participate. Now he and the Kid often found themselves in competition as to who was going to "rule" this robber's roost and be the best-qualified leader of the group. Many tense moments had stirred in the camp until Jessie had come up with the idea of a contest. During the next two years, the two groups, one led by Cassidy and the other led by Kid Curry, would pull off various robberies and whoever was most successful, the most daring, would become leader of all the rest. Cassidy had determined that he would be the one. Now he was giving her a chance to be a part of his doings!

"I'm through eating now, Butch. Really I am." She would have gone hungry just to join in on this plan. Imagine,

44

really being a part of this whole thing. Why, someday she might even be a legend like Jesse James or Billy the Kid or Butch Cassidy himself. That was her thought as she followed Cassidy up the hill. For the moment Jessica was able to put the handsome Corbin MacQuarie out of her mind, little realizing how soon they would meet again.

Chapter Five

Moonlight filtered through the lofty branches of the trees as Corbin rode slowly through the streets of the town. The first thing he had done after Jesse left was to ask about lodging for the night. *Roy's Place,* the wooden sign said. It was not the Ritz but it would do, better than sleeping under the stars in his bedroll, he reckoned. Just a simple room with a good bed was all he really wanted. He was bone-tired.

Quartering Rebel comfortably in the stables at the back, Corbin sought the haven of the small, scantily furnished cubicle. It was a small room of the rudest kind, with a canvas wall at one end. Two chairs and two unpainted wooden shelves and a straw mattress upon a cot were all the luxuries it afforded. A simple room, just as the man had told him it would be.

Pulling off his boots, he settled himself on the hard bed. He folded his arms behind his head, closed his eyes and thought about the day's happenings — the journey, the young lad he'd met. That young cowboy he'd saved from the scuffle had certainly kept him on his toes, he thought. He still couldn't figure out how Jesse had managed to win three pool games in a row. All of his life Corbin had been considered an excellent pool, billiards and poker player. If he weren't such a level-headed fella, he mused, his ego would have been crushed. Well, if the kid was half as good at herding cattle as he was at playing pool, he would have to offer him a job on his ranch. Something about the lad had intrigued him and he wanted to keep in touch somehow.

His ranch—he laughed at that thought. He didn't even *have* a ranch in these parts yet. Furthermore, he had no idea where to find the young cowpoke. He had never asked Jesse what ranch he worked for or if indeed he was working at all. As young as Jesse was, he was probably still helping his old man on a small farm somewhere in the area. Oh, well, Jesse was bound to turn up in Rye Grass Station again sooner or later. Maybe by that time he would have something concrete to offer the youngster. Any lad who could snooker him at pocket billiards would be a definite asset. When he got a ranch, that was.

When Corbin first arrived, he had purposefully done some investigating in an effort to find the perfect site. Hank, the bartender at the first saloon he had stopped at had been a talkative fellow. Corbin chuckled as he thought about his enthusiasm. Most bartenders loved to rattle on, but that one did more so than most. He had told Corbin of a three-thousand-acre ranch for sale in the valley just north of Rye Grass Station. It might be just what he was looking for, he thought. At least it would be a start. The M bar Q ranch in Colorado had close to a million acres. His idea now was to have a smaller, fenced acreage on which to raise high-quality stock. He could start small and increase the acreage later if he wanted to.

From the bartender and the hotel clerk, he had learned what he needed to know about the location of good, available ranch land. The hotel clerk had also let him know that some ranchers in the area were not too friendly to strangers. Those ranchers were most particularly European and eastern investors who bought up good ranch land, rented it out and became absentee owners with no interest except in

47

making more and more money. Cattle barons was what they were called.

Corbin had no intention of becoming an absentee owner. He was determined to build something strong and lasting for himself. Now at twenty-eight years of age, he was still a rootless bachelor eager for adventure. Nevertheless, he wanted a ranch he could live on. Maybe even work on along with his hired help. He had always preferred being on horseback out in the open air.

The Stock Growers Association club membership did not appeal to him. Warren seemed much more inclined to such social events, or at least so it seemed since he'd tied himself to Henrietta. Stock raising was the family business and someone had to represent the MacQuaries, he supposed. If Warren liked that sort of thing, then let him represent the family. Corbin would rather that nobody around here even knew he came from a cattle baron family.

He'd heard talk all day of outlaws and cattle rustlers. Brown's Park seemingly had more than its share. Hell, he just might find an exciting life here after all, he thought as he sat up to unbutton his blue and black plaid shirt. He was a match for any man or group of renegades. The best rule was to just stay clear of them if possible, but be prepared. As to the rustlers, he could hold his own against them. He'd had plenty of experience. There wasn't a better marksman anywhere in the West, and Corbin knew it. Just to be on the safe side, however, he thought it best to sleep with his holster and guns intact, buckled around his hips. A bit uncomfortable sleeping with the extra bulk strapped around his long johns perhaps — but then so was a bullet in the back.

Tomorrow was another day. He needed some shut-eye if he wanted to get an early start. He planned to ride out to see for himself just what the three-thousand-acre spread looked like. The earlier the better. Getting up early was nothing new for him. Back in Colorado, workday at the ranch had begun at sunup and continued until sundown. Nothing worthwhile was accomplished without discipline.

So thinking, he stripped off his Levis, threw them to the floor, then pulled a blanket over himself. He was exhausted but despite his fatigue he lay awake for a long time just listening to the sounds that drifted through the thin hotel walls—the talk, the laughter, the snores, and also the moans that told him the occupants were indulged in pursuits other than sleep. Then at last turning over on his stomach, burrowing his head in the pillow, he settled down to sleep.

Corbin woke before dawn, dressed, gathered his few possessions together, saddled up Rebel and rode out. The stallion was impatient to be off, used to the freedom of galloping long distances, thus he let the horse have his way. Perhaps a good, hard ride would be good for him, too, he thought.

Last night he'd had the strangest dream, one that bothered him even now. He'd been playing pool again but instead of Jesse being a boy, *he'd* been a *woman!* He muttered to himself in contempt, "You stupid sonofabitch, you've been without a woman too long." That must be what accounted for such a crazy notion, and yet there had been something about the youngster that had bothered him. The eyes, too goddamned lovely to belong to a boy—long-lashed, and the most haunting shade of green. And the walk—a slight sway that was nearly undetectable except to a scrutinizing eye.

"Naw. . . ." He pushed the thought out of his mind and targeted his thoughts on what lay ahead, riding northeast and into the sunrise.

Corbin had ridden over the rugged terrain for several hours when he spotted a large spread at the foot of the mountains. Even from quite a distance away he could read the sign. *Sundown Ranch,* it said. There was a good-sized white two-story ranch house and four or five one-room cabins further back. The huge white barn was bigger than the house and very neat and well-kept in appearance. Very impressive, he thought. He estimated there were fifty to sixty horses in the tall-fenced corral near the barn. The string of wooden buildings next to the corral must be for storage of wagons, saddles and such, he thought. The workers here were certainly not lazy. There was lots of activity going on, men pitching hay into the hay loft, an older man driving a small cart drawn by mules, a young girl chasing after a flock of geese, and several men on horseback apparently getting ready to ride out on the range.

It didn't take long before Corbin was spotted. As a small group of cowboys approached, he stiffened with anticipation. By force of habit, he patted the matched set of engraved Peacemaker .45 six-shooters with ivory handles strapped in their leather holsters at his side. They gave him a feeling of security, a feeling that he was ready for anything in case the men were in a foul mood. Out here in the West, a man who did not have a gun and know how to use it would not last for long.

One of the horsemen rode out to meet him, leaving the others behind. He was a heavy-set, barrel-chested cowhand with a sweat-stained Stetson pulled so far down on his head that Corbin could barely see his eyebrows as he came closer. By the way he rode and the fact that the others hung back, Corbin sensed that he must be the foreman of this Sundown Ranch. There was a mark of good horsemanship in the way he sat his saddle and a look of hard-bitten authority in his scowl.

"Got business in these parts, stranger?" the man said in a gravel-toned voice as he blocked Corbin's path. He most definitely seemed less than friendly but Corbin had been forewarned of that possibility.

Maintaining his poise, Corbin flashed the man a wide, friendly smile. "Hank, the bartender at the Crossman Saloon in Rye Grass Station, told me you might be able to help me in locating a small ranch that's for sale hereabouts."

"Old Hank, huh? He talks too much." The foreman did not return the smile but merely sized Corbin up and down several times after he had answered, a bit like a hound scrutinizing a cat and wondering whether to chase it or let it be.

"Oh, I don't know. I found him to be right companionable and helpful. A man appreciates camaraderie when he's new in a town. . . ." He had always had a knack for making friends, or, at least, Corbin had always thought, but this man was as cold as a cube of ice. How should he handle this situation and instigate a thaw? Corbin wondered. One thing for certain, it wouldn't do to be thin-skinned or overly sensitive. Just ignore the hostile stare and hope that a friendly approach, if it were continued, would bring results.

"We don't cotton much to strangers" His leather saddle creaked as he shifted his weight. "If you were wise, you'd turn right around and hightail it outta here. Understand?"

Corbin's patience was thinning. "Look, partner. I mean you no harm." He spoke slowly, trying to maintain his perpetual smile, but he found it more difficult with each moment that passed. "I just arrived from Colorado after one helluva journey. All I want is a little information about a ranch for sale near here. Somebody's gonna buy it. It might as well be me."

The man cocked his brow. "You're not workin' for one of them cattle barons, are you?" As if scrutinizing Corbin from one angle was not good enough, he maneuvered his horse in a circle, round and round where Corbin sat mounted on Rebel. "We don't like foreigners, absentee owners or blue-nosed homesteaders around here. We like it just the way it was before they started coming in, tryin' to change everything."

Corbin shrugged. "I'm no cattle baron and as you can

51

tell by the way I talk, I'm no foreigner—just a good ole American boy, a roamin' cowboy out lookin' for a small place of my own. As I said, somebody's gonna buy that place and it might just as well be me."

Deliberately spitting yellow tobacco juice on the ground at Rebel's hooves, the foreman looked Corbin straight in the eye. "You interested in the ranch for yourself? That the truth?"

"I swear it. You have anything against that?"

"Nope!"

Corbin could see that his attitude was beginning to mellow somewhat. "Don't you agree I should at least have a chance to look at the ranch?"

"Yep. I suppose that's true." He motioned Corbin closer as if he were about to let him in on a secret. "Old Tex, the former owner, got into some trouble awhile back. Tangled with a bank clerk over a bank loan. Old Tex just couldn't help goin' into town to get all liquored up more often than he should have, but then we all go out on a hoot now and then. Anyways, it seems he spent all his money never realizing he owed so much, or so the bankers wanted everyone to believe. When Tex found out what was goin' on, he started shootin' and hollerin', causing quite a ruckus and making accusations. What man wouldn't?"

"I've done my share when I had cause. What happened then?" Corbin was beginning to understand why this man was wary. More than one rancher had become the victim of an unscrupulous banker. It wouldn't be the first time such skulduggery had been instigated.

"After they caught up with him and hauled him off to jail, the sheriff came to foreclose. Some of us think someone put the sheriff up to it. Probably paid him a pretty penny. And now the ranch is up for sale at three times what Tex owed."

Corbin had listened intently, nodding his head from time to time as the man lapsed into a detailed account of the

52

story. It seemed Tex had once been a Texas Ranger who had decided to settle down farther north and work his own land.

"He succumbed to the charms of a pretty young woman, little knowing she was in league with the banker," the foreman continued. "He proposed marriage, only to have her laugh in his face. Trouble was he'd spent a fortune wooing her, money that should have been used to pay back his loan. The banker charged a ridiculously high interest rate, knowing full well it was impossible to raise that kind of money." For someone who had been so closed-mouthed before, now Corbin couldn't get a word in edgewise. Something had changed the cowboy's mind about him, he thought, but didn't know just what it was. It really didn't matter.

"I'm truly sorry," he did manage to say. "I always hate to see a man cheated."

"Yep, it's too bad. Tex was a good cowhand, rough and ready, a lover of good fun and good whiskey. And he was my friend." The man shook his head. "Well, now his cowhands are out of work. I can't use any more help here. Maybe if *you* buy the place, you can put 'em to work."

Corbin realized why the foreman had come around to a more friendly attitude. At first he had resented the thought of anyone buying his friend's ranch. Now, however, he was trying to find work for the laid-off cowboys and viewed Corbin as a likely prospect, stubborn enough to buy the ranch in spite of what he said. He no doubt figured it was better to show a little friendliness just in case Corbin did become a neighbor. Cowboys were a loyal, clannish lot.

"I'll see what I can do." Corbin had received the information he needed. If he intended to buy the three thousand acres of land, he would have to see the sheriff, then get in touch with that banker. It just could be they would both find they had met their match. No one made a fool of Corbin MacQuarie. Knowing what had happened to the

53

previous owner would help when he tried to negotiate.

"My name is Gus. Gus Chittem."

"Corbin. Corbin MacQuarie."

After experiencing a more friendly salutation than the greeting he had received upon his arrival, Gus Chittem offered to ride with him and show him the ranch he was looking for. Corbin rode out from the Sundown Ranch a happier man.

The ranch Corbin was interested in buying was a neighboring property but still a great distance away. Neighbors in these parts, just as at home in Colorado, were miles and miles apart with vast stretches of grazing land for miles and miles in between ranch houses. It was a long journey and as he galloped along upon Rebel's back, he was thinking that he must find a better hotel than the one he had stayed in last night. After being in the saddle for so long today, his back would need more support than that lumpy straw mattress he had been given. It wasn't that he was getting soft, it was just that even sleeping on the ground in a bedroll would have been better than what he had settled for last night. It made finding his own ranch even more imperative.

With Gus beside him, Corbin's mind was relieved as to what to expect from others in the vicinity; thus he took time to enjoy his new surroundings. Over in the nearby field, several prairie dogs barked out a warning at the sound of hoofbeats, their little tails wagging back and forth. He had to laugh at their antics. Some people thought the prairie dogs were a menace, but Corbin knew better. They ate the bad grasses that would kill cattle and had helped the cattle and buffalo herds to flourish. It was true that once in awhile a horse would step in a prairie dog hole and either throw the rider or become lame, but the good the little critters did far surpassed such infrequent accidents. Besides, any rider worth his salt should look where he was going.

"Pesky rodents. No better than rats, I say. Like to get rid

of the whole lot of 'em!" Gus was saying.

"Better prairie dogs than coyotes."

"Hmm! The surrounding hills hold plenty of those snarling predators as well," Gus answered peevishly.

Passing by a lone herder with his three sheep dogs tending a sizeable flock of sheep, Corbin noticed that the herder carried a Winchester repeater. No doubt it was for bagging coyotes, he thought. His suspicion was reaffirmed by his companion's grumbling.

"Coyotes. Only thing worse is *sheep!"*

Riding a bit farther, Corbin saw another herder with his flock. Some sheep were down by the water's edge, knee-deep in water, while others were just crossing the wooden bridge. On farther down, six covered sheep wagons and a sea of sheep grazing on the hillside drew his eye. How many herders were there? How ever many he knew that neither the sheep nor the sheep herders were very welcome in ranch country.

"Woolybacks! Stupid and unpredictable."

Same as some humans, Corbin thought with a smile.

"Damned sheep chew the grass down to a nub, leaving nothing for the cattle. Sooner or later, violence is bound to occur over this. It's happened in other areas of the land, and it will happen again."

Corbin thought how unfortunate it was that Gus was right. Sheepherding and cowherding just didn't mix.

"Bonjour!" Making a show of friendliness, one sheepherder greeted the riders. From his dress and the garments of the others, Corbin could tell that the herders were Basques from the Pyrenees; he'd seen their kind before. They had two strikes against them: their way of making a living and their nationality. Raising his hand he returned their greeting, though Gus rode stiffly by. Those were the "foreigners" Gus had been talking about, he thought. Although he knew he should not feel prejudice against them, he did too. He really didn't want them on this cattle-grazing land any more than anyone else did, and yet in Scotland his ancestors had raised sheep. The incessant baaing continued as Corbin galloped on.

A little farther along the trail he spotted farmers plowing under the best grassland. Once again, Gus bristled. Could it be that everyone was rushing to beat the next guy to good ground and water? That had happened in Colorado but had been settled in the courts. Now he understood what the bartender and hotel clerk had been talking about. The ranchers resented the intrusion. And well they should, he reasoned. The cattlemen were here first. It was cattle country.

Onto these vast cattle-covered ranges, newcomers were descending. Hank had said that they climbed on a horse like they were climbing a ladder, couldn't read brands, and owned eastern saddles. The hotel clerk had called them "nesters." No, they were not welcome here. Whereas cowhands drew fair wages, spent freely, had no family to support and took very little thought of tomorrow, nobody felt they needed these "blue-nosed nesters" around.

In return, the newcomers also feared and disliked the cowpunchers, Gus told him. To them the cowboy was a wild, reckless, hard-riding man who swore and feared neither God nor man. They regarded a cowboy as a swaggering swashbuckler who carried a gun and was quick to use it. Gus had heard the talk in the saloons of how afraid the ranchers and cowboys were that the newcomers would bring conflict into their way of life.

"For generations this has been wild roaring cow country, and we want it to stay that way. The homesteaders are trying to turn it into an agricultural society. Hell, soon they'll bring in their schools, churches and respectable moral codes of conduct, and spoil all the fun!"

"Just as they did in Colorado," Corbin answered somberly. He would have to agree that the homesteaders should stay at the edge of the prairie where they belonged and leave the ranch land to the ranchers and cowboys. He had come here for adventure, but it appeared that he might soon be drawn into some sort of conflict. Perhaps it was inevitable, but only time would tell.

After crosssing the Green River, they entered a well-watered open country with several miles of good grazing all around. The three-thousand-acre ranch was just what Corbin was looking for. Here a herd of yearling cattle could make splendid progress. There would be no need to break the unwritten law by crowding up or trespassing on range already occupied. That was what was causing so much trouble to begin with.

"Here you are, son. This is what you came to see. I've got to get back but you can look around." With a nod of his head Gus took his leave.

Corbin scouted around and came to an old trail which he followed for about twenty miles or so. At trail's end was a one-story log ranch house and a fair-sized corral. It wasn't as fancy as the Sundown Ranch, but with some hard work it could be made into a pretty nice ranch in time, he thought. He could build onto the bunkhouse and easily repair the corral fence. The barn was small, but it would hold enough winter feed for the small herd he intended to start with. This was just what he had in mind. The next thing to do was to get back to Rye Grass Station, go to the sheriff's department and see about purchasing it. He had no desire to get in anyone else's way. He only wanted to mind his own business, and hoped that others would do the same.

Chapter Six

For the moment Jessie was too caught up in the plans for the robbery to think about anything else. After last night's discussions, which lasted into the wee hours of morning, excitement stirred within her. At last she was going with the boys! Finally, they had fully accepted her. It had taken patience and a heap of convincing but she was going with them, thanks to Wade's and Butch's finagling. She couldn't even think of going back to Rye Grass Station to see Corbin MacQuarie as pleasant as that thought was. There was too much work to be done. She had to prepare herself for the upcoming robbery!

In between gulps of coffee, she managed to strap her gunbelt and holster around her waist and shove her short-barrelled Peacemaker revolver inside the holster. The tin cup, now empty, was hastily dropped on the table. After drawing the back of her hand across her mouth to remove the wetness from her lips, she picked up her Winchester carbine rifle, grabbed her hat from a peg on the wall, and bounded out the door.

Wade was just coming up the path to the cabin as Jessie ran down the hill toward him. She flashed him a grin and a wink, then hurried on, calling to him over her shoulder, "See you later, Wade. Don't have time to talk right now. Gotta practice my shootin', ya know."

"Well see that ya don't blow off yer toe while ye're at it, Jess. Be careful, hon. Slow down. Robbery ain't for quite awhile. . . ."

"Blow off my toe," she grumbled. Hell, she'd been shooting a gun since she was ten years old and had first been taken in by this bunch. Wade needed to have more confidence in her. She was about to give him a piece of her mind but his good-natured guffaw told her he was just teasing. Well, let him have his fun. He thought her interest in being an outlaw was just a passing fancy, but he'd see. She meant business.

It didn't take her long to reach the corral, saddle her pinto pony and gallop over the buffalo-grass-covered field toward her favorite wooded spot. All along the way she kept repeating to herself, "I can do it, I know I can." Yep, she was dead serious about proving herself, all right. Men! They thought they could do just about anything better than a woman, except the things they didn't really like to do — cooking and cleaning. She'd suffered their tomfoolery once too often. She'd heard the chuckles when Butch had announced she was going with them this time. Well, she'd show them!

For the next few days Jessie's plan was to improve her marksmanship, her draw and her aim. That was her intention now. 'Course, she knew there was no way she would ever be able to twirl a six-shooter round and round on her trigger finger, cocking and firing at each turn as she had seen Kid Curry do on the day they had first met. Curry and some of the others had exhibited such experience and speed that she couldn't help but admire their prowess. The important thing, anyway, was being able to hit exactly what she was aiming for. She knew Butch's rules. At no time was any person to be killed. Frightened, yes. They could shoot at hats, horses, guns and inanimate objects but never the passengers. It was for this reason she had to be on her toes. She didn't want one of her bullets to go astray.

Jessie urged her horse into a brisk run, heading toward her practice field. She knew this valley like the back of her hand, had ridden back and forth, up and down, more times than she could count. She had ridden in sub-zero weather through ice and snow with cold winds snapping at her cheeks and nose. Also in mid-summer with the sun shining down with all its force. Sometimes she had led pack horses loaded with supplies. Regardless of the conditions, she loved the freedom she felt here, away from the mainstream of cow-country traffic.

Coming now to a wooded area near the creek, she slid off the horse, patted him on the rump to indicate that he should stay to graze, and then headed on foot to a wide-open space just up ahead. The space was filled with rocks, tree stumps and overhanging cliffs. Here was the place where she could take aim at the flowers pushing themselves up through the crevices in the rocks. To clip them off from their stems required concentration and the greatest of skill.

Again and again she took aim, fired and hoped that the tiny flowers would be separated from their stems by her shots. First she got two out of five, then three out of six and finally six out of seven. When she was satisfied with her shooting, she moved back a few feet and tried from a farther distance. She had just lifted her rifle and was sighting it again when she was interrupted by a loud, masculine voice behind her.

"Well, I'll be damned. You really are somethin', you know that? 'Course now, I'd be supposin' there'd be an easier way for a gal to pick a bouquet." When she turned around she saw Billy standing behind her, a sly grin on his face.

"Billy! What you doin' here?" For a moment she'd feared it was Bob Meeks creeping up behind her.

"Just admirin' the scenery," he said, pushing his wide-brimmed hat back from his forehead as he grinned. There was a strange look in his eyes she had never noticed before.

A twinkle, a spark. "Naw. I'm lyin'. I saw you ride out and I followed."

"You followed?" Proudly she said, "I'm getting better all the time, ain't I?"

"Yeah, you sure are," he chuckled low in his throat. Jessie had meant at shooting but it was obvious he was thinking other thoughts. His hazel eyes swept from her hat to her boots, lingering at a point just in the middle. Jessie decided to ignore his bold stare.

"Want to try to outshoot me?" she asked, inviting him to join in the practice. Whatever he was thinking, she thought it best to distract him.

"Naw, Jessie. I'm gettin' bored with hiding out. Being an outlaw can be downright tedious." Once again his eyes danced over her. "How's about you and me ridin' into Rye Grass Station for a little *fun?*"

"Fun!"

"Just you and me together. Ya know what I mean!"

She did, but she was hoping she was wrong. Such an entanglement could ruin a good friendship. "Stop gawking at me like that. Why, you'd think I had a fly on my nose.

"I just like how you look, Jessie. You ought to be flattered that I find you so pretty."

"Pretty!" Somehow the thought that Bill was not taking the robbery as seriously as he should irritated her. Throwing her rifle to the ground, she scolded, "If that don't beat all! I never thought I'd live to see the day you'd act so silly. What the hell's gotten into you Billy? We have a train robbery comin' up and all you do is stare at me and say you want some fun. I've heard of people with clabber milk for brains but I sure never figured you to be one of 'em."

Her tirade caused him to wince, as if she had physically rebuked him. "Aw, don't be mad, Jess," he countered. "I'm prepared. You'll see. When the time comes I'll be ready. In the meantime. . . ." He raised his eyebrows suggestively.

"What makes you so sure?" Oh, but his attentions were

annoying her. Strange, but if it were Corbin MacQuarie acting this way, she'd have a far different reaction. She'd throw herself into his arms instead of backing away. But then, she loved Billy like a brother and Corbin . . . ? "You're as green as grass when it comes to robbin' trains. Holdin' up banks ain't nothin', and you've only done that once. Acted as a lookout, if I remember right."

"Yeah . . . yeah. I kept watch, all right, and probably will again. But train robbin' ain't what I got on my mind right now."

"Get to the point and we'll get this thing settled. Just what have ya got in mind?" As if she didn't know. Well, she'd soon set him straight. At the moment there were more critical things to be done than kissing and pawing.

"Git to the point? OK." Billy put his thumbs in his belt and strutted closer to her, obviously sure of himself. "You're gettin' to be a mighty good-lookin' woman, Jessie. I've been noticin' lately that you're no longer a kid."

She couldn't hide her smile. "I haven't been a kid for a long time, Billy."

"Well, maybe not, but if you get much bigger in the chest you'll have a helluva time posing as a fella when we pull a job," he blurted out. "I caught a look at you when you undressed last night. You forgot to blow the lamp out before you took off your drawers. I really got my eyes full when you took off that shirt of yours. I thought about it all night long, Jessie. Couldn't sleep for the trouble you caused me."

"You watched me!" Picking up a handful of pebbles she flung them at his head. "You . . . you . . . you Peepin' Tom. Why I . . . I never . . . !"

"Neither had I. . . . Ooo Eeee!"

She was flustered, flattered and more than a bit angry, all at the same time. "Is that what you followed me here to says?" Once again she couldn't help but to compare him to Corbin MacQuarie. Since meeting that golden-haired,

62

blue-eyed stranger, she couldn't even think of any other man seriously.

"I really didn't want to say much of anything, Jess. A little action is what I had in mind." He motioned with his thumb. "See that soft green bank over there by the river? It sure would make us a nice soft bed."

He was acting just like Jeff had once so long ago. Was love-making all a man ever thought about? If her first beau had been any indication, it was. She'd known Billy for years. They'd played together, gone skinny-dipping together, teased and taunted. Now he was acting, "just like a cockeyed jackass," she said aloud. "If you're suggestin' what I think you're suggestin', turn around and get the hell out of here, Billy. I just ain't interested." Reaching over, she picked up her Winchester from the ground and took aim.

"Ya wouldn't shoot me would ya, Jess?" His mouth formed an "o" of surprise.

"Sure as hell hope I don't have to." She cocked her gun threateningly, taking delight in bluffing him. He needed to be taught a lesson. A woman needed to be wooed, not taken for granted.

"You won't . . ." He kicked at a rock on the ground, sending it flying. "We coulda been good together, Jess, if you'd given me half a chance. But I guess being one of the boys is just more important to you. You don't know the first thing 'bout acting like a lady. Walkin' around in those britches, actin' like a man, it won't get ya nothin' but trouble. You'll see. And don't say I didn't warn you. . . ."

With that Billy nodded, turned around and left without a word. Jessie watched as he returned to where his horse was grazing alongside her own pinto, mounted his horse and rode off. Now that he had gone she was sorry she'd been so gruff with him. Had she angered him beyond making up? She hoped not. On thinking it over, Billy hadn't really done anything so terrible. She liked him but not in that way. A woman had a right to choose, just the same as a man. Billy just could never win her heart.

She knew what he would probably do now, ride into town and soothe his deflated ego in the cribs or in the arms of one of the saloon girls. Billy wouldn't stay mad long. Besides, he was more hurt than angry. She was sorry about that. His words had just taken her by surprise. None of the others had ever come right out and suggested such a thing to her. They just treated her like any other cowpuncher. That was what she wanted, wasn't it? Of course it was and yet his comment about her not knowing how to be a lady, that she would get into trouble, bothered her.

She knew just what she was doing. It just made things a lot easier if she wore pants. She'd learned three years ago how being a woman could complicate your life. All she'd gotten was a broken heart for her efforts. She wanted none of that. Billy was wrong and she was right. And yet, she hoped that being female wasn't going to make her life difficult from now on. What if it had been Bob Meeks who had seen her undress? She knew for certain he wouldn't have been so easy to frighten off. She would have to be more careful about that in the future. She might know pitifully little about Bob Meeks, but she did know that he was a womanizer, a dead shot with a rifle or pistol, and had spasms of uncontrollable anger when crossed. Yes, if there was to be any trouble, he'd be the cause.

Horse-theft was commonplace. And most cowhands rustled a few cattle now and then. That was hardly any reason to hang a man. On the other hand, the cold-blooded murder Bob had committed was a violent, unforgivable act against two unsuspecting prospectors. It was not even done in self-defense, but just because he needed their horses. No siree, she wouldn't trust that Bob Meeks as far as she could throw him.

The snap of a twig behind her caused Jessie to jump. It was only a small ground squirrel in search of its lunch, but she thought to herself that it might have been a more sinister visitor. She liked this secluded spot, but from now on perhaps it would be a good idea to stay closer to the campsite. Billy's showing up today might have been a good thing after all. Sort of a blessing in disguise. A warning. It had set her to thinking. Billy she could handle . . .

Bob she could not.

Chapter Seven

It was mid-afternoon when Corbin rode back into town, determined to own the rangeland he had visited earlier in the day. It was perfect for what he had in mind, just the right size, and water would be no problem. Two Green River tributaries flowed right through the acreage. Well, he'd just mosey on by the sheriff's, then over to the bank and settle the deal. 'Course, he had no intention of fanning the flames of resentment by throwing his weight around, but he did intend to own that property.

At the moment it was all he wanted, to gain access to the three thousand acres and a few head of breeding stock to start his own cattle breeding business. He could easily run the cattle up to Alberta, Canada to avoid high shipping costs. As to the M bar Q in Colorado, the inheritance he shared with Warren, he'd keep it separate and apart. No one needed to know of his large Colorado ranch holdings, at least until he proved himself to the folks hereabouts. It would be his secret for the moment.

Corbin made a mental list of all that needed to be done once he bought the ranch. He'd need ranch hands, of course, and he would treat them fairly. From what he'd learned from Gus when he stopped by the Sundown Ranch on his way back, the cowboys were having a hard time competing with big outfits. The Wyoming Stock Growers

Association had passed a rule forbidding employment to cowboys who owned *any* cattle, a way to keep a monopoly. Many cowboys had acquired a few cattle of their own, nothing very large, just a few head of strays and mavericks they had come by. Such cowboys were now on a blacklist and denied employment even without proof of any wrong-doing.

Was it any wonder they were easily riled to anger where cattle barons were concerned? Corbin thanked God that Colorado had taken steps to ward off any monopolies by big ranchers. Monopolies were bound to bring about hard feelings, if not downright violence. Tempers in Wyoming were flaring, and why not? They were making the owning of mavericks, or any cattle for that matter, by anyone but the big outfits, a crime. They were actually forcing the cowboys to rustle cattle just to keep body and soul together.

Corbin had talked to enough cowboys along the Rocky Mountain Ridge to know that most of the cowboys felt themselves to be free agents and that no sonofabitch from Cheyenne or anywhere else was going to dictate to them. He was behind them all the way. Certainly they seemed to need a champion. If excitement was what was lacking in his life, this was the place to be, or so he told himself as the town of Rye Grass Station came into view.

Corbin rode through town until he came to the sheriff's office. He dismounted, tied Rebel to the hitching post and with a jaunty strut, spurs jangling, he pushed the thick wooden office door open. The heavy-set, dark-haired man behind the desk never even bothered to remove his feet from the desk. Turning slightly around in his swivel chair, he called over his shoulder, "Something I can do for you?"

Corbin crossed to the sheriff's desk, placing his palms on the dusty surface and leaning forward. "It appears so. I came to see about the Tex Adam's place. I understand it's for sale and I want to buy it." The weight of the moneybelt that hugged his hips was reassuring.

"Well now, I don't know about that," the man mumbled, lazily picking at his teeth with a toothpick. "Someone else was in just a while ago. He was interested too. Offered $1.25 an acre. More than the goin' price." As if to ignore Corbin and give him a sign that their conversation was over, he turned his back and concentrated on the papers littering his desk.

"Well, I'd like a chance to counteroffer whoever it was. I assure you my money is just as good as your prospective buyer's." Corbin wasn't sure he fully trusted the sheriff after talking to the foreman of the Sundown Ranch. It rather appeared that he was either saving the ranch for some member of the Stock Growers Association or was trying to jack up the price in order to make a profit for himself. One or the other. He'd give him the benefit of the doubt. At least for now, however.

"Won't do you a bit of good." The tone of voice was gruff. "That ranch is nigh on to being sold."

"Then unsell it!" What could he do? What more could he say, unless he wanted to take the deed at gunpoint? He wanted that place, and wanted it bad. "I'm a gamblin' man myself. I'll raise the other fella ten cents an acre."

"Twenty!"

"Fifteen and not a penny more." Corbin slapped his hand against the desk top, causing the lawman to jump as if he had been kicked by a horse. He whirled around in his chair, his face marked by his anger, his eyes smoldering a challenge.

"W-who are you to be . . . ?" His voice faltered as he stared at Corbin, taking in the broad shoulders, the hard, lean strength, the stubborn stance. Slowly he got to his feet, his indignation wavering. "Well, I'll be . . ."

"I want that land!" Corbin punctuated his request with another strike at the desk top, so hard his hand stung.

"Corbin MacQuarie!" The lips beneath the dark drooping mustache smiled.

"Yes, I'm Corbin MacQuarie. . . ." Corbin's voice was smooth against the sudden silence. For a moment it would have been possible to hear a pin drop.

"Warren's little brother! Well, I'll be damned. Recognize that MacQuarie profile anywheres." Grabbing Corbin's hand he shook it up and down like a water pump handle. "Long time no see."

Corbin tried to remember where he'd seen this amply girthed man before. "I'm sorry. . . ."

"Art Conners is my name. One of my best friends during my years with the Pinkerton Agency was your brother. He used to bring me to the ranch house again and again for a taste of your mom's apple pie." Art Conners patted his rotund stomach. "That's where I got this, no doubt. In those days I was a mite skinnier, however." The smile seemed-genuine. "I remember you'd just returned from some fancy eastern college or somethin'. You used to beat the pants off me at chess."

Now Corbin remembered. There had been a scandal involving Art Conners but he couldn't remember all the details. Whatever it was, he'd been asked to resign from the agency. And this was the man who was the sheriff. Still, the old friendship just might be beneficial. "Guess it's a small world, Art," he said, forcing a smile.

"Shore as hell is! Well, I'll be damned. What do you know about that?" He offered Corbin his own leather padded chair. "Sit! Tell me what Warren is doin' now. I've sort of lost touch the last few years. . . ."

"He's got himself a new wife and has settled down to being a family man. No kids yet, but time will take care of that." Corbin winked as if to say Warren was working on it.

"Did he marry that cute little trick he met in Chicago? Jenny, I think her name was. The saloon dancer?" Art shook his head and laughed as he held his two hands up to his chest. "She sure as hell had big . . . well . . . sure had a . . . a case on him."

Corbin shook his head "No. He married a girl by the name of Henrietta Smitz. Don't think you ever met her. Warren didn't know her until he got out of detective work."

"Pretty?"

"Very."

"Big . . . uh . . . ?"

"Henrietta has curves in all the right places. A very pretty, dark-haired girl. Soft-spoken unless she's makin' a fuss. Determined but very genteel."

"Hmm." Art placed his hand on Corbin's shoulder in a friendly gesture. "Tell Warren when you write that right after I left the agency I went to work as a private detective for one of the largest cattle ranchers in Cheyenne. His name is Will Floyd. Worked for him until about six months ago. Oh yeah, and tell him I helped put that Butch Cassidy behind bars. He'll get a charge out of that. Seems Cassidy is making quite a name for himself since he got out of prison. It's about time to teach him another lesson, or so it appears."

"Butch Cassidy. I've been hearing that name quite a few times since I crossed over the state boundary."

" 'Course. He's a sly one. Most important outlaw leader hereabouts. Trying to make himself out to be another folk hero. Like Billy the Kid or Jesse James. But I'll corner him one day," he said with a show of bravado. "Tell ole Warren I could use him to do just that."

"I'll tell him," Corbin murmured. In truth he hoped Warren didn't get any ideas about returning to detective work. Two hundred and twenty-five dollars a month and all expenses paid might not seem such a bad deal to most, but Corbin was all too aware of the dangers. The cowhands resented that kind of money being paid when they only drew $25 a month and a bunkhouse to sleep in. Couldn't blame them for that, because cattle herding was hard work; and yet so was chasing outlaws.

Art Conners broke into a tirade, bragging about his

exploits, as if Corbin hadn't heard such stories before; then an uncomfortable silence sprang up between the two men, as if neither knew what else to say. Finally Corbin broke the silence. "Now, about that rangeland I want. Are you going to accept my offer?"

"You and Warren come from a ranching family and have been in this business long enough to know how it works. You scratch my back and I'll scratch yours. That's only fair." The smile Art Conners gifted Corbin with was a bit too wide and Corbin could only wonder what the payoff would be. "Because you are Warren's brother, not to mention a big land-owning *MacQuarie*, I'll let you have it for that $1.25 an acre. The other fella doesn't need to know how much you paid. Some things we keep secret around here."

Those were just the words Corbin had hoped to hear, but he did feel a little uncomfortable knowing he was a favored buyer because his brother was a friend of the sheriff and because of his family name. It also made him uneasy knowing that one of these days Art Conners would expect a favor in return.

"I'll take it," he said nonetheless. One couldn't look a gift horse in the mouth, or so he'd heard it said. "Dunna fash yerself," his father would have told him. Seeing that Art Conners had a map of the area on his desk, he leaned down to take a look at the boundary markings, tracing them with his index finger. It lay right in between two areas that had been marked in red. That fact boded watching. "I've got the money right here," he stated. Calculating in his head, he withdrew the money and carefully counted it. "Care to accompany me to the bank, just for safety's sake?"

"Sure—then we'll get over to the Land Office and make it legal." If Conners seemed a bit too accommodating, Corbin ignored it. He'd just have to keep careful watch. Besides, deep down inside, he knew he would be fair in his dealings with the cowboys. Perhaps another buyer would

71

not. That was foremost in Corbin's mind as he went about the business of paying out his cash and acquiring the deed.

The next thing he had in mind to do was to hire some of the laid-off cowpokes the Sundown Ranch foreman had told him about. He was a man of energy, zeal, and honor and wanted to be well liked in the little town of Rye Grass Station. After all, this was to be his new home. He wanted no part of the public outrage over favoritism shown to prominent families. An understanding of neighbors was vital to the success of any ranching enterprise. He planned to give respect to those who earned it and scorn to those who did not, regardless of wealth. He had no desire to mention his family connections or try to instigate himself into Brown's Park society; to the contrary he intended to stay to himself, at least for awhile.

As he and Art Conners walked from the Land Office he made his wishes known. "I'd appreciate it if we could keep my family's influence in the cattle business as quiet as possible, Art. Think we could do that? At least for awhile?"

"Never had a request like that before." Art Conners looked at him quizzically. "Most people wouldn't want to do it that way, Corbin. But if that's the way you want it, that's the way it'll be. Of course, I can't promise anything. Here in this rugged mountain country, news travels all over the area. It becomes known to every settler, every cowhand, every bartender, every barber, banker, or businessman in town." Art shook his head and looked Corbin right in the eye. "Maybe you should have used an assumed name like some of the others around here."

Corbin laughed. "It's too late for that now. I've talked to too many people, registered at a hotel, and already am known by some in these parts. Besides, most of the assumed names are taken by outlaws and I don't want to be thought of as an outlaw. I just want to be one of the ranchers in Brown's Park Valley. I want to make my ranch a successful one. That's my only aim right at the moment."

Art Conners tried to keep up with Corbin's long strides, shaking his head all the while. "I sure can't understand you. Most people with money are proud of it."

"Yes, I know, but I want to remain anonymous until I'm better acquainted with the territory and the people. I have my own reasons." Corbin's expression clearly told the other man that argument wouldn't do any good.

"Whatever you say." He guffawed. "If I didn't know better, I might think you had somethin' to hide. Sure you ain't running from the law?" At Corbin's scowl he quickly said, "Naw . . . just jibin'. If you're anything like Warren, nobody will ever mistake you for an outlaw. I've never seen anyone quite so dedicated to law and order as that brother of yours."

"I'm just as dedicated and twice as stubborn. Never cared much for seeking a career in law enforcement, that's all. But once I set my mind to somethin' I'm just as single-minded." Corbin's tone held a hint of a warning, just in case.

"I reckon ya are. Yep, I reckon ya are. . . ." Taking out his pocketwatch, the sheriff acted impatient. "Well, will ya look at that! Four o'clock already. Guess I'd better get going. I've still got a lot to do." Their goodbye was amiable, with Corbin thanking Art Conners for his help in settling the matter of the ranch and Conners promising to pay a "friendly call" after things got settled.

Within the next few days Corbin purchased the ranch land, bought one hundred head of cattle from a rancher in Montana, hired a crew of twelve men and was in the cattle business again. His plan was to assist the men in his employ in every way possible, for he felt the cowboys had gotten a raw deal. If he could find Jesse he'd offer him a good job, too. If things were as tough for him as they were for the others in the area, he would need a helping hand.

That kid had really made a lasting impression on him,

one that he couldn't seem to ignore. He liked Jesse's way of thinking, his attitude, his courage and confidence. Not to mention the fact that he was an excellent companion. Corbin laughed to himself every time he thought about the game of pool. Yes, Jesse was excellent company as long as they never played another game of pool again, he thought with a smile.

So far things had gone quite well for him. Not only did he have a great deal of experience in ranching, which certainly showed, but he also had a special knack for making friends easily. The men he had hired liked him and were grateful that they finally had jobs again. Most of the men he had hired were those recommended by the foreman at Sundown Ranch. He and Gus, the foreman at Sundown, had become friends and Corbin listened to his advice on just which men to hire, though he didn't always take it.

There seemed to be a hundred things to do. Until the new bunkhouse was completed some of the men would have to sleep out in the open, but then most of the cowboys didn't mind that a bit. That's the way they slept while on a cattle drive. They were used to it. They preferred it unless the weather turned bitterly cold. Since it was pushing into September, that gave Corbin little time to spare. Winter would be upon them sooner than they knew.

It didn't take the men long to notice that Corbin was not afraid of work. He would pitch right in, doing anything that needed to be done. He hauled hay, chopped and stacked wood, helped in the building of the bunkhouse and had even ridden out with two of the cowboys to bring in a stray which had somehow wandered away from the herd. Just as if he was one of the ranch hands, he had carried a coil of rope and a shotgun in case of trouble. Luckily the rifle hadn't been necessary. For the time being, all seemed peaceful.

One of the newly hired men was the best in the country for finding wandering cattle in the timbered country just beyond. It didn't take him long to prove his worth. Archie Jarvis was his name, and if his attire was a bit shabby—scuffed boots, slightly crumpled Stetson, faded trousers and old leather vest, there was an air of efficiency about him that Corbin liked. He had a feeling it wouldn't be long until they'd be friends, a camaraderie initiated when Corbin accompanied him in search of a stray cow. Archie found the heifer down in a cranny by the river, taking upon himself the trying job of tying ropes to the young cow's hind legs and tugging and pulling until she was free. During the process, Archie had looked over at Corbin and judged him favorably, an opinion that was echoed by the others.

"Looks like you're a hard worker yourself, boss. I admire a man who doesn't sit on his backside. You can count upon my loyalty." Corbin did count on it, and rewarded Archie with the job of foreman.

Sometimes Corbin would join the ranch hands around the campfire at night. He enjoyed looking out over the vast countryside at the bright moon and stars overhead or at the majestic mountains surrounding the valley. Oftentimes coyotes howled or owls hooted in the distance, setting a special kind of mood one could only find out in the open. After the stray had been returned to the herd, Corbin sat with the other men on the rocky hillside and commented on how peaceful it looked—deceptively tranquil.

"It's not bad out here, but throughout the valley we have plenty of trouble when some outsider arrives tryin' to muzzle in and get his fingers in the pie," a man known as "Bowlegs" said.

"Yeah, but we're mighty glad when the likes of *you* come in once in awhile. It's obvious you're no highfalutin' company man," Archie added.

A rather quiet young cowboy named Jim Stonesworth added his two cents' worth to the conversation. "Most of them want more than their share and that means not even stopping at tryin' to be the biggest ranchers around but pressing on to being even bigger and bigger. Oink, oink," he grunted. "Them cattle barons are just as greedy as hogs."

"Don't want none of them kind here!" Archie grumbled.

"No siree!" They all echoed, making Corbin suddenly feel uncomfortable. His serene mood was spoiled and he felt a slight twinge of guilt for not being totally honest with his ranch hands. It was a mood that didn't pass even when a tall, lean, red-haired cowboy took out a jews'-harp and played a winsome melody.

While the others sat around the fire talking, telling stories, smoking and drinking, Corbin did a serious bit of thinking. Once his ranch was established and running smoothly, what then? Surely there was more to life than roping and branding. A woman. Somehow a man's thoughts always seemed to turn to the gentler sex. Yes, it had been a long time since he'd held a woman in his arms and he seemed ready for an entanglement. He'd have to eye the ladies the next time he went into town. Putting his hands behind his head, he looked up at the stars with that thought in mind. And yet, hadn't he learned that love often came when a man least expected it?

Chapter Eight

Jessie squinted her eyes against the early morning sun's glare dancing through the window. Today was *the day*. At high noon she'd be riding out with the boys to intercept the Union Pacific Number Thirty-Four. Now that the time was drawing near she was nervous, though she would never have admitted that to a single soul, not even to Wade. That's why she hadn't slept a single wink all night. Her stomach was tied up in knots, and a large lump constricted her throat every time she even thought about it. She was really going to do it, yes siree, become a bonafide member of the Wild Bunch.

Who knows, she thought, maybe I'll even take on a nickname for myself. Kid Watson? No, too common. Calamity Jessie? Naw. "Southpaw" Jessie? She was left-handed, after all. That one had possibilities.

She wondered, what would Corbin MacQuarie think if he knew she was an outlaw? The very thought troubled her. She hadn't told him, perhaps she never would. Her common sense told her it was best that he didn't find out. Somehow Corbin MacQuarie seemed the type to take the law's side on the matter.

"Corbin MacQuarie," she whispered to herself, as his image danced before her mind. What a hankering she had for that blue-eyed, golden-haired handsome hunk of a man. Hell, she hadn't seen him again, though it hadn't been for lack of trying. Twice now she'd gone into town hoping to just "run into him" only to be disappointed. Corbin MacQuarie was otherwise occupied. Though she hadn't had any luck, however, she had learned a thing or two that made her smile. The handsome blue-eyed Scotsman had bought a ranch to the northeast of town and from the talk it appeared that he was "settling in." Jessie thought perhaps after the robbery was over she just might pay him a call. Friendly like. A welcoming of sorts. Mmm, how she liked that idea!

A loud knock announced a visitor. Jessie had been lying in one spot too long. She moved to ease a cramp that was beginning to twitch in the calf of her leg, wincing at the discomfort, then she bounded out of bed. Not wanting to be caught lollygagging around on such an important day, she tugged her pants on over her long johns and pulled on a shirt.

"Jessie! You in there?" Butch's voice. "Come on out if you are. We gotta get moving. We've only got a few hours before the train comes through. Don't want to have to rush. Wanta make a practice run if we have time."

"I'm comin'. I'm comin'." Her fingers were clumsy as they fumbled with her buttons. Strapping on her holster and running her fingers through her tousled hair she managed a smile as she opened the door.

"Well, now don't you look eager, Jess." Butch grinned, longing to tease. "But that holster sure looks mighty empty. Don't forget your guns."

"I won't." Jessie snorted with indignity. "I was in a hurry to open the door and . . . "Realizing he was just trying to get her goat she met his smile with one of her own. "Wouldn't forget a thing like that, Butch."

"I did once. Yes siree. When I was about fourteen I was in such a dither to accompany ole Mike Cassidy, my friend and namesake, that I tore off without a gun." Plucking her hat from a peg on the wall, Butch plopped it on her head. "Now I feel naked without it."

"I wouldn't have forgotten mine. I wouldn't, Butch. Wade can tell you how many hours I've spent target-practicing." Jessie's eyes swept over the room as she spoke, making certain she hadn't forgotten anything that could become the butt of jesting later on. Her neckerchief. She'd have to use it to tie around the lower part of her face when they approached the train. "I can shoot the petals off a daisy at a hundred yards."

"Is that right?" Butch seemed favorably impressed. "Well, I hope there won't be any need for shooting. I want this robbery to be peaceable. Don't want to rile the good citizens around Rye Grass Station unduly." Pulling out his pocketwatch he clucked his tongue as he looked at the time, then hastened her along.

Saddling her horse, Jessie put her left foot in the stirrup and pulled herself up. The hooves of her pinto echoed Butch's sorrel's as they rode their horses down the sloping knoll to join the others. Jessie thought how from a distance they all looked like a frightening bunch of hooligans, hats pulled down low on their foreheads, neckerchiefs waiting to hide their noses and mouths. There were wanted posters on more than just a few of the gang, offering sizable rewards. Were they dangerous? In reality some were, some weren't.

Wade, for example, wouldn't hurt a flea but his scowl made him look fearsome. Jed Bates spoke in a raspy growl but he too was more bluff than brutality. Billy was in so many ways just a lonely kid. Butch enjoyed the game of outlawing but in reality had a friendly streak that kept him amiable. Grant Tabor was a little too quick on the draw but so far hadn't killed anyone. Kid Curry was a man one ought not to cross. Sundance sometimes let his ego get in the way. Bob Meeks, on the other hand, was a whole different story. His eyes glinted like twin coals in the sunlight, his jaw was set with grim determination. From where she sat her horse Jessie could see his callused fingers brush against his gun as if longing to pull it free. Oh, he was a mean one.

"Well, so you're goin' this time. So nice to have something pleasant to feast my eyes on." Bob's voice was deceptively soothing as he pulled his horse alongside Jessie's mare.

"Keep your eyes to yourself!" Jessie exclaimed tartly.

His smile reminded her of a Cheshire cat's but she knew him to be more weasel in temperament. "Bet you wouldn't be talkin' like that if I were that rancher you've been chasin' after. Bet you'd let him look you over from ass to armpits and do much more than that if he had a hankerin'.'

"What do you know about that?" Jessie was alarmed. She didn't want Bob anywhere near Corbin.

"I got ears and I got eyes. Besides, I followed you into town and heard you askin' about him. Corbin MacQuarie, wasn't that his name?" Taking out his pistol he toyed with the handle, then put it back. "Might run across him some time. Wouldn't that be interesting."

Jessie didn't have time to answer. The ground exploded with the thud of hoofbeats as the gang rode out. Nudging her horse's flanks she hastened to keep up. The last thought that flitted through her mind was the hope that Corbin MacQuarie and Bob Meeks never came face to face.

The clanging of a spoon against an old tin pan startled Corbin out of a deep sleep. His eyes snapped open as he yelled, "Archie!" Well, he'd *told* him to get him up at the crack of dawn, so he didn't have any complaints. "All right! All right! I'm awake. I'm *awake,*" he hollered through the open door. The noise suddenly ceased.

Stretching and yawning Corbin put one foot on the floor, longing to stay abed just a quarter of an hour or so longer but trains had a way of leaving if a body wasn't there on time. Trains! He growled in derision, wishing there was another way to go about his errand, but knowing very well it was the only way. He was on a very special mission that started as soon as he got to the station.

"Stamash!" He mumbled, succumbing to another yawn. The name was Scottish and meant "blind fury," an appropriate name for a prize Highlander bull. Corbin was determined to breed the animal with his newly acquired heifers in hopes of producing a superior cattle stock. Stamash and cattle like him had been bred in Scotland to withstand the harsh Highland climate; thus they were sturdy, stocky, and fleshy, interesting to look at with that long, shaggy brown hair of theirs. A "bonny fine beastie," as his father would have said.

Corbin laughed as he imagined just what Archie would say when he set eyes on the bull. He'd scold and he'd grumble, espousing his opinion that a Wyoming bull would do just as well. His foreman was not one to keep his thoughts to himself. Corbin, however, knew just what he was doing. It was an idea that had taken root in his head a few days ago. He'd already sent a telegram advising Warren that he was on his way and that he would not take no for an answer. The ranch and all the cattle on the M bar Q were half his after all. Borrowing the beast was what he had in mind, however, at least until Stamash had impregnated a major portion of his cows. Then he'd give him back. Until then he intended to see that the bull had a safe ride to Wyoming and was comfortably quartered as befitted so important a "guest."

Perhaps I can even convince Warren to come back with me, just for a stay, he thought. Might do him good to have a short respite from that clinging vine he had married. All night Corbin had wondered what his brother would think of his "little" place. It was a rugged paradise, a man's fulfillment of a dream. He believed Warren would like it.

81

Although they were different in temperament and personal likes and dislikes, Warren and Corbin were as close as two brothers could possibly be. He was anxious to explain his plans to him and get his opinion. Somehow a telegram just couldn't do the needs of the place justice.

Again the racket of spoon on pan disturbed Corbin's solitude. Archie was determined that he would not miss his train. The morning air was chilly on Corbin's nude body as he rolled from the bed. Wrapping a towel around his waist, he washed and shaved then slipped on his underdrawers, a pair of brown breeches, and his boots. He'd put on his shirt, tie and coat later. Taking the rickety stairs two at a time he sought out the kitchen and plopped down in a chair at the table.

"Prepared flapjacks, bacon and eggs for your meal," Archie announced, setting a plate heaped with breakfast delicacies before Corbin's eyes.

"It's enough to feed a horse!"

"Or a bull!" Archie chuckled deep into his throat. "Well . . . I know how them trains are. Don't treat a fella right. Why, you'll be nigh on to starvin' before ya get to Denver. No good food aboard."

"Certainly nowhere near as good as yours, Arch. If you weren't already my foreman I'd hire you on as cook in a minute. . . ." Pouring a thick, oozing coating of syrup on the stack of pancakes, Corbin busied himself with eating. Archie was amazing, all right. There didn't seem to be anything he couldn't do. Mend fences, shoe horses, rope steers. A jewel of a man. A positive treasure. He'd have to tell Warren all about him. It was Archie who, despite all his other duties, had insisted on helping Corbin by taking his telegram to the telegraph office. Archie had even stopped by the train station and picked up Corbin's ticket, just so there wasn't a possibility he would not be able to leave on the morning train. Oh, yes. Of all his discoveries, Archie was perhaps the best.

"Ya all packed?" Archie had a mothering streak in him as well.

"I'm only taking a few things. Don't really need a change of clothing. I kept some of my belongings — shirts, trousers and boots — at my brother's. Besides, I'll be back here before you know it. With Stamash."

"Stamash?"

"You're in for a surprise, Arch." Corbin held out his cup for some of the thick, dark brew that Archie called coffee. It was hot and it was strong. Enough to wake him up and keep his eyes open the whole trip.

"A shaggy brute, is he? Well, I' hope ya have enough money to buy him, Corbin. You've been spending money so fast it makes my head swim. Take my advice and be careful. Don't forget how easily ole Tex got hisself into debt. I don't want ya to do the same thing and end up losing this place."

"Don't worry. I'm watching every penny. Really." Corbin was touched by Archie's concern. They were so very quickly becoming good friends.

"If not, well . . . I got a little stashed away that I could loan ya. . . ."

"Thank you, I'll remember that." The large clock outside the kitchen door chimed the time. "I'd better hurry. I'm not completely dressed yet." Wiping his lips with the end of the checkered tablecloth, Corbin sprang to his feet. He started up the stairs but Archie detained him.

"Don't forget your ticket! Won't go very far if'n ya do." Pulling it out of his trouser pocket he handed it to Corbin. "Union Pacific Train, Number Thirty-Four. Remind me to tell you about my stint with the railroad. Yes siree, I drove those spikes and rails under the blazing sun. Helped lay a web of tracks clear across the country."

"I didn't know you were with the railroad." Corbin patted Archie on the back. "You've nearly done it all."

"Yep. Ten years. Before I made ranching my trade. But

we'll talk of it another time. Stories I have to tell take up more time than you've got this mornin'." Archie shooed Corbin away. "So git. I'm anxious to see this Highland bull of yours."

"Shouldn't take me too long. End of the week at the most, perhaps a few days more. Depending. I'm not planning on a very long stay at my brother's. I have my reasons." *Henrietta.* Corbin hurried upstairs to finish dressing, placing the ticket Archie had purchased safely in his pocket.

Chapter Nine

The train station was crowded with people, surprisingly so for such a small town. There were those without baggage, obviously there to meet arriving passengers, as well as those who were carrying boxes and bags of various shapes and sizes. Corbin noticed several ginghammed and ribboned young ladies giving him the eye and returned their stares with a wide smile.

"Howdy, ladies!" Once or twice he even tipped his hat.

Though he was not overly aware of his appearance, he did hear one young miss comment that he looked strikingly handsome. As he passed by the train station's front window he appraised his appearance. He had dressed in a brown pinstriped suit with matching double-breasted vest, a white shirt, striped green and yellow tie, brown leather boots, and a black bowler with curled brim. Usually he did not care much for dressing up; he was much more comfortable in cotton shirts and Levis. Oh, how he missed his wide-brimmed Stetson; but he had some transactions to conduct at the Bank in Denver before he went to the M bar Q and knew how important it was to make a good impression, especially when you wanted to withdraw money.

The train was late. From time to time Corbin would unconsciously touch the gold watch chain draped across from the watch pocket of his vest to one of the front buttonholes of the waistcoat. Only when he traveled did time enter into his thoughts. Generally, out on the range, things just got done when they got done and there wasn't all the fuss and bother about how long it took.

Corbin felt comfortable about having left Archie, who was now his trusted foreman, in charge of the ranch. He was a good worker, an honest man and had exhibited his loyalty in dozens of ways. Corbin felt that he had left the running of the ranch in good hands and knew that Archie could handle any emergency should any arise. That took a load off his mind and soothed his thoughts somewhat about traveling.

The black smoke streamed from the engine, the bell sounded and the brakes began to screech as the long train pulled into the Green River, Wyoming Station. The train was ten minutes late. When it had finally come to a stop he stepped back as a throng of passengers flocked around the waiting platform, throwing themselves into relatives' arms or just meandering down the steps. Then when a voice called "All aboard!" boarding began. Pushing through the crowd, carpetbag in one hand, ticket in the other, Corbin climbed up the two steps along with the other passengers.

There were two passenger cars. He would be in the one closest to the engine. Not because he had any preference of one over the other, it was just that he had been pushed along in that direction. There were many passengers on this train, which had come from Montana to Green River and was now on its way to Laramie, Cheyenne and on to Denver.

The train whistle sounded; the conductor, in his black uniform and flat-topped hat with a bill in front, called "All aboard!" again. Most of the seats were filling up rapidly. Corbin spotted a seat across from two well-dressed ladies traveling with a little boy of about six years of age. Tipping his hat to the ladies, he sat down next to the child as the train jerked and pulled away from the station platform.

They were on their way.

At first it was noisy inside the train as people chattered, bags clunked together, and passengers meandered about. Soon, however, things settled down and Corbin noted that several of his fellow travelers were playing cards, just snoozing, or simply viewing the scenery, what there was of it. At this point, the beginning of the trip, only low, rolling hills covered with sagebrush and tumbling weeds could be seen. There were mountains in the far distance, however, and Corbin knew that the scenery would improve as the trip progressed further southeast toward Colorado. In the meantime he just laid his head back to relax.

He couldn't help thinking how he really dreaded train rides since his parents' fatal accident when the train they were on collided with another train. They had been returning from a cattle buyers' convention in Boston when the accident occurred. He wasn't cowardly, but he hated being reminded of their deaths, and would have preferred to travel by horseback.

The steady, pulsating rhythm of the train wheels nearly mesmerized him as Corbin settled back in his seat. It was going to be a long journey, but not half as tedious as it would have been on horseback. Well, he'd just hope that this time the damned fools knew how many trains were traveling down the track. Hopefully practice made perfect. That thought made him smile and feel more relaxed. Soon the click of the steel wheels on the rails like the monotonous tick of a metronome lulled him into a semi-sleep.

"Hey, mister, wake up. You're going to miss seeing that water tower. Look how tall it is."

Corbin felt a tug on his arm and glanced out of the corner of his eye at the boy who had his nose pressed to the window. "Water tower, huh?" he mumbled. "Well, suppose you tell me what it looks like."

"Goes nearly all the way to the sky. There's so much to see, but it goes by so fast. . . ."

"You ever been on a train before?"

"Nope!" The child pulled his nose from the window where he had been gazing at the blowing tumbleweeds and turned toward Corbin. "Have you?"

"Quite a few times. Where are you going, son?"

"I'm going to see my granddad." The boy stood up in the seat as if to get a better view of the scenery. "Where you goin'?"

"To Denver," Corbin answered.

"Why?"

Corbin laughed, evading the question of going all that way for a stud bull by saying, "Guess you could say I plan to make a whole lot of *females* happy." He certainly hoped so, for it would prove to be profitable indeed.

"What's your name, mister?"

One of the ladies, a pertly pretty brunette, obviously his mother, grabbed the boy's shoulder gently and pushed him down in the seat, saying, "Sit down and be a good boy and don't ask so many questions." She turned to Corbin. "He has always been a talkative, friendly boy. I hope he isn't disturbing you."

"No, ma'am, he isn't. I like kids. What's your name, son?"

"Andy. Andy Prescott." The boy answered throwing his chest out with pride. "My dad is mayor of Rye Grass Station."

"My name is Corbin. Corbin MacQuarie." Corbin offered his hand in a manly handshake.

Soon Andy and Corbin were the best of friends. The ladies smiled their approval as Corbin pointed out various animals, vegetation, and points of interest to Andy. He was keeping the boy amused and that pleased the ladies very much. A large herd of antelope leapt along through the tall grass not too far from the railroad tracks, causing Andy to jump up and down and shriek with delight, a burst of enthusiasm drowned out in the roar of the train clattering over the tracks. The wheels chanted rhythmically as the train rattled on.

At that same moment, several masked gunmen were riding alongside the last few cars of the long train, keeping well out of sight. Butch Cassidy was with them, but since he had promised not to take part in any robberies within the boundaries of Wyoming, he had only masterminded the robbery. He would take no active part. Thus he would keep the promise he had made to the sheriff when he had been released from prison last year. Everyone knew Butch Cassidy was a man of his word. To him, a promise was meant to be kept and although he would share in the loot, he would not board the train and take an active part.

As the band of nine bandits rode beside the train, Jessie watched as Jed Bates and Bill McCarty, a former member of the Jessie James gang, leaned from their horses, caught the rail of the last car and pulled themselves up. Once on board, they climbed the ladder leading to the top of the train and were now running along the top jumping from car to car.

Jessie could hardly believe her eyes. It was a daring thing to do with the train moving so rapidly and something she would never have even dared. A bit too foolhardy for her tastes, and yet they were successful. As planned, Jed and Bill would stop the train and four of the masked riders would enter the passenger cars. Cleophas Dowd, Butch and Wade would remain outside to cover them. It had taken a month to work out the details but every one had his part in the plan worked out to perfection. Even Billy Morris had straightened up and done his share of target practice. Jessie knew he wouldn't stay mad at her for long.

Jessie was not as nervous as she had been a few days. She had breathed a sigh of relief when Butch sent Bob Meeks on ahead to check things out and make arrangements at Hole-in-the-Wall, Wyoming. He had taken care of the last-minute details as to the time of the train's arrival, how much money was on board and how large a crew there would be and so on. He had also taken care of stashing supplies, food, bandages, whiskey, and other needed items at the hideout.

It had been a welcome relief not to have to put up with his searing stares and pointed comments. But now she was sorry he had returned, for she hated being in his presence again. She still wouldn't trust him as far as she could throw him, she thought. Every lewd glance he flashed her way told her what he had on his mind. The only thing that put her mind at ease was the fact that he would be too occupied with the robbery to take much notice of her. She would have to remind herself constantly to stay clear of him once they got to their new campsite. They would not return to Brown's Park Valley, but would lay low at Hole-in-the-Wall, until things cooled down a bit after the robbery.

"Stop daydreaming. Let's get goin'," Bob was saying now.

Jessie and six others rode furiously alongside the train, keeping well out of view of the passenger cars up ahead. The passenger cars were the second and third cars after the engine and coal car. All together there were about twelve cars on the long train. There were cattle cars, express cars carrying merchandise, and a mail car in addition to a caboose. There was no gold shipment on this train but there would be plenty of money. The payment for the railroad workers in Denver was locked in the safe in the mail car. The entire safe was to be taken off the train, dynamited to open it, and the loot divided when they reached Hole-in-the-Wall. This haul would bring them forty to fifty thousand dollars, or so Butch calculated.

There was little time for talking but plenty was going on in Jessie's pretty head. Lordy, she'd had no idea just how exciting the whole thing would be! Her pulse was beating rapidly, her stomach churned with excitement, and beads of perspiration gathered along her browline just above the red flowered bandana she wore around her face, and upon her gloved hands. She couldn't afford to make any mistakes. This was her big chance and she had no intention of doing less than her best. She could do it, *she could do it!* She repeated that to herself over and over as the horses galloped at top speed to keep up with the train.

Suddenly the train began to slow down and she knew that Jed and Bill had made it to the engine and were now holding the engineer at gunpoint, forcing him to bring the train to a halt. Jessie heard a shrill whistle blast while the metallic shrieking of the wheels on the rails rose above the rattle of the coach-couplings. Bill's hand extended from the engine window, waving a red flag to assure that all was well. That was the signal for them to board. The train screeched and came to a stop out in the middle of nowhere, somewhere near Elk Mountain, Jessie calculated. The next stop would be Laramie, far on down the line.

After firing gunshots into the air to let them know they meant business, the four bandits climbed aboard. Billy Morris and Tom Kilpatrick entered one car. She and, of all people, Bob Meeks entered the other just as planned. Masks over their faces, hats drawn low over their foreheads, pistols in hand, they were cool, calm and a frightening sight. Jessie thought that if she said "boo!" at this very moment more than one of these poor folks would faint dead away. It was an invigorating game, all right. It was downright fun being so much in control. No wonder the boys got such a kick out of this outlaw business.

"Everybody just stay where you are and no one will get hurt!" Jessie rasped, certain she could keep that promise. Butch had been adamant. Not one passenger was to shed even a thimbleful of blood. It was an order. "Frighten them but don't harm them," he had said.

Several female passengers screamed, unaware of Butch's intent for their safety. One looked as white as a ghost; the few children climbed into the arms of the adults, seeking protection, some burying their faces in the bosom of their mothers. Several of the men put protective arms around their ladies but Bob would have none of that. "Arms out, hands in your laps palms up if you know what's good for you," his gruff voice declared. "We don't want to hurt nobody but we will if you try any funny business. Just put the things in the sack and keep your hands where we can see them."

While he kept the passengers well covered, Jessie went from seat to seat collecting watches, earrings, tie pins, cuff links, money and any other valuable items. They were placed in a sack which she held out to each passenger. Since instructions had already been given, Jessie said nothing, just moved up and down the aisles.

Suddenly Jessie stopped in her tracks. Her breath caught in her throat. No! It just couldn't be! Her eyes were playing tricks on her. They just had to be. And yet, there he was. Corbin MacQuarie was looking down the barrel of Bob Meeks's Peacemaker. The man she had thought she would never see again. My God, what now? It was impossible for her to do anything except what she had been instructed to do, though at that moment she would have liked nothing better than to turn around and run. Corbin was hesitating. What if he decided to pull a gun? Would Bob shoot him despite Butch's orders? Her hands trembled at the very thought. Oh, please, let everything go smoothly. She didn't want Corbin or anyone else to incite Bob's temper.

Whatever she did, Jessie knew she could not allow any emotion to be evident in her voice. "All right, mister, let's have that watch, tie pin and any money on your person." She tried to be as fierce as possible, keeping her voice low and raspy so that he wouldn't recognize it. Thank God he did *not* go for his gun.

"Be quiet, everyone," Corbin advised. Damn, if only he had his gun, but he had foolishly left it with his other baggage. Who would have ever envisioned a train robbery, of all things. "Just do as you are told." The command in his voice caused the others to obey without incident.

The items Jessie had asked for were placed in the sack and she proceeded on down the aisle, looking over her shoulder as she made her way. She had finally reached the door as Bob came down the aisle collecting the last of the valuables.

"Went like clockwork! Butch was right . . ." he was saying.

Suddenly a boy darted out in front of him, toward the door Jessie had just opened as she jumped from the train. "Give that money back. It belongs to my pa and ma!" he yelled, tugging at Bob's arm.

"Andy! Come back!" a woman shrieked. "Oh, don't hurt my Andy. Please!"

"Why, you little brat! I ought to . . ." Bob caught the boy by the arm and shoved him hard against the side of the seat. "I'll break your arm and then you won't be so brave." With a vicious grunt he twisted the child's wrist until the boy cried out in pain.

"My arm! My arm! Ouch! You're hurting my arm."

Within moments all hell broke out. Nobody seemed to know exactly how it happened. Corbin jumped to his feet in an effort to protect Andy. "Leave the boy alone! If you want to tangle with anyone, let it be with me!"

Corbin eyed the gunman warily. The eyes between the bandanna and hat brim were hostile. The eyes of a killer. Corbin fixed his gaze on the man, watching warily as he squeezed the handle of his gun.

"Tangle with you?" Bob laughed evilly.

Corbin's blue eyes stared straight into slate gray ones and he could see his sentence in the man's eyes. Even so he would have held his ground had not Andy suddenly sprung free. As he did so, he pulled the mask from Bob's face and knocked his hat off. There were enough wanted posters in the area for everyone on board to know the man's identity.

This man was a wanted murderer. And what of that partner of his? The lad must be a vicious criminal, and a killer, too. There had been enough pictures of this Bob Meeks posted in every town to paper several walls. Not only that, but there was a reward of $1,000 for his arrest and capture.

"So, you know me! That look in your eyes says you do. Damned fool kid. Why, I'll . . ."

It all happened so fast that Corbin's mind couldn't register everything he did. He acted on blind instinct to protect the boy, staring down the barrel of the gun pointed at him as he put Andy behind the safety of his hard-muscled body. He leaped forward, engaging his opponent in a struggle for the gun, as both balanced precariously near the ledge by the door. Suddenly Corbin's shoulder burned with heat. He felt as well as heard the explosion of the Colt .44. A searing pain flashed through his flesh. He felt the pounding of his blood as it poured out of the wound. Through the fog of his throbbing pain, Corbin looked at the outlaw as he felt himself tumble from the train.

Corbin felt himself falling and put out his hands to stop his descent. As his head struck something hard, he focused his eyes on an all-consuming darkness, struggling against the blackness that pressed down on him. Then he could fight it no longer and gave in to the unconsciousness that enveloped him.

"Bob! What have you done?" For an instant Jessie thought Corbin was dead. Dear God, no! Her mind screamed over and over, though she somehow managed to keep silent. Her eyes focused on Corbin's crumpled form, hoping beyond hope. Only the slight rise and fall of his chest helped her keep her composure. Bob would kill him if he knew he was still alive, that much she knew. She'd have to pretend and do whatever was necessary to keep Corbin alive.

"What have I *done?*" Bob mimicked. "Is he dead?"

Jessie's heart almost stopped beating as she feared Bob

would make certain of it, but as she bent over the still form she nodded her head in Bob's direction saying, "He's dead all right." Her own neckerchief had come loose in the scuffle but she was too concerned with Corbin to take much notice at the moment.

Jessie was so intent on Corbin that she didn't see the artist sitting by the window. As she hovered over Corbin, the artist had time to do a rough sketch of her quickly. *Corbin!* She could see the blood on his coat. Jessie's heart rose in her throat as she looked at him. How could she have ever known that her silly thirst for adventure would lead to this?

With much shooting into the air and hollering, the bandits blew open the safe and crammed the loot into saddlebags. Then once more the train got under way, chugging down the tracks.

Butch was mad as hell, that Jessie could see, and rightly so. "You goddamned idiot," he yelled to Bob. "I told you there was to be no killing! Robbing is one thing. Killing is another. How many times have I said that?"

"Guess I got a little trigger-happy." In the face of Butch's anger, Bob was not as cocksure.

"Well, you'd better get your ass out of here. As soon as you get your cut, you're on your own." Showing his disgust, Butch spat on the ground at Bob's feet. "Go on! Git!"

Bob didn't wait around, knowing his neck was on the line. He was in real trouble. Not just from the other members of the gang but from the law. More than one passenger had witnessed the shooting and knew very well who was guilty. Served him right, Jessie thought. She watched as he grabbed a handful of bank notes, stuffed them in his saddlebag and was out of sight in a flash. The cloud of dust that his horse's hooves conjured up was a comforting sight.

"Let's get the hell out of here," Butch ordered. "It'll be awhile before any message can be sent and a posse formed to hunt us down but never mind about that. Just hurry! I'm shamed to say first time any of my gang has marked us with murder." Shootings were something that he had tried hard to avoid.

Jessie nearly told him then and there that Corbin was alive but thought better of it. No, Butch was not a killer, but he would undoubtedly advise her to leave Corbin behind and ride away. That was something she just couldn't do.

While Wade and Cleophas Dowd kept firing in the train's direction, it continued on down the tracks, leaving the bleeding man behind. No one in the train had even tried to find out about the wounded passenger. Obviously they thought he was already dead, Jessie thought. As the train gained speed, she saw Butch examine the haul then shove the loot back in his saddlebags, heard the shots he fired into the air. The Wild Bunch hooted and hollered and rode toward the mountains in the distance at breakneck speed. No one seemed to notice that Jessie had remained behind.

Chapter Ten

Gray clouds of smoke puffed up from the departing locomotive's smokestack like a winsome ghost, leaving a trail as the Union Pacific Number Thirty-Four moved down the tracks. Jessie watched as the locomotive train began gaining speed, at last vanishing into a long, sweeping curve in the roadbed. Everyone aboard must have assumed the man who had been shot was dead; leastwise they wouldn't have left him, she reflected. Either that or they were just plain cowards, every one of them — concerned with their own hides.

And yet when she thought about it, they couldn't have done anything about Corbin anyway, what with the bandits still hollering and shooting in the air, she mused. Butch and the boys had kept up the threatening activity until the train was well on its way toward Laramie, many miles on down the line. She wouldn't have to worry about repercussions for what had been done for quite a while. For the moment she and Corbin were all alone by the railroad tracks.

Alone. Jessie looked down at the unmoving form before her, wincing as she saw the blood still oozing from the wound. The others would be expecting her to catch up with them, but she knew that she simply couldn't leave Corbin here. Hell, even if she didn't have a hankering for him she couldn't do that. There was nobody around to offer him aid and might not be for days. Oh, there was a small ranch with a few horses in a corral just a ways back; but other than that there was nothing but grazing cattle and sheep anywhere around, along with other, more dangerous animals. If coyotes smelled the blood, they would surely attack the unconscious man. He would be too weak to defend himself even if he were to regain consciousness. Therefore she couldn't leave him behind while she summoned help. Corbin could die before help even arrived. She'd have to take him with her but that posed a serious problem.

First things must come first, however. She had to find out how badly he was injured. With that necessity preying upon her mind she carefully removed his tie, his shirt, and vest and examined the wound with gently exploring fingers. Actually the wound itself was not as bad as she had at first supposed it would be. The bullet had passed completely through the fleshy, upper part of his forearm, near shoulder level. No vital organs were involved, thank God! She was relieved to find out that there was no lead to be removed, for she most certainly didn't have the skill for that delicate operation. For a moment when she had seen all that blood she had feared Corbin might be more gravely injured, but lucky for him Bob wasn't the crack shot he supposed.

But the big knot on the back of his head told her why he was still out cold. Actually it was a blessing in disguise, for if he had not been knocked out, Bob undoubtedly would have pumped more lead into him. Certainly Bob had been in an ugly mood. Well, at least he wouldn't be riding with Butch and the boys any longer. Not now, since so many people could positively identify him as having been at the scene of a shooting. He'd be banished from the gang and good riddance to him.

As for Corbin, she'd soon have him feeling good as new.

Jessie looked around, swearing beneath her breath when she realized her predicament. There was nothing with which to clean the bullet wound. That would have to wait for a while; as for a bandage, his shirt was too bloody. Well, then, she would have to use her own.

Opening the buttoned cuff, she ripped the sleeve up to the shoulder seam, then found out that she had to remove her shirt in order to sever the sleeve from the shoulder seam and tear it in two. It would have to do. Wrapping Corbin's shoulder and upper arm as tightly as she could, she then replaced his vest and slipped on her own torn shirt. Picking up the remaining clothing she stuffed it into the saddlebags.

Now what was she to do? They sure couldn't stay there. A posse would eventually be formed in Laramie and sooner or later they would come. There would be too many questions. Besides, she couldn't just leave him at the mercy of the weather. Oh sure, it was pleasant enough now, but the nights were growing chilly and it could rain. No, they couldn't stay there. There was no shelter, hardly even a tree. She would just have to take him with her. But how was she going to move this big, unconscious man? She was only five feet four inches tall. He was well over six feet tall and weighed close to one hundred and eighty-five pounds or so, she would wager. His well-muscled virility certainly presented an obstacle, all right.

Jessie was never one to be bested by problems. Somehow she'd figure out a way. Spying the rope coiled on the saddle, she thought of a plan that might work. She had roped and thrown enough cattle to know how to handle large weights. She would carefully tie the rope around Corbin's waist and use the pummel of the saddle as a pulley. If she could rope and throw a calf as well as any man, she would not allow herself to be bested by this man's size. If she could only get him near enough to the saddle, lift him to a standing position, then get him upon the pinto's back, the rest would be easy.

"Sagebrush!" Jessie whistled for her horse. Trained to

obey, the pinto answered her command, moving to where she knelt beside Corbin. Springing to her feet, Jessie grabbed the rope and knotted it around Corbin's lithe form.

Now that that was done there was still the problem of lifting the big guy onto the horse. She placed the free end of the rope around the pummel so that it slid easily when she pulled on it, then tugged and tugged until she had Corbin in a seated position. Using the horse to lean upon for support, she slid her hands under Corbin's armpits and managed to lift him to his feet, put her arms around his waist to support his sagging body and shoved him over the horse's back just in front of the saddle.

It was quite a struggle, but after two efforts at balancing his bulk had failed, she soon accomplished her task. Corbin's limp body was draped face down, hanging across the horse's back in front of the saddle. He looked to be in a secure though uncomfortable position. Placing her foot in the stirrup, swinging herself up, she mounted Sagebrush, nudged his flank with the toe of her boot and guided him for the distant hills. She did not pressure the horse into a fast gallop but let him select his own pace. The weight he was carrying was more than he was used to. There were ranches on down the road. As soon as she could, she would "borrow" another horse from someone's corral. Horse stealing was her specialty.

The gang had planned beforehand that since the robbery which would take place on the Union Pacific line between Rawlins and Medicine Bow, the members would meet afterward at Hole-in-the-Wall. It was the closest of the outlaw hideouts, just north of the robbery site.

Jessie had always liked the wide, fertile valley with red cliffs on either side. Hole-in-the-Wall was one of her favorite hideouts; the outlaws grazed cattle in the valley between the cliffs and it was a place to plan many future robberies or seek refuge from recent ones. It was really one of the most secure hideaways. There, the penetration in the wall was so small that two men could hold off a large number of pursuers. There was no access from the east and to the west and south one could see for miles across the sea of grazing land. Yes, it was a very secure place to be. The cliffs, caves and overhangs gave excellent protection and many advantages, because most posses did not want to follow any outlaw into this area. It was discouragingly steep and dangerous. Resolutely Jessie headed in that direction.

The sun had climbed high into the sky. High noon, Jessie thought, shielding her eyes against the glare. She led Sagebrush the moderate distance to a corral she had seen farther on down the tracks. There, she went about swiping another horse for herself, a nice palomino. Now, the trip would not be too burdensome.

All along the way tied to the saddle he had remained unconscious, his breathing steady, his face pale. Jessie had ridden at a brisk, steady pace, stopping occasionally to be sure that the bandage she had fashioned from her shirt sleeve had stopped the bleeding and that Corbin was all right. His pulse was strong and from time to time he mumbled. Jessie found that to be a favorable sign that he would soon come around. Hopefully it would be *after* she had thought of some answers to the questions he would undoubtedly raise.

Corbin was still too woozy to know what had happened but he groaned, grunted, and tried to open his eyes as they approached a steep path leading up to a flat mesa. Sagebrush was used to such terrain but the horse she was riding balked; his ears laid back and his nostrils flared, for he seemed to know that the trail was steeper than it looked and very, very rocky. Riding an unfamiliar horse up such a pathway was risky so, Jessie dismounted and led both horses up the path. Sometimes horses could slip or stumble on loose rocks and she didn't want to take any chances with her precious cargo.

Her destination was a small hut built upon the mesa. It offered protection from the cold winds or storms that often swept across the plains in the winter months.

A little further up the canyon, right in the middle of Fork River Basin, was the outlaw cave. If worst came to worst she could ride over there to get help, but for now she did not want anyone to know too much about what had happened. Taking a stranger into the outlaw camp was risky business, for then if he suspected who they were, he might well identify the members of the gang to the authorities and put them all in danger. Besides, in a deeper sense, she didn't want Corbin to know what she had done, that she had been a party to the robbery. He'd scorn her and that was something she didn't want to deal with at the moment. If she could nurse Corbin back to health all by herself, she would have accomplished something for which she could be proud for years to come.

Corbin had helped her when the chips were down. This was the least she could do for him. Perhaps in time it would prove to be her atonement for her part in the robbery. Perhaps he might even find it in his heart to forgive her.

Although it was mid-October and everything was shrouded in muted tones of brown, gray and yellow, anything could happen in these parts from a freak snowstorm to an unrelenting Indian summer. If the weather held out and it remained as nice as it was now, she could easily care for Corbin here in this hut. Somehow the thought of being here alone with him here was downright pleasing.

The more she thought of it, the better she liked that thought. Things might not turn out as badly as she had first supposed. First she would see to his well-being and then she'd check in at the outlaw's stronghold to collect her share of the take. She might indeed have need of some money.

Jessie paused at the top of the trail to get her second wind before heading for the crudely constructed, small wooden hut atop the mesa. As she stood gazing in his line of sight, Corbin's glazed eyes peered at her through half-closed lids. "Who . . . ?"

Her head snapped around as she heard his whisper. "Just stay put for a little while longer. You're going to be just fine. Trust me."

"Jesse. . . it's . . . it's you." Corbin saw the boy's smiling face through a fog. His head felt as if a dozen hammers were pounding in his brain. He was confused, totally disoriented. "What . . . what happened?" he managed to ask in a low, almost inaudible voice.

"It'll be all right. You've been shot, but we have everything under control." She hurried to his side to quiet him. Though he was weak he was struggling, trying to get off the horse. Just like a man to be so stubborn. "Corbin! Quiet down. You'll open up that wound again and start it bleeding."

"Ok! boy." He heeded her warning without further ado, obeying the authoritative tone of her voice.

"I'll get you down." After he had remained quiet for a moment she leaned over toward him saying, "Just put your uninjured arm around my neck and let me help you." Gently she slid him from the horse, then aided him in lowering himself to sit upon the stony ground.

"Jesus, I feel like a horse kicked me in the head," he said, putting his hand to the large lump. "What happened . . .?"

"We'll talk about all that later. Right now I want you to just lie back and rest a spell. I know this ain't exactly a feather bed but I want you to lie back awhile until you're feelin' a mite stronger."

He didn't have to be told more than once. Corbin knew he was as weak as a newborn calf. The boy was right. There would be time for questions once this whirling and stabbing in his head disappeared. "Thirsty . . ."

Jessie left his side only long enough to grab her canteen. "Here, take a sip of water," she said, raising his head and holding the open flask to his dry, parched lips.

He tried to smile but it was more of a grimace. By the expressions flitting over his face, it was obvious he was in great pain. Even so he was very, very brave. Not once did he give in to even the slightest measure of self-pity.

"Think you could make it to that small wooden cabin over there?" She pointed in the direction of a tiny square building a few feet away. It was crudely constructed of raw lumber with a flat roof. There was a stone chimney indicating a fireplace inside. One single, small, oblong window slit was placed up high, next to the door. In this part of the country, windows had to be shipped great distances and so, glass was used sparingly. She would have to remove the long bar latch across the door to keep the wind from blowing it open. The winds in these parts of Wyoming could blow fiercely at times.

"I don't . . . don't know, but I'm . . . I'm willing to try."

"Just lean on me." Carefully she helped him to his feet. "Easy now. Easy." They slowly stumbled along together across the short distance, taking it one step at a time.

Corbin leaned heavily on the boy's small frame. "Whoa . . . my legs feel like jelly." All the while Corbin was sure his limbs would collapse beneath him but pride kept him on his feet.

"Just a little further . . ." It was a good thing that she was a strong woman, Jessie thought. She'd always prided herself that she was strong in mind as well as in physical strength. Now both came in mighty handy.

When at last they had reached the door of the small hut, he sat down to rest while she used both hands to lift the heavy bar latch and set it aside. The door was stuck. It would not open easily. She found a short, sharp stick and removed some of the debris that had blown beneath the door frame.

"As you can see, this windbreaker has not been used for quite a while," she said, smiling at him. "Just takes a little know-how, though." With a final burst of strength, she pushed hard against the door. "Should open now." It still didn't budge. Taking a deep breath, she pushed and pushed and finally kicked it open.

Once inside, she helped him to lie back upon the straw-filled mattress and removed his boots and bloodstained vest. She had taken off his coat and shirt and used his tie to fasten the bandage while tending his wound. The coat and shirt were still in her saddlebag where she had stuffed them in her haste to get away from the scene of the robbery. Such a fancy suit! Now it was ruined.

"Lets take a look at that wound. How does it feel?"

He said nothing, just blinked his eyes a few times and shrugged his shoulders, making a fearsome show of being strong.

"Sore? I expect it is." Unwinding the makeshift bandage, she probed gently. The shirt had stuck to the flesh in some places. That was a good sign that the bleeding had stopped. "Tired?" The look in his eyes told her that he could hardly keep them open.

"Mmm-hmm."

"Sleep, if you can . . ." For now, she would just rewind the bandage and allow Corbin to get some much-needed rest.

"No . . . no . . . I . . . I don't want to. So many questions . . ."

Jessie winced. This was the part she had been dreading. "Well, I have some answers, but now is not the time for talkin'. I just want you to rest and get back your strength. Then we'll have ourselves a bit of conversation."

"I . . . I'm happy that you came along when you did and found me there by the tracks, Jess. But how . . . ?"

"Oh, I was just in the right place at the right time, I suppose. To do a good deed, that is . . ." She averted her gaze as he looked at her. For the moment she just couldn't look him in the eye.

"Those damned bastards just left me there . . ." Left me to die . . . and . . . and I might have if you hadn't come along." He winced and blinked his heavy-lidded eyes again, trying to focus on the youth but having a devil of a time. It was like looking at someone through a fog. Was Jessie really here or was he just imagining it? As if to reassure himself he reached up to touch his companion.

"Well, I am here. That's what's important."

The pressure of a hand holding his gave him proof that he was not just dreaming. Jesse here? "What the . . . the hell you doin' way up here anyway?" It was a long way from Rye Grass Station and Brown's Park Valley.

The moment of reckoning had come. Jessie thought quickly. "Oh, you know us cowpokes get around. We have to grab work wherever we find it. I just finished a wranglin' job and was returning to the Valley when I came to the robbery site," she said in a rush. "But we will talk of that *later.* Right now I'd better go and get your coat and shirt and my coat out of the saddlebag. Soon it will be dark and the temperature may drop. We'll need something to keep us warm." It had been cloudless when they reached the mesa but by the time she did everything she could to make Corbin comfortable and collected a little firewood, the rain began coming down in torrents. Well, that was Wyoming!

She knew the creek would be too high to cross tonight so she determined she would just settle down to a quiet sleep. They were both exhausted. It had been quite a day! Besides, here they were warm and comfortable and anything they might need she could and would get tomorrow.

The small shack was warm and leakproof; that, at least, was a blessing. The only thing missing was some light. There were no candles and the lamp had no oil in it, thus Jessie adjusted her eyes to the darkness as it slowly descended upon the cabin. She had banked the fire so it would burn slowly throughout the night, so the fire did give off a faint glow. It was enough to give her a hazy view of

106

Corbin. She had admired him earlier as he slept and now as she lay down beside him, her imagination danced with dreams of his virile body cuddled next to hers in slumber.

Chapter Eleven

Light danced through the small opening next to the door, flooding the shack with a stream of dancing colors as Jessie opened her eyes. "Sunrise," she murmured, still half-asleep. Out of habit she turned her head to where her bedroom window should be, but instead of the familiar surroundings she was startled to find herself inside a wind-breaker shack. "What the . . . ?" Stretching her arms, she was startled by the contact her hand made with solid flesh.

"Corbin!" She was tangled in his arms and legs, his head resting on her shoulder. It was a pleasant surprise. Some-time during the night they had sought each other, appar-ently for warmth. Despite the fire, last night had been a mite chilly. She and Corbin had lain side by side in a semblance of intimacy. That thought made her smile as she stretched languorously.

"Mmmm. . . ." She wasn't in a big hurry to pull away. He might be unaware of her, but she was achingly aware of him. She was just where she had wanted to be since she'd first laid eyes on him. So, last night had not been entirely a figment of her imagination. His body and hers were indeed intertwined. How could she get up from the straw-filled mattress without awakening him? Did she even want to get up? No, really she did not. She could remain here content-edly in this place with him forever.

A voice which seemed to speak from deep within her consciousness told her that he was the man she had waited for all her life. Somehow, someway, she must make him love her. Love her? So far he still didn't even know that she was a female. Well, that had to end. When he was better, she would see to it that he found out. This she vowed. Being together like this was a good start for a romance.

Jessie's only regret was the circumstances that had led up to this cuddling. Like the pictures in a kinetoscope, images flashed in her mind. The robbery. The gunshot. Corbin lying so still near the railroad tracks. Once again she relived that moment when she thought he was dead.

"Corbin. . . ." she whispered. "I'm so sorry. . . ." For the first time in her life Jessie regretted being a member of the Wild Bunch. Certainly she bemoaned Corbin's misfortune in being at the wrong place at the wrong time. What strange twist of fate had put him aboard that train? She could only wonder.

Careful not to awaken him, she shifted from his embrace so she could look at him. His face was relaxed in sleep; there was no sign now of the pain he had felt when he'd first regained consciousness. Well, he needed sleep. It was a most powerful healer, she thought, reaching out to touch a lock of blonde hair that had fallen across his brow. Her fingers probed further, remembering the knot on the back of his head. That worried her nearly as much as his shoulder wound. It was as big as a goose egg without much sign of lessening in size. Well, she'd have to do something about that.

Carefully, inch by inch, she drew her leg from beneath his sinewy thigh, then took hold of his muscular arm and carefully lifted it from its resting place across her stomach. Just the touch of him awakened a host of sensations she recognized all too well. She was attracted to him with a fervor as potent as whiskey, she thought. A feeling that could lead to a whole heap of trouble if the circumstances

109

weren't just right. She'd have to be cautious and not let her feelings get too out of hand.

Slowly, ever so slowly, she slid from the mattress and stood looking down at the peaceful form resting so comfortably before her. Be cautious, she thought. That was easier said than done. She was downright mesmerized by him. Her gaze roamed from head to toe, appreciating his masculine good looks, the broad shoulders, trim waist, long legs. A splendid specimen all right. What a man! Brave as a bull. He'd not cried out once and she was relieved that he had shown no evidence of pain last night. Apparently he was not in as bad a shape as she had at first thought or perhaps he was just too exhausted.

For the first time Jessie was thankful for last night's rain. Picking up her neckerchief she moved outside and dipped it in a rainbarrel. The cold water would soothe the bump on his head and hopefully shrink it a mite. Walking back toward the bed she smoothed the hair away from his face again and placed the cloth on the injured spot. Though he stirred and moaned in his sleep he didn't awaken, so Jessie took the time just to watch him for awhile.

The dancing sunlight played across his face, shadowing his well-sculpted nose and highlighting his jawline. It was his mouth, however, that held her scrutiny. It had just the right fullness that spoke of lips pleasant to kiss. Her heart hammered at the very thought.

"Here now, girl, get your mind off of that!" she scolded herself. There were other things that took precedence over her amorous thoughts. Getting Corbin back on his feet, for starters. While he was sleeping so soundly, she would ride over to Agnes Cullem's place to get some things they would need.

Prowling about the small cabin like a restless coyote, she made a mental list of all she would need. Agnes was a good-natured widow woman who had taken a shine to Wade. They had grown quite close and spent as much time together as they could when Wade was in this part of the country. Agnes would help and wouldn't deluge her with questions. Agnes knew Wade was an outlaw and that was that. It didn't matter to her. Most of the outlaws had wives or lady friends somewhere along the Outlaw Trail, as a matter of fact. Agnes's place was not far from the shack. Just down over the hill a ways and closer to the creek.

Yep. Agnes is the answer, she thought. Agnes had run a small farm all by herself since her husband died a few years back. It would be well supplied with necessary items.

Taking one last look at Corbin to assure herself that he was resting comfortably, Jessie slipped on her coat, put on her hat, saddled up her horse and rode out. If she hurried she would be back before Corbin even opened his eyes.

It was a short journey. Jessie was so preoccupied with her thoughts that she hardly even realized she had arrived until she saw the fence that marked the boundaries of the place. As she approached the farm, she found the heavy-set, red-haired woman sitting in a rocking chair on the porch, smoking her corncob pipe. Agnes had always been an early riser. She was usually up before the sun and out feeding the chickens before others had even thought of getting out of bed.

" 'Mornin'!" Agnes's green eyes lit up when she saw Jessie astride her horse. Jessie knew it was because she thought Wade would soon come riding up also.

"Good morning, Aggie." Jessie smiled pleasantly. Agnes always made her smile. She seemed to be the last remnant of the pioneer women who had made the West such a strong and promising land.

"Didn't know you and Wade was in Wyomin'," she exclaimed, getting up from the rocker and smoothing the back of her rumpled skirt. Her eyes focused just over Jessie's head, toward the horizon, looking for Wade.

"Yeah, we just can't stay away from this place it seems. Keeps calling us back again. 'Course now I don't suppose

111

you mind that," Jessie teased with a wink. Jessie slid down from the horse's back, narrowly missing a puddle. "That was some downpour we had last night wasn't it?"

Agnes rolled her eyes toward the sky. "Looks to be a nice day today though."

"Sure does. I saw a rainbow riding in. A good sign I'd say." Jessie couldn't help but notice Agnes's expression of longing as she looked toward the direction Jessie had just come from. "Wade isn't with me."

"He isn't?" Agnes couldn't hide her disappointment. "Ohhh, well. . . ." She looked down at her hands, then asked, "Why *didn't* Wade come with you?"

"He would have, Aggie, if he'd known I was comin'. Truth is, he doesn't know I'm here." Jessie's look was imploring. "Sure would appreciate it if you'll tell him I'm back and I'm all right when you see him. Just in case. . . ." I wouldn't want him to worry." Jessie was as nervous as a cat on a hot tin roof. She couldn't let Agnes know that she had Corbin hidden away in the shack just above her place; but at the same time, she didn't want Wade to think something had happened to her and to comb the territory.

"But you're up to somethin'. Is that it? Somethin' you don't want to tell me about now?" The gentle hand she laid on Jessie's shoulder told her she really understood. Agnes was a generous soul who would give folks the shirt off her back if she liked them, and were they to ask for it. Jessie wouldn't hurt her feelings for the world and yet she didn't want to tell anyone about Corbin just yet.

"I guess you just might say that. I just need to keep a secret for now. But when I tell anyone, you'll be the first, Aggie."

"A secret?" For a moment the woman looked puzzled but shrugged her shoulders. "You tell me when you're ready." Taking her arm, Agnes led her toward the porch. "In the meantime I just wonder how I'm gonna tell that old polecat that you're back when I'm not even sure I'll see him. You tell me Wade is back and yet he hasn't come to see me. Hope that spark between us isn't dying. . . . Men! Who can understand them? Sometimes I don't even want to try. Outlawing is all he thinks about. Tomfoolery, if you ask me." She pursed her lips in mock anger, but Jessie knew she wasn't really annoyed. One reason Wade always came back to the woman was because she granted him his freedom.

"Wade just got here himself a few hours ago. We got separated, that's all. He'll come. You know he will."

Her answer seemed to appease Agnes, at least temporarily, though after a few minutes' hesitation Agnes asked, "He's on the run again, eh, Jessie? But if you ain't seen him, how do you know he's all right?"

"Oh, he's a tough old coot. It'll take more than a posse to get the best of Wade. Besides, we all got a head start. You know the lawmen never follow us up here when we're so far ahead of them."

"I know." Agnes eyes twinkled with merriment and a soft chuckle escaped her lips. "Wade says he's gettin' old but he's still quite a man. More than a match for the others, I reckon."

Now that the formalities were over and done with, Jessie just wanted to get the things she had come for and be on her way. There wasn't much time for conversation, as pleasant as keeping company with Agnes always was. She didn't want to leave Corbin alone for too long even though he had been sleeping soundly and hadn't seemed too uncomfortable when she left. The thought that he might get up and wander around tapped at her brain. She'd best hurry back.

"I'm short on grub and I haven't had a chance to get into town." she blurted out, telling a bit of a fib. "Besides, the creek is still too high for the wagon to cross. Think you could spare some beans, maybe a little coffee, and a piece of pork or two?" Without being impolite she decided to get right to the point, knowing full well that Agnes would gladly give her what she asked for.

113

"You and Wade have had a fight, is that it?" Hoping this would still the questions, Jessie nodded. Agnes clucked her tongue sympathetically. "Well, we all have disagreements from time to time."

"From time to time," Jessie repeated. "I could use a candle if you happen to have one around. And maybe a strip or two of material for bandages, some whiskey and a few sticks of kindlin' wood if you can spare some."

"Bandages." The woman's face turned pale. "You need bandages? Did somebody get shot?" Agnes was understandably alarmed. As she hurried towards the door she reminded Jessie of a hen with ruffled feathers. "Maybe I'd better go back to Hole-in-the Wall with you and help out some."

Now she'd done it, Jessie thought. She should have known Agnes would take just the attitude that she had taken. How was she going to get out of this one? She had done more lying since she had come here today than she had done in her entire life. She hated not being able to tell Agnes the truth. If she could trust anybody it was Agnes.

"It's nothin' serious."

"You sure?" Agnes paused in mid-stride, scrutinizing Jessie with her stare. "You wouldn't keep it from me if Wade . . . ?"

"Wade's fine! None of the boys got shot." Jessie grasped both of Agnes's hands and looked deep into her eyes. "If something had happened to Wade I wouldn't keep it from you. On that you have my word." She thought quickly, a story tumbling from her lips. "One of the guys just skinned himself up a mite. Probably wouldn't really have to bandage it at all but you know how squeamish men can be. All bluster and pride until they see a little bit of blood. I just thought if you had a few pieces of clean cloth and some surgical tape handy I could use them and put his mind at ease."

Agnes was visibly relieved. "Just a scratch?"

"Just a nick. But those things I asked you for would sure come in handy. . . ."

"I'll rustle those things up for you in a wink." Agnes relit her corncob pipe and took a few puffs. "Want to come in and sit a spell? You can fill me in on what's been going on since last I saw you."

Jessie shook her head. Ordinarily she'd take the time and indulge in a bit of "woman talk" as Agnes called it, but the thought of Corbin preyed on her mind. "No thanks, Agnes. I'd better be getting back. You know what bears those men are when their stomachs are growlin'."

"Yes, indeed I do." Hurrying inside, Agnes was back in no time at all with even more than Jessica had asked for packed in a basket. Everything except the kindlin' wood, that was. The wood was secured with a small bit of rope so that Jessie could tie it to her saddle.

Jessie thanked Agnes as she mounted her horse, calling out over her shoulder, "Wade will be down to see you as soon as the heat is off. You know he can't stay away from you when he's anywhere near Hole-in-the-Wall."

Apparently that made Agnes happy, for the corners of her mouth turned up in a smile as she raised her hand to wave. "Hope you're right. Bye, Jessie. Tell Wade I'll be waitin' when you see him."

"Bye, Agnes. I'll tell him if I see him before you do."

"And tell the other boys I said, howdy."

"I will. . . ."

Agnes waved and smiled again as Jessie galloped away. Then, scratching her head, Agnes wondered why Jessie had asked her to tell Wade she was all right. If Jessie was going back to the camp she'd be able to tell him herself. Strange, but one moment she had acted as if she would be seeing Wade right away and the next moment she acted as if it might be a while. What was going on here? Why had Jessie been acting so fidgety? Oh, well, she wasn't going to trouble herself about it. Jessie was probably just making conversation. Slamming the screen door behind her, Agnes went into the house to pretty up a mite just in case Wade did drop by.

Chapter Twelve

Warmth engulfed Corbin like a cocoon, light teased his eyelids. The sound of a horse nickering its impatience called him out of his sleep. *Rebel?* His head ached with pain as fiercely as if he'd been kicked in the head, and his mouth felt as dry as dust. Even so, Corbin struggled to regain his senses, opening his eyes slowly, trying to focus on his surroundings. Out of habit he turned his head in the direction where a window should be but instead of the familiar blue curtains greeting his gaze, he stared at unpainted wood. Where in blazes was he anyway? It must be a cabin or shack of some kind. He tried to unscramble his thoughts but the throbbing in his head made it difficult. What he could remember was being on the train when it was held up, trying to protect the boy, feeling the burning agony as the bullet struck him, and then falling. The details were about as clear as mud, however.

"My arm!" He tried to move it but it was stiff and so sore that he winced. "Damn!" How badly was he wounded? Cautiously his fingers explored, satisfying him that it was not as bad as it could have been. He'd been struck, but arms would heal. In some ways he'd been fortunate if he counted his blessings. One thing was clear, however, those outlaws had certainly put a cog in his plans for Stamash. "Have to put myself on the very next train," he mumbled stubbornly.

Pushing at the mattress in an effort to sit up, he was engulfed in a wave of dizziness and sank back down in defeat. His mind was eager but his body wasn't going to cooperate, at least for the moment. He was about as weak as a newly birthed calf. Get on the train? Ha. He couldn't even make it to the door.

"Damn! Damn! Damn!" His frustration was nearly as fierce as his pain. If only he had the strength to go after that bastard who'd shot him he'd make him pay. Instead he had to content himself with mental revenge, imagining what he would do if he were able to come face to face with the men who had held up that train. It was a most unfulfilling vengeance. "Outlaws! Ought to be strung up, every last one," he grumbled.

Corbin had been lying on his back when he awoke and now sought to change his position. Rolling over onto his side, his gaze met the crumpled mattress and it was then that he realized someone else had shared the bed.

"Jesse!" Jesse had brought him here. He'd tied him on a horse and led him away from the railroad tracks. Bits and pieces of what had happened after the shooting slowly started to fit together. He remembered seeing the boy's face when he'd opened his eyes, thought of how Jesse had so gently pulled him down from the horse and helped him inside. And then last night, even in the depths of his sleep, he had sensed that someone was with him. He had heard a voice only inches from his ear assure him that he would be all right.

"Sleep," a voice had said, touching his face with stroking fingers, tending to the lump on his head. He remembered moaning in his sleep and a body hugging him close.

"Jesse?" The thought of such a tight embrace with one of his own sex turned his face the brightest shade of red and yet the more he thought of it the more he wondered about the lad. Damned if he didn't have that notion running

118

around in his head again. This time he couldn't shake it away. Was Jesse a she rather than a he? Certainly the face that was framed by thick auburn hair was comely enough to belong to a woman. Wouldn't be the first time he'd seen a female with shorn curls. The voice, although high-pitched for a male youth, would be pleasantly low and husky for a woman.

Corbin reflected on the fight he'd saved Jesse from. The way Jesse had been swinging out and kicking had been far from genteel. In fact had the odds been less severe he might not have had to intercede in the fight at all. And yet that didn't prove much. He'd always said that a woman riled was twice as dangerous as a man.

He was confused. One moment he chided himself for even thinking Jessie could be other than what he'd first thought. No woman would be able to beat him at billiards! his pride insisted. The next moment he was plagued by the memory of hands as soft as a spring breeze tending him, and he gave in to the other opinion. Male or female, which was Jesse?

He'd have to ask. It seemed the best way of finding out, yet at the risk of angering his new friend. Girl or lad, Jessie had managed to save him. But how? What twist of fate had brought Jesse to the railroad tracks in time to save his life? Coincidence? Could be and yet . . .

Corbin's head throbbed as he thought about it. Touching the knot on his head, he winced. It was little wonder he had a headache. Hell, he was lucky he hadn't cracked his skull wide open. Was it any wonder that he'd been knocked unconscious? Trains! Somehow they sure were unlucky for the MacQuarie family in one manner or other. Even so he was doubly determined to continue what he had started. He'd get Stamash to Wyoming if he had to ride the damned bull all the way back. Yes sir! The way he felt at the moment, however, that time seemed a long way off.

"Ohhh!" The way he was lying had caused a cramp and

119

Corbin moved to ease the muscles of his uninjured arm. He positioned himself on his back again, and taking a deep breath he relaxed every part of his body. Counting slowly he winced only slightly when a spasm of pain tore into him. After reaching one hundred and seventy he was lulled into thinking his strength had returned. He was dressed in his pants and vest so he wouldn't have to worry about that. If only he could make it to the door at least he could get some idea of where he was. That would be a start. If he could manage to get himself on a horse he'd make it back to the ranch somehow.

Gathering up his energy, he managed to sit up this time. Dangling his legs over the bed he smiled as his feet touched the hard earthen floor. He reached out his hand to steady himself, then on shaky legs he sought to stand. Instantly he felt what a mistake that bold move was. His legs were about as steady as a piece of string; his head felt as if it were spinning. Swearing, he slumped backward.

"Damn!" His voice was a croak, a whisper as he fought against the fatigue which threatened to consume him. His exertion had done little but drain the meager strength he had. He was helpless for the moment. And so damned tired all of a sudden. Covering himself up with his coat, he thought he'd close his eyes just for a minute. Just for a brief amount of time. He didn't want to sleep again, he wanted to be awake when Jesse returned so he could ask some questions. Corbin struggled against sleep, but in the end lost the fight and succumbed to the sudden darkness that enveloped him.

Chapter Thirteen

Corbin was still asleep when Jessie returned. Though the sun was out, drying up the puddles and moisture the night's rain had brought, the shack seemed damp as she stepped inside. Now that she had some dry firewood, she could build a real fire and warm it up a little. On top of everything else that had happened to Corbin, she certainly didn't want him to catch pneumonia.

Placing the wood in crisscross fashion, Jessie pulled a handful of straw from a hole in the mattress and threw it on top of the sticks. "That should give it a quick start," she said to herself as she held the lighted match to the straw. Then she laughed softly. "Hope nobody else does what I've just done or soon there will be no filling in the mattress. Would make for a whole heap of disgruntled travelers." Ordinarily she kept strictly to the code of the trail but then circumstances sometimes made it necessary to bend the rules. Corbin was all that was important now and she was anxious to get the hut warmed up quickly for his well-being.

The fire flickered and sparked, dancing up in red and orange flames that mesmerized Jessie as she watched. Damned if she couldn't see Bob Meeks's face there, grinning so evilly. Just like the devil himself, she thought. Certainly what he'd done had caused a whole heap of trouble for everyone concerned. Corbin had a lump on his head and a hole in his shoulder, she'd been put in the awkward position of explaining to the wounded man what had happened, and Butch and the gang would once more be targets for every lawman for miles around.

"Blasted polecat!"

"Uhhh." Corbin moaned in his sleep and her attention was once again drawn to the handsome man lying on the straw-filled mattress. His coat, which had served as a blanket, had been pushed aside and she moved near his sleeping form to cover him up again. Dressed only in his pants and an open vest he was an eye-pleasing sight. Her eyes roamed freely over the partially clad body, appreciating his manly beauty. His skin was several shades darker than hers with a swarthy, natural tan; his shoulders and chest were strong and sinewy with muscles that fascinated her. Jessie stared at his sleeping form, longing to be locked in the embrace of those strong arms and to lay her head upon the thick tawny hair covering his broad chest. A quiver raced up her spine as she remembered last night. Even just the memory was exciting. Oh yes, a girl could get hooked on this one, all right.

Jessie had not felt this way about a man for a long time. In fact, if she were truthful with herself, she had never felt this way about a man before at all. Being with Corbin made her feel . . . content, that was the word. As if somehow she belonged with him. He brought out all the protective instincts within her. Even so, he inspired her passion at the same time. They had only met once before and yet she deeply cared about what happened to him. When she had seen him fall from that train . . . Well, she didn't even want to think about that now.

Am I falling in love with you? She had thought once before that she was in love but what she had mistaken for that emotion, when she was little more than a girl, was nothing compared to what she was feeling now. Oh yes, love could be all clouds, stars and sighs but it could bring heartache, too. She had thought that her heart would break when Jeff had left without telling her goodbye. What would happen to her if Corbin did the same? She wouldn't allow that to happen. She simply couldn't stand it. This was the man she wanted and this was the man she would have—come hell or high water.

She wouldn't let him go. Fate had brought them together again and despite the circumstances she viewed that as a sign. He was meant to belong to her. As if sensing her searching eyes, Corbin stirred in his sleep, a soft groan escaping his mouth again. If he was dreaming, they were far from pleasant fantasies.

Reaching for his coat, she pulled it over his half-nude form. He looked so vulnerable in his sleep, so content, that she vowed to keep constant vigil until he fully recovered. He was not completely out of danger yet. Even though the wound was not as deep as she had at first thought, if it were to fester, complications could occur. As soon as he awakened she would tend to his shoulder, put some whiskey on the wound and rebandage it.

In the meantime, she began to dig through items stored in the corner chest which held emergency equipment. Items were placed there in case a cowpoke, or even several of them, should become stranded. One thing the cowboys were good about was taking care of one another. All too often a man could and did get snowed in during the winter months, for here in Wyoming the storms could be treacherous. Several shacks, such as the one she and Corbin now shared, were scattered throughout rangeland country.

Jessie took inventory of what was within the wooden trunk. There was a blackened frying pan, some well-worn blankets, and some other odds and ends. Corbin would need some hot coffee and some nourishing grub.

"Bull wart, where is a damned coffeepot? Must be one

here someplace," she mumbled, piling one item after another in the center of the room. Two tin cups, spoons, forks, knives, even plates—but no coffeepot. If she'd had any inkling that there wouldn't be one here, she'd have cajoled Aggie out of hers. She hadn't suspected, however, that someone would have run off with the one that should have been here. With an agitated grumble she kept searching. "Oh, here it is," she breathed with relief. Right at the very bottom of the chest was that so-important object.

Jessie had tried to be as quiet as possible but the clatter of utensils awakened Corbin. Just as she retrieved the coffeepot, she heard a deep, throaty laugh and turned to find Corbin's smiling blue eyes appraising her. "You look like a pirate assessing his treasure."

The comparison made Jessie wince. In some ways she supposed that's just what she was. Bandit. Pirate. Outlaw. One and the same. "Sorry I woke you up. How are you feelin'?"

"My shoulder is sore, the other arm is stiff or asleep." He rubbed the knot on the back of his head, "My head aches, my mouth is dry, and I'm starving. But all in all, I'm damned grateful to you that I'm still alive. How did you happen to come along when you did, Jess?"

"Ohh, I just did, that's all." Jessie bit her lip, hastily looking away. "But we'll talk later. I'll put some coffee on, fry up some bacon and eggs and then tend to that shoulder, in that order. How does that sound?"

"Just what the doctor ordered." Corbin struggled to sit up, leaning back against the wall.

He remained silent but Jessie could feel his eyes following her every move as she went about preparing breakfast. As she measured out the coffee, then put the water on to boil, those heated blue eyes made her as nervous as a prairie dog being eyed by an eagle.

He knows, she thought, tortured by the very possibility.

What will I say to him? How can I make him understand I just wanted to have a little fun, to be accepted by the boys? I didn't want anyone to come to any harm. Certainly not him. Just like Butch, I never wanted anybody to get shot.

"Ouch!" She was so flustered that she burned her thumb as she reached for the coffeepot. Ignoring the pain, she poured two steaming cups of coffee but kept a cautious distance away from Corbin as she handed him his cup.

"Thanks. . . ."

"It's good and strong," she called over her shoulder, returning to the fire.

"That's exactly how I like it." He took a sip. "Perfect! But it would be a whole lot more pleasant if you'd come sit beside me, Jess. I have something I want to ask you."

"Sit beside you?" It was coming, she just knew it was. The question she was dreading. Once again he was scrutinizing her. He was going to ask her if she was involved in the robbery. "I'd like that, Corbin, but the bacon can't fry itself."

Using breakfast as an excuse she turned her back on him, busying herself with the duties of cooking the food. That in itself was no easy matter. First of all, she had never been much of a cook and secondly, even if she had been it was awkward cooking over an open fire. Jesse improvised by fashioning a stove top with a piece improvised of iron screen she found in the chest and balancing it on two large rocks. When the bacon was crisp and the eggs turned over just once, she dished up the food. Only then did she come close to Corbin.

"Mmm, the smell of that bacon . . . nearly made me forget how bad I feel. When a man's hungry his stomach takes precedence over his head." Sitting bolt upright he reached for the plate Jessie offered, only to succumb to dizziness.

"Lean on me, Corbin." Putting her arm firmly around his ribs she helped him regain his balance, then going over to the chest took out the old blankets to put behind his head and back, propping him up to a sitting position. An old board was used as a tray so that he could eat without exerting much strength. Only when he was comfortable did Jessie pick up her plate.

The tiny cabin was completely silent except for the sound of the scraping forks and contented chewing. At last Corbin wiped his mouth with the back of his hand and put down the empty plate.

"That was mighty tasty. Thank you, Jess. I feel better already."

She smiled. "I'm glad." She'd been just as hungry as Corbin professed to be when they started yet now her food was only half-eaten. The very thought of coming to terms with what she had done tied her stomach in knots. All the more so when she looked him in the eye.

"Why . . . ?"

"Why what?" Not a flicker of emotion crossed Jessie's face, although she had never felt more like crying.

"Why didn't you tell me?"

"I had my reasons."

"Didn't you know I'd soon find out. I'm not blind, Jess."

Her voice was tight, almost choked. "I know you're not . . . and . . . and I . . . I was going to tell you, honest I was. I just didn't think now was the time or place. I was going to wait until you were stronger . . ."

" 'Course I should have known right from the moment we met." He chuckled deep in his throat. "The way you move that cute little fanny of yours. . . ."

"What!" What on earth did *that* have to do with being an outlaw?

"The softness of your hands, when you were touching me, your eyes, those full lips." He ran his index finger up

126

and down her arm. "That sleeveless shirt exposes the smooth skin of your arm. No boy's would be as smooth as velvet. You're a damned nice lookin' woman, Jessie. I was a damned fool not to have realized it before."

So that's why he'd been staring a hole right through her all this time. He'd suspected she was a female. *Woman,* he'd said. She wanted to throw back her head and give vent to unrestrained exuberance but she kept her poise. "Yep, I'm a woman all right. Now you know my deepest, darkest secret!"

"Your name is really Jessica then, isn't it?"

"Jessica. Yes. Though all my friends call me Jessie."

"Jessie, with an 'i' and an 'e'. A very pretty name." So she was not named for Jesse James after all. "You should have told me you were a woman when we first met, Jessie. I'd have acted a whole lot differently."

"Couldn't see no reason to. Besides, you didn't ask. I just let you think whatever you wanted to think. Sometimes it's just much simpler that way." Her green eyes glinted mischievously. "Thought you might be upset and all, having a woman beat you at billiards."

"So . . . still remembering that, are you?"

She nodded, smiling sweetly, then took his empty plate. "I'm glad to see that you have a good appetite," she said, avoiding the question. "That's a good sign." After a moment's hesitation, she added, "And good sense too. Want more coffee?" Corbin nodded his head yes. She filled his cup, then sat down on the floor near the straw mattress, thoughts racing through her head. He didn't know about her connection with the outlaws. Now that he knew she wasn't a boy she doubted he'd even give it a thought. She was safe.

"Why don't you sit here on the mattress next to me instead of on that hard floor?" he asked, patting the casing with the open palm of his hand. "You aren't afraid of me are you, Jessie?"

" 'Course not!" She was just a bit uncomfortable, that's all. Although her blood clamored to put her arms around him she felt suddenly shy, an emotion she'd never experienced before. Rising from the floor, she took a step toward him. "See!"

"I want to know all about you. How you . . ."

"Shhh." She put her finger to his lips. "There's time for all that later. You aren't going anywhere and as long as you're holed up in here I will be, too. For now we had better have a look at that shoulder."

Taking her hand in his, he caressed her fingers then lifted it to the back of his head. "Feel the size of that goose egg? It's causing me more trouble than the gunshot wound. That thing's as sore as hell."

The touch of his hand on hers caused a tingling within her. If just his touch could bring forth such emotion, she knew something was bound to happen between them sooner or later. There was an electric current circulating here. She could feel it.

"Let me soak that bandage loose and than we'll put a cold cloth on that bump."

On the way back from Agnes's farm, she had stopped at the creek to fill a bucket with water; now stepping outside, she dipped her handkerchief into its cold depths. "The water I fetched should be heated before I wet your bandages, lest it chill you to the bone," she said when she stepped back inside. "In the meantime it will be just the right temperature for your head. It will make you feel better."

As she leaned over to place the cloth on his head, he grasped her wrist again, this time pulling her arm toward him. The pressure of his lips on the palm of her hand caught her by surprise. He was kissing her hand and oh, what longing it evoked deep within her—a pleasurable tingle in the pit of her stomach, a warmth that flashed through her like a spark.

"That's my thank you, Jess . . . until that time when I have enough strength to take you in my arms the way I want to right now."

Always glib and quick to an answer, Jessie was tongue-tied now, as if her tongue was frozen to the roof of her mouth. She could only stare at him mutely as his blue eyes regarded her. The blood seemed to pulsate in her ears, sending another shiver all through her body. He wanted to kiss her. All that was holding him back was that damned lump on his head and his shoulder wound. But he would get better. She'd see to that, and then . . .

The sound of neighing horses brought her back to reality. She must tend his wound and then see to the animals. They should be untied and allowed to graze. Though she hated to leave his side, she put a pan of water on the fire and when it was heated, set about soaking the bandage loose with the tepid water. The wound looked clean and seemed to be healing nicely but the water had started a small amount of bleeding again. Just for good measure she opened the bottle of Old Crow that Agnes had put into the basket and poured some upon the wound.

"God, that burns." he said gritting his teeth and with a grimace of pain in his clear blue eyes. "How's about a drink? That'll help the pain too." She handed the bottle to him. While Jessie changed the bandage he contented himself by drinking from the bottle.

"That's enough now." She reached out to take the bottle from him. "We have to keep this for medicinal purposes, you know."

The liquor had loosened Corbin's tongue. Now he was in a talkative mood. "Jessica, how did you get into the cattle driving business? A woman like you shouldn't be doing such heavy work."

"It's a long story. I'll have to tell you all about it sometime. Just to start with, I was left an orphan and my

129

foster father was a cattle man," she lied. She couldn't tell him too much without revealing that she was really an outlaw.

"An orphan. Poor kid. Must have been hard for you. How old were you when your parents died?"

"About eight. But don't feel sorry for me. I really have loved the life I've led. I like the freedom. I've become self-reliant and I always have been a nature-lover. I'd say I'm in a perfect line of work." Work? There were those who would say it was hardly that.

"Ever been married?"

"Naw. Never had the time and never met the right fella. Oh, I thought about it once but that was a few years back. How about you Corbin?"

"No. Like you I'm free as a bird. Always have been but I was nearly caged once." The thought of Henrietta made him smile. She and Jessie were just about as different as two women could be. The opposite ends of the spectrum. As Jessie finished seeing to his wound Corbin couldn't help thinking that perhaps the next few days were going to be more interesting than he might ever have imagined.

Chapter Fourteen

Corbin knew exactly what torture was. It was lying beside a very desirable woman, being driven by a hunger he hadn't the strength to fulfill just yet. "Oh, Jessie. . . ." He heard his breath, coming quick and rasping, and clenched his fists, fighting to gain control. It was difficult when she was pressed so tightly against him. Well, what had he expected? There was only one bunk and it was a narrow one at that.

Not that he was complaining. Never that. Slipping his arm beneath her head, he held her to him, savoring the warmth and feel and scent of her. He was a very lucky man for more reasons than one. He had escaped death and gained so much in the bargain. Jessie. Closing his eyes he wondered how she would feel beneath him as they made love. His breath became heavier as his hunger for her intensified.

"For God's sake, think of something else," he breathed. Corbin stared into the darkness, remembering how she had looked today. Like a ministering angel, caring for him so diligently. At first he'd needed frequent naps because of his weakened condition but little by little he was regaining his strength. But not soon enough, by a damned sight.

He slept fitfully, his nerves and muscles wound up as

tight as a spring. When morning came he awoke feeling tired and restless. Jessie's hand against his forehead, her murmured words of concern, told him he had talked in his sleep.

"No fever, thank God. You were so restless that I had thought. . . . I'd feared. . . ."

"Its hot in here," he said, knowing very well that wasn't the reason. Last night it had been an agony lying next to her.

"I'll open the door. I should have banked the fire last night but I was afraid you'd take a chill. The nights can grow so cold."

She walked to the door and opened it halfway. The morning breeze teased her auburn curls into a dance around her face, and pressed the cloth of her shirt tight against her slender form, revealing the gentle curves of her breasts.

I must have been crazy ever to have taken her for a boy, he thought. Everything about her cried out that she was a woman. Her mouth was soft and as pink as a rosebud, her skin was smooth and unblemished, the color of dark cream. Though her hair was shorter by far than most women would allow it, it was not unbecoming. Quite the contrary. The tendrils of glossy auburn hair curled about a beautiful face. It was her eyes, however, deep and a jade green, that really drew him. They could be sparkling with mirth one moment, full of warmth, only to become dark and veiled the next as if she were holding some precious thought deep within her that she didn't want to share. Intriguing eyes they were, with brows that were curved at just the right angle.

"Is that better? It's blowing out. It's not too cold on you, is it?"

"A bit. All I needed was some air."

Jessie closed the door and picked up her canteen. "Would you like some water? It's cool."

132

"Yes, I would." She was such a caring person. That had been shown in the special care she gave him. He'd always been so damned independent and yet it struck him suddenly that everyone needed someone to love. As she bent down to give him a drink he realized how much he wanted to kiss her. That was the thought that nagged at his mind each time she came near or passed by.

"Is anything wrong, Corbin? You seem to have something on your mind." She clasped his hand tightly, entwining their fingers.

"I feel about as useless as a three-legged horse! I want to hurry and get on my feet. That's all."

"You will." Much too soon, she thought. Being here with Corbin was so pleasant that selfishly she wanted to prolong the time. "Do you want some coffee?" At the nod of his head she relit the fire, filled the pot with water and coffee and set it on the flames. "I'm going to see to the horses. When I get back I'll fix you something to eat. Breakfast will use up the last of our supplies." Perhaps she'd ride up to Laramie. She couldn't keep relying on Aggie's generosity. "I'll have to see about getting some more."

Lying on his back, staring up at the pock-marked ceiling while she was gone, Corbin wondered, just how he would describe Jessica? Certainly she was different from any other woman he'd met. A pleasing presence. Carefree, smiling. Most certainly pretty. There was a sense of freedom about her that drew him. She seemed the type of young woman who did exactly what she pleased. At least until he'd burdened her with his woes. Certainly being confined with him the last two days must be wearing on her nerves. And yet, she never once complained.

Jessie remained on his mind all day. Even when she was out of his sight tending to the horses or going about the chores, she wasn't out of his mind. Closing his eyes, he could see her as clearly as if she stood right before him. Jessie was slim of hip and long of leg. Corbin had suspected that she did something to bind her breasts until he caught a glimpse of them peeking impudently from her shirt front as she bent over to tend his gunshot wound. A tantalizing sight! Her shirt was far too big and loose, that was how she hid her feminine curves. Now he knew what lay beneath. Firm, perfectly shaped globes. When he watched her more critically he was rewarded as the peaks of her breasts nudged the fabric of her shirt now and again.

"Corbin?"

Looking up he saw her standing in the doorway. For a frozen moment in time their eyes locked and Corbin knew in that instant that she was the woman he'd been looking for all of his life, a woman to cherish, a woman who would be a partner and who would work beside him.

"I didn't mean to be gone so long. One of the horses got loose and I had to chase it down." There was something in Corbin's eyes, the way he was looking at her, that caused Jessie's breath to catch in her throat. Did he have the same twittery feeling for her that she had for him? All morning he'd filled her thoughts, more so now that he knew she wasn't a boy. She just kept hoping.

"And did you catch it?"

"Just barely." She laughed. "He led me on a merry chase. Good thing I'm experienced about these things or we'd both have to ride my pinto."

There were times like right now when she seemed so relaxed around him, like a wiry, wild colt. At other times she seemed on the alert, cautious as if at any moment she was going to run away.

"Mmm, riding double might have definite advantages." Catching her eye Corbin boldly winked.

"It might. . . ." As if his comment had given her

134

courage, she knelt down beside him. "I want to know so many things about you, Corbin." Her forearms leaned on his thighs, while she rested her chin on her hands. "Where you were born, where you came from; things like that, you know. . . ."

"There's not really much to tell. I was born in Colorado. Greeley. You already know I'm part Scottish, that I came here just recently. I have a brother, recently married. My parents are dead."

"I'm sorry . . ."

"They died in a train collision. It's been a long time since I could persuade myself to get on a locomotive. After what happened to me I'd say it was a wise vow. But what about you?" She'd told him that she'd been orphaned. No doubt Jessie had had to work hard her whole life. He to the contrary had been granted every advantage. Damn, if that didn't make him feel a bit guilty.

"I was adopted by a very kind man. His wife and child had died and he was lonely. We've been very good for each other, I think."

"A rancher?"

"Yes. . . ." Jessie was anxious to divert the conversation from her to him again. "But what made you decide to go into ranching?" Every time he wanted to find out about her she insisted that he tell her about himself. Certainly with other women it had been just the opposite. They loved to talk and talk and talk but seldom wanted to listen. It was a pleasant change.

"It seemed the thing to do. Especially here in Wyoming. I'm a man who couldn't be tied down to any desk job. I'm not cut out to be a banker or a lawyer or a teacher."

"Or a barber or a saloon keeper." She laughed softly and he liked the sound.

"You should laugh more often."

"I will if you want me to." She leaned closer. "Corbin, why were you on that train?" It was a question that had deeply troubled her.

"I . . . I was going to visit my brother. Just for a few days." He supposed it was silly to keep Stamash a secret. Certainly Jessie wasn't a cattle rustler. It was just that he didn't want to instigate any more questions. "I haven't seen Warren for awhile."

"Oh. You must be very close."

"Yes, we are. It's always been that way." She was eager to learn about him, so much so that Corbin felt guilty to hold so much back. It was just that he didn't want to flaunt being a wealthy rancher. Not yet. He did tell her all about his new ranch, however, and about his foreman, Archie.

"You'll like him. He has a keen sense of humor and he truly cares." Yes, Archie was a one in a million kind of man who was totally honest. He doubted the man had ever even told one lie. "Right from the first he's proven himself to be a good friend."

"Friends are important. Billy is one of my friends. We grew up together. Now my being a female has begun to cause a bit of trouble."

"He's attracted to you." Strange how that thought made him jealous. He'd never had that emotion before.

"But he'll get over it. It just wasn't meant to be. Billy just isn't the kind of man I want."

"What kind of man is that?"

"One like you." Jessie was without guile. No fluttering eyelashes or false smiles from her. Just honesty. As her eyes focused on his face her emotions were openly displayed and it pleased him.

They contented themselves in conversation, enjoying the time they were together. How much time had passed, a minute, an hour? When he was with her time seemed unimportant. He was mesmerized by her husky voice, intoxicated by the warm pressure of her body against him. It was as if nothing existed beyond the magic confines of the shack. Indeed, suddenly the ramshackled old building seemed like a paradise.

"It's peaceful here," Corbin murmured.

"Mm hmm." Jessie's hand curled around his as she pressed her face against his shoulder. He smelled of woodsmoke and whiskey.

"I like being here with you. You are very special to me, Jessie. I want you to believe that."

"I do. Because I feel that way too. . . ." Stretching out her fingers she stroked his face.

A smile crinkled the corners of his eyes. "I know. I need a shave."

"I'll add a razor to the list of things I need to pick up. We'll be as cozy as two bugs in a blanket. Who knows, maybe you'll never have to leave."

"At this moment I don't want to. You've bewitched me. Jess. . . ."

"I hope so." Jessie snuggled against him, curled into the crook of his good arm, warm and content. It was as if this was what she had been waiting for. This place. This man. This moment in time.

"I want you to be my woman."

"I am already." She placed her hand over her heart. "I feel it right here. Maybe I knew it from the first moment I saw you. I don't know. But it feels right."

"We don't know each other very well and yet somehow it's not important. We know the important things."

His arm slipped around her waist and he gave a long shuddering sigh as she wrapped her hands around his neck, hugging him close. He bent his head and his lips moved gently yet insistently over her cheek. She turned her head so that their lips met. The kiss was long and sweet; she had no desire to pull away, only to cling to him and return the pressure of his mouth. Their lips met and clung, smiled against each other's, then parted for another kiss that took her breath away.

Jessie had been kissed before but it was nothing like this. Corbin's lips pressed ardently against hers brought forth a jolt of sweet fire that swept through her veins like a whiskey chaser.

"Corbin . . ." she murmured against his mouth. She had wanted him to desire her. She had hoped that somehow, someway he would learn to love her. This was a start. Oh yes indeed, this was a start of what she hoped would develop into a sizzling hot-romance. A romance as hot as the branding iron she carried on the saddle horn. If only that would happen she would never again ask for anything more.

Her mouth was warm, sweet beyond his imaginings. "Jessie! Jessie!" He murmured her name, gazing at her soft mouth. "All morning long I've wanted to kiss you."

"And all morning long I've wanted you to."

His wounded arm was aching like the very devil but he ignored it and concentrated on the gently curving body so close to his own, stroking her, caressing her. He enjoyed kissing her. The moment his lips touched hers his body exploded with such a fierce surge of desire that he trembled. He had felt desire before, many times, but never like this. Even so it was tempered with a yearning to give, to protect.

The glare of the early morning sun fell on her bare arm, showing the smooth skin and the slimness beneath that tattered shirt where her sleeve was missing. It was a reminder of what she had done to save him. He ran his fingers up and down her bare arm, sending pleasurable impulses up her spine.

"I still think it must have been a miracle that sent you to the railroad tracks, Jessie. How on earth did you happen to be there just at the right time? Are you my guardian angel?"

For just a moment she stiffened. Angel? Hardly that. If he knew the circumstances of why she was really there he'd certainly agree that she was far from a heavenly being. "I'd like to be."

"How did you happen to turn up at the right place, at the right time?" It was a question she had dodged successfully before but now she couldn't think of a way to take his mind off the question.

"I had heard in town that you were leaving on that train. I guess . . . I guess . . . I just wanted to see you off. In hopes that you would soon return." That answer seemed to satisfy him, for he smiled.

"To send me off? I'm just thankful you didn't run into those outlaws."

"So . . . so am I. I heard the shooting and hid behind a bush. I saw you fall from the train." She clutched his hand. "Oh, Corbin. I nearly died! I thought . . . I thought. . . ."

Burying his face in her hair he whispered, "It's all right. It's all right. We won't talk about it any longer." He nibbled at her ear. "We've got better things to do. Come here, you little minx. Maybe we can get something started."

They lay together upon the straw mattress, kissing and hugging. As time went on, things began to get a bit more serious. Having been with a man once before, with Jeff, she knew all the signs.

"Jessie. . . ." Taking her face in his hands, he looked deep into her green eyes. "You have the most beautiful face I've ever seen. And your skin is like ivory." Once again he ran his fingers up and down her sleeveless arm, causing ripples of desire to stir within her.

Jessie didn't want another casual love affair, she wanted something more lasting. That meant giving her heart but at the same time keeping his respect. "I'm not sure you're strong enough now for such shenanigans," she laughed. "I think I better get up, lest you are too tempted."

"I already am. Last night, Jessie, with you so close I thought I would go out of my head." He tried to unbutton her shirt front with his uninjured hand but had a difficult time of it. "This shirt has only one sleeve. Let's take your arm out of the other sleeve too."

She might have helped him but the sudden pain that flashed across his features told her he'd exerted himself enough. "No. I want you to lie back, close your eyes and rest a bit."

Her body was achingly soft against his. Only reluctantly could he pull away. He didn't have the strength to continue what this would lead to. She knew it and he did too. "Damn those outlaws!" he said aloud and yet had it not been the train robbery he might never have known the potency of Jessie's sweetness.

"Damn those outlaws," she echoed. Searchingly her eyes studied his face. "What would you do if you ran across one of them?"

"Send them straight to hell by way of the sheriff."

"Oh." She wondered if that included her. If he ever found out, would he turn her in? Suddenly she realized she had better cover her tracks. "You're right about this sleeveless shirt of mine. It is almost indecent."

"I didn't say that. I rather like it."

"Still. . . . And you need some new duds." She'd tried to wash the blood out of his shirt in the creek and hung it to dry, but looking at it now, she hadn't been very successful. "Yours are all blood stained. Your pants, your shirt." She'd put on her jacket to hide her tattered clothing and ride into the nearest town to purchase some new garments. Then she could bury her kerchief and shirt, just in case. That way there wouldn't be as many questions asked. Above all she didn't want to leave behind any clues that she had been involved in that robbery.

"You're going to leave?" He gripped her shoulders in protest.

"Only for a little while. I won't be gone long. Laramie isn't too far away. I'll get you that razor so your chin isn't like sandpaper. And you can rest while I'm gone."

"Rest? That's all I've been doing lately." Seeing her stern expression he laughed. "All right, honey. Anything you say. But be forewarned. When I get back my strength I intend to finish what we started."

Chapter Fifteen

Warren MacQuarie slammed the *Denver Post* down hard on the table. the glaring headlines BUTCH CASSIDY'S WILD BUNCH STRIKES AGAIN stood out in bold, black letters, fueling his ire. "That does it. Something has to be done about that blatant *thief*," he called to Henrietta.

She hurried from the kitchen carrying a small tray of blueberry muffins the cook had just prepared. "Really, Warren. I see no reason for you to shout."

"No reason?" His blue eyes flashed anger as he ran his fingers through his bright red hair. "That pack of rats just held up a train. They should all be strung up, if you ask me. That's one way to get rid of a menace."

Her mouth was a grim line of disapproval, casting her face in the profile of an unrelenting statue. "Now, now, Warren. You know what the Bible says. 'Judge not lest ye be judged.' "

"We have gone over and over that, Henrietta. You can't expect me to change overnight. I'm used to speaking my mind. I'm a rancher, not a preacher like your pa. Damn it anyway!" His brows drew together in a scowl but one look at that lovely face with its frame of dark brown curls softened his irritation. His wife was one mighty fine looking woman. Corbin would never know what he had so foolishly thrown away. Or perhaps he did. Was that why he'd just upped and left the ranch?

"Preacher or rancher, I will remind you to keep a *civil tongue* in this house. You know how I abhor profanity." Pointing her finger at him she looked much like a stern teacher chastising a naughty pupil. "Now, what is wrong?"

"A train has been robbed up Wyoming way." For a moment he looked thoughtful. "Hope it wasn't the train Corbin was on perchance. Then again if it was, he'll have a story to tell, I'd wager."

"Well I hope he *wasn't*. I for one am not interested in such stories. Train robbery indeed!" She folded her arms and lifted her chin haughtily. "And while we are on the subject, Warren, your brother really should have had the courtesy to be more specific as to when he was going to arrive. 'Sometime this week' indeed! He assumes he's the only busy MacQuarie, it seems!"

Warren conveniently ignored her tirade as his finger jabbed at the headlines. "Something *has* to be done about that Butch Cassidy and his no-good band of cutthroats." Seeing her mouth draw down in another frown he cleared his throat then continued in a more subdued manner, trying to calm his rage. "Imagine those trainmen just leaving a man to die by the railroad tracks. By the time the posse arrived he was gone. Coyotes might have gotten him or he might have wandered into the nearby hills. Anyway, they're pretty sure he's dead and they don't even know who he was."

"Are you going to become obsessed with that Wild Bunch just because Art Conners got in touch with you again?"

"No . . . no, but well, I sure as hell . . . er, heck wouldn't put up with that kind of tomfoolery even for a

143

minute." Picking up the newspaper he quickly scanned the story again, clucking his tongue in disgust.

"Oh? I suppose you could handle the matter much better?" She turned up her nose haughtily again. "I doubt it, Warren."

"I could!" Tearing off the front page he crumpled it, tossing it back and forth like a ball in an effort to curb his frustration. Sometimes Henrietta could be a trial. But he loved her anyway. Bless her psalm-singing heart, she just didn't understand the matter of keeping the peace.

"Warren. *Warren.* Just because Art Conners ran into Corbin and wrote a letter to you shouldn't affect our lives." Coming to his side she laid her hand on his shoulder. "Oh, darling, I know what's troubling you. What is really the matter. Art Conners helped put Butch Cassidy behind bars a few years ago and your ego is still smarting. But don't feel that way. He boasts about it just to annoy you."

"And God knows that it does. Art was the one who picked up that cowboy and put him in jail but after I gave him all the information. It could have been me." Warren remembered the details all too well. Art Conners was an opportunistic scoundrel who had gotten the promotion at the Pinkerton Agency that Warren rightly deserved. "But whoever would have known one cattle-rustling cowboy would so quickly become a living legend?"

"That is no reason to think that you have been outmaneuvered by Art. You're happy just ranching now and. . . ." Putting her hands on her hips she studied him silently, then said, "You can't stand being bested. *That's* it, isn't it? Your silly male pride."

"Suppose it is?"

"Don't you dare even contemplate what I think you might be." Henrietta glared at Warren as she spoke. She had been afraid that he would someday want to return to the agency and she wanted none of that.

"Now, honey I . . . I like detective work, Henrietta. It's in my blood. You know goddamned well. . . ."

At this point Henrietta corrected him, "Please, *no* swearing, Warren. Using the Lord's name in vain is a sin. When judgment day comes I'm certain you don't want to be punished."

From what she constantly had told him about hell he most certainly didn't. "All right, then. But let me have my say. Please."

"I've never put a bridle on your tongue. Say what you will."

He took her hands in his. "I don't want to make you angry, God knows. I love you. I married you because I did. But you know very well that I'm sick and tired of Bible-thumping and one 'social event' after another."

"Bible-thumping? So that's what you call it." She pulled her hands away. "Going to church and to the meetings and gatherings associated with it are hardly social events but doing the Lord's work."

"Whatever it is you call it, I've gone along with it so far but enough is enough. I'm just not comfortable among your friends." Slowly but surely Henrietta had replaced his friends with those of her own. She dictated every facet of his life from what to wear to what to eat. Sundays when he used to enjoy a game of cards with the boys or a leisurely ride about the ranch were now spent in church. He couldn't smoke, he couldn't drink, he couldn't swear. "A man has to have some say so in his own life."

"You . . . you're sorry you married me. I can see it in your eyes. You just don't love me any more or you would want to make me hap . . . happy." Putting her lace hankie over her eyes, Henrietta wailed.

One thing Warren could not stand was to see a woman cry. Henrietta knew this and put on a performance to equal any actress's. The ploy had worked before. "Honey! I'm sorry." Quickly Warren was on his feet holding her in his embrace. "What happens up near Wyoming isn't any business of ours. I don't care a hoot about what happens to the Wild Bunch."

"Do you mean that?" Her misted hazel eyes peeked through her fingers at him. "You'll put Butch Cassidy out of your mind?"

"We will talk no more about it now if it upsets you so, my love," he said, drying her eyes then holding her close to his heart. He kissed her forehead. Henrietta was a good woman, he knew that. He had chosen her purposely to be the mother of his future children, had been attracted by her virtue. After the saloon girls he'd been with she had been like a breath of fresh air. She was the kind of woman a man married. It was just that sometimes he missed the good old days when he could let go with a swear word or two or even have a drink now and then. Since their marriage his life had changed drastically. But then perhaps it was all for the best. It had been time to settle down.

"No more talk of outlaws?" Henrietta sniffled a few more times and then blew her nose. Her big hazel eyes looked up at him through long, damp, dark lashes, smiling as he nodded. "And you'll take me to the Springs next week as we originally planned? Without any fuss?" she questioned.

The world's richest mining area, Cripple Creek, was near Pike's Peak. At least fifty of the millionaire mining families were still living in the Colorado Springs area. Their beautiful homes and gardens could compete with any, even in Europe. Henrietta was of the mind that she and Warren should take their place among those of like wealth. Perhaps he'd be able to make some investments and increase his own profits.

"Yes, we will go to Colorado Springs if that is what you want." Warren replied. What else could he say without starting another flood of tears? Henrietta knew how to work him all right, but after all, they had just been married six months, he reasoned. All women used such wiles. Once she had a baby in the cradle things would change. She'd be too busy to dominate him.

In a way he couldn't entirely blame Henrietta for wanting to go to the Springs. It was fast becoming the "London of the Rockies," a very fashionable place just seventy-five miles south of Denver. It was a logical meeting ground for the rich and famous to congregate, and it would be a welcome respite from singing hymns.

"Then I'm happy again."

"And when you're happy, I'm happy." Perhaps time would bring her around to understanding that if they were to have a successful and loving relationship, what made him happy had to be just as important as what made her happy. Henrietta had gone to a fashionable girls' school down south and didn't seem to understand much about the ways of men. That they needed to be unbridled once in awhile. She only knew how to get her own way. But then she wasn't the only one at fault. He had given in just because it was much easier than dealing with her tears. If he had spoiled her these past few months, well, maybe he could soon correct that mistake.

Warren's reply was just the one Henrietta had hoped for. He'd given his word just now. Warren never broke a promise. She insisted that they finish their breakfast and then begin plans for the trip. Just as soon as Corbin's visit was over they'd have their "little vacation." *Corbin,* she thought, clenching her teeth. Of all the times for him to return. Well, hopefully he'd hurry and not stay very long. She wouldn't let him interrupt her plans.

In truth Henrietta was still smarting from Corbin's horrid treatment. He'd humiliated her by changing his mind about marrying her. For a moment she'd thought her fine plans of being a rich rancher's wife were thwarted until she'd met Warren. The way he'd looked at her had been worshipful and she'd known in an instant that marrying him would be her new plan. Even so there were times when he was making love to her that she imagined it was *Corbin*. If that was wicked of her, well, she'd just make atonement in her prayers. Rogue or not, Corbin was not the kind of man a woman could easily forget. Somehow Warren just didn't measure up to his younger brother. He wasn't as tall, nor as well-muscled. His eyes weren't as blue. And that carrot-thatch atop his head was thinning, whereas Corbin's hair was thick, golden and wavy.

No, Warren couldn't compare to his brother, she thought. If only she had married Corbin. The day after the wedding it had been her lament. She'd flirted with her former beau just to let him know she still cared, that if he changed his mind she'd leave Warren in a moment, but all she'd done was chase him away. Now he was coming back. Although she tried to pretend that she didn't want to see him, it was not true. Vacation or not, the thought of his coming here quickened her blood. She wanted to look pretty for him, let him see what he was missing, make him want her again. It was all she could think of as she ate her muffins and drank her coffee. And who could say, perhaps she might be able to persuade Warren to take Corbin with them to the Springs. It was an interesting idea.

When breakfast was over, she rose from her chair and hurried away, saying only, "I'm going to look through my closet, darling. I do hope I have something suitable to wear."

After she was gone, Warren pondered over the situation. He really didn't want to go to Colorado Springs but he had to now. But he would just go this once. The way Henrietta talked this was to be the first of many visits but she just didn't understand. He had a ranch to run. Now that Corbin had left he was doubly needed. He just couldn't let the ranch his pa had labored so hard to build just fall into decay.

Whereas Henrietta had servants to do all her chores, he had to oversee his ranch hands. If this got to be a monthly habit, soon Henrietta would be wanting to move to the Springs. No, he would be firm. When Corbin came to visit they'd have a brother-to-brother talk. He needed some advice. Surely as experienced as Corbin was with women he'd be just the one to give it. In the meantime Warren was of a mind to assert his own wishes now and again. One more time he'd give in to Henrietta's pleading — but it would be the last time.

Chapter Sixteen

It hadn't taken Jessie very long to complete the necessary errand in Laramie. With the money she had with her, she purchased some canned goods, foodstuffs and a can opener at the general store. The drug store had soap, a shaving mug and a razor. Old man Brady's Clothiers had most of the other things she wanted, a shirt for herself and two for Corbin. The only thing she had any trouble finding was a tie to replace the one she had used to secure the bandages. There didn't seem to be a tie in all of Laramie. Not one like Corbin had been wearing. She was determined, however, to find one somewhere. Perhaps it would soothe her conscience just a mite for what had happened. Corbin had looked mighty fine in that pinstriped suit and she wanted him to look just as devilishly handsome again.

The people she knew in Laramie were few and far between. She did know the postmistress, Mrs. Jenny Williams, however. It was where Wade once got his mail when the outlaws were in the area. Now she was glad that she had stopped by the post office, for the affable matron knew just where she might find a tie like the one she was trying to replace. A clothier from Texas was giving old Mister Brady some stiff competition.

"And if he doesn't have one, then I know you'll find what you need right here." Reaching under the counter Mrs. Williams brought forth the thickest dime novel Jessica had ever seen.

"Well, I'll be." Jessica picked it up and examined it critically, wondering just what the old woman meant. There weren't any ties between the pages. "Sears Roebuck?" She read many a dime store novel but had never heard of that hero. "Who in hell is he? Never heard of him."

"Sears Roebuck is a catalogue, my dear."

"A catalogue?" Jessie's eyebrows shot up in question. "What's a catalogue?"

"It's like a store in a book."

Throwing back her head, Jessie laughed. "Store in a book. Now that's a good one." Mrs. Williams didn't join in the laughter and at last Jessie decided she was serious. "Let me see."

"It's for people who live far away and don't have the time to come all the way into town. You just find what you want, write down the number and they send it here."

"You don't say." There was a sparkle in Jessie's eye as she viewed the catalogue. Why, some of the things they had in the book were nothing short of indecent—lace drawers and all sorts of unmentionables that made her blush. But there were skirts, blouses, and dresses too. Hats. Fancy shoes. She wondered what Corbin would do if he saw her all gussied up, but remembering Jeff, she shook her head. No, she was what she was. Hadn't she learned that lesson before? And yet. . . .

"Take the catalogue with you. I have another." Mrs. Williams insisted. "Any items you decide to order can be held for you here at the post office until you are ready to call for them. All you need to do is to send the order to me and I'll forward it on to Chicago. When the merchandise comes into Laramie I'll set it aside until you can come in to get it."

Jessie took Mrs. Williams up on her offer. There were a lot more things than just clothing between the pages and she thought perhaps Wade might enjoy taking a look. Why, there were even doors, fences and coffee grinders not to mention all manner of bric-a-brac.

"Sometimes the winter storms in these parts won't allow anyone out and about." Mrs. Williams had said. "But then, I guess you know all about the Wyoming snows and how dreadful they can be. Remember, if you decide you want to order, I'll just keep your things here for you until you call for it, in the spring if necessary."

After Jessie had thanked the woman for her help, she went into the new fancy clothiers Jenny Williams had suggested. Sure enough, there she found a tie. It was nothing like the one that displayed Corbin's exquisite taste—it was yellow with blue polka dots—but beggars couldn't be choosers. It was a bit gaudy, but a tie was a tie after all. Besides, she was lucky to find one. The owner explained they had just had some fancy Wyoming Stock Growers Association shindig last week and most of the ties had been sold. Hastily she made the purchase, exhausting all the money she had in her pockets. All she cared about now was returning to the shack on the mesa and to Corbin. As he'd said, they had started something and she was of a mind to see just where it would all lead.

There was a rosy glow in the west as Jessie headed back. The countryside was almost uninhabited, the scenery wild and picturesque. Jessie enjoyed the ride despite the fact that it was lonely, and barren, ever-mysterious and desolate. This was Powder River country and she knew it like the back of her hand. Earlier she had passed some low log huts which had been roughly thrown together to shelter the workers who cut ties for the railroad. For the last several miles, however, she hadn't seen a living soul. The thought took hold in her mind that this would be a perfect place to hide out if an outlaw ever found it necessary. She'd remember to tell Butch the next time she saw him.

The steep red cliffs stretched east and west for thirty miles, as far as her eyes could see. As she rode through the wide fertile valley, hemmed in by the cliffs, Jessie took the time to examine the purchases. In addition to a white dress shirt and the tie she'd purchased to replace the blood-soaked items, she had bought a flannel shirt for herself and one for Corbin, a gift of sorts. The evenings were turning chilly, winter was coming on. Just plain cotton shirts would have to be replaced by flannel before too long. Besides, it was her way of showing how sorry she was about the situation Corbin was in. She supposed she'd be trying to make it up to him for a long, long time.

Taking the tie out of her saddlebag she examined it, not at all sure he would really like it. About the only thing it would make was a good target, she thought with a laugh. Ties were something the cowpokes hardly ever wore, a bandanna was usually fine for them, so she wasn't a very good judge on fashion. She had done the best she could but she had begun to suspect she might not have made such a good bargain. No doubt the reason it was the only one in Laramie was because no one else wanted to buy it. Well, if nothing else it would make Corbin smile and would be a good source of conversation.

Riding along Jessie was wildly happy. So much so that she thought it must be a sin, considering the penance she should be paying. Instead it was like a dream come true and she had Corbin all to herself. Thinking about their kiss her heart jumped. Corbin's warm lips on hers had reawakened a host of sensations she'd buried for much too long. But, oh, what a spark he'd kindled.

Was it her imagination or were the colors of the mesa more vivid? The air more invigorating? The song of the birds so much sweeter? She felt vibrantly alive! All sorts of ideas bounced around in her head, visions of snuggling up with Corbin and loving him for ever and ever, of "turning over a new leaf," as Wade might have said. She'd never want to be an outlaw again if Corbin took up her time. No siree!

Coming into the home stretch, with the steep uphill grade of the canyon, her pinto stumbled, then caught himself. Jessie slid from the horse and led him the rest of the way. Several good-sized rocks tumbled down the embankment but when the red dust settled, there was an eerie stillness. She looked ahead toward the mesa to see just how much farther she had to go when suddenly, as if from out of nowhere, a lone man on horseback galloped across the wide flat mesa toward the shack.

The sun was in her eyes so she couldn't see clearly. Could it be Corbin trying to regain his strength? If so, she'd give him a good scolding. No, that was impossible. It wasn't Corbin, he was still too weak from loss of blood even to think of such a thing, too weak even to get on a horse yet, let alone ride like the wind. Besides now that she could see better she could tell that the man on the horse was of a slighter build than Corbin, not nearly as large. Had she been followed then and her hiding place discovered? The very thought put her senses on alert.

Slowly she led her horse over the flat-topped mesa, cautiously scrutinizing the visitor. He didn't look like a lawman. Dear God, let her have a reprieve. She thought how humiliating it would be to be arrested right in front of Corbin, but relief flooded through her when she discovered the man astride the horse was Wade. Wade! *Thank God,* reverberated through her mind over and over. Working her way on foot she came as quickly to his side as she could. "Wade! Wade!" He heeded her call. "You gave me such a fright. I thought we had been followed." She wiped her hand across her forehead saying, "Whew . . ." to show her relief.

"What kind of a greetin' is that, Jessica?" Wade dismounted and started toward her, scowling all the while to show his displeasure. He always addressed her as Jessica when she had fallen from favor. "I've been worried sick about you. I'd be thinking you'd be beggin' my pardon for all the gray hairs you've caused to pop out all over my head." If he'd noticed her slip in mentioning "we" he didn't say.

"I'm sorry! Didn't Agnes give you my message?" She knew he had every right to be mad. Of course he was worried. Wouldn't she have been under like circumstances? Even so she kept up a lighthearted banter. "I know you must have been to see her by now. You know she's crazy about you. . . ." Jessie was trying desperately to inflate his ego to smooth his ruffled feathers at the same time.

"She gave me a message that didn't mean diddly squat! She was just as confused as I was. That's what I'm doin' here now. When she told me you had come to her for food and a few other items, I got suspicious. I knew you had to be someplace close by. So's I come to

155

see just what mischief you're up to. I had myself a little look inside."

"Then you know what I went and done." After a few minutes hesitation she added, "Don't you?"

Wade nodded his head but remained silently stern.

"I've got *Corbin MacQuarie* in there, Wade. He was the man Bob Meeks shot," she jabbed her finger toward the shack a few yards from where they stood. "I couldn't just leave him there to die."

"Tryin' to act like a saint, Jess?" Wade asked in irritation. "Well, if you are, let me just remind you that all of them are martyrs." He threw his hand up in the air. "Do you know what you're doing, Jessica? You'll get us all hanged. Bringing him here. . . . Ain't you got a lick of sense, gal?"

"If the sheriff hasn't got us by now they never will. You know as well as I do that there ain't a posse around that wants to ride into Fork River Basin country. That's why we came here in the first place."

"It's true Rye Grass Station has a sheriff with the brains of a titmouse, but Bob Meeks stirred up a hornet's nest and there are a whole heap of folks crying out for revenge. I always credited you with good sense, Jessie, but if so then why the hell were you so foolhardy as ride into Laramie? The rest of us wouldn't do such a damned stupid thing."

"Stupid? *Stupid?*" Now she was getting her dander up. Nobody, even Wade had ever dared to call her stupid. "Because I had to, that's why. Bob Meeks and his trigger finger put me in a pickle. I had to get some things. Nobody knows me in Laramie. Why is it so stupid for me to ride in there? You always sent me into Rye Grass Station to get supplies because nobody ties me in with the gang. If it's so damned stupid to show myself, why'd you do that?"

156

Wade had to acknowledge that he shouldn't have said what he said. "Well, I probably shouldn't have phrased it that a-way." He looked at her apologetically and reached out his hand to pat her on the shoulder. "It's just that Bob Meeks is so well known here in Wyoming. His wanted posters are plastered on all the walls and trees from here to Salt Lake City. They're offering a $12,000 reward now. Butch is sorry he ever allowed him to ride with the Wild Bunch much less take part in the train robbery."

"So? I'm not Bob Meeks. What does Bob and his wanted posters have to do with my riding into Laramie? Nobody even knows I'm one of the Wild Bunch." Once that might have irritated her but now she was relieved. What Corbin didn't know could assure a long-lasting relationship with the handsome rancher. She hoped he'd never find out about her misdeeds. She wanted to let him think of her only as his rescuer.

"That's just it, Jessie. That's why I was so gol-durned worried. One of the passengers on that train sketched a *likeness* of you. It was in the *Cheyenne Gazette*. You're just as wanted as Bob. Nobody knows if it was you or Bob that pulled the trigger."

"What?"

"They are looking for a boy of your description who may have killed and disposed of the body of one of the train's passengers."

Jessie's eyes opened wide in disbelief. "Guess I was lucky I wasn't apprehended just now in Laramie," she said, her voice quivering as she thought of what might have been her fate. Being behind bars wasn't a very soothing prospect.

"Soon that sketch of you will be hanging on as many walls and trees as Bob's posters. You're in bad trouble if you're seen in Cheyenne, Laramie or anywheres near any of the other towns. By hidin' Corbin MacQuarie the way you're doin', you're making it worse. Nobody's seen him. Everybody assumes he's *dead*."

"Dead?"

"Dead. And that makes you a suspected murderer."

Jessie was absolutely flabbergasted. A killing hadn't even been committed and yet she was already being suspected. That put a whole different light on the matter of her relationship with Corbin. She didn't know what to say. What could she do now? Take him back and let him tell his story was one possibility and yet it would ruin everything if Corbin found out she was one of the outlaws responsible for his misery.

Still, if he didn't show up pretty soon, her neck would be in a noose for a murder that had never even been committed. Come to think of it, it seemed that the clerk in the last store she was in asked a lot of questions. Did she imagine it or did he really look at her in a strange way, as if he wondered if he'd seen her before?

"I have to keep Corbin here a while longer, Wade. I just have to. Please don't ask me to explain. I have my reasons." She was so close to fulfilling her love that she wasn't about to take the risk of losing him. One moment of happiness, that was all she wanted.

"If he is really hurt bad, Jessie, you know we can't call a doctor in." Wade misunderstood the situation.

"It's not as bad as it might have been. All that blood made it look really bad. Bad enough to convince Bob that he was dead, but I stopped the bleeding and the wound is getting better. But . . . but he is still so weak. That's why I need to keep him here. I can handle it, though. I'll get him through. I can handle it all by myself. I just want you to promise me that you won't tell Butch or any of the others." Corbin MacQuarie was a danger to the gang and although she knew they wouldn't kill him, she didn't want to be responsible for any ill will. If she was really careful she'd tend to Corbin, spend a bit of time with him, then take Corbin far away. No one ever had to be the wiser.

"What can I tell them then?" For all that he was an outlaw, Wade hated to tell a lie. "They already wonder why you haven't shown up at Hole-in-the-Wall."

Jessie thought for a minute then came up with, "Tell them I'm with Agnes. They know we're friends. They won't question that. Just tell them I'm helping her with a few chores at the farm for a day or two. I'll get over to the hideout as soon as I can." There was a softness in her eyes as she looked in the direction of the cabin, a look Wade detected.

"And your share . . . ?" Wade didn't like what was shaping up one bit. Remembering how Jessie had carried on about Corbin MacQuarie that day not so long ago when she had returned from Rye Grass Station with supplies, he supposed there was more to this than met the eye.

"You can pick up my part of the loot if you will. I trust you to make sure I'm not cheated of my due." Turning her back for just a moment she concentrated on her saddlebags. Without realizing it she was whistling.

"Jessie, Jessie, Jessie! You know I'd do just about anything in the world for you." He shrugged his shoulders. "OK. You always did have this old codger wrapped around your little finger. I'll promise not to tell, if that's the way you want it to be."

"Thanks, Wade."

"I just want you to be careful. Bob thinks Corbin MacQuarie is dead, but if he were to find out differently there's no telling what he might do. He can be mighty loco. Might make you the scapegoat for his misery. Be careful."

"I will. I promise. I know you're right. Bob could be dangerous if he learns he's been crossed, but there's no way for him to find out as long as nobody but you and me knows what happened." She put her finger to her lips. "It will be our secret."

Wade put his arm around her shoulder and drew her close. "Take care, honey, and don't get yourself into a situation that will cause you any pain." She knew just what he meant. His word of caution was aimed at her heart. Wade knew all about Jeff and the wound his perfidy had caused. But Corbin was different.

"I'll be careful."

"Goodbye, Jess."

She tweeked his cheek. "Don't act as if we're never going to see each other again. I'll be back with the gang again before you know it."

"I hope so." Wade gave her a peck on the forehead, put his foot in the stirrup and swung into the saddle. Even though he referred to himself as an old codger he was still a good specimen of manhood. Before he started out for Hole-in-the-Wall he leaned over and said, "If you need me for anything you know where to find me, Jess."

"Thanks, Wade. You're the greatest pa a girl ever had. . . ." She watched Wade disappear out of sight, feeling a myriad of emotions bubble up inside her. As long as she lived Wade would be a part of her life. But now there was also Corbin. There were two men she loved now. If only she hadn't made such a muddle of it all." It was her only regret.

She sighed, thinking what had been done, was done. Whatever happened, there was no turning back. Not now. Jessie stood quietly for a long time, staring at the gathering shadows. Then, collecting her packages, she headed toward the shack just a few yards on down the trail.

Chapter Seventeen

Rain drummed against the roof, keeping time to Jessie's heartbeat. It was a dreary night, one that matched her mood. She had never felt so desolate in all her life.

She'd ruined everything, she thought miserably. Corbin would find out who she was, what she had done, and any chance for happiness she might have had would be swept away. A lump rose in her throat as she reflected on what Wade had told her and she swallowed it with difficulty. Now the enormity of what she had done was all too clear. Silly, silly girl! She had traded her happiness because of her stubborn insistence that she could be "one of the boys." Well, she'd been included in their robbery all right. Now she would have to pay the penalty.

Mechanically Jessie went about doing the chores and seeing to Corbin's recovery. She trapped a rabbit for supper, fed and watered the horses, fetched water from the creek, gathered wood, changed bandages and even brewed up some sage leaves to help relieve the soreness from Corbin's arm. She ate, worked, and even played cards with Corbin, but her mind was preoccupied with other matters. Even as she skinned and cleaned the rabbit for tonight's meal it had been difficult for her to concentrate. She could hardly think of anything except what Wade had said.

It seemed so unfair that she had a price on her head for a crime that hadn't been committed at all. Nobody had been murdered. She really hadn't done much other than hold a sack and point a pistol. If the truth were known she had really saved the victim's life. But that was just it. The truth couldn't be told without letting the cat out of the bag. She was an outlaw. Not just any outlaw, but a member of the Wild Bunch.

Well, she had asked for it. She had wanted to become as famous as Butch Cassidy. Well, now perhaps she would be. She'd wanted so badly to have her name and picture in all the papers. Well, that sketch of her would be plastered far and wide. That thought no longer pleased her. Now that she had met Corbin and knew that she had a chance with him, the idea of being an outlaw no longer held as much charm. What had been so important just a few weeks ago no longer seemed important. Indeed, it might well be her undoing.

Corbin MacQuarie was so special. She'd never felt like this before. He was everything she had ever wanted a lover to be. He was handsome, strong, intelligent, witty and loyal. A gentleman. It was something Jeff had never been. But how loyal would Corbin be if he found out she had deceived him about her occupation? What was she to say? I love you, Corbin, but would you wait for me until I get out of jail?

Corbin had made a point of accepting her just the way she was. He hadn't even suggested once that she wear petticoats or ribbons. It wasn't that she dressed in men's garb that posed the problem. He didn't seem to mind. Even if it had made a difference that could be changed easily enough. Not only could her appearance change but it would have to change soon if she did not want to be arrested and sent to jail, she mused. They were looking for a young lad, not a young girl. That in itself was going to cajole her to put on a skirt. Only problem was she was damned if she did and damned if she didn't. Right now she could not afford to be seen in any of the towns buying feminine attire or anything else, but on the other hand she couldn't be seen dressed as she was.

"I'll have to hide out here until I turn old and gray," she mumbled beneath her breath.

And what about Corbin? How could she keep him from seeing the wanted poster with her likeness on it? He was sure to see it when he rode into town to catch the train. He would undoubtedly recognize her as the lad they were looking for and then what? Once she started asking questions the whole story would have to be revealed. It would be stretching good luck to think she could talk her way out of this one with a glib answer. The man who sketched her picture knew she was with the outlaws. Besides, she didn't want to build her life with Corbin on one lie after another. If it came right down to it she'd have to tell him the truth.

He'd never want to see her again. It was a devastating thought. She'd come so close to finally having what she wanted only to spoil it by her childish actions. And yet, if somehow she could persuade him to travel on horseback to Rye Grass Station, perhaps all would not be lost. There were enough townspeople either in Butch's pay or friendly to the Wild Bunch that the posters could easily disappear without Corbin seeing them. Yes, that was it! She had to keep him as far away from any other town as she possibly could—at least until the furor died down.

Her face was flushed from the heat of the fire and

because of her thoughts. Damn that nosy artist! Why hadn't he minded his own business? She was no murderer. He would have seen that if he'd had eyes in his head. And yet, there had been a lot of confusion, what with Bob shooting Corbin and all. Maybe it wasn't all that easy to tell what really happened. Even so, his timing was awful. Just when her dreams could all come true, some two-bit artist trying to make a name for himself had to sketch a picture of her. If only he'd been a photographer, it might have been different. A man with a camera couldn't have gotten a picture of her because she would have had to pose for a long time in order for him to take it. That was something no outlaw would do unless he'd lost his mind. But sketching was something that could be done quickly. And it had.

The outlaws had always felt safe that nobody could take their picture unless they wanted it, she mused as she put lard in the frying pan. Butch had mentioned several times that he wanted to pose for a good picture of himself someday to replace that prison photograph. He had even talked about having a portrait taken of the gang as a group. If his picture was going to be in all the papers, he had joked, he at least wanted it to be a good likeness of himself. Well, let Butch have his face in the papers. From now on she wanted no part of such notoriety.

From his perch on the bunk, Corbin watched her work. Without understanding why, he noticed she had put distance between them. He'd noticed her change of mood the minute she'd stepped through that door this evening and could only wonder at its cause. Well, whatever was bothering her he'd soon ease her mind.

"Is something wrong, Jessie?" Though his voice was soft it sounded like a shot in the silent room.

"What?" His question sliced through the fog of her despair.

"You've been greasing that same spot in the frying pan for a long time now." He punctuated his sentence with a chuckle.

"Oh . . ." She turned to look at him and saw that he was lying on his side with his head on his arm. As she whirled around he pushed himself to a sitting position, trying to get up.

"Do you need some help?" he offered.

"No! No, stay put. I'll have dinner cooked in a blink of an eye. I promise. It's just that the moisture from the rain keeps putting out the fire." She forced a smile. "And I didn't think you'd want to eat raw rabbit."

"No, I like mine cooked, Jessie. Jessie!" He repeated her name in that tone that told her she was special to him. "You're an exceptional woman. Is there anything you can't do. You ride, you rope, you cook. How is it that no one has roped you yet?"

"I didn't want to get all tangled up." Her body tensed as tight as a bowstring.

"Never?" His voice was soft and husky and she knew what he was thinking.

"Well now, I might. . . ."

Jessie knew that Corbin was sincerely interested in her. His every word and the look in his eyes attested to that. He hardly took his eyes off her whenever she was in the shack with him. But soon he would be well enough to return to his ranch near Rye Grass Station. It was hard to tell how many days they had left together. Certainly he was a man who could not be held down to a bed for long. What would she do then? What would happen when they parted? They might never see each other again, especially if she was caught and put in jail. It made these moments together all the more precious.

You want him to make love to you, she thought. Then don't let your thoughts and worries stand in the way. Tomorrow was tomorrow and tonight was tonight. Wade had always told her not to borrow trouble. "Today has enough troubles of its own. Take care of them and let tomorrow's troubles take care of themselves when the time comes," he liked to say. Maybe she was just worrying too much and should take things as they came, or so she contemplated as they ate supper.

Maybe Corbin would never find out about her part in the train holdup. It was a possibility. Maybe she would have a second chance. One thing she had made up her mind to, however, was that she was going to try to change her way of living. Outlawing had been exciting when she was a kid. Now she was a woman full grown and had found her life's treasure. Although she hadn't known him for long, one thing she knew for sure was that Corbin MacQuarie was her treasure. A good man was hard to find. She had laughed at Laura Bullion for following Ben Kilpatrick around and wearing her heart on her sleeve. Now she saw all that in a different light.

Jessie stepped outside, ducking the rain as she fetched a bucket of water to use for the evening's dishes when they were through eating. As she approached the shack, she could hear music and thought for a moment she was losing her mind. Was it real or had she been doing so much thinking that she was beginning to imagine things? Opening the door slightly she peeked around it and saw Corbin sitting up, leaning against the wall strumming a guitar and singing a love song.

"Oh, Jessie is my darling, my darling, my love. I would not want another. . . ." he sang out loud and clear. His fingers moved along the neck and strings of the old guitar she'd noticed under the bed. It seemed he could play the instrument without much effort.

"So . . . ! You're musical!" She continued watching and listening and when he had finished the song she clapped her hands with glee. Her somber mood was forgotten for the moment "You're pretty good on that darned thing, Corbin." Even the gunshot wound didn't seem to hamper his playing.

"I used to chase away the coyotes, keep them from the campfire this way." He smiled as she laughed. "There, that's what I wanted. You look twice as pretty when you lift up the corners of your mouth." He started to lay the guitar aside but she pleaded with him to hear another song. Corbin complied, giving her a rendition of "Old Folks at Home." "Stephen Foster, though Archie thinks I wrote it. I didn't tell him any differently."

Jessie giggled. Putting the pan on the stove she wiped her hands on her pants leg and came to his side. "It is dark and gloomy in here with the rain. Shall I light another candle?" she asked.

"No, it's dark and gloomy in here but you're my sunshine. Your smile gives off just enough light." He held out the guitar. "While you were gone today I passed the time in mending the neck of this old broken thing with a little of that surgical tape." He thumped the neck of the instrument with his finger. "Good as new."

"And very useful, as I see."

"Helps me while away the time when you're not in here. And perhaps I can say in song what is in my heart." He strummed a chord. "Like the cool night air caressing my face, like a brook whispering in the night. The girl who draws my heart and soul will never leave my sight."

His voice was a pleasant baritone, though his playing left a bit to be desired. Even so, Jessie was enchanted. No one had ever sung to her before. If the words didn't quite rhyme, if a chord here or there was out of tune, it didn't matter. It was what he was telling her in the song that deeply touched her.

"It's beautiful, Corbin," she said when he was through.

"No. I'm clumsy of finger and a lousy poet, but the meaning is there. You're very special to me, Jessie." He put the guitar back under the bed. "And while I'm thinking of all the good things you are, let me say thank you for all you've done for me. Jess, I want to thank you for saving my life." He plucked at the sleeve of his shirt. "And for the new duds."

"That plaid shirt looks real good on you, Corbin. The blue in the plaid matches the blue of your eyes. Guess that's why I chose it in the first place. You don't find a light blue plaid like that very often. And . . . it suits you."

"Matches my eyes does it?" He smiled, showing the even white teeth that had fascinated her that very first time they'd met. "I am more comfortable in it. Flannel. It's good and warm too. You know what, though?" She shook her head no. "I wonder where in the hell you got this tie." He held it up by the end. "Even in this dim light the damned thing is nearly as bright as a copperhead snake." He laughed and shook the tie to let her know he was just teasing.

"Don't you be funnin' me now. That tie was hard to find."

"I know and it was thoughtful of you, Jessie, to buy me a tie and all the other things. It really was. Hope you don't mind my teasing you a little bit. It shows I'm feelin' better and besides, you're always such a good

169

sport. I like that about you." After a slight pause, he added, "Come to think about it, I like a lot of things about you."

"It's probably the last tie in the whole town of Laramie. I thought you'd need it when you wear your dress-up duds to go back to Rye Grass Station on the train." She had purchased the clothes before she knew that her picture would be plastered all over that town and other big towns. Now she was hoping he would *not* take the train. " 'Course now, like you said, trains can be mighty unlucky at times. The more I think about it the more I think it's wiser if you come back to Rye Grass Station for a spell."

"I can't. I had an important errand in Colorado. A matter of romance, you might call it," he joked, thinking of Stamash.

"Oh, I see. . . ." Jealousy was like the sting of a bee, making Jessie wince. So, he'd been going to see some girl.

"No, you don't see." Corbin read her thoughts and decided to reveal his plan. "My brother has a ranch in Colorado and I was going to borrow his bull to . . . well . . . build up my herd."

"Oh!" That revelation made her feel a whole lot better. "Well, maybe you could wire your brother from Rye Grass Station and he could make the arrangements."

"We'll see. Right now there are other things on my mind." Slowly his eyes caressed her, starting from her auburn curls and sliding down her arms. "I think I liked *your* old shirt better." His grin was a sly one. "The one your wearing's nice but I can't caress your lovely bare arm now."

"Why not, Corbin?" she teased, feeling in playful mood. "This shirt is removable just like the other one was."

"Oh, it is, is it?" he laughed, reaching out to grab her hand.

"Yes. . . ."

It was an invitation he couldn't refuse. His arms reached out to draw her into an embrace. "Oh, Jess! Jess!"

Her hands pressed against his chest and slid up to clasp him around the neck. She looked up at him, studying his face, running her fingers through his unruly golden hair. "Never did give you that shave. But I will."

"My face is as gritty as sandpaper. I don't suppose I should kiss you. . . ."

"I don't mind. I don't mind at all." She leaned her head forward, brushing his lips with her own.

"Jessie. My Jessie!" His whisper was like a breeze against her lips, warming them, teasing them. Thinking of what was to come she moistened her lips with her tongue. Then he was kissing her, his mouth hard and demanding.

"Corbin. . . ." The fusion of their lips swallowed any words she might have spoken. And then there was no need for words.

He held her face in his hands, kissing her eyelids, the curve of her cheek, her chin, her mouth. His tongue traced the outline of her lips then stroked and teased the edge of her teeth. Their eyes met and Jessie's heart began to hammer at the glitter of raw desire she saw in those sapphire blue eyes. She craved his kisses, his touch, and wanted to be in his arms forever.

The bed was hard but now it seemed as welcoming as a soft feather bed as he drew her unresisting body with him. They landed with Jessie on top but gently he rolled her over until they were lying side by side.

His lips played as seductively on hers as his fingers

had plucked the guitar strings, sending a blissful music through her soul. Desire flooded through her, obliterating all reason.

"Jessie!"

Kissing didn't satisfy the blazing hunger that raged through him and swiftly he pulled at the buttons of her shirt. Before Jessie had time to realize what he had done she was pleasantly surprised to feel his warm, seeking fingers on her naked breast. Lightly, teasingly, his long fingers stroked and caressed the peaks until they hardened. Jessie couldn't hide the moan that escaped from her throat. She wanted to be naked against him so that his hands could roam at will. With that thought in mind she pressed against him, blending herself into every curve and angle of his body.

"We've got to stop this, Jessie!" Taking a deep breath Corbin willed himself to be a gentleman but it was increasingly difficult. His desire was raging out of control, like a forest fire. He wanted her so very much.

"Stop? No!" Jessie all but shouted. They might have only this one time together. Carefully so as not to disturb his wound, she worked at the fastenings of his shirt, her hands trembling in their eagerness. Corbin followed her lead, undressing her slowly, savoring what lay beneath the plaid flannel shirt. Then his arms were about her as he brought her soft curving flesh hard against his chest, caressing the tips of her breasts with his own. It was an erotic experience awakening Jessie to the full depths of her sensuality. Only Corbin had ever aroused such an urgent need within her. What she had felt for Jeff had been puppy love; this was the real thing.

"Your skin is as smooth as a new leather saddle."

"Yours isn't. Your chest is prickly." Her fingers roamed over the stiff hair that trailed from the area between his nipples to his abdomen, stroked and fondled him as slowly and deliciously as he had explored her breasts. Her hands slid over muscle and the tight flesh as she sought to familiarize herself with every inch of the tall, muscled length straining against hers.

Jessie watched the expressions that chased across his face and felt the same hot ache of desire. It was like a spring coiling up inside her, awaiting release. Moving away from him for just a moment she brazenly slipped out of her denim breeches, her drawers, pulled off her boots, then leaned over him. The sight of her silken smooth limbs, her proud jutting breasts, was his undoing. Corbin's breath came out in a short gasp as he viewed the loveliness presented to him.

A powerful, fierce emotion exploded between them as he gathered her into his arms again. Passionately they clung to one another as Corbin whispered her name over and over again. His warm breath tickled her ear, his tongue caressed the soft flesh of her ear lobe. Then he concentrated on the soft fullness of her breasts again.

"Most certainly not a boy," he murmured.

"What?"

"I was just thinking about that first time we met. How could I have been so blind? If I'd only known then how beautiful your body was I never would have said goodbye that day." He paused in his exploration. "Jessie . . . Jessie are you sure? I don't want you to have a moment of regret for what we have done."

"I'm sure. I want you Corbin. More than I've ever wanted anything in my life." She wanted to tell him that she loved him but knowing how such words could often frighten a man, she held back. "I want you."

Slowly she peeled off his shirt, taking extra care with his arm. His hands assisted hers, tugging at his pants, pulling them over his buttocks and down the strong column of his legs. His maleness was firm swelling with his need for her. He was so strong, so powerful. The thought of what was to come made her tingle all over. It was right. She knew that deep in her heart. He was her man and she was his woman. It was as simple as that. A thing that had started in the Garden of Eden.

Her arms went about his neck, her legs encircling his hips as she pulled him toward her. Slowly Jessie undulated her hips, and experienced a shock of raw desire as she felt the probing length of him slipping between her thighs.

"I swear, it's never been like this before, Jessie. Oh, Lord." His hands captured her buttocks, cupping them, pulling her up against him.

Their eyes met and held in an unspoken communication that said she was ready and so was he. "Are you sure you're well enough?" she whispered.

"I'd have to be dead not to want to love you now. . . .

Even so, Jessie knew a way to love him that would make it easier for him, less strenuous. For just a moment she was poised above him, then slowly she lowered herself, straddling him, easing herself down upon his elongated hardness. She kissed him, fusing their two naked bodies together in an embrace so intimate that it left her breathless. Closing her eyes she began to move up and down, rising and falling, intent on giving him pleasure. Corbin covered her breasts with his hands, his fingertips exploring as they joined each other and became one flesh. The spasms of pulsating pleasure th followed were like nothing Jessie had ever felt before. She should have been embarrassed she thought, for being so very brazen, and yet being with him seemed so right. There was nothing shameful in loving a man and giving your body in love.

Corbin's breath was ragged. She was so warm, so tight around him. He arched up to her, sighing softly at her movements, giving himself up to the intensely powerful world she was creating. Oh yes, she was a woman all right. And what a woman. Passion seemed as natural to her as breathing. It was a moment he would never forget, for he knew her desire was prompted by love. He felt it too. Something more than the joining of bodies was going on here. His heart, his soul would be forever in her keeping.

"Corbin . . . ?" There was uncertainty in her voice. "I don't want you to think . . . I mean . . . you're . . ."

"Special. So are you, Jessie. More so than you know." Wrapping his arms around her, he rolled them over, still locked together. This time Corbin took the lead. If there was pain in his arm he didn't notice. Nor did he care, at least for the moment. Tangling his hands in her red-brown hair he brought her to the edge of an imaginary cliff, hurling them both to fulfillment.

In the drowsy afterglow of their love-making, they held each other close, a companionable silence arising between them. Then as the hours deepened they immersed themselves in conversation, the love banter that exists between two lovers. The flickering candlelight cast a soft, golden glow over them, weaving a spell. They touched each other gently, wonderingly, each knowing that something wonderful had passed between them tonight. It was a love that would not soon be forgotten.

Eighteen

In her wildest dreams Jessie had never thought she could be so happy, and yet she was. So much so that the world outside the tiny cabin just seemed to melt away. She wouldn't think about anything but Corbin. A moment like this might never come again. Was it any wonder that she reached out to snatch at the dizzying opportunity offered to her now? In the two days that followed their first love-making, Jessie never once regretted initiating their union. She had never known desire until he kissed her, never imagined what love could be like until she looked into his eyes. If she was shameless because she couldn't wait for him to make love to her again, well, so be it. Love had a special set of rules.

How could I have ever thought anything was important compared to this, she wondered, looking at him with renewed adoration. He had taken off his shirt and tie and sat bare-chested, looking in a small piece of mirror, engrossed in his busy act of shaving. As if she minded his whiskers one little bit, Jessie thought with a smile. Last night had been a wonder beyond compare. Oh yes, Corbin was getting much stronger. He had proved that beyond a doubt whenever they were together.

"Ouch! Damn it, I nicked myself."

"Want me to help?" Before he could answer she whisked the razor out of his hand and finished what he had started. Seeing a small scratch in his chin she wet her finger with her tongue and dabbed at the blood. "Poor Corbin—another wound."

"Hopefully it won't impair my prowess," he joked. Taking her hand he laid it on his cheek. "Oh, Lord, how I'm going to hate to leave here."

The very thought brought a mist to Jessie's eyes and yet she knew the time was drawing nearer. They couldn't hide away here forever. Even Adam and Eve had been chased out of paradise. "Oh, Corbin, let's not talk about that."

"OK, we won't." He held out his arms and she walked into them, encircling his neck with her arms, winding her fingers in the waves of his golden hair. For an endless time she clung to him as if to keep the world at bay, to keep him near her. At last he pulled away, holding himself an arm's length away from her. "What are we going to do now?"

"Something special."

"Mmm, I'm all for that."

Jessie ignored his meaning. "Tell you what. I just bagged another rabbit for supper. It's a nice warm day. Real Indian summer weather. Let's go out, build a fire and sit a spell while the rabbit cooks. We can look at the sunset and you can get a little fresh air. Fresh air will do you good and maybe you could try walkin' a little too."

"Fresh air? Damn, I haven't been outside this cabin in so long I hardly know what the world looks like." He sat on the edge of the cot trying to put his boots on but he couldn't manage without her assistance. When he stood up his legs were a little wobbly. "I haven't had boots on for so long I almost need to learn to walk all over again," he joked. "I know cowpokes don't like to walk

177

unless they have to, but this is ridiculous."

"You can do it." Putting her arms around his waist she led him to the door. "Come on now. Just head for that beautiful sunset out there." Taking hold of his elbow she guided him through the door. "Think you can make it without my help?"

"I'll try." Once outside, he walked slowly and made it to a lone pine just a short distance from the shack before he stumbled. Quickly he caught himself.

"This tree will give support to your back."

The pine tree was a few feet from the edge of a cliff overlooking the valley below. A breathtaking sight. A smoldering red sun hung low in the sky, touching the mountains with a muted scarlet light. Corbin's eyes were riveted on the scene as he lowered his body to a sitting position. Jessie took a seat beside him.

"The ground isn't all that soft. Wait here and I'll get the saddle blankets. Be right back." She hurried back to the shack, grabbed the blankets, the skinned rabbit and some firewood. She hurried back to his side and as Corbin fixed a comfortable resting place for them, Jessie started a fire and spitted the rabbit over the flames. Then she rejoined Corbin.

Looking out across the valley Jessie shaded her eyes and watched as the setting sun danced across the horizon, illuminating the clouds and the steep rock formations in the distance. Here and there gray smoke curled up toward the sky, giving evidence of other camps in the valley. Other than that, there was little sign of other persons anywhere about. It was quiet, peaceful and romantic. The kind of evening poets always wrote about. They sat together, his arm around her shoulder, hardly saying anything, enjoying their camaraderie. There was something very stirring about the silence and the countryside. They both felt it.

"I feel so free here, so unencumbered. Without a worry in the world." Corbin squeezed her hand. "But all this must end, Jessie."

And then where were they going to go from here? she wondered. Perhaps this *was* her last chance at happiness. This was the man she had thought she could never have and yet he belonged to her for this moment in time. She wanted to make the most of the time they had together. Wade had cautioned her about getting too involved, he thought Corbin MacQuarie would break her heart; but this time she had to prove Wade wrong. Life was for living, not for worrying. She would throw caution to the winds and simply handle tomorrow's troubles tomorrow. For now they were here—and they were together.

There was something sensual about the utter quiet. It was like an enveloping blanket surrounding them, bringing them together. Corbin was caught up in the magic, but slowly his thoughts came together and he tried to sort things out. Just where did Jessie fit into his life? Certainly she was too fine a woman to love and leave. She had inched herself deeper and deeper into his heart as each day passed by. She was a woman he could share his life with but did he want to make such a commitment now? Was it too soon to know the depth of his need? And—what about Jessie? How did she feel about him?

What is he thinking? Jessie wondered. Was he reflecting that this blissful isolation they shared couldn't last forever? Was he as taken with her as she was with him? Had the passion that passed between them meant as much to him as it had to her? He was a man with strong hungers. Had she just appeased his appetite or was there a deeper feeling for her buried within that muscular chest? She watched him and she wondered.

It was Jessie who broke the silence, though she didn't put her thoughts into words. Instead, she made small talk. "That's Big Horn Mountain in the distance and Wind River Range, those rolling hills over there," she said pointing in their direction.

"Its a desolate valley, rimmed as it is by those steep rugged buttes and bluffs . . . but beautiful nonetheless," he replied. Then he caught her off guard when he asked "Is it true that for better than thirty years this valley has been ruled by outlaws?"

"Outlaws?" She quickly tried to avoid further questions by making it appear as if she knew nothing about it. "That's what they say. Don't know if there is any truth to it."

"I've heard there's a place hereabouts that's part of the Outlaw Trail." Corbin hadn't been able to forget what had happened to him. He wanted to find those renegades and have them brought to justice before they fell on another unsuspecting group of passengers.

"Outlaw Trail?" Jessie shrugged her shoulders. "I suppose it is considered a lawless area, but more men have been killed playin' poker than in robberies. It's the gamblers who do most of the killin' around these parts. Take Wild Bill Hickock, for example. He was killed just about twenty years ago in Deadwood while playin' poker. It was a gambler who shot him in the back, not an outlaw." Her loyalty to the gang members prompted her to defend them. "Besides, folks hereabouts don't really think the outlaws are all that bad."

"Well, they are!" Corbin didn't like the idea of her sympathizing with them in any way.

"They haven't bothered me."

"Well they might!" he snapped. "I really don't like you coming up to this place. It worries me, Jessica."

"Oh, bull wart." Just like a man to start dictating to her and trying to control her life, she thought. Telling her where to go and what to do. For a moment she bristled. "If I hadn't known about it, where would you be?"

He squeezed her hand. "Hey now, don't get angry. I was only concerned for you."

She regretted her blustery mood. "I'm not afraid. I'm fast on the trigger, set a horse real good and I'm clever as the next man. And another thing, I hardly ever trust someone until I know them." Jessie got up from where she was sitting, definitely of a mind to change the subject and get back to the romancing before they had a fight and spoiled everything. "Look there," she said pointing skyward. "The moon is comin' up. We had better eat before it gets dark. That rabbit should be good and done by now."

They shared the rabbit, then sat looking off in the horizon for a while. The fire died down but it was just too nice to go back inside. The full moon had risen. In the distance a pack of timber wolves could be heard howling. It was a reminder that it was wild territory. Untamed. Corbin rolled his shirt sleeves up above the elbow and leaned back against the tree trunk, not any more anxious than she to leave the serenity. Enacting a truce, Jessie resumed her place beside him, laying her head on his shoulder.

"That moon looks almost silver. Doesn't it, Corbin?" Jessie remarked. Corbin turned, his eyes soft, smoldering, almost hypnotic. She had a sudden longing to entwine herself in his arms.

"Its about the prettiest sight I've ever seen, except for you. . . ." The sight and smell of her was intoxicating as his eyes feasted on her beauty. "That silver moon is casting lovely shadows on that pretty face of yours." As he spoke, she raised her head and looked up at him with gentle green eyes that radiated what was in her heart. Placing his index finger gently beneath her chin he lifted

181

her face upward to meet his kiss.

She felt vibrantly alive as he kissed her, her whole body responding to the memory of the pleasure she found in his arms. His full lips captured her lower lip gently between them and he ran his tongue over her lower lip. It was titilating and exciting.

Jessie's arms encircled his head, her breast crushed against his massive chest. Both their hearts were beating like drums. It was as if a magnet was drawing them together and neither could resist the deep stirring, churning, wanting sensation that they were feeling.

She was a fascinating woman, Corbin thought. A blending of strength and softness. Oh, God, how he wanted her. Right from the moment he had realized there was a woman beneath that flannel and denim he had been drawn to her, had fantasized about holding her warm and naked next to his body. Sweet and spicy, that's what she was. As she reached out to brush a lock of blonde hair from his eyes, he pulled her to him again.

"God, you're beautiful. Have you any idea how much I desire you?"

"Mm-hmm." Only a fool could not have known what he wanted and she wanted it, too. "Just about as much as I'm tingling all over for you, I expect."

He pulled his partially unbuttoned shirt over his head; his boots and other items of clothing quickly followed. Jessie unbuttoned and removed her shirt with as much ease as if she were about to go skinny-dipping. He knew her body as well as his own. There was no need to be coy.

"Corbin. . . !" Jessie's heart was racing.

He took the one exposed breast in his hand and softly caressed it. She did not pull away but leaned close to his nakedness. His mouth closed over the peak of her breast and he ran his tongue gently over the surface. He felt a desperate hunger to caress every inch of her. Love her as she'd never been loved before, even by him.

"I want you, Jessie. Oh, God, how I need you." He bent forward, his lips claiming hers over and over again. His tongue pushed past her lips to explore the moist sweetness of her mouth in a lingering series of kisses. She was breathless when at last she pulled away.

She removed her own boots, her Levis and her knee-length muslin drawers, then turned around baring her complete nakedness to his eyes. He kissed the peaks of her breasts again until she gasped. Her hands in turn caressed his hair, his face, his chest. She pulled him closer and closer until they were lying facing each other side by side upon the soft blanket, the embers of the fire illuminating their bodies.

His voice was husky with desire. "My darling, darling Jessie. . . . My sweet little minx." His hand moved down the flat plane of her belly, down each long, shapely leg and back up again in casual, heated exploration.

Her body pleased him. Her long, slim legs, firm, full breasts, narrow hips and trim buttocks were always delightful to the eyes. Her skin was soft and smooth. If only it could always be like this, he thought. But sometimes things happened to destroy happiness. It was a thought he pushed far from his mind.

"I love you, Corbin. . . . she whispered so softly she doubted he could hear, but she meant it with every beat of her heart.

He was her man. And oh, what a man She wanted no other. With a contented sigh she ran her hands over his chest hair, his flat stomach and down his inner thigh, increasing her boldness as he groaned with delight. Closing her hand around his maleness she wanted it, welcomed it and was awed by the tremors that shot through her. Only by blending together could they appease this all consuming ache that spiraled through her.

She arched against him in sensual pleasure. "Corbin. . . ." His name was like the song the breeze whispered.

Soon their bodies were blending and becoming one in a rapture that seemed to capture them and lift them to the supreme ecstasy again and again. She moaned with pleasure as he whispered his love for her and her body responded to his sweet magic words. Surely she would die if he stopped now. They had found each other. This was meant to be. The whole world was this man loving her so gently. She arched her hips to meet him and he wildly capitulated to the softness she offered. Then it was as if a raging storm descended, hurling them together in its depths.

Jessie was not really certain when it ended or when she returned to reality. She was shaken. She felt marvelously happy, cuddled in his arms.

In the quiet aftermath of their love-making, they clung together desperately. Neither wanting to separate from the other. Neither wanting the ecstasy to end.

They remained naked and caressed each other for a long while. Finally, they pulled the second saddle blanket over their naked bodies and drifted off to sleep, her head resting on his chest, his strong arms cradling her as if to never let her go. And as they slept, the bright silvery moon shone down upon the two lovers as if to bless their union.

Chapter Nineteen

Choking puffs of dusts rose from the road as the carriage rounded the last bend, heading for the M bar Q ranch house. Henrietta MacQuarie put her delicate lace hankie to her nose, voicing her irritation. "Not so fast, Robert! You're jiggling the packages. I don't want to send them scattering all over the road."

"Just anxious to get home. Sorry, Miss Henrietta." The carriage driver was contrite.

"Well, watch yourself unless you want to be out of a job." She was in an understandably foul mood, she thought, and all because of Warren's brother. So far he hadn't showed up at the ranch house and the delay was ruining all her carefully wrought plans.

"Yes, ma'am." Knowing well that she meant her threat, Robert slowed the horses down to half their pace. Henrietta MacQuarie was a woman who at all cost must be pleased.

At last the ranch house came into sight, a large sprawling "L"-shaped dwelling painted a light brown, surrounded by a series of outbuildings and cattle pens. An undistinguished-looking building, Henrietta thought with a sniff. The white door, eight green and white window boxes were her doing, the only "woman's touch" about the whole place. This spring she was determined that Warren make good on his promise to plant more trees and put in a garden. That was the thought that preoccupied her as the carriage slowed to a halt. Warren was just going to have to concede to her good judgment more often. Certainly it was time that big, ugly structure looked more like a home.

Alighting from the carriage she carried an armload of her purchases inside and plopped them in the hallway for Charles to take up to her room. She'd purchased an array of hats, gloves, shoes, and dresses to replace those in her closet that were so sadly out of fashion. She was *not* going to Colorado Springs looking like a pauper.

As she passed by the hall mirror her eyes flickered appraisingly over her reflection. She was wearing one of the dressmaker's new creations. Yes, the blue dress fit perfectly. The white lace and piping gave just the right touch and complemented her figure to perfection. The neckline was just right. Not too daring but with just enough décolletage to make it interesting. It might do Warren some good were other men to give her the eye.

The morning had gone smoothly enough, even so she was in a "mood" because of an argument with the dressmaker over one of the outfits she'd ordered. The red dress had looked cheap and gawdy, more like something a saloon girl would wear rather than a proper matron. In the end, however, Henrietta had kept it anyway, considering it a bargain that she had talked the woman down to half-price. The wicked thought tugged at her brain that she would wear it when Corbin came. One thing he had always admired was her figure.

"If Corbin ever arrives," she mumbled peevishly. She

186

was beginning to wonder if he was ever coming. And yet they had not heard a word to the contrary. How like Corbin to flaunt courtesy. No doubt he was dallying in Denver or along the way. Perhaps it was with some woman or other. The longer she thought about it the angrier she became. By the time Warren entered the house, slamming the door behind him, she'd worked herself into a rage.

"You're back," he said, kissing her on the cheek in greeting.

"Just where is your brother?" she snapped back, pulling away from his embrace.

Warren's jaw tightened. "We've been over this before, Henrietta. There are things that can happen that a man has no control over. Ranching can be a precarious business. A drought, a sudden freeze, illness in the herd. Something's come up to postpone Corbin's arrival, but he'll be here. It's for us to be patient." He couldn't resist adding, "Aren't you the one who is always telling me that patience is a virtue?"

"This is different. Your brother's lack of courtesy is endangering all our plans, as well you know." Colorado Springs was a good four-day trip from the ranch's location. The very fashionable place was just seventy-five miles south of Denver. "Just what are you doing about it?"

"I did the only thing I could do. I wrote a letter to him to let him know I understand that something has come up. I told him he would always be welcome, but to let me know his plans."

"His plans? *His* plans! Don't you care about what *I* want at all?" In a swirl of skirts and petticoats she turned her back on him, lacing her fingers together in front of her as she sat on the velvet covered settee. Her

187

stinging silence was a signal of the potency of her displeasure.

"Henrietta, please understand. . . ." A rap at the door interrupted his train of thought. With a disgruntled sigh he listened as Henrietta's "butler" announced their visitors.

"Miss Belinda Marshall, Mesdames Alexandra Crampton and Cassandra Jackson."

"Oh, dear, I'd quite forgotten I'd invited them today." They would have no time to argue over the matter of Corbin, not with three of her friends here.

"Damn!" Of all the people in world he wanted to have to endure at this moment it had to be those three. "Prune faces," he breathed.

"Warren, hold your tongue." Rising from the settee Henrietta hurriedly instructed Charles to make tea as she passed him by, then led the women into the drawing room. No one would have suspected that the women were sisters, but they were, though Belinda Marshall was as tall as her sister Alexandra was short and Cassandra was as dark as they were fair.

Cluck, cluck, cluck, the ladies talked on. Their conversation turned immediately to gossip, who was courting whom being the favorite topic. Warren thought how boring it all was, how small the world was that these women lived in. His eyes darted to the doorway, wishing he could make his escape, but knowing that to do so would insure a stern rebuke from Henrietta and the danger of being locked out of the bedroom in punishment.

Uncomfortably sandwiched between Belinda on the left and Alexandra on the right as they sat on the red velvet settee, Warren listened to the women, suddenly realizing why they were often referred to as "hens."

188

"Your tea, Belinda." Taking the silver tray and teapot set from Charles's hands, Henrietta poured the beverage.

"Thank you, my dear." The cup swayed precariously on the saucer as the thin, long-nosed woman balanced it in her bony fingers.

"Alexandra!"

Alexandra Crampton glanced up nervously from the newspaper she was reading to take the proffered cup from Henrietta's hand. "Sorry, but I was fascinated by something in this morning's paper."

"What?" Henrietta craned her neck to see.

"They have a sketch of the boy they think shot that man on the train. Why, just look at those malevolent eyes. He looks like a murderer. Take a look, Henrietta."

Henrietta tore the paper out of Alexandra's hands and stared at the picture. "Obviously an outlaw," she said, scanning it eagerly. Not that she had any real interest in the story. No, it was because she wanted to show Warren that without *his* help the investigation was proceeding quite well. With that purpose in mind she thrust it into his hands.

"Dreadful. Just dreadful," Alexandra exclaimed, setting the teacup down and scanning the newspaper again. "When a body can't even travel without something like this happening, why I just don't know what's gone amiss in the world. Of course, we all know that Wyoming is Godforsaken territory so I suppose such things are to be expected."

"They're not civilized like we are here. That's for a certainty," Cassandra added with a disdainful sniff.

"I'm surprised that brother-in-law of yours packed up and headed there. But then I always did think he was rather wild." Alexandra's hands moved to her breast,

189

fluttering like two trapped doves.

"He *is* wild!" the other sister snorted indignantly.

Henrietta sighed, taking a sip of her tea. It was a bit too sweet and she realized she had been so intent on her thoughts that she had put in two spoonfuls of sugar instead of one. It was all the talk of Corbin, she reflected. Why did he still have the power to rattle her nerves so?

"Reminds me of an outlaw himself, at times," Cassandra added snidely.

"I beg your pardon, madam." Warren shifted in his seat, indignantly coming to his brother's defense. "Corbin is as law-abiding as *I* am. If you are even hinting. . . ."

"Oh, forget about Corbin! Warren always defends him no matter what he might do." Henrietta smiled sweetly. "Besides, what happens in Wyoming isn't important at all. But what I have to tell you is. Warren and I are planning a visit to Colorado Springs."

"The Springs!" The sisters' voices echoed each other. They were notably impressed.

"Why, I was just reading about it the other day." Cassandra was quick to show her knowledge. "The article said that Colorado Springs was the brain child of a Civil War general, William Jackson Palmer, who had seen that easterners could be lured to the Pike's Peak region just as they had been lured during the gold rush years."

"People are pouring in from all parts of the world. Even the Western Railroads are advertising the health, adventure and romance of the Rockies." Henrietta lapsed into a tirade on the virtues of the area.

Warren sat back blocking out his wife's rambling by concentrating on his own thoughts. He really didn't

190

want to go to Colorado Springs and it was obvious Henrietta was just flaunting the trip, so he had to go now. But he would just go this *once*. The way Henrietta talked this was to be the first of many visits. She'd even hinted at moving to the springs, asking him if the M bar Q really meant so very much to him. Once it hadn't but now it did. It was his family's heritage, an inheritance from his father that he would never completely let go. Not even for Henrietta.

Henrietta. Henrietta. It seemed he usually built his plans on what she wanted. Sometimes he wondered why she had married him in the first place. Once they were married she had demanded a cook, a maid, a butler, and a laundress. By her every word and action she proved that she didn't like being a rancher's wife and yet, she had insisted that he give up his law enforcement career and go back into ranching. Why? Just what was it she wanted? Did she love him or did she just want a ring on her finger and a matching one in his nose? During these past few days he had begun to envy Corbin's freedom.

And yet. . . . Suddenly the wheels in his head starting turning. Perhaps he could use Henrietta's love of travel for his own gain.

"Warren!"

Henrietta's shrill voice shattered Warren's thoughts into splinters and he looked up into her scowling face. "What, darling?"

"Belinda was asking you a question. The same one I want answered. Just when are we going on this so-called vacation of ours?"

Warren refused to cower this time. He looked unwaveringly into his wife's eyes. "When *I* say we are going," he answered matter-of-factly.

"Oh. . . !" Rising angrily to her feet, Henrietta tipped over her cup of tea. "Now see what you made me do." Dabbing furiously at her new blue dress she cast him a scathing look, expecting his apology but receiving none. "Its stuffy in here. Belinda! Alexandra! Cassandra! Come, I'll show you the garden I'm planning for next spring." In a whirl of blue Henrietta left the room, followed by her friends.

After they were gone, Warren pondered over the situation. There were times when he wished he could get away from his wife, if only for a little while. He supposed there were those of his friends who would say, "The honeymoon was over." Well, time would tell whether or not he had made a mistake. It was still not too late to go back into detective work again. If he could get Corbin to return. Would he?

Thinking about Corbin's coming for Stamash, Warren had to admit that Corbin wasn't wasting any time in trying to build up his new ranch. Well, that was Corbin for you. Didn't let any grass grow under his feet. From the letters he'd received he could say one thing for his brother. He knew what he was doing. After all, hadn't it been Corbin who had done the superb job of selecting a foreman and all the other cowpokes who worked the M bar Q? Corbin had always loved the ranch their father had built. Why then had he so suddenly just upped and left? The answer had come to him before but he had refused to listen. Now he did. Henrietta. It had started with the flower boxes and Corbin's refusal to go along with her whim. Henrietta's pouting had driven a wedge between the brothers. Now Corbin was starting all over in another state.

But Corbin should be here and not I, Warren thought guiltily. Corbin's heart was in ranching, not his.

If Corbin had left because of Henrietta then the answer was simple. Keep her away from the ranch as often as possible and let Corbin have all the say.

"That's it!" he whispered. It was the only answer. Hell, Corbin was more cut out for this kind of life than he would ever be. Perhaps when Corbin arrived he'd talk the matter over with him and try to convince him to come back. With Corbin running the ranch he could be happy, Henrietta could travel whenever she wanted, and Corbin would be back where he belonged.

Reaching over, Warren picked up the newspaper and scanned the story about the robbery, again feeling the longing for adventure prick him. He'd catch those robbers, he thought as his gaze touched on the main suspect. Such a young boy to have already murdered a man. It was a sad thing when those so very young were lured into being outlaws.

The more Warren thought about it, the more he was tempted to give detective work another try. There was big money to be made in private detective work. Cattle rustling was becoming a real menace, not to mention other outlawry. Some of the cattle ranchers paid as much as $225 a month and all expenses. Those ranchers belonging to The Wyoming Stock Growers Association paid even more. Or so Warren had been informed by the friends he still kept in touch with, those who were still doing detective work.

It wasn't even the money, really. He was actually quite well fixed for money. It was the adventure, the excitement of tracing down an outlaw and bringing him to justice, that he missed. He had been shot at and even injured a few times but once a lawman always a lawman. Or so it seemed. What he loved most was horses, adventure and guns.

193

Why hadn't he realized how different Henrietta's likes were from his own? Socializing was all right, he guessed, but there were so many other things he would rather be doing with his time.

Henrietta was a small, demurely elegant young woman. And even though he loved her, she was splitting him into two people: a tough empire builder determined to bring law and order to the West, and a cavalier doomed to see to his lady's every wish. He was just going to have to take the bull by the horns on this matter and exercise his own wants. Surely he had some rights in the matter of how his days were to be spent. After this trip to the Springs, he would lay down the law in his marriage. He just had to.

Just because Henrietta loved to hobnob with the elite and to drink tea as the English did was no reason for him to have to do the same. She enjoyed the beautiful homes, the theater, opera, concerts and the company of witty, well-educated, well-bred people and so did he, within reason. But lately she seemed to want to spend every Sunday at church socials and every Saturday evening dancing that new rage, the gallop, and eating French chocolates just so she could brag to her friends when they came to tea. Henrietta was slowly but surely becoming a snob. Even the ranch house didn't seem good enough for her lately.

Colorado Springs was just a symptom of what was happening. She had assured him that powerful tycoons from Amsterdam, The Hague, Paris and London could help him in his business dealings. What she said was true but, after all, he was a college graduate with some measure of wealth himself. He did not want to think that Henrietta was only interested in him because of his money. No, she loved him in her way. After all, she, too, came from a well-to-do-family didn't she? It must just be that she was not totally a western woman. Warren had always taken his money for granted and didn't like to make show of what he had. Henrietta was of a different frame of mind. It was not that they didn't love each other. The problem was whether or not they could come to some agreement about any number of things that had been weighing on Warren's mind lately.

Once again Warren's eyes were drawn to the newspaper article about the robbery suspect. Now that he thought about it, that boy had the look of a born killer in his eyes. Witnesses said that he shot a man in cold blood when the man had protected a small child. Hell and damnation! What was the world coming to when someone could get away with that? Warren was just itching to use his new Smith and Wesson frontier double action .44 revolver. Butch Cassidy had been quoted as saying that he and his gang could evade any pursuers. Warren wanted to prove that remark false. Newspapers were bringing the outlaw fame. Hell, he was about as well known as the president lately, he and all those of like kind. It was disgusting!

Henrietta is wrong! I am needed, he thought. There were books of laws and officers to enforce them but keeping order in a frontier town was not an easy thing to do. Warren wanted to change that. Only the six-shooter stood for peace and only a good marksman could control any howling, rowdy mob. It further irritated Warren that sometimes gunslingers, gamblers, and even saloon operators could become peace officers. The more he thought about it, in fact, the more he had convinced himself that he was indeed needed farther west. If only he could make Henrietta see that.

Warren, passed up and down the long room thinking

195

how bored and restless he was. Right now Corbin was enjoying the sights and sounds of the true Old West. Wyoming was where the excitement was. "Damned brother of mine always knew how to live," he said, pounding his open palm with his closed fist.

But he knew what he would do now. As soon as he got back from this trip, he was going to begin doing some of the things he wanted to do. He might even write to the Pinkerton National Detective Agency. He knew his worth. They'd want him back again. He had courage, could handle a gun, and was excellent when it came to tracking a thief. Why, he'd soon have that young scoundrel in tow, the one who shot the passenger. Unlike the other lawmen Warren wasn't afraid to ride the Outlaw Trail. If he had his way he'd ride right in there and tackle the whole Wild Bunch. He'd soon have them in jail where they belonged. Yes, the West needed men who knew the mountainous terrain. Men like him. Here on the ranch he was wasting his time, but not for long. No, not for long.

Chapter Twenty

It was dark in the cabin except for a slice of moonlight drifting in the window. A stillness hung over the room. Corbin and Jessie lay in each other's arms, snuggled against the chill of the night, weary but satisfied after a glorious night of love-making. His head was a pleasant weight on her shoulder. She felt the warmth of his breath on her neck, his hard, warm body curled around hers.

"Jessie. . . ." Corbin reached out and gently touched her cheek. She could feel the heat of his eyes blaze into hers as he said, "I have a confession to make."

"A confession." If they were going to spend the time that way she had a few to make herself. "What?" she asked uneasily.

"For the last day or two I haven't been feeling as poorly as I've been letting on. My arm is healed, Jessie, almost as good as new in fact, thanks to your loving care."

She chuckled softly. "I wondered why the boiled sage leaves hadn't relieved the soreness quicker."

"I haven't been truthful because I just didn't want to face the fact that it's time to leave." His arm tightened around her waist as if to hold onto her forever. "To-morrow I have to go."

"I know." It was the time she had been dreading.

While living in this isolated place, Corbin and Jessie had developed an unusually close, cheery, loving relationship. Now the time had come to face reality. With the first rays of the sun they had to go their separate ways, at least for a little while. There was no room for sentiment. He had a ranch to manage and she had to keep out of sight, at least until the furor over the robbery died down. Each had responsibilities to themselves and to others.

"You're mighty special, Jessie." His lean, long form caressed hers and she was conscious of his nearness with every nerve, every muscle of her body.

"You are special to me too, Corbin. You were, right from that first time I laid eyes on you. All the way up the canyon I thought about you, but my feelings sort of . . . of frightened me."

"Frightened you?" As if to give her comfort he leaned his head forward and kissed her on the fore-head.

"I was afraid of falling too hard and getting hurt again." Somehow the story of her romance with Jeff just tumbled past her lips. How she had gussied up for him, trusted him, let him make love to her only to have him ride away without a word of warning.

"I'd never do that, Jessie. What we shared together is very, very special." His whispered words warmed her, then he kissed her. Not with hunger but with a gentleness that touched her heart.

"You're so special to me that it hurts. Corbin. . . . Corbin. . . ." She had been so brazen, so bold in her love-making with him that she had been afraid he'd

198

think her a wanton woman. Certainly she had acted that way, but only because she knew how precious their days together were. "Besides Jeff, you're the only man . . . I'm not. . . ."

"Hush. It's not important." His mouth, hard and demanding, fastened on hers, stealing her breath away, swallowing any other words she might have said. His kiss kindled that oh-so-familiar fire deep within her. Tomorrow they might have to part for awhile, but there was still the rest of the night.

Corbin's lips seemed to be everywhere, her lips, forehead, neck, and shoulders. Pulling his face to her breasts he cherished each peak, making gentle, poignant love to her, molding her, shaping her, joining her body in the timeless rhythm of love. When he entered her she felt her heart move and knew at that moment that Corbin's love was the most important thing in her life. And with that thought came the hope that somehow, someway tomorrow would not be the end of their romance.

Even so, the morning came all too quickly. If only she could lasso the sun and keep it out of sight just a little while longer, Jessie thought, watching the bright rays filter through the tiny window. And yet perhaps it was better not to prolong her heartache. With that thought in mind she eased herself from Corbin's grasp, rolled out of bed, dressed and absently combed her fingers through her hair. She had known that this moment would be difficult to endure but she had not counted on so much pain.

"Jessie . . . ?" His low, throaty voice stirred her. Would it always be that way when she was with him? Just a touch or a whisper sent streaks of pure fire through her. "You're beautiful in the early morning light."

She didn't answer. The lump in her throat was just too large to enable words. Instead she busied herself tidying up the room and gathering their belongings together. Still, she couldn't prevent her eyes from straying once or twice in his direction.

For over two weeks now, they had been tucked away from the main thoroughfare. Nobody had business up in this narrow, lonely valley. Once they had seen a herd of wild horses stirring up the dust as they made their way through the valley down below. At first she had thought that some wranglers were chasing them but no wranglers appeared. The windswept narrow canyon ran downhill for miles. It was a totally isolated place. It had been just her and Corbin. Now he was going.

"You could go with me, you know. I thought about it some after you were asleep. Would you like to, Jessie?" She hadn't been expecting such an invitation.

"I would like to. . . ." But she couldn't. Right now her image was undoubtedly strewn from Denver to Laramie to Salt Lake City and back again. Even after it was found out that Corbin was alive it would still implicate her in the robbery. "But I . . . I can't."

"Why not?" Corbin couldn't hide his disappointment. He fully had been expecting her to say yes.

"Because . . . because I can't, that's why. I . . . I've got a job to do. I've hired on. . . ."

Jessie had told him it was her job to catch wild horses such as these then lead them into chutes, strap halters over their heads and with the help of other cowboys holding lead ropes, to break the horses. "And I'm good at it, too." She had said proudly. "I learned that if I put a burlap sack over a stubborn horse's head, he will be easier to tame."

"Then change your plans. They'll understand. I would if you'd hired on with me." Rising from the bed he came to her side, cradling her in his arms as if he thought that would make a difference. "Now, stop talking foolishly. Pack your things and when I ride back to the ranch I'll take you with me. Of course, Archie will be surprised but . . ."

"I can't!" She shook her head vigorously, her misery mirrored in her eyes. There was nothing she could say that would make him understand, unless she told him the whole story and that was a thing she couldn't do. Better to live with dreams than to shatter what they had shared with the truth.

"I'm asking you to marry me," he blurted out, surprised by his own statement.

"I . . . I can't leave Wade. Not yet."

"I see." Never had his pride been so deflated. Here he had always been the one to avoid such entanglements before and now when he'd at last met the girl he wanted for his wife, Jessie was rejecting *him*.

"No, you don't see. You can't possibly understand." Jessie couldn't hide the mist of tears that sprang to her eyes.

Corbin's mouth trembled as he tried to smile. "Yes, I do. You're young, Jessie and you want your freedom." His voice was carefully controlled. "While you enjoy having me for a lover you're not too anxious to have me for a husband." Grabbing up his pants he stiffened his back and held his head erect, feigning an nonchalant attitude. "Well, that's the way it goes." He swore beneath his breath when he realized he was trying to put both his feet through the same pants leg.

"Corbin . . . ?" She didn't really know what she could say without giving herself away. "I . . . I just need time, that's all."

"Then I'll give it to you. I've got my ranch, after all. Those cattle can't herd themselves. When you want to come to me, when you've made your decision, let me know." He hurried into his shirt, boots and vest.

"Are you hungry, Corbin?" His icy disdain was more upsetting than his anger might have been, and she was tempted to tell him all.

"I'll get something to eat later. Don't trouble yourself." Now that he was well enough to ride, Corbin had to get back to his ranch, the Rolling Q. He had been away far too long already. Warren and Henrietta must have been frantic when he did not show up at the Colorado ranch as expected. The first thing he must do when he got back was to get in touch with Warren.

"Then I guess it's goodbye, at least for a while," Jessie whispered.

"Yep, I reckon it is." Corbin tried to lighten his mood. Even though he had wanted Jessie to return with him he tried to understand her position. She just felt she could not leave until the job she had been sent to do was completed. He respected her for that. Both of them had responsibilities that had to be met and that was that.

The sun was already much higher in the sky than he wished it were. He had wanted to get an earlier start but leaving Jessie was not an easy thing for him to do, even though his ego had been pricked. Besides she really was such a loving soul, giving him one of her own horses.

Jessie flushed under the scrutiny of his gaze as he thanked her for giving him the palomino. He had no idea that it was stolen. She watched as he threw the saddle blanket and saddle over the horse's back, fastened the cinches, then stepped away for a minute. "Are you sure you can get another saddle for yourself if you give me this one?" he asked. " 'Course now, you're probably a lot better at riding bareback than most of us are." He stepped close to her, wrapping one of his big strong arms around her while he smoothed the hair back from her face with the other. "Aw, Jessie, I hate for you to be up here all alone. Won't you reconsider going with me?"

Jessie shook her head. "In answer to your first question, Yes, I can get another saddle from the ranch where I work. Most of the time the cowboys furnish their own saddles but if I need one they will provide it." She didn't tell him that they were easy to steal. In answer to your second question, I can't go with you, Corbin. I just can't. Not until I finish what I started. And I won't be alone. I'll be back with my outfit in Cheyenne." She couldn't say Hole-in-the-Wall and reveal the location of their hideaway. "They sort of look out for me. You know how close cowboys are to those with whom they ride the range." What she was saying wasn't entirely untrue. Only the part about going to Cheyenne was a lie.

"Yeah, I know how close cowboys can be. Only don't you think it's about time you fessed up to being a woman?" Jealousy prodded his words. She had given her body to him and that made him feel possessive. What if she found someone else?

"I thought you didn't care how I dressed or acted. That's what you said. I am what I am. I have my reasons for how I talk, how I dress, and how I act. It's not your place to make any changes."

"I know." He shook his head, regretting his words. He didn't want to part after an argument. "Even

203

though I've fallen in love with you, I have no right to dictate. You know what you have to do and I know what I have to do." Jessie could see the disappointment in his eyes and once again she was tempted to tell him the whole story. She was hurting him without really meaning to.

"You'll never know how hard it is for me to stay behind. I am in love with you too, Corbin. I don't have to tell you that. But . . . but I just have my reasons." Standing up on tiptoe she wound her arms around his neck, squeezing him tight. "But it ain't exactly the end of the world."

"You could have fooled me," he said with downcast eyes.

"We'll be together again as soon as spring comes. Things should have settled down by then."

"The spring?" It sounded like a lifetime. The winters here were long and hard. The snows would be coming soon and it would be difficult to travel any meaningful distances.

"Unless we have an early thaw, I'll be back in Rye Grass Station about calvin' time." Jessie was certain that by then the whole incident of the train robbery would have blown over. Then she'd woo Corbin and look forward to a happy ending.

"All right. I'll hold you to that promise." He reached out for her. "Come here you little minx," he said teasingly. "We really did get something started all right. We did kindle quite a fire didn't we? Maybe it'll take more than that snow that's coming to put out the blaze we've begun." He kissed her long and hard then stood back looking into her sad green eyes. Placing his foot in the stirrup, he swung into the saddle, trying to maintain his calm. He wouldn't make a fuss, wouldn't beg. She had a right to the same freedom he'd always treasured. He'd just hope with every beat of his heart that they would meet again. "Thanks again for the horse. I never really don't cotton much to takin' trains. Somehow trains don't bring me much luck. You're right about finding another way back to Denver."

"I'm right. Trust me." Jessie forced the corners of her mouth into a smile.

"Whoa." The palomino was a bit edgy after being confined for so long. "What did you say this horse's name was?"

Jessie thought hard. She had no idea about the name, the horse being stolen and all. "Sunbeam," she answered, looking up at the sun.

"Sunbeam! Sunbeam!" Corbin concentrated all his efforts on getting the animal under control. After the horse stopped dancing and prancing and had calmed down a little, Jessie stood on tiptoe and he bent down for one last kiss.

"You're some woman, Jessie. Damned if you're not." He grinned at her, then winked. "Let's not remain separated for too long, you hear. Come to Rye Grass Station as soon as you can."

"I will!" Putting her hand to her lips she blew him a kiss. "I will, Corbin, you'll see . . ."

Jessie watched as he rode down the hillside and out of sight, blinking back the tears that threatened to spill from her eyes. Some outlaw she was. She had seen men writhing in pain from gunshot wounds, some who had never recovered. She had seen men shot down in cold blood. She had been followed and hounded by many a posse and only the love for this man could make her cry. She loved him desperately. Devotedly. Right now she felt that any sacrifice she would make would not be enough. She had found what she wanted. Corbin loved her because she was no clinging vine but a self-reliant young woman. With him, she could be herself and not have to pretend.

Still, she couldn't just turn her back on Wade and the others and walk away. They had been like a family to her. They had helped her through many rough times, and she was wanted for murder. And yet when spring came she would have to make a decision and she already knew what that decision was. She no longer wanted to be with the Wild Bunch. From this moment on she was going to play it straight and hope she could put it all behind her. Certainly Wade would understand when she told him she was determined to change to a respectable way of living.

"It will all work out," she murmured, watching as the cloud of dust grew smaller and smaller. It would be just fine. There was one thing in her favor, Corbin had decided *not* to take the train. For awhile, until the truth was revealed, posters would be all over the trains and the train stations but there was a chance that he would not even see them. This way, he would be riding directly to Rye Grass Station following the valley into Vernal, Utah. He would hardly go through any towns, large or small. When he got back, people could see for themselves that he was alive and well and would realize that there had been no cold-blooded murder. Then, the furor would die down and she would no longer be wanted for murder. When she was no longer wanted, the posters of her would come down to make room for the real cold-blooded killers. God only knew, there were plenty of that kind around. Soon people would forget and she could take her place back in society.

I'll grow my hair, just to be safe. Yes, it was undoubtedly a good thing that winter was coming and that she would remain out of sight for awhile. By the time they got together again, everything should be cleared up. She'd dress in feminine attire, just to fool any of those who might still remember. She'd change her way of living, all right. So much so that the foolish artist who sketched her would not even recognize her. And then, at last, she'd be free to love.

Chapter Twenty-one

It was a dark and cloudy day, the rumble of thunder as fearsome as Archie Jarvis's grumbling. "Something's wrong, I tell you. I know it. I sense it with every step that I take. Corbin said he was gonna send a telegram. Well, where the hell is it?"

"No news is good news, Arch," Bowlegs insisted.

"The hell it is!" He'd sent Bowlegs into town to find out if there'd been a mixup, but when the ranch hand returned instead of calming Archie's fretting it only stirred it up all the more. At the Crossman Saloon the bowlegged cowboy had found out that there was a train robbery the very same morning Corbin had set out on the train.

"A robbery!"

"Whole town is talkin' about it. 'Course now nobody at the Arrowhead Saloon is saying much," Bowlegs answered. " 'Course everyone in Rye Grass Station knows them employees are loyal to Cassidy and his Wild Bunch."

"S'pose they was as tight-lipped as as a spinster." Archie mumbled beneath his breath. "They always are when it comes to blowing the whistle on anything

208

Butch Cassidy has a hand in." His brows shot up in question. "It was that bunch of renegades that done it, wasn't it?"

Bowlegs' head wobbled up and down. "Yeah. Law might never have known if not for Bob Meeks. Seems someone on the train identified him from that poster that's been making the rounds of the town. Either he or one of the others of the Wild Bunch shot a man. Fell right from the train he did. Dead as a doornail."

"Huh!" Archie's scowl spoke of his opinion of the gang but for the moment he made no more mention of Corbin, that was until the cowboy who delivered the weekly mail left several letters from Warren MacQuarie in the box. Although it was not in Archie's nature to snoop, he nevertheless promptly opened the letters. Archie knew that Warren would not be writing if he and Corbin were together at the M bar Q as they had planned to be. Something must have gone wrong. With that thought in mind, Archie decided to check things out for himself.

Archie Jarvis rode into Green River, Wyoming just over the line from the ranch. He couldn't remember just which train Corbin had taken but he was determined to find out. With that thought in mind he stepped right up to the stationmaster, a rotund man who semed to be busy counting money, ticket stubs, or something or other.

"Ahem!" It was near the noon hour, a train was in the process of leaving. Archie tried to exercise his patience, realizing the stationmaster was busy. Trying to keep himself entertained, he scanned the wanted posters on the wall. The train station was gathering quite a collection, including one of Bob Meeks and another sketch that looked strangely familiar. "Hmmm." He

209

could have sworn he'd seen someone from the Arrowhead Saloon busy taking that poster down from the trees and buildings in Rye Grass Station. "Another one of the Wild Bunch," he snorted, standing there with his hands in his pockets to stare at it awhile.

The train whistle sounded, smoke poured from the engine and the train was under way. As soon as it was on down the track, Archie strode casually over to the ticket window again and said gruffly, "I know you're busy, but let's get down to business . . ."

He never managed to get the remainder of his sentence out of his mouth for the uniformed, white-haired old man behind the counter looked up with startled blue eyes and said, "Don't shoot. Please don't shoot." It was obvious by his expression that he did indeed think Archie was there to rob the ticket office.

"Shoot? Hell, I'm not even carrying a gun." Taking his hands out of his pockets Archie proved that to be true. "Just calm down. I have no intention of shooting." When the stationmaster gave a sigh of relief, Archie proceeded. "What I do want is some information about the train that was recently robbed near Elk Mountain. I haven't heard a word from my boss and it's got me worried. Did that train arrive in Denver?"

"Yes, sir. It did. And only an hour behind schedule," the man answered proudly.

"I see. So it wasn't delayed or anything like that? Or rerouted?"

"No, sir."

A queasy feeling starting curling up in Archie's stomach. A premonition. "Do you remember a man by the name of Corbin MacQuarie? A pleasant, handsome yellow-haired fella wearing a pin striped suit. . . ."

"Mr. MacQuarie. Yes. Yes, I remember him. It was a

frightful thing that happened. Just frightful. That's the reason I was so jumpy just now. Everyone around here has been on edge and on guard since that horrible day."

"You're sure you remember him then? He got on his train?"

"Oh yes, I'm sure. We had a good conversation about Creede, Colorado. You see, I used to live in Creede. We talked about the old days in those parts of Colorado." He whispered behind his hand, "Colorado used to be rather wild, you know."

"No, I didn't."

"We talked about Tincup, Colorado, too. Tincup was where the first seven sheriffs were murdered about twelve years back and one man shot down just for watering down the whiskey. I remember talking to him about Bob Ford, the killer of Jesse James, who was gunned down in Creede, Colorado. We both agreed that Colorado has had its share of crimes like other mountain towns throughout the area. He told me that Denver, Greeley and Colorado Springs have cleaned up their towns but that there is still plenty of outlawry and violence of every kind in out of the way places. . . ."

"OK! OK!" Archie wondered if this old man had talked Corbin to death. "Then he *was* on that Union Pacific Number Thirty-Four?"

"It was him all right." The old man's face puckered up. "I remember how bad I felt when the two ladies and the little boy attested to the fact that *his* name was Corbin MacQuarie. That's the reason I remember the name so well. Because of their testimony. And when I got the description of the murdered man's brown pin-striped suit. . . ."

"What?" Archie's face paled. Leaning against the counter he grabbed the man by his shirt front. "What

211

did you say?"

"I said I got the description of the man murdered in that train robbery. He was wearing a pinstriped suit. It was Corbin MacQuarie all right."

"Good God!" Archie's hands were shaking as he let the man go. So, he was right! Something terrible had happened to Corbin.

"I almost became ill enough to vomit just thinking about that nice young fella. He said just before he boarded the train that he would see me again and we would finish our conversation when he came back this way from his trip to Denver. Now we never will."

"No, you never will." Archie shook his head, a part of him refusing to believe what he'd just heard. Corbin MacQuarie was so young, with his whole life ahead of him. To have been shot down in the summer of his years seemed the very worst travesty of justice. "Poor Corbin. Poor, poor Corbin," he whispered.

"I'm sorry."

"Yeah, whole lotta people going to feel the same. He was a special sort of fella. A damned good boss!" Archie clenched his fists trying to maintain his emotions. He couldn't cry like some damned woman. He had to keep his head and do what Corbin would have wanted him to do. "You really have been helpful. I sure thank you for telling me all those things. Guess I had better send a telegram to his brother," he said more to himself than the stationmaster. "Can I send one from here?"

"Just write down what you want to say on this yellow pad," the man answered, thrusting the tablet into Archie's hands, "and I'll see that it gets sent right away."

"Mighty obliged." Archie made the telegram as brief as possible, telling Warren MacQuarie the few details he

212

had learned from the old stationmaster. Then there was nothing left for him to do, nothing really that he could say but that he was sorry. Corbin MacQuarie was dead and there wasn't anything he could do, though he would have if he could, the Good Lord knew.

Leaving the train station office, he swung into the saddle and galloped just as fast as he could back to the Rolling Q. His heart was heavy as he traveled and he hung on to the hope that there had been some mistake as to the identity of the murdered man. The more he thought about it, however, the more everything just added up. Corbin had never arrived in Denver because he was dead. The man who had been shot *was* Corbin MacQuarie. The question was, what was going to happen now?

Chapter Twenty-two

Warren MacQuarie settled himself back in his leather chair and took a sip from his brandy snifter, his eyes resting on the mantelpiece where his collection of guns resided. The last two days those guns had beckoned to him with the poignancy of a woman's arms and yet he knew it was all just a silly dream, an illusion. If he even suggested to Henrietta that he wanted to return to the Pinkerton Agency he'd be locked out of the bedroom forever. No, it was time he faced the fact that he'd been hogtied by that little filly the moment he'd said, "I do." From now on everything was going to be *her way*.

"Warren!"

At the sound of her voice he hurriedly hid his brandy beneath the seat of the chair. Damn, just for once he wished he didn't have to react as if he was committing a crime by enjoying his manly comforts, but that was the pattern they'd settled into. Even with all of his stoic musing he could not help chuckling, however, as what appeared to be a walking pile of clothes came through the door. A melodious voice drifted over the pile of dresses. "Warren, help me make a decision."

"What's the matter, honeybug?"

Rising to his feet he helped her lay the garments on a big overstuffed chair. "I don't know which dresses and hats to take." Her mouth drew down in a pout. "Since you limited me to only one trunk."

"Well now, honey, we're only staying five days. I hardly think we need to take your whole trousseau." He'd given in on the Colorado springs excursion but he was going to remain firm on this.

"But I want to make you proud of me."

"You will. You always do." With a smile he assessed her voluptuous body with an appreciative gaze, anticipating tonight. He'd given in just as she'd known he would and agreed that come tomorrow morning they'd go ahead with their plans, Corbin or no Corbin.

Although Warren wanted to see his brother, he'd given Slim Reinker, his foreman, the authority to do whatever was necessary in arranging for Stamash to go with Corbin to Wyoming for awhile. Warren supposed the ranch could go on just as well without him while he was in the Springs. Slim knew the ropes and would keep the newly hired cowpokes plenty busy. Winter was right over the horizon so there was a whole lot of haypitching that needed to be done. The cattle would be fed from the barn's hay loft. Each cow would eat half a ton before spring showed its face again. Not to mention the fifty saddle and work horses that needed to be fed.

"Look, Warren. This black suit and feathered hat will be perfect for traveling, don't you think?" She held them up for his inspection. "And I can wear this coat with the fur collar and matching fur muff for ice skating on Palmer Lake."

"Ice skating? For God's sake, we haven't even had any snow." Warren knew now beyond a doubt what she was really planning: to make Colorado Springs their winter home. Well, he didn't like that idea one bit.

"There will be in a month or two." Leaning over she kissed his lips. "Don't be such an old grouch. We'll have a wonderful time, you'll see. Someday you'll thank me, Warren." Clutching a green feathered hat to her bosom she whirled around in glee. "Oh, it will be such fun. I can hardly wait."

"Henrietta . . ."

She touched her fingers to his lips. "Don't say a word and spoil it. Oh, Warren I know you'll enjoy yourself, too. Why don't you take up polo, darling? Henry Van Winkle thought you would be a marvelous polo player when you last talked to him. Why, I'll bet you sit a horse prouder than any other man down there . . ."

She rambled on and on and not wanting to spoil her enthusiasm, Warren simply agreed. She had him wound around her little finger. She knew it and now so did he. Crossing his hands over his chest, Warren shook his head as he walked over to the window. What would Corbin think if he could see him now? Would he say, "I told you so"?

For a long moment Warren stood at the window, pondering the situation. He watched as a man dismounted in front of the stables and strode up to the door. As the man came closer he recognized his foreman and thus he opened the door before Slim even had time to knock.

"You got the payroll?"

"Uh huh!"

Something was deeply troubling the man, Warren could tell that at a glance. Usually smiling, Slim's eyes were downcast, his frown as wide as a gully "OK, what is it? What's wrong?"

In answer Slim reached into his pocket, handing Warren a telegram.

"You stopped by the telegraph office. Bad news?" Some gut feeling told Warren at that moment that somehow it involved his brother, but even so he wasn't prepared. When he read the words he couldn't help the howl that rent his lips, a wailful sound like a wounded animal. "Nooo!" He doubled over as if someone had struck him, then sank to his knees.

"For the love of God, Warren, what is it?" Henrietta tore the telegram from her husband's hand and read it herself.

"Corbin . . ." he somehow managed to say.

"Corbin killed? Oh, no!" Somehow she couldn't imagine him dead. "Killed in that train robbery?" Bowing her head she felt a sincere moment of grief. Corbin had been so alive, so strong. It just didn't seem fair. "I'm sorry." But not so much so that she wanted it to affect her life in any way. In horrified anger she watched as her husband walked over to the mantel and collected his guns.

"Damn them! Damn them to hell!"

"Warren, what are you doing?" She skillfully maneuvered herself to block his way. "I won't let you . . ."

"For once, my dear, you have nothing to say on the matter." Clenching his jaw he strapped on his guns.

"If you go, I'll never speak to you again. I mean that, Warren."

"Then I'm afraid we'll both have to suffer through a silent marriage." Before she had time to back away, he kissed her on the cheek. "There are some things a man just has to do. Please try to understand."

217

Without another word Warren followed Slim out the door and to the stables. He was on the next train to Green River, sending a telegram ahead to Art Conners, the sheriff. Conners met him at the station with a saddled horse, and they rode back to Rye Grass Station together. From there they went on to Corbin's ranch, the Rolling Q.

It was a sad-faced group of cowboys who greeted them. Corbin's crew had liked their new boss and expressed their grief to Warren. Somehow they just couldn't think of him as dead.

"Don't know whether or not I'm a gonna like his brother as our next boss," he heard one young cowpoke whisper.

"Just because he's Corbin's brother doesn't make him the same as Corbin." Warren heard them talking among themselves about how most ranchers had cut pay from $35 to $25 per month and abolished free room and chow at the bunkhouse. Corbin had done neither. His cowhands received $35 a month and he had promised to build them a brand new bunkhouse.

Warren wasn't sure that he would sanction that. To his mind Corbin had been much too generous, but then one of his brother's faults had been that he didn't fully understand the value of money. Warren did. Living on his Pinkerton salary that time he was estranged from his father had taught him a great deal.

"You hungry, son?" Archie appraised his new boss with a critical eye. If he didn't miss his guess the ranch would be sold right out beneath them. There'd be a whole lot of cowpokes out of work again. Such a sad, sad thing. Corbin had somehow made them part of his dreams. "Right now we don't have a chuck wagon cook and sort of take turns fixin' the grub. 'Course now I

218

seem to be doin' more than my share, but no never-minds. Besides, we'll get a cook later if you feel we need one."

"I'm not hungry!" Warren took refuge from his pain in silence. What did this old codger know about how he felt? What it was like to lose a brother?

"No, I don't suppose you are." Archie looked at Corbin's brother warily. The brooding, silent type was what this Warren MacQuarie seemed to be. Not made from Corbin's cut of cloth, but then few men would be. But then it was time to get it through his thick head that Corbin was gone. In the meantime he wasn't even sure that they would all have reason for a cook. Nor was Warren MacQuarie giving them much cause to hope. "You expect to keep the ranch?" He wanted to know, as much for the others as for himself.

"Don't know yet." Warren didn't even want to contemplate what to do with his brother's ranch.

"I see." Archie thought that somehow Corbin would want his brother to keep it. "He was so proud of the place. I want to tell you how much I respected your brother," Archie felt enshrouded in his own sorrow. "I remember how Corbin told me before he hired the men that he wanted competent, experienced ranch hands, not worthless saddle bums who couldn't be trusted. He had been willing to pay for that type of man and even went further, he had been willing to help with the *work*. How could anyone not like a gent like that?" They all had to agree that he was a special man and they might never again have a boss like him. No siree, Corbin MacQuarie was one of a kind and would not be easily replaced.

"My brother was a fine man and I intend to get his killer." Reaching in his pocket Warren pulled out the

219

sketch of the young boy who had so cruelly murdered his brother and skewered that face with his stare. He would never, never forget that face.

Looking at him, Archie could feel Warren MacQuarie's pain, but cautioned him nevertheless. "Careful, son. Vengeance can be a two-edged sword, or so my mama used to tell me. Remember that, son."

Chapter Twenty-three

Jessie rode along the barren, lonely, mysterious strip of land toward the camp at Hole-in-the-Wall. As she approached the great basin surrounded by red cliffs, two men stood guard at the one entrance. It was a hole in the rock formation leading to a giant basin on the other side where robbers grazed stolen cattle. It was a veritable paradise with a small settlement of their own consisting of cabins, corrals, bunkhouses and plenty of space for the storage of food and other necessary commodities.

Suddenly a series of shots hit the ground beneath her horse's hooves, causing the pinto to rear and nearly throw her. Taking her hat off she waved it in the air. "What are you damned fools tryin' to do? Save the lead. You might need it later on."

The two men standing guard, Coyote Bo and Al Folsom, put their rifles down as she came nearer and shouted simultaneously, "Jessie? Jessie Where the hell have you been, girl?"

"Wade told us some cock 'n bull story about your being with Agnes at her place helpin' with the chores for a few days," Bo spouted.

"Yeah, and we believed it until a couple of days ago when Agnes herself rode up here to find out what was goin' on," Al added.

"She's been livin' with Wade in that cabin over there since about Thursday night," Bo guffawed knowingly, shaking his head in the direction of the cabin he had mentioned.

"Agnes is here, huh?" Jessie thought she would have to do some fancy talking to explain her whereabouts the past couple of weeks but the two men didn't question her further. In fact, they seemed much more interested in what Wade and Agnes were up to.

"Yep, Agnes is here all right and I want you to know Wade's been actin' like some damned fool kid again." At his last remark, Bo winked as if he knew some secret and Al just chuckled.

"We even had a dance here the other night. Several of the young dudes got real brave, rode into the Wind River ranches and come back here with some *wimmen*."

"Wade really got somethin' started." Al added with a snigger.

"Should have been here, Jess. It was some shindig. Lasted till almost four in the mornin'," Bo continued.

Jessie sat astride her pinto while the two cowboys told all about it. "Sounds as if you did need me around here to keep you fellas in line," she said as she placed one foot in the stirrup, swung the other leg over the horse's back and eased herself to ground level. "Guess I'd better get over there and do a little chaperoning." She laughed and the two men guffawed again as she took purposefully large strides in the direction of the cabin Coyote Bo and Al had pointed out.

Jessie walked up to the cabin door and knocked but there was no answer. She knocked again then waited a few seconds. She was just getting ready to knock again when Wade's voice finally sounded out, "Who is it?"

"It's me, *Jessie*."

Like a flash Wade was there to open the door, pulling up his suspender straps.

"Jessie. Goddamn. You're a sight fer sore eyes. Didn't know but what you'd ride out of here with the Prince Charmin' of yours and I'd never see you again." He grabbed Jessie by the shoulders and held her out at arm's length to look her over. "My, my, my, but that smile tells me that you're happy."

"Happy as a warthog in a bed of clover. Oh, Wade . . ." She couldn't help the blush that stained her cheeks and laughed gaily in unison with his chuckle. "It must be sinful to be so contented and so in love."

"In love, is it? Jessie, I don't know if . . ."

Agnes came from behind a blanket that was strung up on a line in front of the bed to block the view from the window. "It's good to see you again, Jessie," she said sheepishly. Obviously Jessie's entrance had been ill-timed.

Jessie couldn't help but smile. It was obvious what had been going on before she arrived. "So you and Wade did find one another again," she said softly. "Didn't I tell you he was drawn to you like a bee's drawn to honey?"

She was happy for Wade and for Agnes, too. They were two lonely people who really did need each other. Actually, they had much in common. Both had lost their spouses quite suddenly and had never cared to remarry. Besides, now that Wade had Agnes, it wouldn't be so hard for Jessie to tell him about her plans for a changed life style.

"Yep, I chased her until she caught me," Wade

223

joked.

Agnes took her pipe out of her apron pocket, lit it then gave Wade a playful shove. "He knows a good thing when he sees it," she said with a teasing gleam in her eye.

Wade put his arm around Agnes and drew her close. "All joking aside, Jess. Agnes 'n me's gonna get hitched. She wants me to stop this damned business I'm in and settle down at her place."

"Settle down?" The situation couldn't have been more perfect if she'd planned it. Here all the way back to the hideout she'd been wracking her brain to think of how she was going to tell Wade that she intended to leave the gang for awhile, and now it was all going to be made easy for her.

"Now, Jess, I know how much it means to you being an outlaw and all. . . ." Wade looked at Agnes and she looked at him in silent agreement. "But it will be much better for a young woman like you to . . . to well . . . you can live there with us and. . . ."

"Live with you?" Jessie threw back her head and laughed. "Whoa! Just a minute. Not so fast. I've heard it said many a time that three can be a bothersome crowd." Coming up behind them she put one arm around each of them and hugged them tightly. "I'm tickled to death about the two of you. It's the best thing I've heard in a long time. But I've got some plans of my own."

"Plans?" Agnes was completely surprised.

"This'll make it a lot easier for me to say what I came to say. I want to go out on my own for a spell. I'm leaving the Wild Bunch, too, you see."

"Leaving Butch and Sundance?" Wade looked suddenly puzzled. "Happened kinda sudden, didn't it, Jess?

ACCEPT YOUR **FREE GIFT** AND EXPERIENCE MORE OF THE PASSION AND ADVENTURE YOU LIKE IN A HISTORICAL ROMANCE

Zebra Romances are the finest novels of their kind and are written with the adult woman in mind. All of our books are written by authors who really know how to weave tales of romantic adventure in the historical settings you love.

Because our readers tell us these books sell out very fast in the stores, Zebra has made arrangements for you to receive at home the four newest titles published each month. You'll never miss a title and home delivery is so convenient. With your first shipment we'll even send you a **FREE** Zebra Historical Romance as our gift just for trying our home subscription service. No obligation.

BIG SAVINGS AND **FREE** HOME DELIVERY

Each month, the Zebra Home Subscription Service will send you the four newest titles as soon as they are published. (We ship these books to our subscribers even before we send them to the stores.) You may preview them *Free* for 10 days. If you like them as much as we think you will, you'll pay just $3.50 each and *save $1.80 each month* off the cover price. *AND you'll also get FREE HOME DELIVERY.* There is never a charge for shipping, handling or postage and there is no minimum you must buy. If you decide not to keep any shipment, simply return it within 10 days, no questions asked, and owe nothing.

MAIL IN THE COUPON BELOW TODAY

To get your Free ZEBRA HISTORICAL ROMANCE fill out the coupon below and send it in today. As soon as we receive the coupon, we'll send your first month's books to preview Free for 10 days along with your FREE NOVEL.

— F R E E —

B O O K   C E R T I F I C A T E

ZEBRA HOME SUBSCRIPTION SERVICE, INC.

YES! Please start my subscription to Zebra Historical Romances and send me my free Zebra Novel along with my first month's Romances. I understand that I may preview these four new Zebra Historical Romances Free for 10 days. If I'm not satisfied with them I may return the four books within 10 days and owe nothing. Otherwise I will pay just $3.50 each; a total of $14.00 (a $15.80 value—I save $1.80). Then each month I will receive the 4 newest titles as soon as they come off the press for the same 10 day Free preview and low price. I may return any shipment and I may cancel this arrangement at any time. There is no minimum number of books to buy and there are no shipping, handling or postage charges. Regardless of what I do, the FREE book is mine to keep.

11-89

Name _____
(Please Print)

Address _____ Apt. # _____

City _____ State _____ Zip _____

Telephone ( ) _____

Signature _____
(if under 18, parent or guardian must sign)

Terms and offer subject to change without notice.

If that MacQuarie fella has anything to do with your plans you'd better remember you ain't knowed him as long as I've known Agnes here."

"Wade!" Agnes poked him in the ribs. "Let the girl be. She has a right to follow her heart." A smile cut across the woman's face from ear to ear. "I'm happy for you, honey."

"So am I," Wade agreed, though his expression belied his words. "Can't say I ain't disappointed. We kinda wanted you with us. We had it all planned out."

"Yes Jessie, you're a part of our life and a part of the plans we've been talkin' over. We really want you there too." Agnes added, taking Jessie's hand in both of her own. "But if your heart is taken then don't let him get away. I didn't. . . ." She winked suggestively.

Wade wasn't as agreeable. "I say you don't know a thing about that MacQuarie fella. I don't want you to end up with your heart in pieces, Jessie."

"It won't." She had to make him understand. "He feels the same way about me that I feel about him. And somehow it seems with odds like that I just can't lose." Suddenly overcome with emotion she threw herself into Wade's arms. "You know you are just like a pa to me, Wade. I couldn't love you more if you were. But a man like Corbin MacQuarie only comes once in a gal's life and I just can't let him go. I want to make myself respectable so I can claim him."

"Respectable?"

"I'm going to take my share of the loot and make something of myself. Oh, Wade, that thing about the wanted poster has me more addled than you know. I just don't want Corbin ever to find out about . . ."

"He might!" Wade held her at arm's length shaking his head. "And then what are you gonna do, Jess?"

225

She lifted her chin stubbornly. "I'll just have to cross that railroad tie when I come to it. I'm gonna have to hope that he doesn't. Besides, once he's back at his ranch it will all blow over. By the time I see him again there won't be anyone in this world who would ever tie me in with outlaws. You'll see."

"Then you won't live with us?"

"No. But you'll still be as close as kin. I could never forget how much you mean to me, Wade." She hugged him again, longer this time, then embraced Agnes. "And Agnes, you've been as kind and considerate as any mother could ever have been. You'll both always be considered my parents. I just think it's about time for me to move on. To try my independence." She laughed. "To tell you the truth, Aggie, your ranch here in Wyoming is just too far away from Rye Grass Station, Utah to fit in with what I have in mind. Too far from Corbin."

"He must be a fine man. Tell me all about him."

Jessie did, telling Agnes the story of their first meeting and of her time with him in the cabin. "He's the kind of man to make a woman sigh. I never thought he'd give me even a nod but he did. Wanted me to go with him and I would have if I could."

"What do ya plan to do then if you aren't going to him? Where will ya live? What will you do? Who'll look out fer ya?" Wade was bombarding her with an endless stream of questions.

"I plan to get a respectable job and lead a respectable life. What do you think of that? I've grown up, Wade. Seeing what can happen when a body goes outside the law made me think. I like Butch and the boys. They've been family but just like you I think it's time for me to move on."

Both Agnes and Wade nodded in agreement. "Calls for a celebration. Let's see what we've got to cook up for a feast," Agnes said as she headed toward the cook stove in the kitchen area, busying herself by looking in the cupboards.

"I got yer share of the loot in that tobacco can under the bed, Jess," Wade said. "There was more'n we figgered. Nine thousand for each of us. The whole haul was over eighty thousand dollars." He grinned. "And there are those who say crime doesn't pay." He drew in a sigh. "Makes a man a bit leery about going straight. Sure ain't gonna make that kind of money any other way. But it will last for awhile."

"Should keep us well fed and clothed for quite a time," Jessie answered, trying to push away the prick of guilt she felt at knowing it was stolen money. Looking over to where Agnes stood, way across the room, she asked, "Want me to help you with the cooking? I've gotten quite inventive the past few days."

Agnes shook her head. "No. You ain't seen Wade fer quite a spell. You 'n him's got a lot to hash over, it appears. You talk and I'll cook."

While Agnes puttered about the kitchen Wade and Jessie pulled up a couple of chairs and talked about old times, good times, bad times and whatever else came to mind. Jessie thought that Wade had never looked more contented.

"She's good to me, Jess. I never thought I'd meet a woman like my LaVerne. 'Course now, nobody can ever take LaVerne's place, but when a man gets older, he needs a little motherin' now and then."

"And I sure ain't the motherin' kind. Am I, Wade," she teased.

"I didn't mean that, Jessie." Seeing that she hadn't

taken offense he continued. "You're just a young 'un. You could use a little motherin' yerself. I guess I wasn't the motherin' kind either but we got along pretty well, you and me. Maybe what I'm tryin' to say is now we will both have someone to take care of us. That doesn't mean that we can't go on carin' fer each other though. Does it? I'll always be here any time you need me."

"I know. And you know I'll always be there if you need me, Wade. Wherever I may be." Laying her head on his shoulder, Jessie closed her eyes, tired after her hours on horseback. She didn't open them again until Agnes called them to supper, a tastily prepared meal of steak, potatoes and gravy. Agnes even placed a lighted candle in the center of the table to make it appear more festive. Oh yes, Jessie thought to herself, this woman is exactly what Wade needs. I hope everything turns out half as well for me. Damn, but she missed Corbin already. She thought she could wait three whole months before seeing him again, but could she?

It was a question that plagued her as the day gave way to night and she sought her own hearthfire in the cabin Butch had assigned to her. The first thing she did, after lighting the oil lamp and kindling a fire in the wood stove, was to sit down on the bed and put her head in her hands. She was feeling so alone without Corbin. They had been together constantly for almost two weeks. Twelve glorious days. She had become used to having his arms around her. Now, suddenly he wasn't there. Dear Lord, how she missed him. And yet, if she could get through this night, each day would become a little easier. Or would it? She really wasn't sure.

At last, blowing out the lamp, she took her boots off, put her hat and guns on a chair next to the bed and reclined, fully clothed. She looked out the window at the moonlight, feeling miserable without Corbin. Was he missing her as much as she missed him? She hoped that he was.

Without even bothering to undress, Jessie continued thinking a long, long time. Then at last she fell asleep, her head resting against the bedpost, propped upon two feather pillows.

Corbin rode across the endless valley toward the dark gray horizon. There was a strong chill in the wind now that the sun was down. Pulling his coat collar up he galloped onward, looking back now and again. The clouds all seemed behind him. Clear skies up ahead encouraged him to gallop faster and faster. As he rode, he spotted some wild mustangs in the distance and his thoughts turned to Jessie and the others like her who rode the range for months in pursuit of animals such as these.

"Jessie. Jessie. Jessie." Even the rhythm of his galloping horse seemed to call out her name.

A little farther on, he came to an old shack in the flats and thought of the love they had shared in a shack much like that one. In fact, almost everything he saw reminded him of Jessie. How he hated to leave her behind! Jessie was a woman different from any of the others he had ever known, not pretentious or overbearing. She was her own person and he admired that, a free spirit full of life and love. What a treasure he had found when he found her.

"Oh, Jessie!" If only he had been able to persuade her to come with him back to the ranch, but she had been so adamant about going her own way. Still, her promise had been that they would see each other again. He hoped that the winter would not be too severe and that soon they would be together once more.

It was a long and lonely ride. Corbin was in a hurry to get back to his ranch but although he had pressed the horse hard, he knew he would not get to Rye Grass Station until sometime tomorrow. A horse just couldn't compete with the speed of a train and he had come a long way into Wyoming before the robbery. The horse needed a rest.

Pulling the palomino to a halt, Corbin prepared to camp for the night at the mouth of a cave. The cave would offer protection from the wind chill which could become very cold after sundown. Bedding down in the open in this kind of weather was really not a very appealing idea.

Going to the mouth of the cave he fired several shots into it to be sure that no fierce animals were inside, then he hobbled the horse, fetched some water from the nearby waterfall and watered the palomino. The cave was warm and cozy. After he spread out his bedroll, he climbed under the covers and placed Jessie's Winchester rifle right beside his bed. Lord, what a generous woman she was. She had given him her horse, a saddle, and her own Winchester rifle. All of those things were costly items. Someday he would make it all up to her.

I'll have a special saddle made, he thought, liking the idea more and more as it repeated through his brain. A hand-tooled saddle with real silver trimmings. He'd put it on ole Sunbeam for when he returned the horse to her. A special gift that could say what words might not convey, that he was grateful and more than that, that he loved her.

The primitive howl of a coyote came from the direc-

230

tion of the cave's entrance and Corbin was instantly on alert. Propelling himself up on one elbow he grabbed for the rifle. His eyes scanned the darkness warily, but all was quiet again.

Probably there was more danger from the two-legged creatures than from any predatory animals, he thought. So far he had not met up with any unsavory characters, but in this outlaw country anything might happen and it paid to be prepared. Sleep with "One eye open," as his brother might have said.

His last thoughts before falling asleep were of Jessie. He hoped she was now safely back in Cheyenne with her outfit. He most surely didn't like her being in this lawless place, but the lady had a mind of her own. Ah, yes, she was a strong-willed woman with as much grit, courage, and determination as anyone he'd ever seen. Somehow he just knew she would be all right.

"Jessie. . . ." Closing his eyes he fell asleep with her name on his lips.

Chapter Twenty-four

The sound of laughter, neighing horses, barking dogs, shots and wild "yahoos" disturbed the early morning quiet and Jesse's slumber. "It's impossible to sleep after seven o'clock in this infernal place," she mumbled into her pillow, pulling the covers up over her head. It was no use. The activity going on around her cabin, the clatter of pots and pans from the cookshack, the grating of boots on the hard ground as the members of the Wild Bunch went about the morning chores, forbade her continued repose. "Ohhh!" she groaned, stretching her arms and legs in irritation, but just as quickly she modified her mood. "Aw, hell, I probably wouldn't have slept much longer anyway," she conceded as she sat up in bed and placed her feet upon the floor.

The habit of early rising was far too well established even if it had taken hours for her to fall asleep. She'd spent a restless night, awakening several times, Corbin's face haunting her dreams. She'd been worried about him, hoping he'd be safe on his journey. If anything happened to Corbin . . .

She had no need to worry. He was a man who could take care of himself without her watching over him.

232

Even so he sure did bring forth her protective feelings. She wanted to wrap him in the safety of her arms and never let him go. Oh yes, she loved him, all right. And she was sure of one other thing. She had never felt that way about Jeff, she had only thought she did.

There was a world of difference between pretending and the real thing. Just as there was a difference between being truly happy and just supposing that you were. The emotions and sensations that Corbin had aroused in her were like nothing she had ever experienced before and she wished shamelessly that he was here right now so that they could share those wondrous feelings again.

Had she really been that wanton woman who had given herself so unabashedly to him? she wondered. Had her fingernails really raked his back in endless ecstasy? Had her voice moaned his name? Yes. Yes. Yes. It had been the most glorious time of her life, waking up next to him, his belly pressed against her back, his legs entangled with hers. Oh, how she missed him this morning.

As she washed and dressed she reflected on their time together, studying her body and face in the mirror as if somehow she expected a change in the image staring back at her. Her eyes had a definite sparkle, her mouth had an upward slant but her body still looked the same. The change in her was inward not outward—a contentment knowing she had found someone to love and who loved her.

Jessie looked out the window. There was no more commotion going on. While she had been going about dressing and reminiscing, the boys had gone their own way, undoubtedly to the cookhouse so that they would be first in line for breakfast. Why couldn't they have done that a little earlier and allowed her to sleep, she thought with a wry smile. Donning her wide-brimmed Stetson, she took her gunbelt from the chair where it was hanging, fastened it around her slim waist and walked out the door. She was so used to doing things for Corbin that she felt lost now. A bit like a fiddler who had lost his bow.

Sitting on a large rock she contented herself for a while picking up pebbles and tossing them at a tin can the boys used for shooting practice. It was just one more reminder of the tumultuous life she had been living. How had she so quickly become disenchanted with the kind of life that had once meant so much to her? The answer was Corbin.

Not that she felt any different about her friends. No. She could understand what had driven them to outlawry—greedy ranch owners who had cut their wages in half, forcing those who wanted to survive into rustling and theft. Now the outlaws had such tight control over certain areas in Utah and Wyoming that the law seemed almost powerless. They'd built cabins and corrals and established a string of strongholds that were impregnable. Hole-in-the-Wall here was just such a fortress, a natural hideaway.

The towns around Hole-in-the-Wall were "Hell on Horseback," or so people said. Before the Union Pacific Railroad had established a route through Wyoming, most of them had been early military forts, stage stops or small clusters of settlers living close to each other for protection from marauding Indians. Some towns were nothing more than a saloon and a few prostitutes' cribs.

The larger southern Wyoming towns, such as Laramie, Casper and Cheyenne, had better law enforcement and jails. But up in this Powder River region there weren't even any jails. It was every man for himself and the one with the quickest draw was the winner.

After being with Corbin and what had happened on the train she realized that this way of life was wrong for her. Now that she had met Corbin she was anxious for things to change. Just as soon as she had breakfast she'd confront Butch and tell him what she planned to do. He'd understand. He'd have to.

"Jessie? Is that you all growed up, Jess?" He came from the direction of the corral gate, his hips swinging with that self-assured strut he always affected. Of all the men she'd ever wanted to see again, he was the last.

"Jeff!"

For several days, or so Wade had told her, more and more outlaws, some members of other gangs, had been arriving at Hole-in-the-Wall. They had all been eager to join Butch and the Wild Bunch now that Butch was proving himself to be a true leader. Everyone, it seemed, wanted to climb aboard his bandwagon. Some of the outlaws were people she had never seen before. Some had brought in their common-law wives and lady friends. Hole-in-the-Wall was getting very crowded. It made her all the more anxious to leave. Of all the people who had arrived at Hole-in-the-Wall, none had surprised her as much as running into Jeff Collins, however. She had never expected to see him again.

"I'll be damned. It is you, Jessie." He smiled that oh-so-cocky grin as he came closer.

"The last thing I heard you were in Montana. What are you doin' here?" He had changed or was it just that in comparison to Corbin he was left wanting? At fifteen she had thought he was the best-looking man she had ever seen. Now he seemed to slump over when he walked, his skin was sallow, and there was a large scar across the bridge of his nose. Not only that, but the dark, drooping mustache he sported now made him look evil.

"What am I doing here?"

"That's what I asked. What are you doing here," she challenged hotly.

"The same thing everybody else is doing here. This is the best hideout in the entire West. Any posse approaching this place can be held off by just a couple of men."

That was true and it meant security for the outlaws. There were caverns for hiding, passages for escape. The only entrance was a long, narrow gorge that was guarded by rifle-carrying outlaw sentinels and easily concealed from view when the gang members placed a large, loose rock at the opening. When a band of outlaws was being followed they had only to roll rocks back in place after they had passed through the niche called "Hole-in-the-Wall," and the posse following would be left behind looking foolish and feeling baffled. It was almost as if the men disappeared by magic. There was no evidence of any trail behind the rocks.

"Then you're a wanted man."

"I might be . . ." He shrugged his shoulders. "Yeah, I am. But then, I'm not the only one. From what I seen in the papers you've made quite a reputation yourself."

"What? What did you say?"

Slapping his knee he guffawed. "Aw, come on Jessie. It's what you've wanted all along. Well, now your face is just about as well known as ole Bob Meeks. Hell, you even made the *Denver Post*."

"No!" Her first thought was Corbin. Dear God, don't let him see.

He scrutinized her, cocking one dark brow. "Did you kill him?"

"I didn't kill anyone! It was a mistake, that's all. When he comes strutting into Rye Grass Station everyone will see." Jeff made her feel ill at ease and she was all the more determined to get as far away from here as she could go. "I'm innocent."

"Won't make any difference. Once your face is known you'll be blamed for every wrongdoing from here to Utah. Believe me, I know . . ."

"They won't hang anything on me, I'll get myself a lawyer."

Jeff laughed uproariously at that. "What few lawyers there are here have never seen the inside of a law school. Only those in the bigger towns have anything besides clabber milk for brains." It was true. The so-called lawyers in and around Hole-in-the-Wall just fooled everyone by hanging out a hastily painted sign.

"Butch Cassidy has hired himself a good lawyer in Cheyenne."

At least if anything too drastic happened to any of the members of his gang, they would have legal representation. If they had a chance to go to trial, that was. Most of the justice around the Powder River area, if one could really call it justice at all, was unofficial. Vigilante groups of citizens would just decide to lynch somebody and then carry through with it. Thank God most of the Wild Bunch were well liked throughout these parts. Butch had worked on a ranch hereabouts when he was younger and would not steal from any of the Hole-in-the-Wall Valley ranchers. Oftentimes he helped them when he could. Sometimes he even gave them money to get them through a hard time. He was well liked here all right. That thought gave her at least some comfort. And yet with all the publicity about the robbery, people just might be a bit riled up.

237

"Hell, Jess, I decided almost a year ago to come here first chance I got. This Powder River country is my kind of country."

"Guess just about every gang anywheres around has heard of this place then, huh?" Jessie wished that Jeff hadn't. Hole-in-the- Wall was just too small for the both of them.

"You bet your sweet ass they have. I have been in several hideouts in Montana and Idaho. This place is the only one anybody talks about anymore. Butch has made it into an outlaw's paradise." He paused in his praise of the hideout for a moment then stretched his hand out to her. "Come on over here and set on the corral fence with me. We'll catch up on what's been going on." He climbed up then gave her a hand. "Hasn't really been so long since you and me was lovers. Want to pick up where we left off?" As he leaned over to kiss her, she pushed him off the fence but that didn't stop him. He brushed off the seat of his pants and started to climb upon the fence rail again.

"Now just a cotton pickin' minute. You don't need to think that I have just been sittin' around waitin' for your sweet, tender kisses for three years."

"Well, no Jessie. I . . ."

"And I suppose you're gonna tell me that all you have been doin' since you left Wyoming is pinin' away over me." He nodded his head "yes." "You always was a damned liar and probably always will be."

"Now . . . now, Jessie, just calm down," he sputtered. "I've had my ups and downs but I always have loved you I . . . I swear it's true."

"Ha! You forget thet I am no longer a lovesick fifteen year old girl."

He whistled appreciately. "Sure as hell you're not.

You're even better lookin' now than you was then."

When he tried to put his arms around her she shoved at his chest with the toe of her boot. "I've learned a lot about men these past three years and I know enough not to listen to sweet words from any lying, mangy coyote."

"Now, Jess." Once his smile had been boyishly charming, now it looked devious. "Couldn't we just share that nice little love nest you're livin' in over there all by yourself?" He pointed in the direction of her new home. Even now the curling smoke escaping from the chimney made it appear very homey.

"*You* can live there! Because I don't intend to. I'm leaving this place. I'm gonna get me a job."

"A job?" He snickered, he chuckled, and then he threw back his head and laughed out loud. "A job. That's a good one." When at last he slowed his laughter down to a giggle he asked, "And just what do you plan to do?"

"Well . . ." The truth of it was she didn't really know. Just what kind of skills did she have? "I can rope and ride and . . ."

"Nope, you can't get a job on a ranch somewhere. Not with winter coming on. Winter is a slow time for ranch hands. No one would hire on another mouth to feed, especially one who is a *woman*."

"Then I'll do something else. Work in a store or something . . ."

"And take the risk that one of the clientele has seen that sketch of you? Come on now, Jess, you've got better sense than that. You better think of someplace where you can hide that face of yours. Work the night."

She knew what he meant by that remark. He was eluding to the fact that she could become a prostitute, one of the "fallen angels" as many of the gang members called them. No! Better outlawing than that. And yet the truth was there really wasn't much in the line of work for any woman in these parts except saloon work or entertaining gentlemen. The girls in the cribs and saloons had been very good to her so she didn't mean to look down her nose at them, it was just that she was the kind of woman to love one man and only let that man touch her in that manner.

Jeff's comments bothered Jessie and yet she stubbornly clung to her dream of going straight so that she might look Corbin squarely in the eye the next time she saw him. After she ate breakfast she sought out Butch but he told her much the same thing.

"Stay here, Jessie. You'll be safe here," Butch said, his blue eyes staring earnestly into hers. "We're family!"

Though she tried to make him understand, argued with him hotly, Butch had the upper hand. If she mingled among the citizens she took the risk of being found out and possibly arrested, he told her. At least until spring honest employment would be difficult if not impossible to find. If she spent any of the loot from the robbery, on the other hand, she might arouse suspicion as to just where it came from.

"It just makes more sense to stay." Butch laid his long-fingered hand on her shoulder and squeezed affectionately. "You'll be snug as a bug right here. We've got enough food to last the winter and warm shelter."

"Butch . . . I . . . I can't stay . . ." She was losing the argument and she knew it. His square jaw was ticking in a way that clearly told her he was losing his patience.

"I'm sorry, Jessie, but I just can't let you go." There, he had said it.

"Can't let me?" So it wasn't really a matter of choice

any more.

"I've got to think about the good of the gang. If you were to get caught, and well you might with that sketch of you all over the territory, you might in some way endanger the rest of us. Come spring . . ."

Come spring! it was the same thing she'd known all along. Hadn't she said as much to Corbin? Damn that artist! How would she ever have guessed that one man could have so easily ruined her life. Now she would have to stay with the outlaws even though she really didn't want to. An imposed exile of sorts. How ironic life could be.

"I heard, Jessie." Jeff's voice was husky. "But don't take it so hard. Now you and me can love each other again."

"Love? Man, that takes gall. I mean real gall. No, we can't, and let's leave love out of this conversation." Jessie kicked at a rock, sending it skimming. "Go back into the hole you crawled from and leave me alone." Damn but if he didn't remind her of a snake. "If we're both gonna be living here at Hole-in-the-Wall, we might just as well get a few things straight right now. I ain't no fool and I ain't gonna be fool enough to fool around with *you.*"

"You weren't the fool. I was, but I didn't have any idea where I was goin' when I left you, Jessie. I was just young and restless. Wanted to move on. I never could stay in one place for very long."

"Did you also forget how to use your voice? If I remember correctly, you didn't even say goodbye, leave a note or anything."

For the first time he sounded sincere. "I didn't mean to hurt you." He held out his hand to her but she pushed it away.

"Let's just let a sleeping dog lay."

"I've just come out of the pen in Montana. I need friends. I need a woman, Jessie."

"A friend I can be, your woman I can't be, Jeff. I've found someone else, you see." Closing her eyes Jessie fought against her tears. All her dreams had been deflated so quickly, just like a hot air balloon when it was struck by lightning. For the first time she wondered if she really had any chance for a life with Corbin or if she was just whistling in the wind.

Chapter Twenty-five

Corbin had been up long before dawn. He'd saddled up, tied up his bedroll and had ridden out with Jessie's Winchester close at his side. Now he was glad that he had that gun. A man never knew when there might be an open blast of gunfire. Already he had experienced such an encounter. A few miles back he had ridden by a small corral alongside the trail. A man had come from out of nowhere shouting something about a stolen horse and had begun firing at his head. The damned fool had nearly creased his hairline with one of the shots. Corbin had decided that the man was either drunk or wanted to steal Jessie's horse. It only proved how dangerous Wyoming could be. He was glad he was on his way back to his own ranch in Brown's Park Valley. The only thing that marred his enthusiasm, however, was that he was leaving Jessie behind.

Now Corbin rode through a sunlit morning, anxious to reach Rye Grass Station ten miles away. He was beginning to see familiar landmarks and knew that the distance to his final destination, the ranch, was narrowing. What a story he had to tell Archie. There weren't very many men who were rescued by a woman like Jessie. He was looking forward to his foreman's congenial company, though he supposed that by now the train robbery would have been told and retold. No doubt Arch would be surprised to see him still on the Wyoming side of the state line. Well, he'd just have to explain it all and tell why he had come back to the ranch without that damned bull.

"Stamash," he grumbled. It had been his idea of bringing the Highlander bull here that had put him on that train in the first place. As soon as he got into town he'd send a telegram to Warren explaining what had happened and why he had never shown up. Stamash would just have to make the trip unescorted.

Little did Corbin know that at this very minute, his brother, Warren, was at the Rolling Q in Brown's Park Valley, mourning Corbin's death and seeking revenge for the deed. Warren and Sheriff Art Conners were in the process of planning to join U.S. Marshal Joe Lefors's posse. Joe Lefors was coming to Cheyenne from Waco, Texas and the two of them, along with a few others, were to meet him in Cheyenne in a day or two.

Lefors was dedicated to cleaning up the territory by ridding it of Butch Cassidy and the Wild Bunch and had personally called for twelve men. Both Warren and Art Conners had been included in that call by the big Texan. All three of them had worked at the Pinkerton Detective Agency together before going their separate ways. Of the three, only Warren had not continued with a career in law enforcement, though Art was now trying to convince Warren to get back into it again. Henrietta and he had fought over his wanting to resume such a career but now after the train robbery and his brother's death, Warren's mind was made up. Although he knew it embodied many dangers, the rewards were many. Just like Lefors, he wanted to rid the West of outlaws, beginning with the young bastard who had so cruelly murdered his brother.

Unaware of the seething vengeance brewing in his brother's heart, Corbin meanwhile reached Rye Grass Station and pulled the palomino to a halt in front of the town's hotel restaurant, dismounted and tied the reins. He was hungry, because he had ridden since sunrise with an empty stomach. He was just not being as skillful at trapping rabbits as Jessie. Now the thought of coffee, steak, and a couple of fried eggs hastened his steps.

Passing between the tables he took his seat at the far end, his back to the door. Taking off his hat he thumped it against his thigh to dislodge the dust of the road, then placed it on the chair beside him. Hoping to tidy up his appearance he ran his fingers through his hair and straightened his tie, smiling as his gaze caught the yellow spotted with blue polka dots. It was a pleasant reminder of Jessie and those magical days they had spent together. Sadly it made him realize just how far away she was, but if he had his way they'd be together again and soon.

"What'll it be, mister?" A tall, skinny woman with gray braids forming a coronet atop her head inquired.

"Coffee, black and strong, steak cooked rare, and two eggs sunnyside up. And rolls if they've been baked fresh this morning." He flashed her a grin. "I've been riding long and hard this morning and have worked up a fearsome appetite."

"Hmm. Out-of-towner. Then you've missed the excitement hereabouts."

"Excitement?"

"Man from a ranch near here was killed in a robbery. There are those trying to stir up more trouble by gathering up a posse to avenge his death. They'll be ridin' through here soon, I expect, trying to get the folks in

245

town to rally." She wiped the table with the end of her apron, never once taking her eyes off his face.

"And will they?" The way she was surveying him so wide-eyed he supposed he looked like the man they were after. He was dusty, ragged, and hadn't had a chance to shave.

"They won't! Cassidy's got his fingers in the town, you see. As for me I'm a great believer in minding one's own business." Strange, but she seemed to be issuing a warning. Shrugging his shoulders Corbin wondered which side of the dispute she was on, the outlaws' or the posse's. He'd remember to ask Archie about the situation when he got back to the ranch.

His hunger was soon appeased and after the third cup of coffee Corbin got under way on his journey back to the ranch again. Now from the top of a hill about half a mile away he could see his ranch; the gray smoke streaming out of the stone chimney was a welcoming beacon spurring him on to gallop even faster homeward.

There seemed to be quite a commotion going on, as if somebody had just stepped on an ant hill. As he drew nearer, he could see the corral where a group of men was assembled. All of them seemed to be scurrying about saddling and watering horses and placing packs upon the backs of mules.

"What in tarnation is going on down there?" he said aloud to himself. "Come on, Sunbeam." Gently he slapped the horse on the neck with the reins. Damndest horse he ever saw, it didn't even know its name.

Corbin urged the horse into a fast gallop, slowing its pace somewhat as he came in view of the corral. Sunbeam neighed, drawing the attention of the men. As he approached, all eyes turned in his direction. The faces of the men were drained of color; most of them looked as if they were seeing a ghost.

Archie was the first to break the silence. "My God! Is it really you, Corbin?" he asked, brushing his hands across his eyes as if trying to banish a mere vision. Then shielding his eyes with his hand, he squinted. "Couldn't be anybody else," Corbin answered with a grin, hardly realizing the reason for all the fuss. "Unless there's someone else pretending to be me."

"I never thought I'd see you again." Archie hurried to his boss's side as Corbin dismounted. "Dang me, if you ain't about the grandest surprise I've had in a long time." The other men moved back out of the way as if still weren't sure their eyes weren't playing tricks on them, but Archie enclosed Corbin in an emotional embrace. "Welcome back, son. Welcome back." After a few minutes Bowlegs, Rawlings and the others gathered around them.

"We thought you was dead," Bowlegs blurted out.

"Dead?" Now Corbin understood the poignancy of Archie's greeting.

"The sheriff was here and this posse was gettin' ready to go out and avenge your murder. We was goin' ter join 'em," Kelly, another of the hired hands, added.

"Never mind all that." Archie stepped forward with a big smile on his face. "Let's just give a loud shout. He's here and he's all right." They all took their hats off and threw them in the air as they shouted, *"Whoopee!"*

Corbin couldn't help smiling at the wonderful welcome he was receiving. He supposed it wasn't every day a man got a chance to welcome someone back from the dead. "I'm sorry you all thought I'd gone to meet my maker. To tell you the truth, for awhile I *was* in heaven. I was shot, it was true, but then I was rescued by a most beautiful creature. That lovely angel nursed me back to health, and here I am."

247

"He sounds a bit delirious to me," Bowlegs grumbled. "Women. Bah! Angels. Ha."

"Angels! Sure. Sure. That's what they all say when they have had a close call like the one you had," a tall, thin, balding man Corbin had never met, obviously a new ranch hand, added.

"Believe it or not, that's the way it happened. But that's another story." Corbin eyed the members of the ranch posse. He knew some, others he had not yet met. Probably ranch hands from neighboring ranches, he thought. Well, now they'd have no need to go out riding.

"Come on in and we will find a cook to fix us up a meal. Archie . . .?"

Archie stepped forward to offer his services as usual. "Its difficult to talk to men with empty stomachs. But first of all, Corbin, I gotta tell you that your brother was here earlier."

"Warren here?"

"I sent him a telegram when I thought you'd been killed in that robbery." As quickly as he could, Archie related the tale about his journey to the train station, how he'd been told about Corbin's murder and the events that had followed.

"So that's the posse that woman was talking about." She'd been talking about *his* death and Warren's intent for vengeance. "I've got to ride into Rye Grass Station and set this matter straight. I was shot, but obviously not killed. There's no need for Warren to get his dander up."

Archie put himself in Corbin's path. "Naw. You've already ridden a long ways. I'll send Cooper with the message. He'll send your brother hightailing it back here. Right now it's for you to just relax and to tell us all the story."

248

All through the meal the men barraged Corbin with questions, anxious to know all the details of the robbery. Corbin had never suspected that people would think he was dead. But, of course, it all made sense now as he thought about it. That was exactly what they would have thought when they hadn't heard from him. He should have told Jessie to send a telegram when she went to Laramie that first day but he hadn't thought of that. His mind had been on other things. For just a moment her sweet face flashed before his eyes and he felt a stab of longing. But soon he would be with her again. He wondered what Warren would say when he told him he'd found the girl he wanted to marry. Well, wasn't he the one who had told him it was time for Corbin to settle down? He had a feeling his brother would be pleased.

After breakfast the men pushed their chairs back from the table, took out cigarette papers and Bull Durham packets and rolled their cigarettes or reached into their vest pockets for a cigar. In honor of the celebration welcoming Corbin "back from the dead," Rawlings even spiked several cups of coffee with whiskey.

"I know you was wonderin' what we had planned when you rode up awhile ago," Archie said when the chatter had died down. "I'll try to explain it to you. U.S. Marshal Joe Lefors is comin' up to Cheyenne from Waco, Texas to go after Butch Cassidy and his gang. We was just gettin' ready to go to Cheyenne to meet him. When your brother thought they'd gunned you down he put himself in the detective business again."

"Well now he can go back to his ranch and forget the whole matter." Corbin smiled knowingly. "I'm sure Henrietta will be relieved to have him back home and Butch Cassidy can sleep easier."

"Cassidy, ha!" Kelly wiped the top of his head with his

hand. "The very thought of his boldness brings out the sweat. He's just becoming much too bold. Mark my words he'll soon be bothering us here. Thousands of dollars' worth of cattle have been stolen by those no-good renegades, brands burned out and their own brands substituted. I hope somebody catches them this time."

"We haven't had any trouble with cattle rustling." Corbin turned to look at Archie. "Have we?"

"Not so far. Some around here say he seldom bothers anyone in this area. Rye Grass Station being his town and all. I've heard it said that any rustling is from some of the ranchers themselves fattening their herds with stolen stock."

"And blaming Cassidy?" Corbin asked.

"Yep. But from what I've heard there's no doubt he robbed that train," Archie snorted. "And because of his tomfoolery you got wounded. Don't forget that."

Corbin scowled. "I won't. Oh, no. Cassidy has long been a nemesis of my brother's and therefore of mine. Started when he held up the San Miguel Valley Bank in Telluride, Colorado. Warren followed him to the Colorado border and nearly nabbed him. Would have, too, if it had been legal to cross over the border and get his quarry. I remember how frustrated my brother was. Then Art Conners caught Cassidy in Fremont County and brought him in to Laramie. Had him put away for awhile until Cassidy bargained with the governor for a pardon."

"Yeah and once he was out he wasted no time getting a new gang together. Now he is undisputed leader of that Wild Bunch. Trouble is nobody knows exactly where they hide out. They are somewheres in Jackson County, Wyoming, though, they're sure of that."

"Jackson County. Isn't that near the place where the robbery took place?" When Archie nodded Corbin felt a stab of pure, unbridled fear. That's where Jessie had said she was headed. Damn, how he wished now that he'd insisted she come back with him, even if he'd had to carry her swearing and screaming all the way. She was smart and she was tough but a woman just wasn't any match for those who worked outside the law. "Archie, I want you to do some inquiring and see if you can find out what ranch a *Jessie Watson* is working." The only way to relieve his mind was to make certain that she was all right.

"Sure, boss." Archie's brows shot up. "Is that the name of your angel?"

"Yes, it is." Corbin had an idea in mind to have Warren stop by on his way back to Colorado just to check up on her. It was an idea, however, that would just have to wait for awhile. When Cooper came back he told Archie and Corbin that Warren had already ridden out with Art Conners and their posse. Trouble was that no one really knew just where they were going. What made it a more complicated matter was that Joe Lefors had just sent a telegram. After having been warned of an impending snowstorm and knowing just how vicious such blizzards in Wyoming could be, he had decided not to come to Cheyenne until after the spring thaw. If the posse went after Cassidy, they would be doing so all alone.

Chapter Twenty-six

Despite the isolation of the hideout at Hole-in-the-Wall, it was not a lonely place for an outlaw to be. As a matter of fact, Jessie thought with a disgruntled sniff, it was getting a bit too crowded. Outlaws came and outlaws went, an odd assortment of fast-buck merchants, whiskey peddlers, land speculators, bunko artists, tinhorn gamblers as well as the usual tightknit group of Butch's followers and their ladies. The winter snows had finally curtailed the arrival of any more gunslingers, which pleased Jessie. There were more than enough already.

Names like Deaf Charley Hanks, Harry Tracy, Black Jack Ketchum, Tom O'Day, William Tod Carver, Bob Lee and Dave Lant took their stations in the ranks then just vanished, either to die under the guns of sheriffs or posses or to molder in the prisons nearby when they were caught.

As for Jeff, she was not surprised when one day not too long after their conversation he just came up missing. Wade said he'd heard he got into a gun battle in Buffalo, a small town outside Hole-in-the-Wall in which several desperados had been killed. Violent death was no stranger in this Wyoming country, thus she had shed no tears for him and supposed him to be lying in an unmarked grave somewhere. Still, she was glad that she had seen him again just to help her put her feelings in perspective and to know beyond a shadow of a doubt that she had never loved anybody until she met Corbin.

The valley itself was a quiet place. The grassy slopes were now snow-covered and the bubbling ice-cold streams solidly frozen over in some places. In the early morning and late evening hours, fierce, moaning winds often swept over this Powder River country causing severe drifts and whirling clouds of snow to form.

Jessie put down the bucket of water she had just fetched from the nearby stream and turned around to view the landscape. The scenery was spectacular and she found herself wishing she could share it with Corbin. It looked like a huge snow sculpture accented by well-worn paths, some animal tracks and the slow-flowing streams resembling snakes as they curled and crept across the white background. What a glorious sight, she thought to herself. Indeed, she had plenty of time to just gaze upon its beauty and wonder what Corbin was doing right now. With little or no work to do, except to feed and care for the winter-sheltered animals, there was plenty of time to do as one pleased.

As she stood looking at the winter wonderland before her, she knew that she would soon have to tell Butch Cassidy of her plans for the future. Oh, he'd tried to talk her into staying with the gang come spring but Jessie had made up her mind and once she did that there was no changing it, as Wade had often declared. Corbin MacQuarie was her chance for happiness and she wasn't going to let him go, not after what had passed between them.

253

As for Butch, his plans were working into hers without his really being aware of the fact, for he and some of his closest companions were already planning to move on to Brown's Park Valley at the first signs of spring thaw. He had planned to have Wade, Agnes and Jessie with his small caravan on the move south into Utah. There he planned to rendezvous with other riders to await the transfer of the herd coming up from another station in the south. They would then drive the cattle up to Montana, Idaho or even into Canada and sell them there. It would be Wade's last job with the gang, or so he said.

Jessie was well informed on the workings of the rustlers' syndicate and in that way managed to help keep an eye on Corbin's cattle. Every time she could she talked the boys out of coming anywhere near the Rolling Q. Even so, she had not yet told Butch that it was because of a rancher that she was disenchanted with the life she was leading. Not that she was being cowardly about telling him, it was just that lately so many other problems had seemed to be taking up a great deal of his time and she hardly ever saw him.

In fact, she had noticed that Butch himself was not as interested in rustling now that he had successfully made such a big haul in a train robbery and so easily, or so it seemed to him. He spent a lot of time with the Sundance Kid and Wade told her that they were already planning the next robbery to take place somewhere in Utah. Why settle for an apple when a goodly portion of the whole pie was available, seemed to be his reasoning. Though it promised to make her rich if she went along, however, Jessie intended to remain true to her vow to go straight.

Jessie followed a well-worn path back to her cabin door. She took the bucket of water into the cabin so it wouldn't freeze over during the night. There was nothing worse than having no unfrozen water for coffee when she got up in the morning. She pulled a chair out and sat down for a while to rest, her eye catching sight of the catalogue on the shelf. She laughed quietly to herself and thought of how she had changed as she pulled it down.

There was a time, not too long ago, when looking through the catalogue at the pretty clothes would have been the last thing she was interested in; now looking through her "dream book" occupied a great deal of her time. She wouldn't be able to get into Laramie until the thaw but since the postmistress there had promised to keep her purchases until she called for them, she had actively started her order form with the thought in mind of sending the list with one of the fellas when they went into Laramie.

As she glanced over the pages, her fingers toyed with her auburn hair which had grown to shoulder length, another change that Corbin had inspired. Right now her hair was bothersome, but more often than not she tied it back when she had work to do. One thing was for sure. No one would ever guess she was the "boy" in that sketch when she was finished. With her new clothes and longer hair she'd look every inch the proper "lady." Once that might have horrified her, but now she found the thought pleasing. Corbin was so masculine that he brought out a desire in her to be more feminine once again. How like a man to turn a woman's head and make her start wanting to look and smell like a flower. But what the hell! When Corbin saw her he couldn't help but be surprised. It would be fun just to see the expression on his face. He'd never take her for a lad again. Perhaps her laying low the past few weeks would eventually pay off.

"Oh, Corbin. . . ." Only a few more months of this horrid snowy winter and she could be on her way back to Rye Grass Station. Until then the only thing she could count on were her dreams and her memories of Corbin's kisses. If there were any ladies in Rye Grass Station who'd decided to set their cap for him, why they'd better keep their distance come the first of April!

In a minute or two she was going over to Wade's to eat dinner and visit for awhile. Even though she had her own place, the three of them ate all of their evening meals together, sometimes at her place but most often at Wade and Agnes's cabin. Agnes was an excellent cook and Wade took great pride in her accomplishment. "You can learn a thing or two from this lady of mine, Jess," he would say. She knew he was right about that. Indeed, she had learned some cooking tricks from Agnes, just one of the other things she suddenly taken an interest in. "The nesting urge," as Aggie called it.

"The way to a man's heart is still through his stomach," she would say giving Wade a playful hug while winking at Jessie.

Jessie was glad she was able to spend so much time with them, though she often teased Wade about staying with the outlaws when he'd intended to live at Aggie's cabin. He hadn't made any secret of the fact that *she* was the reason, though Jessie knew she was well past the age when she needed chaperoning. When spring came, they would be separated for awhile but she just had to go ahead with her plans for a new life, as painful as parting from Wade would be. She had made up her mind and wouldn't change it now. Someone had told her once that "it wasn't smart to change horses in mid-stream." She liked to keep a tight rein on her determination just as others kept on their mounts while crossing a stream. She guessed that the phrase was just as fitting in this instance.

The temperature was falling as she walked toward the other cabin. She knew that she was expected for dinner so she opened the door without knocking and stepped inside. Taking off her hat and holding it aloft, she said a cheery, "Howdy, folks."

"Howdy, Jessie." Expecting Wade to come out of the bedroom, Jessie's eyes darted in that direction. "Wade ain't here yet." Agnes gave her an affectionate pat on the shoulder and a big smile.

"Ain't here? This night ain't fit for man nor beast. Where'd he go?"

"He's the guard at the entrance today."

Jessie knew that during weather like this only one guard was necessary at the entrance of that narrow gorge called Hole-in-the-Wall. Sometimes when the weather was very severe there was no guard at all. Any man not already comfortably situated within the confines of the valley retreat would have to be insane to attempt to get in there. In bitter weather, Hole-in-the-Wall was a secure winter wonderland for those inside the valley walls. Even so there had been talk of some fool Pinkerton agent doing everything he could to track them down. That he was coming much closer than anyone else ever had was a source of chattering in the hideaway. It was one more reason to put Butch a bit on edge.

Jessie and Agnes chatted for awhile about the subject, both concerned lest Wade get in some kind of trouble, but not long after Jessie arrived, Wade came in from out-of-doors. His whiskers were white with frost, his nose as red as a cherry. "It's g . . . g . . . gettin' d . . . d . . . damned c . . . c . . . old out there," he said, stamping his feet hard to get his circulation flowing. "That fire looks mighty invitin'." He threw his gloves aside and rubbed his hands together in front of the fireplace as Agnes helped him off with his boots. Picking up the coffeepot he found it empty and grumbled a bit but Agnes, always one to spoil him, immediately put on another pot.

"Got to have my coffee to fool myself into thinking I'm warm," he said with a good-natured laugh. "Or I'm an old grouch. Now little lady," he said, addressing Jessie, "what have you got to say for yourself? Still plannin' on hogtying that MacQuarie fella come spring?"

"Hogtying him?" Jessie thrust out her chin. "Why, to the contrary, I merely plan to make myself visible so that he can hogtie me. That's Aggie's suggestion and it seems a good one."

"That so?" Wade looked in his new wife's direction. "Well, that's how she got me." He chuckled low in his throat but just as suddenly his mouth tugged into a frown. Actually, Jessie, it ain't no joke, your havin' eyes for this MacQuarie fella I mean. We've got a few lawmen in our pay, spies if you will. I've heard somethin' very distressin'. It seems one of those Pinkerton agents is named "MacQuarie." Damned fool is hellbent on catching *you*."

"Me?"

"Somethin' about his brother being murdered."

"I didn't kill anybody."

Wade shrugged his shoulders. "I know that and you know that, but apparently that damned smarty pants Pinkerton fella hasn't heard the word yet. Ranting and raving every place he goes about how he means to trap the whole Cassidy gang and bring them to trial." His thick brows drew together in a frown. "Talk like that will get the damned fool killed."

Agnes's call to dinner quieted the conversation but Jessie couldn't put the matter from her mind no matter

258

how hard she tried. She remembered Corbin saying something about a brother and the prospect of his being on her trail was upsetting. Carrying her bowl to the table, she sat down, hunching her shoulders; she picked up her spoon but suddenly lost her appetite. How much longer was she going to have to pay for one mistake? Why should she be punished for what so many in the gang had done? It just didn't seem fair. Hell, she nearly was of a mind to give back her share of the money but Wade talked her out of such a silly move. She might need it to begin her new life, he told her and she had to agree. It was a nest egg. A sizable one at that.

After dinner Agnes did all she could to lighten the mood in the cabin. She was optimistic. Where Wade saw thunderclouds she saw rainbows and at last Jessie was soothed into being hopeful that when all was said and done, things really would settle down. Sitting before the fireplace and talking, Jessie felt her mood mellow. The food, fire, and drink had a soothing effect. Taking off her boots she sat wiggling her toes inside her stocking feet, thankful that for the moment Wade and Aggie were here to keep her company. Come spring, she would not see her foster father as often. Maybe not at all for long periods of time. He had been so kind, so good, so caring. The only thing that really tugged at her heart-strings was the fact that he was getting older. If he hadn't taken up with Agnes, she knew she could never have left his side. Seeing how quickly Agnes had put the coffee on for him when he came in from the cold and the way she had helped him remove his boots had warmed her heart.

While Agnes and Wade discussed the pattern of the new quilt Agnes had just finished, Jessie studied their faces. It was obvious that Agnes loved Wade. She was always at his beck and call. Could she be that devoted to Corbin or was it against her nature? Agnes had a more motherly way. A more matronly attitude. Would she be more like Agnes in years to come? She really didn't know. Still, she reminded herself, while she was with Corbin for that short time at the small shack she had waited on him in much the same way as Agnes was now waiting upon Wade. Right now if only she could be with Corbin, she had no doubt she would do anything in the world for him. She guessed part of love was trying to please your man, if he also did the same for you.

"Yeah, well I remember when you and Billy was just kids. You've grown into a beautiful woman, Jessie," Wade was saying.

"Sometimes I sort of miss Billy," Jessie said, remembering. She never had any romantic feelings toward Billy but had always felt protective of him much as a mother must feel about protecting her child. It was just that he could be such a little boy at times. "I haven't seen him since the day of the robbery."

"Some people said he has become a tinhorn gambler in the saloon owned by that gal in Lander he took up with. I heard that he now wears his six-shooter gunfighter style, the holster tied to his thigh with rawhide, and that he always wears a black hat at a cocky angle."

"Is that right?" Jessie had a feeling that one of these days Billy was going to get in a whole lot of trouble.

"Yep. He's gettin' too big fer his britches," Wade added, seemingly wanting to evade the subject. "Hope he don't end up like Bob Meeks."

"What ever happened to Bob Meeks?" Jessie asked, "Not that I really care. Just curious, that's all. Since it was his doing that got me in trouble in the first place. Him and that trigger finger and temper of his."

"Nobody really seems to know. After the robbery he just sort of vanished into thin air. He got his cut and then vamoosed."

"I wouldn't fret if I never saw him again." Jessie squirmed in her chair as if to show displeasure at the thought. "Those moods of his scared me to death. They really caused a shiver to run up and down my spine. And those black eyes of his were penetrating in their gaze. Whenever he was anywheres near, it was almost as if you could feel the leashed-up violence just waiting to explode."

Agnes had been listening and finally said, "Guess that's one of the men I never met. Is that the one you told me about, Wade?"

"Yeah, that's him all right. His single action .45 was always near at hand. He was as fast on the draw as any man I ever saw. The one thing that always worried me was that he seemed to have utter contempt for human life."

"Well, like Jessie, I'm not sorry that he moved on then," Agnes said, shaking her head from side to side as she spoke. "A man like that around here with nothin' to do during the winter months could cause a whole lot of trouble."

"Come to think of it, he didn't seem to have any friends, did he, Wade?" Jessie questioned, shuddering as she thought of the way his eyes always seemed to undress her.

"Naw, he was sort of a loner. Cassidy was the only one he really seemed to like very well. He had a sort of calming effect on Bob, it seemed. All he needed to say was 'Let up on that squeezin' trigger finger, Bob and let him alone,' and ole Bob would do it."

They sat around talking about old times and what the

future might bring for an hour or more before Jessie noticed Wade's head nodding and his eyelids beginning to droop, and decided to leave. "Guess I'd better be gettin' over to my place. Have to make out an order from my 'dream book,' she confided to Aggie.

"Here, let me help you with that mackinaw," Agnes said, rising from her chair to hold the coat open so that Jessie could slip her arms into the sleeves.

As Jessie started out the door she suddenly realized she hadn't put her boots on. There she stood in her stocking feet. "Bull wart. Just goes to show you how interesting conversation can divert a gal's attention." They both laughed as Jessie struggled with her boots.

"Jessie, while I'm thinkin' of it, can I just take a look at your Sears Roebuck Catalogue one of these days? That 'dream book,' as you call it?"

"Sure, Agnes. Just remind me next time you come over." Walking over to the chair, she kissed Wade on top of his balding head. His eyes were closed but he opened them slightly and smiled up at her, then closed them again. "Bye, Aggie. See you tomorrow."

She opened the door and stepped out into the crisp, white snow and walked homeward over the well-trodden path. The snow squeaked beneath her boots with every step she took. As soon as she stepped inside her own cabin, she lit the lamp, threw some more wood on the well banked fire and pulled the Sears Roebuck catalogue off the shelf on the wall. Sitting down at the table she nibbled on the end of her pencil as she pondered over the merchandise.

It was difficult to make up her mind between the kersey cloth jacket for $5.95 or the one for $4.95. Finally, she decided on the jacket for $4.95. Not because it was cheaper but because of the stand-up, high-fashion

262

collar and the new fan back. She wrote the number 63478-ladies jacket-size 34-royal blue-price $4.95 in the proper columns under catalogue number, item, size, color, and price.

She had no trouble with the hats. She had made up her mind on that a week ago. The shepherdess shape in castor-color silk-finished velveteen with the draped silk around the crown and two oblong pheasant feathers caught into a pretty buckle was her choice. The full rosette of royal blue ribbon would match her new jacket. It was an interesting hat, but could she ever grow to love it as much as she now loved her tan Stetson? Number 62886-ladies hat-castor color-$2.95 she wrote in the proper columns on the order blank.

Jessie turned the pages again to the capes, feeling frivolous. She would certainly love to own one of those plush capes, and after all, with nine thousand dollars burning a hole in her pocket she didn't have to worry. The $15 one with the storm collar of fur would fit very well over her new jacket. Yes, that was the one she wanted. Number 63550-ladies plush cape-size 34-$15 she wrote.

She chose two skirts, one of black manchester cloth for $1.95 and another of royal blue mohair for $3.15. Next came two waists, one of royal blue taffeta with white inlay front for $4.50 and one garnet-colored velvet with detachable high collar for $2.65. Next came six pairs of muslin drawers at 45¢ each, two cambric under-skirts at $1.95 each, a bosom protector and an adorable pair of black vici-kid high buttoned shoes for $2.00. The description said that they were as soft as glove leather. Well, she'd soon see. There were ten buttons and scalloped buttonholes. If she was going to dress up she might just as well do it in style.

Would she have to order one of those horrid corsets? She would order one but she wasn't sure she would like wearing it. She didn't know much about corsets. "Guess the one for the slender form and extra-long waist would be best," she mumbled aloud to herself. Her waist was only 23 inches and besides, it was the only one that had shoulder straps. The others were strapless and that worried her a mite, lest she have to keep tugging them up. The one she chose had six front-closing hooks and was only priced at $2.98. Even if she decided not to wear it it wouldn't be too much of a loss at that price. She would add it to the other items on her order and ask Agnes about it tomorrow. If Agnes thought another would be better she could change the order before sending it in.

Dressing like a lady was going to take some getting used to, but it had to be done sooner or later. If she was going to use her femininity to foil that Pinkerton agent she might as well do it up right. Besides, she couldn't let some better dressed-woman run off with Corbin. Not now. Not now or not ever. It was one thing for him to admire her when they were alone in the cabin and to say he liked her flannel shirt, but what would he do when he compared her to the women in Rye Grass Station? She was sure that Corbin was sincere in telling her of his love for her but she wasn't about to take any chances this time. He wouldn't just up and vanish one day like Jeff had. No siree!

Before closing the catalogue she looked again at the musical instruments and another thought popped into her mind. She'd order a guitar for Corbin. He'd liked playing that broken one at the shack so well that she bet if he had one of his own he would sing more songs to her. His singing had set just the right mood. She tapped her pencil on the order blank, sorely tempted. No, she wouldn't order it now. It would be too hard to carry. She would wait until she was back in Rye Grass Station and order one for him then.

When she had completed her order and signed the form, she folded it, placed it in the envelope but did not seal it in case she wanted to change the corset or Aggie wanted to order some item or other. Sometime within the next few days someone was bound to go into Laramie and she would send the order along with that person. On any given day, a visitor was sure to ride into camp to get some grub, a fresh horse, and be on his way again.

"And it will take a while to arrive from Chicago," the woman had said. Jessie would place the order as soon as possible.

Jessie felt pleased with herself as she placed the catalogue back upon the shelf. "Corbin, my dear," she said as she blew out the lamp and undressed, "it won't be long now. Just about two and a half months until spring and we will be together again." It sounded like forever no matter how she tried to convince herself otherwise. "Please keep on loving me, darlin'. I'll never stop loving you. I'll be there as soon as I can."

Chapter Twenty-seven

The sky spit icy rain and snow. It was bitterly cold. So cold that Warren MacQuarie's breath came out in white clouds and the wind struck his face into numbness as he rode along. Even so he continued his quest. It was an obsession that could only be quenched when he saw that young killer hanging from a rope. He would only be satisfied when the so-called "Wild Bunch" was safely secured in their cages.

He could read the headlines now. *Pinkerton Agent Arrests Notorious Outlaw Leader — Butch Cassidy.* It would make what he was going through now worthwhile. It would make him a hero.

I have to find their hideout before the snows fall harder, he thought. Once the weather stayed snowy and cold, the drifts could get to be as high as four feet and travel would be impossible. He had to find it. He had to find that entrance that hid Hole-in-the-Wall.

He knew he was galloping through outlaw country. Almost anywhere along the way through the deep ravines and desolate canyons he might encounter cattle rustlers, horse thieves, bank or train robbers, murderers on the run or any number of men with prices on their heads.

Right now he knew how important it was to keep his wits about him. A man almost needed eyes in the back of his head in this country. Just this morning when he'd stopped by one of the ranch houses he'd heard a familiar tale. Stolen cattle. In hopes that the tracks might lead them to the infamous Hole-in-the-Wall, Art Conners and a few of his boys had accompanied Warren but the hoof marks had blurred into oblivion before they'd gone a half a mile.

Now, after several hours of travel, Warren could finally see the smoke of a fire which acted to spur him into a faster gallop. Instead of it being an outlaw's cabin, however, he found Art Conners' men ambling about.

"Damn! That does it for me. I'm going back," Bud Davis was saying. One by one the men were deserting to return to their warm hearth fires at home.

"We're never gonna catch up to them. Either they are a whole heap smarter than the usual outlaws or they're just plum lucky. Either way, I've had it," another man added.

It was chilly, even inside the cabin. Snow lay deep in the northern exposures and had blown into drifts on the trail. The men pulled up the collars of sheepskin jackets, jammed their hats down over their ears and toasted their hands and faces before the flames of the fire crackling in the hearth.

"The fact is that life around here can be cut short at any time."

One of the newcomers, Felix Gastes, looked as if he had lost his last friend when Bud Davis made that remark. Felix was a short, thin man with a carefully trimmed mustache and black hair parted in the middle, a dead giveaway that he was a bartender. His eyes seemed to be questioning whether or not he should have volunteered for this mission in the first place.

"Something bothering you, Felix?" Warren asked, feeling understandably irritated.

"Well . . . uh . . . sort of . . . I do have a lot of problems right now. My wife is in failing health and, and . . ." He chafed his hands before the fire nervously.

"And the thought of trailing outlaws is scaring the hell out of you. Isn't it?" Warren questioned. That was all they needed on a trip through outlaw country. They would be better off if the city slicker would just return to his duties as bartender in Price and forget the detective work. Lord almighty, what would happen next?

"I hired out for a price to lay a killer out cold and stiff," the bartender answered. "Now I'm not so sure that I like becoming a hired gun."

"Let's just say that under some conditions the law just looks the other way. Nothin' really wrong with that." Art Conners was quick to defend their position as he glanced slyly in Felix's direction. "I've spent a good share of my life trying to bring outlaws under control."

"Yeah, but that Cassidy bunch is becoming quite bold," one of the men added.

"The governors of Utah and Colorado have agreed to hand-pick a select squad of law officers from each state to go after the Wild Bunch. The only trouble is that the governor of Wyoming has faith in Cassidy's promise and doesn't believe he had anything to do with that train robbery in which your brother was reported killed," said Conners.

"Cassidy was responsible all right," Warren argued. "I have a gut feeling about that."

"The Denver newspapers are beginning to hammer away at Butch Cassidy and the Wild Bunch. I was reading about him even before this last robbery," Art Conners continued. "Hate to have some damned outlaw getting that much attention. Next thing you know they will be making him into a hero of some kind or other."

"Remember, thousands of dollars worth of cattle have been stolen by those outlaws, brands burned out and their own brands substituted," Warren grumbled.

"Even if they didn't have anything to do with train robbery and we gave Cassidy the benefit of the doubt, the time has come to put an end to this whole damned mess of stealin' and rustlin'," hissed a voice muffled by a red and black plaid woolen scarf.

"We've been warned to stay out of here but even if we have, we're determined to go in after 'em," Art Conners declared.

"What you're telling me is that you are planning a raid like the one that gunned down Nate Champion five years ago. Joe Lefors led that one, didn't he?" Felix asked. "If I remember correctly the people were up in arms about the killing of Champion and probably would be about that Cassidy fellow, too. Don't know why, but sometimes these outlaws are really well liked."

"Oh, they know how to buy their friends all right." Art Conners said with a sneer.

They had been sitting around the fire for quite a while when Warren glanced out of the window of the small cabin. "It will be getting dark soon. Better just bunk down here for the night and get an early start in the morning." Noticing that Felix hadn't been saying much, Warren added, "Maybe Felix here will decide not to go after all."

Later that night while a game of poker was in progress, a messenger rode in with a telegram. "Been tryin' to track you down, Mister MacQuarie," he said. "Your brother. He isn't dead after all."

"He isn't dead!" Warren let out a hoot that shook the

roof as he read that the news was true. "Corbin's alive and basking in front of his fire at the Rolling Q."

Somehow Felix's face seemed to reflect his thoughts on that matter. He was obviously relieved. "Then there's no need to continue on. We can bag these renegades come spring when it's warmer. Let them hibernate a while. We'll catch them climbing out of their holes."

"Guess it would be difficult to try to track down them outlaws in this awful Wyoming snow," Art Conners said. The others soon agreed with him. A meeting would take place after the spring thaw. Joe Lefors knew the Wyoming territory and had no desire to leave Texas for Wyoming just now, but he'd join them all come spring.

It was a good thing, too, for in the morning the snows swirled and continued falling. The men were stranded there with no hope of even getting to the train depot in Rock Springs, Wyoming just over the border. The only way to go was back. Blizzards farther north were notorious all over the West. It was there that so many Mormon families had frozen to death on their way to Salt Lake in the 1860s. Art's followers didn't want to be another statistic. It was difficult to do any tracking in the snow. It was cold and miserable. Some of the men insisted they go back.

Warren was in a jovial mood as he sipped his coffee. Corbin was alive! Another thing that egged on his pride was that he had found a clue he'd not been expecting. He had a gut feeling that someone was giving the Wild Bunch a bit of competition in the matter of rustling. It piqued his curiosity to know just who.

Pulling the collar of his mackinaw up, settling his dripping Stetson further back on his head, he pushed out the door and busied himself with doing a bit of his own investigating.

No doubt Henrietta was enjoying herself, skating on the lake in Colorado Springs. He'd sent a telegram to her, explaining his delay, his hope to find his brother's killer, but she hadn't responded and he could only suppose that she was still incensed with him. Ah, well, he'd have it out with her when he got back home.

With that thought in mind he poked about in the snow, surprised by what he found, a piece of cut lariat and a branding iron. Bending down he picked up the objects and examined them. He didn't know just what evidence they would be or how they would fit together in the puzzle he was creating, but he pocketed them nonetheless.

Warren didn't see the rifle aimed at his back. He didn't know the danger until he heard the sound of the shot. Then it all happened so fast. His heart hammered with adrenaline but it didn't hurt, not yet. He turned slowly, a stunned look of surprise as he saw the face of his killer. Then he felt the slicing pain as another bullet tore through him. Like flames of white fire the agony came as he fell to the ground gasping for breath. He felt a hot flood of warmth wet his hand as he groped behind him, then he shuddered as he fell sprawled upon the snow.

Part Two: The Outlaw Lady

Rye Grass Station, Utah
Spring 1897

Lord of the far horizons,
Give us the eyes to see
Over the verge of the sundown
The beauty that is to be.
—Bliss Carman, "Lord of the Far Horizons"

Chapter Twenty-eight

A dazzlingly bright blue sky unfurled over Rye Grass Station like a welcome banner, heralding in the long-awaited days of sunshine. Spring had arrived slowly, reluctantly. The streets of the town had seemingly taken forever to change from knee-deep snow into ankle-deep mud. Then suddenly as if by magic the storms had lifted and in their wake the buds and blossoms had made their long-anticipated appearance.

Corbin MacQuarie looked up at the clear, boundless azure heavens and thought how deceptively calm it made him feel. It belied the turmoil that even now raged within his heart whenever he allowed his thoughts to touch upon his brother. Warren had been murdered most foully, shot in the back by a coward who hadn't even given him a chance to defend himself. Killed by a member of the Wild Bunch, or so Art Conners had told him.

"Damned thieving pack of coyotes!" he swore aloud as he walked slowly down the boardwalk. Even after three months' time he still felt the pain of his loss. Images hovered before his eyes like a mirage. Art Conners' story of a dark-clothed stranger taking aim and firing, not once but twice, unleashed Corbin's misery anew and he gulped back a wrenching sob. That Warren had been shot avenging *his* supposed death made the murder of his brother an even harder burden to bear. Now something much stronger than a love for ranching drove him on.

Grief had turned to anger and a resolve to do for Warren what Warren had vowed to do for him. Namely to avenge his death. With that thought in mind he had sought Art Conners out and asked to be deputized. Though the sheriff had given Corbin a dozen reasons why he shouldn't take on such a task, Corbin had been adamant and in the end had been granted his star.

On a cold, wind-torn morning with Jessie's Winchester in his saddle sheath and a Colt .45 strapped to his waist, Corbin had set out with a small group of men toward the barren, lonely and desolate area where Warren had been killed. The thought in his mind was of tracking down Butch Cassidy and his band of outlaws. Instead his journey had been anticlimatic and he had come back discouraged and empty handed. Still, he had not given up. Someday, somehow, he would be successful and would bring the Wild Bunch down.

In the meantime Corbin had spent every waking moment either at the ranch or in doing what he could to help maintain peace in a more than slightly tainted town. Rye Grass Station was far from peaceful. There were Saturday night saloon free-for-alls, shootings in the streets and arguments that all too often ended in fist swinging. When men were coupled up arguments seemed to brew more frequently. Most annoying of all, however, were the constant episodes of cattle rustling. Archie Jarvis counted five of the Rolling Q's prime cows missing. The cattle thieves always seemed to be one step ahead of any lawmen. Whoever was leading the gang that struck Rye Grass Station and the surrounding area ranches was no fool.

And if the outlaws and rustlers weren't enough, Corbin had learned that here in the northern tip of Utah, winter could well be an enemy, the cold, snow, and ice an unrelenting danger. Stories of horses and cattle freezing to death made him take extra precautions at the ranch. Rumors of avalanches in mountain passes and acres and acres of ice and snow curtailed any efforts to search for Warren's killer.

Storm had followed storm, shrouding the area with white. Keeping warm seemed to become the prime focus for existence. Corbin's excursions into town became less and less frequent and a sense of loneliness had at last taken hold. His mother, his father, and now Warren were gone, leaving him a very saddened man. He had no family. If not for Archie's cheerful devotion and Bowlegs' hovering loyalty he knew he might very well have gone mad.

All in all it had been a hectic, miserable, unrewarding winter. Even with all that had happened, however, Corbin hadn't been able to put Jessica Watson far from his mind. Was she still as pert and pretty as he remembered? Would he ever see her again? Or was she just an illusive dream that hovered just out of his reach, taunting him. It was a question that haunted him as he made his way to Art Conners' office. And yet, it was spring, Corbin thought — a time for rebirth and new beginnings as well as a continuation of those things left undone.

The dirt road of the town was clogged with wagons, buggies, and horses as the citizens came out of their hibernation. Dodging the wheels of a milk wagon, Corbin crossed the busy thoroughfare, elbowed his way through the meandering throng and pushed open the door to the sheriff's office. He found Art Conners sitting at his desk, head down, eyes fixed in concentration on a stack of handbills before him.

"You look busy. Have time for a chat? Bowlegs told me you wanted to talk with me next time I was in Rye Grass."

"Just rummaging through my collection of wanted posters." Art motioned to a chair next to his desk. "Sit down. Sit down." He watched as Corbin took off his hat and lowered his lithely muscled frame into the armless leather chair. "I'll get right to the point. I want you to give back that star."

"What? Never." Corbin pounded his fist on the desk. "Not until my brother's killer is found and the Wild Bunch is dispersed and properly punished."

"Your heart is in ranching, not in chasing outlaws. You're cut from a whole different kind of cloth, Corbin." Art adopted a placating kind of tone. One might have thought he was talking to a child. "Now I can understand the gut-wrenching sorrow you must have felt because of your brother's death and all. But Corbin, I think you should leave sheriffing to me. You have a ranch to run and you're gonna be mighty busy now that spring is here."

"My foreman, Archie Jarvis, can handle things while I'm away," Corbin answered stubbornly. He wouldn't be swayed in this matter.

"Leave this business to those who are experienced in it."

"I'm getting experience!"

"There's another kind of learning that comes from knowing the ropes — and that's what you're lacking. You can't find out how to deal with outlaws by reading law books. Nor can you buy your way out of trouble," he said, eluding to Corbin's wealth.

Corbin's jaw ticked warningly. "I can handle myself as well as any man."

Art threw up his hands in exasperation. "Why the hell does a college-educated man want to waste his time roaming all over with a bunch of flea-bitten cowboys when he can relax before the hearthfire of his ranch?" Crumpling the handbills he thrust them out for Corbin to see. "Look at these. Men like Kid Curry, Cassidy's second-in-command. Black Jack Ketchum. These men are killers. You're a rancher. You're no match for the men whose faces decorate my walls."

Corbin held one up for inspection, reading the name. "Ben Kilpatrick, alias the Tall Texan."

"Train robber. Rustler. Has boasted that he will never be taken alive."

Corbin looked closely at the picture, wondering if it was this man who shot his brother. Certainly the pale yellow eyes looked cruel. He studied the face for several minutes then turned to the next pictures. Harry Tracy. Kid Curry."

"Both killers. Tracy is one of the finest marksmen around. A gunfighter, for God's sake." The sheriff shook his head. "Now, I've been humoring you because of what happened to your brother and all but think, Corbin. . . ."

Seeing the unflattering sketch of Jessie, Corbin crumpled it up. "What's this still doing in here, Art? I told you there'd been a mistake." He tossed the sketch in the wastebasket. "First of all that's a woman not a boy, secondly she *saved* my life and thirdly Jessie wouldn't even know an outlaw if she spotted one. Get rid of it."

"No." Art retrieved it out of the wastebasket. "I'm going to hold onto it for safekeeping just in case. Your brother had it in his pocket when he died."

"So. . . ? Warren hadn't heard my side of what happened. He thought I was dead and that *she* shot me. But it was all a ridiculous mistake." Quickly Corbin repeated the story of how Jessie took him to one of the tiny cabins to recuperate. "But now you know what happened and that if Jessie hadn't come along when she did I'd have been buzzard meat."

Art gave a low whistle. "Just like that. Came along out of the blue."

"That's what she said. She had a job as a ranch hand nearby."

"Mm-hmm. Well, I, for one, am not convinced. I don't believe in coincidences. I just don't buy her just coming upon the train by accident as you were being shot. I smell a fish in the stew."

"If you knew Jessie you wouldn't give it another thought. She's a pretty, spunky, young woman. Open and honest. You're wasting your time if you think she'd spend one minute of her time with bastards like these." In a moment of anger Corbin threw the wanted posters down. "Cassidy. Sundance. Kid Curry. Black Jack Ketchum. Hardly the kind of company a woman like that would even look at."

"Maybe you're right and then maybe she knows more than

she's sayin'. I only know I gotta keep what happened in mind and have her watched whenever she's within my sight."

Corbin scoffed at that and thought how if the whole idea didn't rile him so he'd have a good laugh with Jessie about it. Outlaws indeed! "Well, I'm not so desperate to find Warren's killer that I'm going to pester innocent people." Putting his hat back on his head, Corbin stood up. "And another thing. This star," he tapped it with his finger, "is staying right where it is until Warren's killer is hanging from a tree."

"And that just might be sooner than you think. I've heard tell that Cassidy's bunch is leaving their winter quarters." He laughed loudly, ominously. "The gang holed up for the winter but they'll come out of their hiding now. Even skunks got to seek the fresh air sometime." Reaching over he patted Corbin on the shoulder. Seeing Corbin's unrelenting, stone-faced look, he let out his breath in a long, deep sigh. "OK. OK. Get yourself killed. Let's you and me not fuss and squabble. Keep the dad-burn star if it means so much to you."

"Thanks, Art." Corbin's gaze traveled to the stack of handbills where Jessie's sketch lay at the top. It was an un-flattering drawing that didn't capture the soft lines of her face and yet it looked enough like her to bring forth a deep longing within him. Jessie. Oh, how he wanted to see her, touch her, kiss her again. Even after all this time he hadn't forgotten how sweet their love making had been. Perhaps with her enfolded in his arms he could forget his pain, at least for a moment. For the first time in weeks a gentle emotion touched his heart, pushing away his anger and it was Jessie, not Warren, that filled Corbin's thoughts as he left the sheriff's office behind.

Chapter Twenty-nine

The smell of blossoms and wild grass filled the air with an enchanting aroma and Jessie paused from time to time to breathe in the fragrance as she rode along. Spring! Oh, how she had thought it would never come. And yet here she was at last approaching Rye Grass Station and anticipating a whole new life for herself. Was it any wonder she felt so light of heart?

Jessie had ridden part of the way with Butch, Ben Kilpatrick, Elza Lay, Wade, Agnes and a few of the other members of the original gang who were making plans to return to Utah and complete some unfinished business, namely the holdup of the Castle Gate Pleasant Valley Coal Company. Butch had tried to cajole her into joining them but she had steadfastly refused. That was not the way to go straight, she had insisted. Thus, she had left them at the junction and continued on to Rye Grass instead of going on to the hideout at Cassidy Point with them. When she arrived in the town she wanted to be alone. Things were still a bit too tumultuous to take any chances.

A posse had been out for nearly a month looking for outlaws, making them all a bit jittery, but had not captured anyone. Nevertheless many of the outlaws had struck out for other places just as soon as the spring thaw had come.

The idea of a posse on their trail didn't make them very interested in hanging around Hole-in-the-Wall when there were so many other places to go where they could work and carouse until next winter. The skeleton crew of the original members always hung together though, and they were the ones who had gone on to Cassidy Point with Butch.

Jessie said a tearful goodbye to Wade, cautioning him to be careful. He in turn told her to take care. "Don't let that Corbin MacQuarie break your heart, girl," he had said, ruffling her newly grown crop of longer auburn curls.

"I won't. I'm hopin' that we'll be even half as happy as you and Aggie are . . ." Rising up on tiptoe she kissed his balding head. "Now, you be good and listen to Agnes and I'll see you in the autumn if not before. You hear?"

Wade and Agnes were only going to stay until the job at the coal company in the valley near Price, Utah was over and then Wade had promised Aggie that he would return to her small farm in Wyoming, give up outlawing, and settle down. No more Wild Bunch, he had said. There was only one little matter that had caused argument between them, however. He had promised Butch that he would help with this one last job first, despite Aggie's angry protestations. One last job and then he would give up outlawing forever.

Jessie had parted company with the caravan, turning around to wave now and again until the fork in the road put the others out of sight. The road had been dusty, the rest of the journey lonely, but now she had arrived at Rye Grass Station. Where could she go? She knew several people in the town but their connections with Butch and the others gave her pause. If she was going to make a clean break she would have to be entirely on her own, entirely honest.

It was at about 7:00 P.M. by her reckoning. Thundering past the door of the newly built Main Street Boarding house, gawking as she passed the beautiful three-story building, she thought what a comfortable place it appeared to be. It was a fine addition to the town's present buildings.

As she rode on down the main street, she made up her mind that it was there that she would live, at least until she knew just what direction her feelings for Corbin would take her.

Giving her pinto, Sagebrush, over to a livery stable, she unpacked her saddlebags, asking permission to leave her saddle, saddle blanket and heavier carpetbag with her clothes in it at the livery until she could call for the bag in the morning. The livery owner was very glad to be of help. He said that would be all right and that he would take good care of her things until she returned. Grabbing the lighter carpetbag that contained a change of clothing and the nine thousand dollars she had received as her share in the robbery, she leisurely ambled back to the boarding house for a better look.

Many changes had taken place in the old town during the time she had been away. One of the streets had been cobbled, new signposts had been driven up and there were several small new buildings besides the boardinghouse — an eatery and a new saloon to give the Arrowhead added competition. Walking leisurely down the road she appraised the site of her new home. The carpetbag she was carrying held just a few clothes and the money, thus was not extremely heavy. Even with it in hand she was agile, able to bound up the wooden staircase of the boarding house and pull the massive double doors open. Inside it smelled of strong soap, beeswax and cooking. Agnes would have approved of the housekeeping.

A bell above the door tinkled as she stepped onto the lush gold and emerald carpet. It was even as impressive inside as out, maybe more so. As she walked down the long hallway toward a room at the end of the hall marked Manager — Mrs. Simmons, the four silver lamps hanging from the ceiling gave a dreamy appearance, the light reflecting off the green and gold striped draperies.

It was such a luxurious place that she wished now that she had taken time to put on a skirt. She had been tempted to

283

change as soon as she had picked up her order in Laramie, to ride into town in style; but her need for comfort had told her that such finery should not be worn while traveling by horseback. Riding a horse in a skirt had been unthinkable. Somehow now, however, she wished she had changed from her Levis and cotton shirt into her new clothes before coming here. Instead they had remained in the carpetbag where she had so carefully placed them. Now it was too late to change clothes. The manager would just have to take her as she was, or listen to her explanation.

Pausing only a moment, Jessie tapped lightly at the door with the nameplate. A stout, elegantly dressed elderly woman with snow-white hair piled atop her head answered the door, squinting in the dim light.

"Good evenin', ma'am" Jessie began, shifting from foot to foot and thrusting her free hand in her pocket. "I'd like a room." As she spoke, she glanced at a poster attached to the wall and discovered that the rooms were usually rented a week at a time. "I may be here longer than a week, but I'll take it a week at a time if that's all right."

"Yes, young fella." Taking note of Jessie's denims and large-brimmed hat, she thought Jessie was a lad for just a moment. "Come in and we'll sign the agreement."

"My name is *Jessica*. Jessica Watson," Jessie said as she stepped inside the well-furnished room. She licked her lips nervously, the memory of her wanted poster coming back to haunt her. "I'm a woman, not a man," she blurted out. "I'm dressed this way because I've just ridden into town on horseback all the way from Laramie." She took off her wide-brimmed Stetson and held it in her hand, shaking her hair as she did so.

"Well, so you are—and a very attractive young woman at that. I'm sorry about my mistake, my dear. I couldn't see those beautiful auburn curls and I didn't have my spectacles handy when you knocked at the door." Fumbling around she came up with her glasses and balanced them on her nose. "Oh, now I can see that pretty face of yours."

"Pretty?" Jessie blushed at her remark. "Oh, I don't know about that."

"Yes, you are. Very, very pretty." Extending her hand she introduced herself. "My name is Marie Simmons. I only have five woman tenants so it will be nice to have another." Taking a ring of keys from a peg on the wall she led Jessie up a flight of stairs. "All of the young women are on the second floor, so we might just as well let you look at a room on that floor, too. Just to keep it companionable."

"That's fine," Jessie answered, following along behind.

"We ladies seem to get along well. You will be welcomed by all, I'm sure. Do you want room *and* board?"

"Yes, ma'am, I will."

"Ma'am? No, no, no." She winked. "You should call me Marie. All the others do."

"Marie . . ." Jessie was sure she would be happy here. The woman seemed very friendly. "I will want both room and board Mrs . . . uh, Marie. What's the price?"

Mrs. Simmons pulled a pad and pen from her apron pocket and quickly figured it out. "Eight dollars per week and that includes breakfast and dinner. Most don't eat lunch here but if you want it, that will be a dollar per week extra."

Reaching in her carpetbag Jessie withdrew a roll of bank notes, sixteen dollars' worth, and handed it to Marie, just to assure her space for awhile. Money was really no problem with over nine thousand dollars, her share of the robbery money, in the carpetbag. She'd use it to buy a little luxury for herself and keep a nest egg besides . . . If she was going to change her way of living, this would give her a good start. The way things had been going so far was very encouraging.

"Come along then and we'll get you settled in," Marie said, leading the way up a wide, carpeted stairway. She smiled pleasantly. "I'll have one of my boys carry that bag for you if you would like."

"No!" Jessie clutched it protectively, then relaxed. "No,

thanks, Marie. I can handle it myself. It's got my drawers in it so I wouldn't want to . . . let . . . well . . . you know . . ." Jessie wasn't about to let anyone else anywhere near her money. "Besides, this bag isn't really that heavy."

Marie hesitated in front of one of the rooms, "Number twenty-seven. This will be your room." Opening the door, she lit the lamp for Jessie then smiled broadly as she stepped outside again. "Have a good night's sleep. We serve breakfast at eight. Don't be late or all the breakfast rolls will be gone."

"Thank you. Good night, Marie." Jessie closed the door and suddenly felt very alone and vulnerable. She had never really been completely alone before, she realized. The outlaws had been her friends but now she would have to make new acquaintances. Women friends. That was a novel idea. Aside from Aggie she'd never associated with many of her own sex. Their talk of babies, cooking, and sewing just hadn't interested her. Now, however, things were going to change, or so she supposed. Certainly she couldn't occupy herself in the things she used to take pleasure in, the saloon or the billiard hall. Hopefully Corbin would occupy her time.

Moving toward the bed she lifted the quilt to peer at the fine linen sheets. She pushed on the mattress, then sitting down, bounced on it once or twice. It was soft and inviting and she was bone-tired after the long day's ride. Pulling off her boots, then throwing her hat on a nearby chair, she leaned back against the pillows and closed her eyes.

Jessie had been lying down only for a short time when she heard the sound of galloping hooves under her window. Living with the outlaws had sharpened her senses and reflexes, thus she reached for her carpetbag without even thinking. Removing her .45 and her holster belt she placed them over the back of a chair within a hand's length for quick access. If any trouble occurred, she'd be prepared.

Moving in the direction of the window, she pushed the

draperies aside and looked out at the cloudless sky. It was dark by now but there was a frosty moon. It's light outlined the form of three horsemen riding down the middle of Main Street hooting, hollering, and shooting. To her, this was nothing unusual. The cowboys were back in town after a long, hard winter and were just letting everyone know it.

And yet, I probably should hide the money, just in case, she thought. Opening her carpetbag she took out the dress, shoes and hat inside and draped them over a chair, then pulled out the wad of bills and bag of coins. The perfect hiding place for the bulk of money seemed to be under the mattress, at least for the time being. Feeling pleased with herself, and more secure, she climbed back into the bed and put the disturbance out of her mind. She had more serious thinking to do. About Corbin, for one, thing.

It had been three long months since she had seen him. Never for a moment during that entire time, however, had she forgotten his handsome face, his strong arms or the excitement of being with him. There was no doubt in her mind that now that she was once again in Brown's Park Valley, she wanted to see him. But how could she arrange to do so without looking obvious? It would be just too forward for her to go riding out to the Rolling Q and nonchalantly announce, "Well, here I am." No, she couldn't do that. His feelings for her might have changed in three months. He might even have a new love.

No! No! her mind whirled then poised on the brink of losing all control. She mustn't even think such thoughts. And even if he did, she could hold her own. Jessie was confident. All gussied up, she really did look rather fine. Enough to turn his eyes in her direction again. Besides, she would pull all the hair from the head of any woman who got in her way now, she thought with a slight smile. Hell, she might even pull all the hair from *his* head if she thought he'd cast his eyes elsewhere. A girl had to hang on to what was hers. She would just calm down, stop thinking for now and figure things out tomorrow. With that vow whispered she contented herself in counting sheep and drifted off into a fitful slumber.

When Jessie awakened in the morning she luxuriated in the cool, clean smell of the sheets, the comfort of the mattress. After days in the saddle she felt pampered to be sleeping past dawn and yet the bright light streaming through the window told her it was way past that time. She felt refreshed, rested, and very, very happy with herself. Sitting up in bed she reassessed her room now that it was light, and thought that when all was said and done she really had been quite lucky to find such a liveable room. Staying here wouldn't be bad at all.

Quickly she rose and washed in the basin of water on the commode then glanced out the window. Her room was on the second floor right across the street from the dry goods store and she could look right down on the street scenes below. It was still much too early in the morning for too much to be happening down there, but once again around midnight last night someone had ridden down Main Street shooting at everything in sight. She hoped that it was just some cowboy feeling his oats after having been cooped up in a bunkhouse someplace all winter long. Trouble was something she just didn't need right now.

Walking about in her bare feet she looked at every nook and cranny. She really liked this room. It was well furnished with a big wardrobe closet, a nice brass double bed with a feather mattress, a small desk, a stand with an oil lamp on it, two easy chairs and a mirrored vanity. She was entranced by the pewter washbowl and water pitcher with a delicate blue floral design on it, for it reminded her of one her mother had had once. Ah yes, this was living. Perhaps being a lady wouldn't be so bad after all.

Remembering that Marie had said that the rolls would be all gone if she was late, Jessie went about her morning toilette. As she stood in front of the mirror in her new underwear, crimping her shoulder length locks with a curling iron, she thought once more of how she should approach Corbin. She wanted him to know that she was in town but didn't want to call on him at his ranch. Aggie had given her good advice, that a woman should chase a man but let him think he was the one doing the pursuing.

I could send him a note or buy him another gaudy tie and have it delivered, she thought with a half smile. Or a new guitar? Or maybe she could just watch and wait, hoping he'd come into town for supplies or a shave. Walking to the window in her drawers and bosom protector, she raised the shade and contented herself with looking down upon the early-day crowd. Cowboys. Drovers. Shopkeepers. A blacksmith. Those going to work and those just loitering about until the saloons opened their doors. Rye Grass Station was steadily growing into a thriving little town, she thought with a sigh.

Jessie dressed in a dark blue linen skirt and white shirtwaist. The blouse needed a bit of ironing, she noticed in the mirror, but it would have to do, at least until after breakfast. Brushing her hair back from her face in a cluster of ringlets she tied it with a white ribbon. No one would mistake her for a boy today, she thought with a sniff. Passing by the window, she bent over to retrieve her boots, scolding herself for not having thought to bring a dainty pair of shoes to go with her new womanly duds. Glancing down at the street she took one last look when suddenly the tall, lithe figure of a man caught her eye.

Certainly the broad shoulders between a green and black plaid shirt, the face beneath the Stetson looked familiar. Were her eyes deceiving her? Certainly not. There was Corbin MacQuarie walking along the board sidewalk in front of the blacksmith's. She would have known him anywhere. What a stroke of luck. With great haste she finished dressing, putting on a jacket and a narrow-brimmed, feathered hat, and bounded down the stairs without stopping to eat breakfast despite her hunger.

Once outside the building, she slowed her pace a little but her eyes followed him. Was it her imagination or had he gotten a little thinner? Strange, but usually men got fatter in the winter, what with staying put and exerting little energy. And his mouth — instead of smiling, there was a grim tenseness in his lips. It appeared that it had been a difficult winter for him.

"Corbin!" she breathed. Her heart beat wildly. Although she was dying to see him, she didn't want to appear overly anxious. She wanted to make their meeting appear to be coincidence. An oh, so pleasant surprise. With that thought in mind she traced his steps at a safe distance. Corbin turned the corner, Jessie turned the corner. Corbin crossed the street and she did likewise.

He was going toward the blacksmith's shop. Jessie couldn't very well follow him there without being obvious, she thought. Oh, no. She would just drop into the dry goods store and buy a few things while she kept an eye on him through the big plate glass window. That seemed an amiable solution until suddenly she lost sight of him. For just a moment she had thought she'd lost him and, quickly paying the storekeeper, she hurried outside to get a better look. Just as Corbin came bounding up the steps in front of the store, Jessie was stepping down. The packages she was carrying went flying through the air at the impact of their collision as she was hurled headlong into his arms. With her hat askew atop her glorious curls, she looked up into his astonished face, swallowed hard and said cheerily, "Well, fancy meeting you here."

"Jessie!" They both laughed so hard they nearly cried but just as quickly he sobered. "Oh, Jessie, it's so good to see you again." He held her at arm's length in order to look at her. "You look gorgeous. Really gorgeous."

"Do I?" It sounded so good to hear him say it, and yet she was troubled by the look of sadness in his eyes. What had put that look of disillusionment in his eyes and furled his brows? "Corbin . . . ?" Her eyes asked a dozen questions.

"Oh, Jessie. Jessie." He squeezed her tightly and brushed her forehead in a quick kiss. "Let's go someplace where we can be alone. Someplace where we can talk. We have a lot of catching up to do."

"Want to go over to the saloon and shoot a little pool?" she quipped, reminding him of that time when they had first met.

"No, not today Jess." He laughed and yet soulfully it sounded hollow. "Besides, dressed as you are they wouldn't let you in. You'd have to go in that side, 'wine entrance,' for ladies and then we couldn't be together."

He was right. There were several advantages in dressing like a man. There were still so many places a *lady* just couldn't go. It reminded Jessie of just why she had donned denims and men's shirts in the first place.

"We could go to the livery stable, hire a carriage, take a picnic lunch and drive up the canyon a ways," she suggested. Oh, how she had dreamed these long months of Corbin touching her again, smiling at her, whispering her name.

Corbin was all for that suggestion. "What an intriguing idea. Although I hate to let you go for even a second, I'll see to the carriage if you see to the food and we will meet back here in half an hour. How does that sound?"

It sounded perfect. A place where they could be alone. "I'm living right over there in the Main Street Boarding-house. Why don't you see about the carriage, then come on over there? I'll fix a basket of food and then meet you in the sitting room." As he started down the street she called to him, "Oh, and Corbin, if you don't mind, the livery stable owner has a large carpetbag of mine. Can you just throw that in the carriage too?" He nodded but he didn't smile. It was as if his mouth hadn't curled up in that direction for awhile. Something has happened, she thought. As soon as they were alone she would ask him.

Jessie hastened across the street and into the boarding-house kitchen. She met Marie Simmons along the way and told her what she was up to. "I'll pay you for the food!"

"Don't worry about it — you gave me quite an advance on your board, my dear. So, your first day in town and already you have a young man." Marie was a romantic at heart and listened while Jessie told of her first meeting with Corbin.

"He asked me to marry him once . . ." The two of them filled a basket with many culinary delights, including a bottle of Old Crow just for old time's sake. Somehow the basket of food and the bottle of whiskey brought back memories. Something was troubling him, but she'd make him forget all about it. To make him smile again was a compelling force leading her on. He seemed withdrawn and yet it didn't appear that the love they had felt for each other then had diminished one little bit over the past few months. No, it was something else that was troubling him.

As soon as the basket was filled, and with Marie's blessing, she went into the sitting room to await her lover's return. She did not have to wait too long. His tall masculine form came through the front door with a spring bouquet in hand, a gesture that deeply touched her.

"I just couldn't resist picking these for you. They were growing in abundance out behind the carriage house. The blue ones match your suit and the green leaves are a brighter green, but still the color of your eyes." Jessie was not unaware of the way Corbin's eyes lit up at the sight of her. Nor was she unaware of the way her heart still pounded when he was anywhere nearby.

"Flowers." It was the first time she'd ever received flowers from a man . . . "Oh Corbin, what a sweet thought. Thank you so much." She sniffed each blossom in turn, enchanted by their fragrance, that was until they made her sneeze.

"Your carriage is waiting, my lady Jessica," he said extending his arm. Putting her arm through his, she walked with him toward the rented carriage. Marie gave Jessie a wink as they passed her in the hallway.

"Do you like the way I look, Corbin?" She smiled, completely unaware of how seductive that smile was. "Really?"

"Really! Not to say I didn't like you in your denims just as well. In that skirt I can't see your cute little fanny . . ." At last the corner of his lips turned up, but the smile didn't touch his eyes.

"Corbin . . . ?" She wanted to ask him what had happened but now didn't seem the right moment.

He helped her up onto the carriage seat, spanning her narrow waist with his hands, then he climbed up beside her. Their eyes met and touched in a caress as their bodies brushed. Compulsively Corbin's fingers closed around hers. "Oh, God, Jessie. It's so good to see you again."

Dancing sunbeams shadowed the hollows beneath his eyes and she stared in fascination at the way the light played across his hard jawline and chiseled nose. It was his mouth, however, that riveted her attention. She found herself remembering the texture and pressure of those warm, knowing lips against her own.

"I missed you, Corbin." There was no need to be coy, the truth just tumbled from her lips. "You will never know how much." As if it were the most natural gesture in the world her hand sought out the column of his neck, her fingers caressing the firm, sinewy strength, moving to his shoulders.

Corbin responded to her affection. Holding her face in his hands he kissed her eyelids, the curve of her cheek, her mouth. His tongue traced the outline of her lips as he drew her up against his chest. "Jessie. Jessie. Jessie." Being with her again was like a balm to his tortured soul. For a seemingly endless moment in time they contented themselves by holding each other. Then Corbin moved away.

"We'd best get going . . ." In preparation for making himself comfortable for the ride, Corbin took off his jacket before taking up the reins. It was then that Jessie realized she'd seen a badge pinned to his vest. A badge! With a startled gasp her eyes popped open in astonishment. There fastened to the brown leather was a shining silver star. There was no mistake. Corbin MacQuarie, the man Jessie loved, had become a lawman while she was away from him.

Chapter Thirty

The carriage ride up the canyon was a pleasant one. For a time Corbin forgot his troubles as he basked in the warmth of Jessie's passionate soul. She had a zeal for living, a knack for sharing laughter, a passionate nature that charmed him. Breathing deeply of the fresh air, he paused to listen to the song the birds were singing and hummed a similar tune himself.

Jessie sat proud and tall on the carriage seat, her face framed by wisps of red-brown hair that the breeze whipped free. Corbin's eyes caressed her, realizing just what a rare, sweet, unspoiled young woman she really was. There was only one Jessie. Perhaps that was why he had so quickly fallen in love with her. Surely her guileless beauty seduced him, attracted him as no other woman's coy and practiced wiles could. The light wind swirled about her as they rode the bumpy roadway, molding her dress against the slender length of her thighs and the gentle curve of her breasts. Was it any wonder that instead of appreciating the scenery, Corbin was taking special delight in looking at *her?*

They rode to Cold Spring Mountain. Corbin reined in the team, hitched the horses to a tree and walked around the carriage to her side. She started to scramble down but he put both hands around her waist and aided in her descent. Jessie was giddily conscious of the warmth emanating from his hands. Her stomach fluttered like the wings of a butterfly but not because she was hungry.

"Come on, "I'll show you the place I used to go with Wade when I was a little girl. . . ."

Corbin picked up the lunch basket and followed her up the slope of a hill to a meadow, a secluded spot near a stream shaded by an old gnarled oak tree. It was there he set down the basket. Taking out a small red-and-white-checked linen cloth that Marie had given her, she spread it upon the ground and began laying out their food, fried chicken, baked beans, hard-boiled eggs, cheese, a small loaf of bread and a small jar of pickles and the whiskey.

"Just for the memories," she felt compelled to explain, thrusting the bottle into his hands.

"For medicinal purposes, of course." Corbin took the whiskey with a half smile as he caught her gaze. "You remembered our time together in the cabin."

"Yes, I remembered." I've thought about it very vividly all the time we've been apart, she thought. It was the only thing that had helped her survive those lonely months.

The mountain breeze carried the scent of wild flowers and pine. Corbin shaded his eyes against the sun's glare and appraised the scenery. It was a truly romantic setting with cottonwood, ash, and box elder trees growing thickly along the stream. As he watched a flock of birds winged high overhead and swooped to make the trees their resting place.

"Beautiful." A word that could have been used for her as well. Although he had loved her just as much when she was wearing trousers, seeing her looking so feminine

296

was very stirring.

"It's a little bit like looking down from heaven. . . ." Jessie sighed.

"Like heaven. . . ." He hunkered down beside her, trailing his fingers over her hand and up her arm. "I should have thought to bring a blanket. Your pretty new clothes."

"I don't mind sitting on the grass."

"Nor do I." He lay down on his side, leaning upon one elbow, watching as she finished unpacking the basket. He didn't say anything for a long while and Jessie honored his silence, though she wondered at his mood. Reflective. Sorrowful. She sensed a certain tension in the way he held himself, although he was trying to hide it from her with a mask of false good humor.

"Are you hungry?" she asked at last. Her gaze moved slowly over his face, longing to see him smile.

"As hungry as a coyote in a prairie dog town!" He opened the bottle and poured the contents into two small cups he found inside the basket, handing one to Jessie. "But first, a toast. That we will never be parted again."

"That we will never be parted." Clinking the cups together, they drank to that hope.

Jessie sat beside Corbin, her skirts spread out around her like a large fan. She tried to make herself comfortable, wishing she had on her denims. She handed him the small loaf of bread and he broke it in half, giving them each an equal share. Then he sliced the cheese into wedges with his pocket knife.

"Oh, bull wart! I forgot the forks," Jessie exclaimed in annoyance. Well, luckily most of it was finger food. Picking up a chicken wing, she nibbled at it thoughtfully. Although they had been apart for three months, nothing seemed to have changed in the affinity she felt for him, the deep affection. If anything, she loved him all the more. Ah, absence does indeed make the heart grow fonder, Jessie thought to herself. She had heard that phrase before but never truly believed it until now. Being with Corbin seemed to be a natural way to spend her time.

They ate in silence but she was aware of his gentle scrutiny. Suddenly a shot rang out in the distance and just as suddenly his thoughts seemed to be somewhere else for a moment. His mood changed radically as if the sound had reminded him of something. She read torment in his eyes and wanted to comfort him but she wasn't sure just what to say and so the moment passed.

"I missed you, Jessie. . . ." he said at last. A brown squirrel edged closer and Corbin threw it a small piece of bread. Collecting it like a rare treasure, the tiny animal scurried up a tree.

"I thought the winter would never leave. . . ." She watched as he unfastened the top three buttons of his shirt, revealing his tawny, curling chest hair, and rolled up his sleeves in an effort to make himself more comfortable. Jessie's eyes were pulled in his direction. His virile presence was always exciting.

"I wish the winter had never come!" He sounded bitter and once again she wondered what had happened to wipe away his contentment.

She made an effort to cheer him up, saying brightly, "If not for winter there would be no spring. I guess there has to be a little hardship to appreciate the good all the more." Her eyes softened and she lifted her hand to touch his face. "What made you decide to be deputized, Corbin? You never said you were interested in being a lawman before."

His shoulders tensed as he raked his fingers through

his hair. The look on his face clearly showed that he didn't really want to talk about it. Nevertheless he blurted out, "One of the Wild Bunch shot my brother! The damned coward killed him in cold blood. Shot him in the *back*." He clenched his hands into fists. "I decided to go after vengeance in a legal way."

Jessie bit down hard on her lower lip. An outlaw had murdered his brother. Dear God! Which outlaw? Which of the men she knew had done such a terrible deed? They were a rough lot, yes, but except for Bob Meeks, few of them were killers. Butch tried hard to keep a measure of peace.

Her stomach curled tightly. "Corbin, I'm sorry . . . !"

His eyes were veiled. "It was a shock. Warren had been out of law enforcement ever since his marriage. I keep wishing I could do something to bring him back, to turn back the clock and do something to protect him." He ached to lay her on her back in the warm spring grass and blend with her body, to let her sweetness help him to forget. Instead he contented himself with just sitting next to her.

"How . . . how did it happen?" Though she had in no way been involved in the deed she couldn't help but wonder how it would affect their future. Would she ever be able to tell him the truth about herself now?

"Warren was out looking for the man who shot me. He was trying to avenge my murder." His eyes narrowed, then darkened. "Isn't that damned ironic!"

She knew how it hurt him to talk about it. "Then he didn't know you were alive and he . . . ?"

"I tried to reach him. I sent a dozen messengers but with the snow . . ."

Once he started telling the story, the words poured out and he couldn't stop. He told of the agony of hearing

299

the news, the raging anger that spurred him to pin on the star. "For three solid months all I held in my heart was hatred. It even pushed away my tender feelings for you, Jess. I was goaded into braving storms I would have avoided before. But so far it hasn't done me a damn bit of good. Those blasted outlaws do their dirty deeds with impunity, laughing in our faces all the while."

"Not laughing, Corbin. . . ." Certainly she wasn't. Not now. Not ever. And yet she remembered how she had joined with Butch and the others in mocking the posse that was searching for them. Dear God, she'd never realized Corbin was with them.

He gritted his teeth. "I really don't want to talk about it any more. Please understand." He stood up and left her, walking in the direction of the carriage. A few minutes later he returned with his jacket under his arm. He had gone to get something to make a pillow to cradle their heads on while they lay side by side. Jessie was relieved to see that he had pushed aside his painful memories at least for the moment.

"Why don't you make yourself more comfortable too," he said softly. Jessie complied, unbuttoning the prim-high-waisted jacket and pulling it from her shoulders. Corbin's gaze moved down over her breasts. He wrapped his arm around her and leaned back against the pillow his jacket formed. Jessie snuggled against him, curled into the crook of his arm. She pressed her face against his shoulder. Somehow she'd make it up to him if she could. *I'll never do anything dishonest again. I'll give up outlawing forever, only please, dear God, don't let him find out what I have done.* If he ever learned now that she had lived among the Wild Bunch he would never forgive her.

"Jessie. . . ." He moved her hand around to his lips

and gently kissed the palm. He stared down at her face somberly. "Oh, sweet Jessie, you give me hope." Just looking at her and touching her deeply affected him.

Her eyes seemed to burn his with green light as they misted with tears. He was very dear to her. She would have never wanted to cause pain and yet somehow it seemed the deck was stacked against them. Twice now the men whom she called her friends had brought harm to Corbin. If only she could bring his brother back—but all she could do was to share his pain.

"You're crying. Don't cry, Jessie." He groaned and caught hold of her, tangling his fingers in her hair, his mouth hovering just inches from her own.

"Kiss me. I want you to, Corbin."

He didn't need another invitation. Bending his head, he moved his lips gently but insistently from her nape to her mouth, uttering an imprecation as his mouth claimed hers in a lingering kiss. His heart stopped, then surged with a liquid heat. He wanted her, God knew, but he refused to fall upon her like an animal. He had far more finesse than Stamash, after all. Besides, it was more than love-making he wanted. Understanding, love, gentleness, and a sense of permanency were what he longed for.

For an endless time they lay locked together. Time stood frozen as they explored each other's mouth. This was what she wanted, Jessie thought. To be with him like this. For now, for the next ten years. For a lifetime.

"Marry me, Jessie."

Jessie thought for a moment that it was her own inner voice whispering, but it was Corbin. "What did you say?"

"I said, marry me. We can stand before the preacher today."

"Today?" Although it was what she wanted more than

301

anything in the world, she shook her head from side to side. "No." Once again she was denying not only Corbin's wish but hers as well, and yet what else could she do? She would never marry a man under false pretenses and yet were she to marry him now that was exactly what it would be. He thought her to be a respectable girl, one who made her living roping cows. How cheated he would feel when he learned the truth—and then he would hate her. Oh, she'd seen such things happen before.

"This time I won't take no for an answer." As if trying to tempt her he traced a path with his tongue from her neck to her ear lobe. "Say it. Say that you will. You shouldn't be staying at any boardinghouse, no matter how fancy it is. You should be living at the ranch with me." He gave a long, shuddering sigh as he brought her hard against his body. "Well?"

She didn't answer and her silence troubled him. Was he being foolish to think they could begin again where they left off? Three months was a long time and yet it hadn't dimmed his feelings any. But what of Jessie?

"Is there someone else?"

"No!" She answered that question very quickly. "I love only you, Corbin."

His entire body relaxed at her response and he nuzzled her hair. "Well, then. . . ."

Her heart was in her throat, her knees felt weak, her hands were all a-tremble. She wanted to act recklessly, to tell him yes and take her chances, and yet when she answered it was in a breathless voice talking sense. "I need time to think. Marriage is forever, Corbin. At least it would be for me."

"Time?" Why was it the thing he wanted so very much seemed to be eluding him? Any other woman would have said yes, but not his Jessie. Perhaps that made her all the

302

more precious. "How much time?"

"I don't know," she answered truthfully. At least as long as it took for her to make certain that her past could be put behind her forever.

"I'll give you all the time you need," he said, stroking her cheek, "but I'll give you fair warning that I intend to woo you with a vengeance meanwhile."

"I want you to." Tomorrow. Tomorrow she would let reality touch her, but for now it was a lovely spring day and they had the whole day to be together. The happiness of the moment would have to suffice and keep her satisfied until she could give him her answer.

Chapter Thirty-one

Jessie awakened to the sweet fragrance of flowers. With a drowsy smile on her face she sat up in bed, hugging her knees, and let her eyes scan the room. When all was said and done it seemed she had the same soft streak as other women had for green leaves and bright posies. Corbin had been true to his word to pay court to her ardently. He had sent her flowers, so many that they filled her whole bedroom, and bestowed on her so much candy that she thought surely every candy jar in town must stand empty. She couldn't help but feel happy and content. The world was a much happier place now that she was in love.

Love. It was not tangible, yet Jessie thought at times that she could nearly reach out and touch it. It enfolded her, warmed her. Though she had always valued her independence there were times when she was overcome with a fierce desire to follow Corbin to the ends of the earth if necessary. To tread in his footsteps, to share in his dreams.

And he wants me to be his wife, she thought. It was the answer to all her hopes. Hadn't she loved him from the first moment she'd seen him hovering over her after chasing those bullies away? Yes. Even then she had known how very special he was to her. Why then hadn't she shouted out "Yes!" emphatically when he'd asked her to marry him? Because the sight of that badge had addled her and reinforced her fears that Corbin would find out she'd roamed with outlaws. Certainly he was in a position to learn what she had done. But would he? Could she possibly be so clever that he would never be the wiser? Could she bury the past and start all over again?

The feelings that stirred inside her breast for Corbin were certain to plunge her into turbulent waters and yet wasn't he worth the risk? He wanted to *marry* her! Determinedly she shoved aside the dark misgivings that entered her mind and clung to her gentler feelings. She did love him. Right now that was the only important thing. Her mind, her heart, the very core of her being, longed for him. Her answer must be yes.

The days she'd spent with Corbin had been the most blissful and contented of her life. They had gone for long rides in an open-topped buggy and for walks in the moonlight. Just being with him made her smile. The hours seemed to fly by as the sweet harmony that had first blossomed between them now flourished. There was a romantic side to Corbin that deeply touched her. When she was with him she felt special. He said over and over again that there was "just one Jessie" and that she belonged to him.

Life couldn't get any more perfect than this, Jessie thought. And all the while the idea of saying "I do" became all the more alluring. Jessica MacQuarie. It sounded perfect. She found herself absent mindedly scribbling it over and over every time her hand held a pencil or a pen. Mrs. Corbin MacQuarie.

Though she'd always prided herself on having her feet planted firmly on the ground, unless she was riding that was, Jessica seemed to be floating now. Indeed she was so intent on her thoughts, that she didn't even realize she'd gotten out of bed until she found herself staring into the mirror.

"Moonstruck," she said aloud, remembering a term Wade had always called it. Oh, yes, she was moonstruck. A soft laugh escaped her throat as she splashed water on her face.

She dressed feeling an intoxicating burst of happiness, knowing full well the reason she was up before the sun even touched the sky. It was because she wanted to spend every waking moment with Corbin and thus had told him to call for her when the first light of dawn peeked over the horizon. Today was special. Corbin was taking her to his ranch. He had told her that he had a surprise for her.

A surprise. Well, she had one for him, too, she thought, pulling a buff-colored leather riding skirt over her hips and lacing it up the side. She'd been doing a whole heap of thinking, running the matter of saying yes to him over and over again in her mind. Today she was going to give him that answer.

There was an urgency in her movements as she returned to the mirror to "gussie up," as she called it. She wanted to look as pretty as he was always telling her she was. Maybe because of that her hand trembled as she brushed her hair, a hundred strokes, so it would shine. Impatiently she tried to arrange her unruly curls into a semblance of order. They seemed to have gone askew so she brushed her hair a dozen times more, until the crown of her tresses lay flat and smooth. She wasn't about to give in to ribbons or hair pins but she did renege on using two combs to hold her thick auburn hair back from her face.

Critically she assessed herself in the mirror when she was finished. The "V" cut of her blouse emphasized her bosom, the wide belt showed off her slim waist. There wouldn't be a man in Rye Grass Station who would take her for a boy today.

Her skin looked flawless, a result no doubt of Marie's urging that she use buttermilk masks at night. A small dusting of freckles had all but disappeared. She pinched her cheeks just as Marie had told her to do, bringing a hint of pink, then licked her lips to make them glisten. She was ready, and just in time, too. She could hear footsteps coming up the stairs. Though she was expecting Corbin, the tap at the door made her heart beat as steadily as a drum nonetheless.

" 'Morning," he said, bending his head to touch his lips to hers in a gentle, lingering kiss.

" 'Morning." There was a sparkle to his blue eyes that she hadn't seen before, not since his brother's death. It made him all the more handsome. "You seem in a cheery mood. I'm glad."

"I am." Without saying another word he took her hand and led her out of the boardinghouse, down the street along the boardwalk into the stables. There her pinto stood in a stall, already saddled with the most beautiful hand-tooled leather and silver creation she had ever seen. "For you. In remembrance of the saddle you so unselfishly granted to me."

"Corbin!" From the looks of the handcrafting it must have cost a fortune. She couldn't help worrying that Corbin had spent too much. Could he really afford anything so fine, what with the expense of his ranch and all?

"You like it? It's a California saddle. Shorter and lighter than the one you had."

"Like it?" Jessie had never seen anything so fine. She ran her hands from the cantle down to the silver stirrup. Carefully crafted and lovingly maintained, a fine saddle was often one's proudest personal possession. "Of course I do. But you . . . you shouldn't have."

"I wanted to." Though she had never said so, Corbin had the feeling that Jessie had had to go without some of the finer things of life. He wanted her to have such things now. He wanted to spoil her.

She threw her arms around his neck and hugged him hard. "Thank you. Thank you." Except for Wade, no one had ever given her such an expensive present before. She was deeply touched. He had shown over and over how much he cared. She was the luckiest girl in the world to have Corbin MacQuarie's love and well she knew it.

"It was just a little something I had made to show you how very dear you are to me. You are, you know, Jess." Undeniably she held his heart though he doubted if she even realized how much. Indeed she was a wonder of continued delights. He enjoyed being with her, getting to know her for the determined, honest, loving young woman that she was.

Ah yes, Jessie was everything he'd ever wanted in a woman. She had strength yet with a certain softness, she was sweet but with just the right amount of spice. She was trusting without being naive, companionable but never demanding, anxious to listen to his point of view yet never afraid to voice her own if she disagreed. Not only was Jessie the only woman in the world for him but she would make a good wife to a man whose life was ranching.

He watched now as she pulled herself up on the horse from the left side, relieved to see that his measurements had been accurate. There was just the right distance from horn to cantle to fit her well-curved bottom. The saddle couldn't have suited Jessie better if she'd been born in it.

"Oh, Corbin, it's perfect. And so beautiful I could cry . . ." She blinked back her tears.

"I spent the night in town last night just to be near you," he smiled, "and so we could get an extra early start to the ranch. Hope you aren't too hungry for breakfast. I thought we'd wait until we got to the ranch. Archie makes flapjacks that are as light as a feather."

"Then come on! Care to race me through town to the signpost?" With a shake of her head she offered him a challenge.

"The signpost it is." Pulling himself up on his own horse, he followed after her. The early morning silence was broken by the sound of pounding hoofbeats. Corbin guided Rebel at a frantic pace over the uneven road in a wild ride. As he followed after Jessie he couldn't help but hold an admiration for her horsemanship. It was all he could do to keep a horse's length behind her. When at last they came to the signpost he couldn't deny that she had won. "That's mighty fine riding, woman."

"If there is one thing I can do well, it's ride," Jessie stated proudly, her breath coming in deep gulps as if she and not the horse had run the pathway.

Corbin reined in beside her. "Why did you stop?"

She giggled, a joyous sound. "Because I don't know where I'm going from here. I've never been to the Rolling Q. Guess you'll have to take the lead."

"I guess I will." Corbin looked at the lovely auburn-haired woman beside him, feeling a surge of pride. Somehow he'd convince her to marry him. It was at the

309

moment his greatest desire.

A blaze of sunshine gilded the sky as they rode the many miles, steadily climbing the ridge of the hills that led to the ranch. The trees were just beginning to show their leaves and from a distance a labyrinth of streams was visible slicing through the high pastures. It was a bold panorama.

Against the stark blue, cloudless sky the buildings that formed the Rolling Q stood out like a welcome fortress. Three or four of the ranch hands were visible in the walkways between the corrals, others were tending the horses. "Well, here we are," he said proudly.

"Oh, Corbin . . ." Jessie was clearly impressed, though surprised by the size of the ranch. Indeed, she fell in love with Corbin's ranch right from the start. "Corbin, I knew your ranch would be nice, but not anything as elaborate as this."

"Only shows what good, hard work will do." He pointed to the largest structure. "That's the ranch house," and to a long, narrow one-story building about a quarter of a mile away, "and that's the new bunkhouse. And I've got maybe a dozen or so line shacks scattered around for when the men are out gathering strays. But then you'd know all about that."

There were a number of smaller buildings too, and pole fences that enclosed the corrals and walkways. It looked like a small village from the hillside. And milling about was the most important thing of all, Corbin's herd of cattle. A healthy herd, Jessie thought, as they urged their horses closer.

"Allow me to show you my pride and joy. The reason I was going all the way to Colorado," Corbin said, heading for one of the enclosures. A large, reddish brown, shaggy-haired bull raised his head as they rode up. Stamash. My brother's foreman sent him here by rail to stay on the Rolling Q for awhile."

"That's Stamash?" He was the most unusual bull that Jessie had ever seen. "You told me he was shaggy but I never realized that he would actually have such long, thick hair." It covered his back and fell into his eyes, making the animal look a bit comical at least until he ambled regally over to the fence as if to return her scrutiny.

"The winters in the Highlands are brutally cold. The cattle and the horses have a thick covering to protect them. I've heard about the brutal winters here, the kind that wiped out so many herds a few years back. I'm hoping by breeding Stamash here with some of the cows I can produce a herd that can withstand the winters."

"And will the calves have his shaggy coat?" Jessie reined in her horse alongside the fence and leaned down for a closer look. Oh, yes, Stamash was fascinating all right. She couldn't help wondering what Wade would think of him.

"The calves we've produced on my brother's ranch in Colorado were a duke's mixture. Some resembled their mothers, others were a combination. But every once in a while we produced an animal that looked a great deal like him. Big, strong, longhaired, and with a fearsome stamina." Corbin's arm swept towards the large beast. "What do you think?"

"I think he is wonderful." As if thanking her, Stamash made his voice heard, a deep throat noise that was echoed by a few of the cows. "And I'm anxious to help when the calves are born." She lowered her eyes from Corbin's suddenly steadfast gaze. "I guess that's my way of telling you that my answer to your proposal of a few days ago is *yes*."

311

"You will marry me!" Corbin didn't even try to hide his joy. Taking off his Stetson he waved it in the air, whooping so loud that it brought two of the cowboys to the corral.

"Something wrong, boss?" The one with outwardly curved legs glanced at Jessie in curiosity.

Corbin shook his head. "No, Bowlegs. I was just expressing my pure undiluted exultation that this little lady has just said she would be my bride."

"Bride?" The large mouth opened wide as he dropped his jaw. "Ya don't say." Jessie sensed that he was staring and turned in his direction. Embarrassed at being caught looking, Bowlegs turned his eyes away with the muffled oath that he wasn't going to like it much.

"A woman *here?*" The younger of the two ranch hands wrinkled his nose. "She'll be wanting ruffled curtains at the windows and lace doilies on the tables."

"Now don't look as if you've just tasted a pickle," Corbin laughed. "Jessie here isn't like most women, are you, Jess honey?"

"Hell, no." Jessie cocked her head, letting the breeze ruffle through her hair. "I won't try to change your habits, boys. I won't make you give up your whiskey or poker, won't tell you not to spend all your money on Saturday night, won't make you dress up on Sundays." There was a subtle hint of mirth in her eyes and in the corners of her mouth as she grinned. "I'll let you swear when you feel the need. I might even join you in a few oaths when times are bad. There might be times when I'll lend a rope or a hand when you have a stubborn horse or calf."

"Jessie is no city woman. She knows all about ranching," Corbin explained.

"Is that so . . . ?" Both men expressed more interest in

312

the woman astride the pinto, taking note of the soft curves of her figure and the slender lines of her legs. "Well . . . mayhap it won't be *too* bad." Jessie took that as a compliment.

Corbin nudged his horse's flanks, moving Rebel away from the bull pen. "Come, on Jessie." He winked at her. "It's time for you to meet the man who keeps us all in line. Archie Jarvis, my foreman." They rode a short distance to the bunkhouse and there dismounted. As if being forewarned that they were on their way, the foreman was already walking in their direction to greet them. As he drew closer he lifted his forefinger to the wide brim of his tallcrowned, black Stetson.

"Howdy, ma'am."

Corbin dismounted, then aided Jessie, tying the horses to a large post. "Jessie, this is Archie. Archie, this is the young woman I've told you so much about."

"Pleased . . ." This time Archie Jarvis doffed his hat and bowed in Jessie's direction. "Damned if you ain't jus' about the prettiest thing I ever did see." He swatted Corbin on the arm playfully. "Well . . . ? What did she say? Don't make me stand around here guessin'."

"She said yes."

"Well, I'll be." Archie chortled his delight, then enfolded Jessie in a bear hug. "Welcome to the Rolling Q, little lady." He seemed genuinely pleased. "Ole Corbin here has had some mighty bad things happen of late but lookin' at your sweet face I'd say his luck is changing for the best." He pounded Corbin on the back. "I'd say you was mighty lucky now."

"Perhaps the most fortunate man alive." Corbin caught Jessie's hand and squeezed it affectionately.

"Well then, when's the big day?" Archie's brows shot up in question.

313

Corbin's gaze poignantly searched Jessie's face. "I'll leave that to the lady, but I'm hoping she won't keep me waiting very long." Oh, how he wanted to be alone with her, to give full vent to the passion he had been keeping so tightly in control. Purposefully Corbin had avoided making love to her, waiting for her decision, but now she had told him she would become his wife. He knew the perfect spot to initiate their love-making again.

It was to that very spot he led her after breakfast, a secluded area several miles from the ranch house. Some of the pines had been cleared away to build a new bunkhouse for his ranch hands but along the stream there was a blanket of greenery. Not only were there cottonwood trees and ferns, but there were bear cherries, raspberries, gooseberry bushes, wild grape, and wild current. There was a clear rushing mountain stream across which an immense pine log had fallen, forming a bridge. Taking Jessie's hand, Corbin guided her cautioning her watch her step so she wouldn't tumble into the water below.

The small clearing lay still in the early morning sun, undisturbed by anything but a flock of bluejays that fluttered and took to the air as Jessie and Corbin interrupted their solitude. Surrounded by a clump of trees it was a perfect lover's nest.

"Corbin . . . ?" His name was smothered by a deep, leisurely kiss as his mouth claimed hers. Her mouth opened to him as she closed her eyes. His kiss left her weak and filled her with that familiar tingling sensation, a heat that centered from the womanly core of her and spread all the way down to her toes. It was the kind of kiss she had been so hoping for, the kind that was a prelude to the wonders they had shared in that tiny little cabin in Wyoming.

Corbin drew a rasping breath as he lifted his mouth

from hers. "That's just to show you how happy you've made me by saying yes, Jessie." Corbin realized that what he had always wanted was someone who really cared about him. Jessie did. Each day they had spent together reaffirmed how important she was to him, how important they were to each other. Taking her hand he pulled her down to sit beside him on the bank.

"Mmm. It's so peaceful here." Jessie leaned her head against his shoulder, wishing so very much that he would make love to her. During the past few days they had spent the time in kissing, caressing and cuddling but she wanted more.

"I am blissfully content." His lips caressed her forehead, then moved down her temple to kiss each closed eyelid in turn. He lifted her hair from her nape with stroking fingers, tracing a path to her ear. The touch was followed by warm, exploring lips that sent shivers up and down her spine. They lay side by side looking out at the churning water. The ground was hard, the grass prickly, but they hardly noticed.

"Somehow I feel as if I really do belong here. With you . . ." She drew her head back to look up at him, her eyes shining with a special glow.

With infinite care, Corbin brought his mouth down to capture her lips again. Slowly he unfastened the buttons at her throat, putting forth a tantalizing invitation. "Have you ever gone skinny-dipping?" he asked.

Jessie blushed but answered truthfully. "Billy and I used to go to a secret pool all the time when we were little but then when he took to staring, I didn't go there any more." She arched toward him as he moved over her, caressing her. His lips traced a fiery path down the curve of her neck to her just-bared shoulder. "Mmmm. Oh, Corbin, don't stop what you are doing. . . ." His touch warmed her as surely as did the sunshine.

"You taste good." Deftly he removed her blouse and brought his head down to kiss the soft mounds of her breasts, gently taking a rose-tipped peak in his mouth, savoring it. Soft moans of pleasure floated around them and Jessie suddenly realized that they came from her own throat. Her hands clutched at his hair as she pressed against him.

Unmindful of the rocks and twigs, they lay side by side, contenting themselves in the pleasure of touching, of kissing. Weeds tangled in her hair but she shook them loose with a vibrant toss of her head. Then her arms went around his neck, answering his kisses with sweet, wild abandon.

"Oh, my darling, darling Jessie." Rolling over on his back Corbin reached for her hand, drawing her up to her knees. A quiver of physical awareness danced up and down her spine as he brushed his lips against her hair. "This means I love you." He nuzzled her throat. "And this." His mouth traced a path from her collarbone to the tip of her breast. "And this," but then he pushed her away. "We had best go for that swim while we are able," he said with a grin.

They walked side by side to the water, a spot where fallen trees and rocks formed a sparkling pool. A gush of water bubbled over the barricade to form a narrow waterfall that journeyed on downstream.

"I have to warn you," she said playfully, patting his face with the tips of her fingers, "that I'm as good at swimming as I am at riding a horse. Want to race?"

Jessie removed her shoes and stockings, then slipped her dress over her head. She stood in just her drawers and breast protector, then ever so slowly she removed these, too.

"You little imp." He patted her on her now-bared bottom. "All right. I'll race you across the pool and back."

She watched as Corbin stripped off his own clothes, couldn't take her eyes off him, the broad chest with its thick hair, the flat stomach, the lean, taut flanks from which sprang that part of him that gave her such ecstasy. His muscles rippled with strength as he moved, radiating a virility that was very stirring. "And what will be the stakes?" she asked breathlessly. Jessie trailed her foot in the water, expecting it to be cool but in fact the water was rather warm.

"Whoever wins can name a date for the wedding. Agreed?"

"Agreed." She sprinted into the water with Corbin close behind. The water was deeper than she had anticipated and her head went under the water. She came up sputtering, but soon gained on Corbin's lead. Her body was lithe and strong from years of using her arms and legs, and she soon caught up with him. Her strokes were powerful, but though she came within a hand's length, Corbin won.

"Next Sunday," he called out triumphantly.

"Sunday?" It was so soon. She would have preferred to wait until after Butch and the others pulled the coal company robbery so Wade could be present. Perhaps, after all, it would be better if he didn't attend the ceremony. It would not be wise. Wade would understand.

"You said the winner could choose."

"So I did. Sunday then." A sudden melancholy swept over her, a prick of fear. Marriage was what she wanted but the idea was strangely frightening, too. To belong to someone forever. Oh, how she wished that Aggie could be here so that they could indulge in a little girl-talk

317

before she said her final "I do's."

Pushing himself through the water with strong, bold strokes he closed his hands around her shoulders, pulling her to him. The buoyancy of the water aided him as his arms captured her in an embrace. Mmm, Sunday. I can hardly wait." His eyes were drawn to the soft swelling of her breasts and he bent his head to kiss her there. "And then we can spend every day of the spring and summer here together."

"Together . . ." It was a word that held the promise of everlasting happiness. Jessie's slim form floated toward him and they blended their bodies in an intimate caress, the water intensifying the sensual allure they had for each other. Beneath the water he stroked her belly, her thighs, then moved to the soft hair between.

Lifting her arms she encircled his neck, wound her fingers in his damp, golden hair. For an endless time they clung together, their wet bodies touching intimately as the water swirled around them. Corbin's probing maleness replaced his hand, slipping hotly against her thighs, then teasing the entrance to her softness. He held her to him for endless moments while spasms of exquisite pleasure sent rippling waves through her, a feeling mirrored in Corbin's expression. For a timeless moment she stared into the depths of his dark blue eyes. Glorying in the closeness with him it seemed to Jessie that at that very moment her heart moved with love.

"Ahhh, Jessie." He lifted her from the water and hastened to carry her to the bank. There he pulled her down beside him on the soft grass. "You little minx. You're the only woman who has ever touched my heart, my soul, my body this way. With liquid fire."

The moments that passed were a soul-ravaging maelstrom of kissing, caressing and touching, culminating in an unstoppable tidal wave of desire. Wrapped in each other's arms they gave vent to the all-consuming passion that steamed between them. Jessica felt dizzying sensations course through her blood, like the sparks of a radiating fire, consuming her as she felt the firm touch of his hardened flesh entering her moist womanhood. She writhed under his touch, arching up to meet him as he rose over her, seeking the softness of her body.

When he glided into her it seemed to be the most natural, blessed thing in the whole world. She clung to him, her arms around his neck, her legs locked around his waist, answering his movements with her own. Corbin was her mate. The lines of separateness blended. She was incapable of holding any part of herself from him. She had to love him with all the strength of her devotion because she could give him no less than her whole self.

With her hands, her mouth, her body, she demonstrated the full potency of her love and he returned her affection in full measure. On the sun-washed grass she gave her heart to him and found a haven of passion and love. In the peaceful silence of the clearing they loved each other, their bodies joined, their hearts touching. He knew just how to touch her, how to bring her to the peak of pleasure again and again.

Jessie knew as they lay naked together that she was indeed a fortunate woman. She had soared above the clouds and she was racing toward the sun, there to burst into a hundred tiny sparks of flame.

Corbin gazed down upon her face, gently brushing back the tangled curls from her eyes. "Jessie." She was his now as surely as if they had already spoken the vows. Whispering words of love he made gentle love to her once more, watching her eyes as he brought himself within her once again. He saw the wonder written upon

319

her face that anything could be so glorious, and in that moment he was filled with a complete sense of contentment. The world was theirs for the taking. There was nothing that could ever come between them, or so he thought.

Chapter Thirty-two

Stars glittered as brightly as diamonds in the black sky. The warm air carried the pleasant scent of wild flowers and newly mown hay. The night breeze held the song of owls and crickets. Side by side Corbin and Jessie rode along the path to the stables; they felt contentedly sated and glowingly happy, though Jessie expressed some concern as to what they were going to say to Archie to explain their long absence. In truth, the hours had just slipped past them while they were blissfully entwined.

"I think Archie will understand," Corbin said with a smile, sliding from Rebel then politely coming to her side to give her a hand in dismounting. "He's not so old that he doesn't understand what it is like to be in love."

"He'll know what we were doing!" The cool night air caressed her suddenly burning cheeks as she led her horse through the thick wooden doors that Corbin had just opened.

"Mm hmm, he'll probably guess. Just one look at our grins and the sparkle in our eyes will give us both away." As she passed by him he reached out to run his hand over her delightfully curved derrière. "There won't be a man on this ranch who won't envy me. I want them to know."

"Corbin!" Jessie had never in all her life been shy but suddenly she was. "I . . . I don't want them to think I'm . . . well. . . you know. . . ."

"They won't think you're anything other than pretty and passionate." He brushed against her with a sigh. "Damn, but I am a very lucky man" The way that he said it, with such fierce pride, swept away any embarrassment she might have felt.

"Loving you is as natural to me as breathing," she said softly, struck by the wonder of it all. In just seven days' time she would belong to Corbin forever, to bare his children, share his life, work beside him. There would be a lifetime of glorious days like today.

She was in a reflective mood as she unsaddled Sagebrush, a mood that continued as she strolled hand in hand with Corbin to the house. The warm glow of happiness that she felt deep inside radiated from her eyes. As she looked at him from time to time, there was no need to say a word. What they felt for each other was like a current, flowing from one to the other. For them there were only two people in the world at the moment, at least until Archie's voice rumbled forth.

"So . . . there you are!"

"Here we *are*," Corbin answered, giving Jessie's hand a squeeze as he picked a telltale leaf from her hair.

"I was afeared you was gonna miss the wing ding. And it being in your honor and all." Archie winked knowingly at Jessie but in a manner that said he heartily approved of the day they'd spent together. Jessie had a feeling that she sincerely was going to like the grizzled old foreman.

"Wing ding? What wing ding?" Corbin's gaze moved toward the barn where lanterns flickered gaily, revealing a small group of the ranch hands gathered together.

"Wellll, when you gave me the news this morning, about Miss Jessie here marrying you and all, I took it upon myself to arrange a cookout and barn dance. To announce it formally to the boys and some of the neighbors." He pointed to where a chuck wagon had been set up a few yards from the barn. "I made sonofabitch stew, 'cause no one can make it like I can, and the cook made cowboy beans, red bean pie and sourdough biscuits."

Corbin didn't mind at all; in fact, he definitely approved. "You did fine, Arch. Just fine." It seemed like a good omen that Archie had taken to Jessie so quickly. Besides that, it would also be a good time for his ranch hands to become acquainted with his soon-to-be wife, for they would be in a jovial mood. His men worked hard and any change from the monotony was always welcome.

"Mm-mmm." Archie gave Jessie a gentle nudge. "Better hurry on up before the food's all gone. Them wranglers is hearty eaters." As he walked toward the chuck wagon with them he proudly talked of the great pains he had gone to to make certain the gathering would be a success. "Got us a good soundin' band—a banjo player, two fiddlers, one being myself, an accordian, a washboard player and ole Bowlegs is gonna play the jews' harp." As if by cue the band begun a lively tune. The music floated on the breeze and soon had Jessie's toe tapping.

Corbin left Jessie for only long enough to heap two plates with food, then he returned to her, whispering in her ear, "I told you Archie would understand. What's more he likes you, but then I knew he would."

"And I like him." As she ate she chewed thoughtfully. "He reminds me a little bit of Wade in the way he walks and grins." Jessie hadn't realized how hungry she was

323

before, but now she savored the stew and biscuits. "Besides, he's a good cook," she mumbled with her mouth full. "Wade makes sonofabitch stew but it's not as good as this."

"Archie cooks when he has the time, less now that we have a full time cook. Now the boys will be expecting some home cooking once in a while. Good thing you practiced up on rabbits," Corbin teased in reference to their time together in the tiny cabin when that had been their usual fare.

"A friend of mine named Aggie's taught me a few things." She lifted her chin pridefully. "I had plenty of time on my hands this winter to learn how to please a man's stomach. You just might be surprised." Finishing up the food on her plate she diligently picked up a handful of dirt and wiped the plate clean, roundup style, then set it on the old barrel that was being used to collect the soiled dishes.

"I doubt you'll have to cook much, Jess. If I have my way you'll be spending your time by my side." Corbin's eyes softened as they touched on her.

"That's where I want to be." Jessie laughed, lowering her voice conspiratorily as she confided, "To be truthful I just don't have much hankering for being in the kitchen, unless that's where I'll find you." Wrapping her arms around his waist, Jessie was content just to stand beside Corbin as he finished his meal.

"Ooo-eee, just look at you two lovebirds." Fiddle in hand, Archie was busying himself, pulling at the pegs and plucking at the strings to get the instrument in tune. "Just lookin' at you makes me feel a whole lot younger. I might even try a dance or two."

"Not with my girl you don't." Corbin wrapped his arm around Jessie and pulled her closer. "I want to keep her all to myself."

"Then I expect you might have a bit of quarreling on your hands, son. From what I hear the boys are lining up inside, just waiting to dance with your soon-to-be missus." He pointed toward the barn door where several young men loitered about glancing every now and then at Jessie. "Sportin' their best shirts and breeches. Combed their hair every one. Hell, Bowlegs even shaved off that prickly stubble on his chin." Archie chuckled, turning to Jessie. "Usually we can't even get him to take a bath, but he was the first one in line at the tubs today. Yes sir, looks like we're gonna have a whole heap of changes around here. At least we'll have the cleanest ranch hands in all of Utah."

Archie led the way to the barn, a huge weather-worn structure of rough-hewn lumber painted a light brown. Inside were stacks and bales of new hay, placed around the room to act as benches or piled neatly in the hayloft for those who wanted to look down on the doings from above. Corn meal had been sprinkled on the floor to make it smoother for dancing. "Guns, please . . ." Archie had instructed one of the newer ranch hands to collect the guns at the door, just to make certain there wouldn't be unnecessary trouble. While they were inside the barn their holsters would be empty but when the men went outside they could retrieve their weapons again.

"Sometimes a man gets all liquored up and starts a fight," Archie explained to Jessie. "This way we won't be burying any of the fellas. Good ranch hands are hard to replace."

A few of the ranch hands had brought young women. Corbin recognized two of his neighbor's daughters wearing brightly-colored calico and a local school teacher bundled in her shawl, as well as a few of the town's bawdy women showing off their décolletage. Jessie was amiable to each of them, welcoming every guest with a show of natural charm that would have put the haughtiest society matron to shame.

Corbin was well-pleased with the reception Jessie was being accorded. It didn't seem that there was even one ranch hand who wasn't taken with her. Everywhere she wandered through the throng she was greeted warmly and with enthusiasm. It promised to be a pleasant and fun-filled evening.

Jessie danced the first dance with Corbin, a simple, rollicking dance called the "circle of fire" in which everyone joined hands and moved first in one direction, then in the other. Faster and faster the music played until the dancers were nearly flying over the floor. When at last the music ended Jessie was breathless, yet she didn't have even a moment to rest. A blonde-haired ranch hand pulled her out onto the dance floor for the Virginia reel. Next came another ranch hand, and then another.

"Swing your partner, now do-si-do your corner lady and promenade her home," sang a booming voice, putting them through their paces. Corbin recognized Gus Chittem from the nearby Sundown Ranch as the man doing the calling. He recognized someone else as well. For some reason or other Art Conners was here, though his shining silver badge was not visible.

"Spying on Jessie," Corbin said beneath his breath, irritated by the notion. It was apparent that it was for exactly that reason the sheriff had come, for his eyes followed Jessie everywhere. Corbin wished suddenly that he'd ripped that ridiculous sketch from the sheriff's hands when he'd had the chance and torn it into shreds. Jessie an outlaw indeed! It was so utterly foolish that mirth soon pushed away his anger and he found himself laughing.

"It's good to hear you laugh like that, son," Archie said, pausing from his playing to rosin up his bow. "You've been wearing frowns much too long." Tucking the fiddle securely beneath his chin, Archie moved his bow back and forth in a rousing melody, accompanied by the banjo and jews'-harp.

Squares formed quickly. Corbin saw Jessie wave at him from the middle square and he waved back. Everyone around him began to clap their hands and he joined in. As the music played on, the dancing moved faster and faster and the caller talked faster and faster. With a frustrated laugh the entire square fell to the floor in an exhausted, giggling heap.

Jessie was having the time of her life. What was more important, however, was the feeling that she truly did belong here. Archie gave promise of being a confidant and friend and the other ranch hands seemed more than willing to accept her. She'd even been able to give one young cowhand some advice on how best to break a spirited young colt by hand-feeding it, talking to it soothingly and earning its trust. She cringed to think that her silly, silly fears had nearly made her act so cautiously that she might have lost Corbin forever. Instead she was soon going to be his wife. It was a heady thought, like being lightheaded from drinking too much whiskey.

"Dance?" A tall, skinny cowboy held out his hand but Jessie shook her head. She had danced herself into exhaustion and needed a breath of fresh air. She looked around for Corbin to accompany her. When she saw him talking to a stocky man with a long, curling black mustache, she stepped outside alone.

The night air was cool with just the right hint of a

breeze that stirred through Jessie's hair. Looking up at the sky she could see the Big Dipper and she tried to calculate the time by its position near the North Star. On clear evenings a man riding night herd could tell quite accurately when to come off shift by the position of the Big Dipper as it rotated around the North Star. By Jessie's figuring it was ten o'clock.

As she looked up at the stars she had plenty of time to think of her future with Corbin. A wedding. I have to prepare for a wedding, she thought. Everything had happened so fast that the thought hadn't really settled in her brain until now. She didn't even have a proper dress. There were so many preparations to make. Oh, how she wished that Aggie were here. If she remembered correctly she'd need something borrowed, something blue, something new and something old as well. And a bouquet . . .

Putting her hands behind her back Jessie strolled the path behind the barn deep in thought. She barely noticed the man that stepped from behind a bush until he grabbed her by the wrist. "Jessie, it's me. Don't make a sound."

"Billy!" Of all the people she had expected to see here, he was the last. "What in tarnation are you doing here?"

"I might ask the same of you."

So he didn't know, she thought. Well then she wouldn't tell him everything. What she planned to do with her life was none of his business. "I m here at a barn dance with a . . . a ranch hand."

"Well, if you've got your eye on any of the cattle here you'd best look elsewhere. I've already made my pick." He swaggered a bit as he walked around and around her. "My, my, my, if you don't look pretty, Jessie! You look so fine that if you treat me right I just might be tempted to cut you in on the deal."

"No! Please. Get out of here." She pushed at his arm. "Far, far away, Billy. If you tangle with the owner of this ranch you'll wish you hadn't." Dear God, she had to do something to stop him. She couldn't just stand by knowing he was going to steal from Corbin.

"I'm not afraid!"

"Well, you should be. Corbin MacQuarie has been made a deputy. A lawman, Billy. You'll find yourself dangling from a rope." Jessie's eyes searched the darkness. Was Billy alone or was he with someone else? The last she'd heard he had left the Wild Bunch and was working on his own.

"Don't matter. We have a lawman on our side, too. As a matter of fact, he's the one paying Ross and me good money to do our stealin'." Just as always, Billy was pridefully cocky. He was even so bold as to press his lean body against hers. Holding a handful of her auburn hair in his fist he held her head still as his mouth moved toward her for a kiss. Jessie tried to pull herself free but only by turning her head away was she able to escape his lips.

"You leave me be, Billy," she warned, clenching her hands into fists and beating at his chest.

"You gonna scream?" Although he could have forced her to kiss him, he let her go. "Bring the whole ranch down upon me, I don't care. Scream," he challenged.

She wanted to, but her apprehension about Billy being caught, and then giving her away as well, stilled her voice. She was in a quandary and well she knew it. "No. But I'll give you fair warning, Billy. If you dare to take one animal from this ranch, I'll see to it that you're found. I swear that I will. There are other ranches in the area. Leave this one alone."

He thought a moment, then shrugged. "All right. If it means so much to you, Jess." For just a moment she saw a glimpse of the old Billy in his eyes, but as if fearing she might see his vulnerability he stuck out his lower lip. "I'll take some cattle from old man Chittem's place instead. A steer is a steer."

"Oh, Billy. Have you ever thought of . . . well, just going straight? Of making your money honestly? The law's beginning to tighten up a bit. Squeezing in a little harder each day."

"Working?" He succumbed to a fit of low, throaty giggles. "Oh, Jessie, you are too much." In an attempt to demonstrate his newfound skill he drew his gun, twirling it by the trigger before sheathing it in his holster again. "Hell, I'll always be an outlaw and so will you."

"No. Not me. Wade and I are going straight. And so should you unless you want to dangle from a rope." In frustration she turned her back on him. Just as Wade had told her, she could see that Billy was just the kind of boastful fool that would get himself killed.

"If you ask me it's that so-called Pa of yours that you had best be concerned about. He's the one who will hang."

Jessie whirled around. "What do you mean?"

"Trying to hold up that Pleasant Valley Coal Company is just plain stupid. It's been tried before and every time the robbery has failed. And it will again. Just wait and see. Mark my word, Jessie. It's Butch, Elza and Wade you should be warning and not me. I know what *I'm* doing. Obviously they do not! If they did they wouldn't be walking right into a trap."

"A trap? What do you mean?"

Billy didn't answer, despite her frantic questioning. Taking off his hat he made a mocking bow. "Until we

330

meet again, Jessie. Next time I see you you'll beg for my kisses and my help. Just wait and see." Billy replaced his black hat, placed it low on his brow, dodged behind the same bush he had appeared from and disappeared from her view.

Chapter Thirty-three

The moon was ringed by clouds that seemed to take on threatening shapes as they rolled ponderously through the sky. Jessie stared out the small window at the darkened valley, troubled by her thoughts. She had spent the night at the Rolling Q, a restless night of tossing and turning.

Seeing Billy, knowing that he had cattle rustling in mind, bothered her and made sleeping difficult. Because of that reason she had suggested to Corbin that she stay until dawn and then ride back into town. In that way she thought to somehow protect him. He had been more than agreeable, though he had reluctantly given in to her plea that she use the guest room just to maintain a semblance of propriety. If the truth were told it wasn't for that reason at all but because she just wanted to be alone. She had to do a powerful lot of thinking about the situation.

"Damn Billy!" she swore. He had ruined everything. The cry of a faraway coyote shattered the stillness of the night and added to her mood of melancholy.

Hours earlier, after talking with the young outlaw, Jessie had gone back to the barn, but the giddy feeling of happiness and belonging had been dispelled by his words. Billy had brought her back down to earth from her cloud with a resounding thud.

Like a prowling tigress protecting her mate, she had stalked the grounds, keeping watch, but Billy seemingly had kept his word and moved on. There didn't seem to be any signs of disturbance. When all seemed peaceful, Jessie had sought the haven of her bed but sleep had not come and so she had spent much of the night pacing the hardwood floor. Billy's face was emblazoned in her mind. He loomed before her mockingly, his lips twisted into that taunting smile.

A chill breeze from the distant shadowy mountains ruffled the curtains. She shivered, wrapping her arms around her nude body. Billy had known very well that what he said about the coal company robbery would bother her. He'd meant it to. No doubt he was having second thoughts about leaving the gang. That was it. He was merely being vindictive. Somehow she sensed that he had always been more than a little bit jealous of Butch. The usually smiling outlaw was what Billy wanted to be. Hadn't he tried to emulate him all the time he was growing up? But Billy wasn't and never could be Butch Cassidy and now perhaps he knew that. In every way he fell short. And yet his manner had been so cocky. Disturbingly so.

"I know what *I'm* doing," he had said. "Obviously they do not. Holding up the Pleasant Valley Coal Company is just plain stupid. It's been tried before and every time the robbery has failed. And it will again, just wait and see." Why, the tone in his voice had sounded as if he wanted the robbery to be unsuccessful.

His taunt that Wade and Butch were walking right into a trap reverberated over and again in Jessie's mind. Was

Billy just talking or was he privy to some vital information? The more she thought about it the more she realized she couldn't take the chance that Billy was just jabbering. She had to ride into Price and warn them, just to be on the safe side.

But what about the wedding? She had told Corbin that she would marry him on Sunday. Would she have enough time to ride all the way to Price, talk to Wade and return in time? And what would Corbin think if she didn't? Would he be understanding if she stood him up at the altar? Would he listen to her explanations? She didn't want to take the chance that he would not. Marrying Corbin was the answer to her dreams.

And yet, I can't be so selfish as to think of only my own happiness when Wade's life is involved, she thought. If she didn't go and if Billy was right and Butch and Wade were riding straight into a trap, she would never forgive herself. What chance would she have for contentment then?

Jessie's body was as taut as a bowstring as she walked back and forth, her footsteps keeping time to her heartbeat. Her decision was a foregone conclusion. She owed Wade a great deal. He had taken her in and given her much more than food and shelter. He had given her love. She just couldn't turn her back on him now. She would ride into Rye Grass Station, change clothes and ride posthaste to Price. It was the only thing to be done.

By sunrise Jessie had her journey all planned. Hurrying to dress she opened the door and made her way down the hall, her eyes examining Corbin's home as she walked. Just like him it was rugged—wood, brass and leather with no frills. The only concession to luxury was a thick, tan carpet in the den. A man's home.

She could smell meat frying as she headed toward the

kitchen, but she was surprised to find Corbin and not Archie standing in front of the stove, turning bacon in a skillet.

" 'Morning, sunshine."

"Good morning." Her eyes felt dry and heavy, she ached in every bone. She was certain that her face must be ravaged from her lack of sleep but she tried her best to sound cheery.

"I missed you last night." Corbin plucked a cup from a peg on the wall and filled it from a large, steaming coffeepot. As he bent over her he couldn't help but notice how tired she looked. "I almost came to your room and crawled into bed with you but a promise is a promise. . . ." She looked at him as he spoke and he could see dark smudges beneath her eyes. "Jessie, is something wrong?"

"Wrong? No." For just an instant she had an urge to tell him what was bothering her. To take a chance on telling him about her past, but her fear of losing him overrode her need to talk it out. "Just a bit too much moonshine last night. I should have known better," she replied. In truth she'd only had one mug. There were times she'd partaken of much more.

"Or too much love-making yesterday." His eyes roamed her face and he felt a gentle stirring in his heart.

Jessie sighed. "I don't expect a woman could ever get too much of that. It's a wondrous feeling to be loved." She cocked her head pointing at the stove. "But I didn't think you ever spent time in the kitchen."

"I don't but this morning is special. Somehow I wanted to make breakfast for you. Just a way of showing you that I care." He touched her nose with the end of his finger. "But don't get spoiled. Just like you I don't much relish burning up pots and pans."

335

Despite his protestations Jessie had to admit that he had cooked the bacon and eggs just the way she liked them. His flapjacks, however, tasted a bit strange.

Corbin noticed her puzzled look. "Ran out of flour so I had to use corn meal."

"Corn meal?" Determined not to hurt his feelings when he was being so sweet, she covered them with syrup and ate every bite.

Finishing the meal she got to her feet. "I hate to eat and run but I'd best get an early start. There are a hundred things I've got to do."

"Like finding a wedding dress?" He dimpled as he grinned. "I already took care of that." At her surprised look he said, "I took the liberty of procuring the services of a dressmaker. I was taking a gamble that you would say yes."

"And I did."

"And you did." Taking her in his arms he nuzzled her neck. She was a woman to cherish. "And you have made me the happiest of men because of it." His mouth took hers in a hungry kiss that left her breathless. "Oh, Jessie. Jessie. I want to make you happy," he whispered when the kiss ended.

"You already have."

"Sometimes I love you so much it hurts." Corbin gave her a searching look, then looked away. When he looked at her again she was watching him closely.

"I'd never do anything to hurt you, Corbin. Please believe that." Suddenly she had nothing more to say and she felt strangely awkward. "I . . . I like Archie," she blurted. "And Bowlegs." She had taken an immediate liking to the tobacco-chewing, short, grizzled little man. "He told me his legs are permanently bowed like that because he's spent too many years upon a horse."

336

"Bowlegs can be a bit cantankerous at times but he's been more than a ranch hand. He's been a friend."

"And friends can be as valuable as gold." She had a faraway look in her eyes.

Seemingly out of the blue Corbin asked, "What is Wade like?" He remembered her saying that Wade reminded her a bit of Archie. The weathered, friendly face perhaps.

"Wade?" His question stunned her. It was nearly as if he could read her mind, had known just where her thoughts were.

"You said last night that you doubted that he would be able to come to the wedding. Is that what's bothering you, Jess?" Strange, but she very seldom talked about the man who had raised her. There were even times when she had a worried look in her eyes when he asked too many questions about her early years. Usually so open and talkative about so many things, Jessie was strangely closed when it came to her childhood.

"I was thinking about Wade, yes. He just got married. He's going to live on a small farm in Wyoming. There's so much to do that I'm certain he won't be able to come." She tried to lighten her mood. "I'll just have to find someone else to give me away."

"Archie will do it. He's a romantic at heart as I'm certain you've already found out." Corbin concentrated on his own breakfast, watching as Jessie cleared the dishes away. She made the offer to wash them but he shook his head. "We have such a pile of dishes already from last night that two more won't matter."

"Then I think I better be on my way." Now that the time had come she was reluctant to leave. She chided herself for being so foolish. She'd be with Corbin again. This ranch was soon to be her home.

337

"Can't you stay . . . for just a while longer?"

"No." By the time she got on the road it would be late enough already. "Although I'd like to . . ."

"All right. I won't tease." Even so he pulled her closer for one last kiss, his lips lingering on the soft fullness of her lower lip. Then hand in hand they walked to the stables. She decided to take the palomino since it was a faster animal. Corbin promised to watch over Sagebrush for her.

He helped her saddle "Sunbeam," then helped her to mount. "I still feel I should go into town with you." He felt a sudden, strong urge to protect her despite her strength. Jessie at times seemed as gentle as a wild deer, her eyes wide and mysterious, and yet at other times she was more like a cat who would fight if it was cornered.

"Come with me? No." His coming along would only complicate matters. "You have a ranch to run. I've already disrupted things enough."

"And yet you did have fun last night?"

"Yes . . . ! Oh, yes." She clung to him, overcome by a sudden fear that somehow her dreams would disintegrate before her very eyes. It was a feeling that she quickly banished from her mind, as she said a poignant goodbye.

The sun was peeking through the tree branches as Jessie left the Rolling Q behind her. It was a lonely journey which seemed much longer without Corbin to delight her with his presence. Once or twice she nearly took the wrong pathway but the years of riding the hills and valleys nearby came to her aid. Soon she could see the rooftops of Rye Grass Station. With a feeling of urgency she guided her horse to the stables, then walked up the road to the boardinghouse. She'd have to remember to tell Marie that she was getting married and wouldn't be needing her room after Sunday.

The boardwalk was crowded with the townspeople going to their jobs. Jessie spotted two barbers, a seamstress, and a blacksmith walking elbow to elbow down the main street. Johnny, from the saloon where she'd beat Corbin at billiards, offered her a friendly wave. Two of the girls from the boardinghouse who owned a millinery shop nearly collided with Jessie as she swept through the front door. Offering apologies, she took the stairs two at a time, fumbling for the key that she kept in her pocket.

It was strange, but as soon as she opened the door she had an eerie feeling that something was wrong. She sensed it in every nerve and sinew of her body. It was a feeling that was quickly proven to be justified as her eyes scanned her room.

It had been ransacked, as if a tornado had struck. Clothing was strewn about, her Sears Roebuck catalogue ripped in shreds. The closet was torn apart, the drawers of the little bureau beneath the washbasin pulled out and emptied of their contents. The bedcovers had been dumped in a heap on the floor, causing Jessie the greatest alarm. The money! Her share from the train robbery. Frantically she ran to the bed, thrusting her hands inside the mattress. She sagged with relief at the touch of the crisp paper bank notes and bills. It was there. It was still there. Whoever had put her room in shambles had not been as thorough as they had supposed.

Who would have done such a thing? *Billy* was the name that came to her mind. Who else would have cause to search her room? No one. But Billy must surely know that she would have the money with her. If he was down on his luck, what would keep him from trying to make off with it? He had seen her at Corbin's ranch, would have surely known that she would be occupied for quite awhile.

"Billy, you little coyote." It was a score she meant to settle with him. The only thing that tempered her anger was that he hadn't succeeded. And what should she do now? Take the money with her? No. It was a long, hard ride to Price. Put it in the bank? Hardly. The bankers weren't fools. She'd arouse questions having so much money on her person. Find a new hiding place? Her eyes darted from wall to wall trying to find a safe spot but she couldn't seem to find one that suited her. Then her gaze traveled to the mattress again. So far the money had escaped detection hidden where it was. Perhaps it would be best to just keep it there, at least until she returned. She'd tell Marie to keep a watchful eye on her door.

Mumbling every swear word the boys had ever taught her, Jessie straightened up the room. After what had happened here she knew her decision to ride to Price was the right one. Hell, if Billy would do a thing like this there was no telling what else he might do. He'd said something about keeping company with a lawman. What if he couldn't hold his tongue? Maybe the reason Wade and Butch were heading for a trap was because Billy had spilled the beans.

Jessie popped two buttons off her blouse in her haste to change her clothes. Her fingers were all thumbs as she unlaced the ties of her riding skirt. She exchanged her garments for the plaid shirt and breeches she had sworn she'd never wear again—then tucking her hair under the brim of her hat, she slipped from the boardinghouse to the stables.

Chapter Thirty-four

The heels of Corbin's boots made a staccato sound as he walked down the boardwalk of Main Street. He was in a foul mood, brought on in part by confusion and disappointment. Jessie was gone, had seemingly vanished out of the blue, and the lady at the boardinghouse didn't have any idea just where she had gone. His only consolation was that she was obviously coming back. Her clothes, her carpetbags, a Colt .45 and a large leather pouch holding a few of her possessions had been left behind.

Two days had passed since the party at his ranch and he had felt an urge to see her. With that thought in mind he had ridden into town like a lovesick swain only to be told that Jessie hadn't slept in her room for two nights. He had felt a rising panic, fearing for a moment that something might have happened to her. Upon going to the stables, however, he had found the palomino gone and the youngster who swept out the stalls had remembered seeing her head in a southerly direction. She was riding in a furious gallop, or so he had said.

And she didn't even leave me a note, he thought in annoyance. No word of goodbye, no explanation, no promise to be back in time for their wedding. All he could do was wait and hope with all his heart that his impetuousness hadn't frightened her away. Was it possible that Jessie had gotten cold feet, had decided that she wanted to keep her freedom? Certainly it had been *he* who had pushed the matter of her marrying him. When Henrietta had done likewise to him, hadn't he found the first excuse to leave town?

But this was different. He loved Jessie and she loved him. He couldn't believe otherwise, not after the long, passionate moments they had shared. Jessie would return. He had to believe that — or go mad! Patience wasn't one of his virtues but he had to give in to it now. There was no other way. In the meantime he wanted to have a long talk with Art Conners.

Entering the sheriff's office he found the lawman in his usual place, sitting with his feet propped upon his desk, hands behind his head. The slam of the door startled him and he swung his feet quickly to the ground, his hands poised at his gun handles.

"Oh, it's only you." Relief was etched on his face.

"Only me."

Art shrugged his shoulders. "I didn't mean any insult. It's just that . . . well . . . got myself a new prisoner and I'm a bit jumpy. He's sworn that his buddies will bust him out." The sheriff was always a bit edgy about a shoot-out. He was slow on the draw, but once his gun was clear of its holsters he could shoot the feathers off a duck. Problem was that with most outlaws speed was the main concern. All too often a man would shoot, then talk about it later.

"No offense taken." Though Art indicated a chair, Corbin remained standing. "I didn't have much of a chance to talk with you the other night at the ranch.

342

Hope you don't think I'm a poor host."

"Naw! I saw the way you were looking at that cute little filly you're taking to the altar so I didn't intrude." There was a pause and then he asked, "Are you sure you know what you are doing?"

"Quite sure." Corbin's mouth was set in a grim line as he remembered the way the sheriff had been staring at Jessie that night, watching her every move. He'd brushed it off that night because he was so happy, but now the reminder was a source of irritation and one of the reasons he had stopped by. "Look, I know a man hates to say he's wrong but I think it's time you fessed up to having misjudged her."

"Wrong?"

"Yes, wrong."

"Oh, but I'm not. Not at all . . ." The look of smug satisfaction upon his face riled Corbin anew.

"I'm gonna give you just two seconds to either make some explanation or offer an apology for that statement." Corbin raised his fist threateningly. "No one talks like that about Jessie. No one!"

"All right then, I'll spell it out. That little gal you're aiming to marry is an outlaw—a member of the Wild Bunch."

Once the accusation had made Corbin chuckle, but not today. Grabbing Art by the shirt front he brought him nose to nose. "You're either crazy, a fool, or a liar. Which is it?"

Pulling free of his grasp Art looked daggers at Corbin. "You're the one who is a fool if you can't see it. It's about as plain as the nose on your face. Ask some of the people in this town and they'll tell you about the company she used to keep. She strutted through town in those breeches as if she was hell on horseback. An errand boy for the outlaws was what she was. Getting their supplies for them when it wasn't safe for them to show their faces. And God knows what else she might have done for them. . . ." The implication was all too clear, an insult that lit Corbin's fuse.

"Why, you." A well-aimed punch to the jaw sent Art stumbling to the floor. "Take it back or by God you won't get back up." He wielded his doubled fist threateningly.

Rubbing his jaw Art glared up at his assailant. "Because of my friendship with your brother and all I'm going to forget that you did that and let bygones be bygones. I'll make allowances for the fact that a man isn't quite rational when his heart is in the keeping of a clever woman." Taking out his ring of keys he waved them in the air. "Here, take these. Open the second cell. I've got myself a prisoner you just might find interesting. A man you just might recognize and who will corroborate my suspicions. Man named Bob Meeks. Wanted for holding up that train you were on, among other things."

"That name doesn't mean a damn to me. . . ."

"It *will!*" Art challenged. "Go on! Talk with him. Or are you afraid of what you will find out?"

"I'm not afraid of anything," Corbin countered.

"He might have an interesting story to tell you about your precious Jessie Watson." Art was slow in getting up and when he did he side-stepped Corbin cautiously. When it looked as if Corbin's fury had subsided he stepped closer, holding out the ring of keys.

Corbin took them from Art's hand, then pushed through the thick wooden door that separated the jail cells from the sheriff's office. Slowly he walked by the string of cells. In the first was Buck Cratchet, the town drunk, sleeping off another binge; in the second, a man

344

in a red plaid shirt and brown hat was hunkered down in the corner, his face to the wall. Corbin ran the keys across the bars to get his attention.

"I'm not answering any more questions, you sonofabitch!" the man snarled, turning around. Corbin looked at the beady eyes of the man, the snarling mouth and recognized the man at once. How could he ever forget him? It was the man who had shot him, all right.

"That's him, isn't it?" Art came up behind Corbin.

"Yes, he's the man who shot me. But that doesn't prove a thing. A man might say anything to save his own hide. I wouldn't take the word of such a man. There's no way he knows Jessie. No way at all!"

Like a baited snake the man hissed, "Oh, yes I do. Jessie Watson. A little hellcat who's too big for her trousers. Wade Slatter's adopted brat! Butch Cassidy's little prodigy."

The name "Wade" caused Corbin to flinch for just a moment but just as quickly he recovered his composure. He wouldn't give anything a man like this said any credence. He trusted Jessie, had absolute faith in her. No matter what some two-bit renegade said, he wouldn't listen.

"You're grabbing at straws if you listen to someone like him, Art. You've been a lawman too long. You're beginning to see an outlaw behind any tree. I've said it once and I'll say it a hundred times if need be. Jessie is as honest as *I* am and I trust her. So give up your little game and leave her alone. Or you and I are going to have some serious trouble."

"She's one of us, I tell you," Bob Meeks shouted out. "I got a score to settle with that little vixen. Why should she be walking around free when I'm behind bars? If you want proof then find out what she did with her share of the money we took that day. Nine thousand dollars was what she was given. Same as me!"

"Now I know he's lying." Corbin turned his back. "Conners, you are a fool! And I'm an even bigger one if I stay here another minute listening to such rubbish."

"I don't think so. I think he's telling the truth." The sheriff yanked the keys from Corbin's grasp. "When I find that money I'll prove to you just who is being foolish."

"She's got a cut of the money, I tell you." Grabbing hold of the bars Meeks rattled the door of his cell. "She's one of the Wild Bunch. She and Wade Slatter."

"And I'm Jesse James!" With that Corbin turned on his heel. A tirade of loud oaths rang in the room as he slammed the door behind him.

Chapter Thirty-five

A sullen gray sky hovered over Castle Gate, a tiny town near Price, Utah where the soil gave way to stretches of unbroken rock and flat-topped mountains. Jessie sighed deeply as she scanned the small town for any sign of Butch's, Elza Lay's or Wade's horses. She had to find them as soon as possible, before it was too late and they put their plan into action. Billy's taunts urged her on.

Wearily she raised a hand to her brow only to encounter a sodden mass of auburn curls. It had been a long, hard ride, complicated when Sunbeam had thrown a shoe. She had been lucky enough to find a blacksmith in the little, nearby town of Hannah who had replaced the shoe, but the delay had cost her valuable time.

Riding into town she noticed how ramshackled it looked close up. Only a few of the wooden buildings had been painted and the paint was peeling on most of those. Of the five or six of the larger buildings only three bore signs. The Ace Saloon, Dry Goods, and Ralph's Butchers. Looking on down the street to the far side of town, Jessie could see a large rock formation. Beneath the rocks stood a two-story building with a huge sign above it. The letters were large enough to read even from where she stood. *Pleasant Valley Coal Company*. There it was, the object of her quest. By the way the town was situated so close, it appeared the town existed because of the company. Perhaps that was why it had been built right smack dab in the middle of nowhere. Well, she couldn't stand around gaping all day, she thought, moving on. She had to find her friends. With that thought in mind she had no choice but to visit the buildings one by one.

Jessie started with the Ace Saloon, going into each building on the way down the street. Seeing a second saloon at the edge of town, she thought to try it. She should have looked there in the first place, because it was right down the mountain from the coal company but she hadn't noticed it at first. It was smaller and not as colorful as the Ace. Its strategic location, however, made it a good bet that Butch would be using it as a lookout.

The usual hitchrail was in front of the saloon, so sliding off her mount, Jessie looped the reins of her horse over it. She didn't even bother to use the stairs but climbed up and over the rail to the building that bore a scrawling sign that said Bart's. Pulling the door open she stepped inside and scanned the smoke-filled room for any sign of Wade or the others.

The discordant, tinny sounds of a piano drifted through the room as a piano man busied himself with his tunes. It was early, so the bar was only partially filled, but that didn't stop the drinkers from elbowing their way to the long bar. Bart's was obviously the hub of this tiny town, or so it appeared from the patronage. It was a place for miners to spend their hard-earned money.

Jessie spotted Butch right away by the way his tawny-haired head was cocked at a familiar angle. His stance, the way he held his hat, all gave him away, at least to her scrutinizing eyes. He was at one of the gaming tables. He'd probably gotten into another poker game and lost, she thought. Despite his skill at so many things, Butch just hadn't learned how to play the game.

"Jess!" As she came near he nearly jumped out of his chair, he was so glad to see her. He explained to her that he was clean out of money and asked her for a loan. "Just until we finish our . . . uh . . . job," he said.

"Sorry, I can't help you, sir," she answered, carefully avoiding calling him by name. "You see I had a bit of trouble on my way here. Horseshoe and all. I gave nearly all the money I had to the blacksmith. I was gonna borrow some money from *you*."

"Is that so?" He was clearly disappointed but just as quickly flashed her the boyish grin that always warmed a woman's heart and made him so popular with the ladies. "Aw, Jess, I promised the boys that I'd bring back three bottles of Old Crow. One for each of us. I hate to break my word." He turned the pockets of his denims inside out. "I had a full house. I thought I couldn't be beaten."

Butch walked over to the bar to plead his case before the bartender and ask for credit. All the while the bartender kept right on polishing glasses with a large towel that doubled as an apron. In the end Butch had talked the bartender into giving him credit with the promise that he would send the money back to him. Though the bartender looked as if he doubted he would ever see the money, he gave Butch the whiskey anyway. Jessie knew that the man would be repaid. Butch was like that. He had a crazy sense of fair play. Here he was planning a robbery, and yet in the very same day he was worrying about incurring a debt and giving his word that he'd make good on his bill.

While Butch was busy with the bartender, Wade and Elza returned from what they called a "fact-finding" mission. Like Butch they were surprised but happy to see her. Wade gave her a bear hug.

"You'll bring us luck, I just know it Jess. You can partner up with me and . . ."

"I didn't come to join in, Wade. I came to warn you." Putting her finger to her lips she nodded her head in the direction of a table in the back room where they could have at least a measure of privacy. Wearily Jessie plopped down in a chair and Elza and Wade did likewise.

"Now what's this about a warning?" Elza asked.

Jessie told them about Billy's unwelcome visit to Corbin's ranch, about his taunts and his warning that they were walking straight into a trap. "He was grinning all the time he said it. I wouldn't be the least bit surprised if he might even have some part in it. You've got to get out of here."

Wade's expression was troubled and thoughtful. "I don't think Billy would side with the law, if that's what you mean."

"He said there was a lawman he was doing some stealing for. It made me awfully uneasy."

"Well, he can be a skunk all right," Elza mumbled, nervously tapping his toe, "but I don't believe he'd set us up to be hanged. He might know something, however."

As soon as Butch was through with the bartender he came over to talk and give his viewpoint on the matter. No matter how Jessie tried to convince him to forget the robbery, Butch's mind was made up. He was certain that they could succeed where the others had failed. "We're gonna get our hands on that payroll," he said, his blue eyes twinkling merrily. "We were gonna wait for awhile to pull the job but now it appears we'd better speed things

350

up a bit." So it was decided to do it right away.

Both Wade's and Elza's assignments had perfected their plan. On their way to the coal company, Wade had gone on ahead of the others to Price and Castle Gate, where he had studied the telegraph lines. It was his assignment to find points where they could cut the wire and leave the coal company helpless to send for the posse to help. It was of extreme importance to isolate Castle Gate from the sheriff's office at Price.

Wade sensed Jessie's deep concern. "Aw, Jess, it's perfect. The chance of a lifetime. Aggie and me won't ever have to worry about money again. I can't back out now!" Wade explained to her that the Pleasant Valley Coal Company was situated below a large rock formation, somewhat secluded from the town.

"I know. But it's not so secluded that it can't be seen from up the road a ways. I spotted it from there," Jessie said, her voice sounding harsher than she intended. She didn't want to scold.

"I've done a lot of investigating. The outside steps leading up to the office above on the far side of the building gives us the perfect setup. Nobody from the town can see anything that's going on from there."

"So I rode all this way for nothing?" Jessie put her face in her hands, so weary that all she wanted to do was put her head down on the table and sleep. Such a long, hard ride and yet they were going to be stubborn, foolish, and do the robbery anyway. She might have been angry if Wade hadn't been so enthused.

"I've done a lot of investigatin'. The large payroll is never delivered to the office on the same day. They stagger it. But the men are paid *every two weeks*."

"No doubt the delivery times have been altered to confuse the likes of us. I'm telling you, Wade, it seems to me

351

to be risky business." Jessie tried to talk some sense into his fool head but he was having none of it. The thought of "one last grand and glorious robbery" had turned his head.

To insure success Butch had ridden into Castle Gate and posed as a saddle bum looking for work. He had made his headquarters at Bart's and was usually seen lounging in the saddle when the afternoon train came in.

"The manager thinks he's smart, all right. But I've been watching. The paymaster delivers a signal. When the payroll is delivered a whistle is a signal for the workers to come to collect their pay." Wade told her that he had watched the paymaster come and go and had found that he brought the payroll in himself.

"Yep, he and two guards, each carrying a sack of money. One man for each of us to tangle seems fair enough," Elza Lay added.

Wade had figured out that the thirteenth day of the May was the next date for the money to be delivered and had told Butch they should strike then, but now it appeared the strike, would be *today*. The paymaster had left town on Tuesday and would return three days later by his calculations, which was this very morning.

"Today? Isn't that rushing things?" Jessie couldn't dispel her fear. "What if everything went wrong because they weren't ready?" Jessie just wasn't convinced. "I don't know. I just don't like it." Since meeting Corbin, Jessie just didn't view things the same way. Before, she had adhered to the boys' way of thinking that a steer here or there missing from a herd didn't really make that much difference. But Corbin's entire operation revolved around one bull—Stamash. He'd sent all the way to Denver for the animal. Not only that, he kept careful count of every animal in his herd.

Butch had said that it served the cattle owners right, losing an animal now and then. It was payment for the greed they had exhibited. Rustling was caused because their "pinch penny" ways had put many of the ranch hands out of work. He had said the cattle ranchers were a lazy lot, living off the work of other men. And yet Corbin was not like that. The ranch hands had told Jessie just how hard he worked.

And now they planned to rob a payroll. Hard working men would be cheated of their rightful due and this bothered Jessie. Robbing from the rich like frontier Robin Hoods was one thing but the matter of the coal company was another. No matter what she said, however, Butch, Elza and Wade could not be swayed. So Jessie went along with the express purpose of looking after Wade and making certain there wasn't any undue trouble.

Butch hid beneath the outside stairway leading to the second floor, where the paymaster had his office. Elza and Wade, who were hidden nearby, closed in. It was as quiet as a grave. The only sound was the ticking of a clock. Inside, a balding clerk in a scruffy brown suit looked up.

"Hand over the money," Jessie heard Butch's muffled voice say. Looking through the window she saw that he was holding a six shooter level with the paymaster's stomach. He looked deadly. Was it any wonder the man didn't argue but quickly handed over the money bag?

One of the guards started to run but Wade stuck out his foot and tripped him, sending the man sprawling to the ground. Wade carefully picked up the moneybag the man had dropped.

Elza pointed his .45 revolver threateningly, demanding the other guard to give up the money he was carrying.

Again the money was surrendered without a word. The guards and the paymaster knew they had no chance with three armed outlaws.

"Telegraph wires have been cut so help will be slow in arriving," Butch informed the men, insuring their cooperation. "Just do what we tell you and nobody is gonna get hurt. Stay where you are until we're well out of sight."

Butch backed away, past the inner office where Jessie could see two men sitting at a desk, one angrily thumping his desktop with stubby fingers. Jessie watched to make certain he didn't reach into the drawer and pull out a gun. That at least she could do for the boys.

As soon as Butch was gone the clerk hurried into the room, bent over and said something into the stoutest man's ear. "Shit!" she heard him respond. "All of it?" He stood with his thumbs hooked in his vest pockets, eyeing her from the doorway. Turning on her heel she quickly followed after the others, taking the steps two at a time.

Butch and Elza ran to their horses, swung up and galloped out before anyone could respond to the paymaster's shouts for aid. Their chortled shouts of glee let it be known they were well pleased with themselves. It was one more notch in Butch's ego.

"You fellas go on ahead," Wade said, trying to hide a limp. When he had tripped the guard he had twisted his ankle but he didn't want them to worry. "I need to say a word to Jessie before I ride on. Meet you back at Cassidy Point in Brown's Park. Don't worry, I'll be all right." He waved them on when they paused and turned around. "Go!"

"We'd better hurry, Wade. Here, lean on me!" Putting her arm around his waist and looping his arm over her shoulder, Jessie acted as a human crutch, helping Wade

354

hurry as fast as he was able. All the while she kept looking over her shoulder.

"My last job, Jess. But it's gonna make it possible for me and Aggie to live happy ever after."

"Happy ever after. . . ."

It was a struggle to get Wade up on his horse, but at last she was able to give him a hand up. She mounted Sunbeam and together she and Wade rode through the town. They guided their horses east, turning onto Main Street, then they headed north. Their destination was Spring Canyon. They moved quickly, quietly, hopeful that they would not be pursued. Suddenly Jessie looked behind her. She had no idea where the four horsemen had come from but they were like black specks coming closer and closer.

His horse was in a full galloping stride as Wade drew his gun and fired. "Jessie, get back!" he yelled. Gunfire echoed behind her and she looked back warily.

Jessie urged her horse off to the right out of the line of fire, but soon the entire valley was reverberating with shots. Jessie found herself right in the middle of the melee. Hugging the neck of her mount, she nudged the animal into a run. Glancing behind her she saw that a bullet had sent Wade's hat flying from his head. She saw a second rider sliding a rifle out of his saddle holster. As he shouldered the weapon Jessie screamed out a warning. "Wade, watch out!"

She watched in muted horror as Wade's horse was shot out from under him. The animal screamed, a shrill, high-pitched whinny of pain, and went down. Wade went down sideways and rolled clear of the flailing horse. Only by the greatest of skill did Jessie miss riding him down.

"Wade, are you hurt?" Jessie stared in horror. Slipping

355

off her own horse she ran to him. Wade's doomed horse lay on the ground, hooves pawing at the earth in its death run.

"Drop flat, Jess!" Wade's command reminded her of how vulnerable she was and she dropped to the ground. Rolling to one side she got up on one knee behind an old abandoned water barrel. Temporarily blinded by a blast fired right beside her, Jessie triggered off an unaimed shot from her Colt.

"Wade!" Jessie screamed. She saw him take cover just before a string of rapid shots struck the very spot where he had been. Jessie knew the tricks of evading enemies. She did not get to her feet but crawled on hands and knees towards shelter.

"We've got to hold them off and hope Butch and the others have heard the shots," Wade called out, leveling his pistol. Then the worst thing possible happened. Wade's gun jammed. He could not continue to fight. The spray of bullets sent the dirt dancing up. He was working himself away from his pursuers, ducking from rock to rock or hiding behind the trees. Water splashed and wood splintered as the bullets sought their mark.

There was only *one* horse. Jessie knew she had to make a quick decision. Wade was wanted by the Pinkerton agents and the sheriff in Heber City, Utah for the crime he had been charged with so long ago. If he was caught she had no doubt in her mind that he would hang. She, on the other hand, might very well be able to talk her way out of this difficult situation.

"Take the palomino, Wade, it's the only way. Take it and get the hell out of here!"

"Not without you. We'll ride together."

"And we'll be caught before we go a mile. Too much weight together." She insisted and at last he gave in to

356

her logic. Jessie would merely claim that she had gotten into the middle of the situation as a mistake. "Hell, I'll insist I was just taken as a hostage." It might work. She watched with a grim look on her face as Wade struggled upon Sunbeam's back. When he was safely out of sight she came out from behind a rock with her hands up, only to be immediately pushed to the ground and set upon by two of the men.

"It's all a mistake. I had no part in that robbery. I just got in the line of where you were going," she choked.

No one would even listen to her explanation. Every time she tried to speak she was told to keep quiet or suffer the consequences. Jessie suffered the every indignity the four men could muster and in the end she was tied up, thrown over a horse and marched off to jail. Still, she tried to keep her calm. The Wild Bunch had their own attorney, Douglas V. Preston. He was in Butch's pay and Jessie had no doubts that he would be sent to bail her out. But what of Corbin? He'd think she had stood him up at the altar. Oh, dear Lord, what was she to do? She had played heroine, perhaps only to ruin her own happiness. That was the thought that tormented her as she heard the cell door bang shut.

Chapter Thirty-six

The sun was hanging low in a cloudless sky. Corbin urged Rebel up a rise, reined the horse to a halt and stretched wearily in the saddle. Though it was early he was already tired, a result of pushing himself unmercifully, working until he was exhausted. It was his way of trying to alleviate the anxiety that nagged him about Jessie. It was Saturday and already she had been gone five days without even one word.

Corbin had searched the area, had ridden as much as fifty miles along the road the stable boy said he'd seen her take. Then he'd backtracked and chosen another road. Then another and another. There had been no sign of her and finally he'd returned to the ranch. Fearing that she might have come to some harm he had even initiated the help of Art Conners, but the sheriff had also come up empty-handed. At last Corbin realized that all he could possibly do was to wait and hope that come Sunday Jessie would return. It was the only thought that kept him going.

"She went to fetch her adoptive pa," he said softly to himself. It was a possibility he was counting on. A wedding was a special time in the life of a woman. When all was said and done she'd just flat out decided Wade was going to be there. The stubborn little gal had gone to get him. Come Sunday she'd show up with that cute little smile of hers and cheerfully say, "I do." That moment, Corbin knew, would be the happiest moment of his life.

Corbin looked down upon the cattle grazing on the rolling land, acres that stretched to the eastern horizon, and he thought how much his new ranch meant to him. With effort and determination he had turned the crumbling ranch house into a home, rebuilt the herd and made the Rolling Q a success. Even so he would have given it all up just to know that Jessie was safe, to have her here beside him.

He watched as Archie came into sight, riding around the corner of the barn and heading for a few of the steers. Archie paused for just a moment and waved cheerily to Corbin, then went on about the business of moving a few stragglers across the water to join the herd. Archie and several of the ranch hands had spent their hard-earned pay on new boots and fancy shirts just for the wedding. Oh, how he hoped they'd have use for them.

Corbin hadn't told Archie, Bowlegs or the hands about Jessie's disappearance. They had been so happy for him, so exuberant that he hadn't wanted to spoil their cheery mood. In preparation for the wedding Archie had even decorated the ranch house, "a welcome for the little woman" as he had said. Laughingly he had even told Corbin that if he were only a few years younger he'd have given him some serious competition for her hand. Old or not, however, Corbin knew his foreman was more than a bit smitten with the auburn-haired beauty. It made him doubly proud.

Corbin's thoughts were interrupted suddenly as he

spied a cow and her calf break from the herd and head for an area of rocky ground. Fearing injury to the animals, he touched his heels to Rebel's side and urged the big horse to follow after the calf and its mother. His hemp rope whirled overhead in a whistling sound, then as his arm flicked forward the loop shot out and settled neatly over the cow's horns, enough to make the animal pause. Seeing that its mother had stopped, the calf followed suit.

"Careful. Careful. Don't want either one of you breaking your leg." Taking off his scarf he used it as a flag to wave the cow and calf back toward the herd. Strange how even in the midst of saving those two animals he'd thought of Jessie, remembering how she'd often pridefully boasted about her prowess with a lasso. "Aw, Jessie," he muttered to himself. All he could hope was that Art could temper his foolish prejudice toward her for just long enough to be of some help. The sheriff had access to ways and means of locating missing people, a web of telegraph lines to other areas of the state. If he couldn't help in this matter, then no one could.

As if his thoughts had conjured him up, Corbin saw Art coming, riding his mount so hard that he sent sprays of bright water into the air when he crossed the stream. Corbin's heart leaped up to his throat. He had a bad premonition. Jessie! Art was coming to give him word about Jessie. Not a man to pray very often, he did so now. Please, dear God, let her be all right. Don't let anything have happened.

"Come on, Rebel!" Nudging his heels into the horse's flanks he galloped at top speed to meet the oncoming sheriff. "Jessie!" was all he said as he came alongside the other man.

"Yeah, I found her all right." There was a half smile

twisted on Art's lips that Corbin didn't like at all.

"She's not hurt?"

Again that smile in answer.

"Damn it, you bastard! Don't smile at me like some demented jackass. Tell me where she is!" Frantically his eyes scanned the horizon on the fragile hope that Jessie was with him.

"She's in Price, Utah."

"Price?" Corbin was confused as to why she would be there, but the thought that somehow she'd gone to get her pa still gave him a sliver of hope. "And she's coming back!"

"As a matter of fact I'm riding there as soon as I'm through talking with you. Gonna bring her back. Yes siree!" As if in a show of bravado Art rode past Corbin, then turned in a narrow semicircle and jerked his mount to a halt. "That little gal of yours is gonna be my guest for awhile."

"You're talking in riddles. What is it? What has happened?" Instead of answering, the sheriff reached in his pocket, pulled out a yellow piece of paper and handed it to Corbin. "A telegram!"

Corbin read the telegram twice, then crumpled it up and threw it on the ground. He could see the words emblazoned before his eyes. ROBBERY AT PLEASANT VALLEY COAL COMPANY. Stop. HOLDING A YOUNG WOMAN WHO FITS DESCRIPTION. Stop. ACCOMPLICE TO THE DEED. Stop. NAME — JESSICA WATSON.

Chapter Thirty-seven

Corbin called on every ounce of self-control he could muster as he followed Art through the open doorway that led to the jail cells. In truth he wanted to beat that smirking face to a pulp but doing that he knew wouldn't help Jessie in the least. Taking a deep breath he forced his temper to cool into a more manageable level. Somehow Art had framed Jessie. How, he didn't know, but if he kept his wits about him he would find out. Rob the Pleasant Valley Coal Company indeed!

Damn, if only I hadn't told him Jessie had left town she might not be in this fix, he thought placing the blame for her predicament on himself. He should have known that Conners' ego would goad him into doing anything possible to prove himself right. Hadn't Warren always complained about Conners' conceit and underhanded ways when they'd been together at the Pinkerton agency?

Jessie was in the cell farthest from the door, separated by a wall form the one inhabited by the outlaw Bob Meeks. Chilling laughter echoed from beyond the bars as Corbin passed by the man who had shot him. "I told you so . . ." a raspy voice taunted. "Jessie Watson's gonna hang alongside me. You'll see." It took all of Corbin's self-control to ignore him.

The keys jangled. The thick iron door creaked open and Corbin feasted his eyes on the woman he so loved. Sunlight streamed in through the high, barred window to illuminate the narrow bed. Sitting forlornly on that small cot with her legs drawn up to her chest and her head resting on her knees, she looked like a wounded fawn. Even the sheriff's loud "Ahem!" didn't cause her to look up.

"Jessie . . .?" The sound of his voice brought forth a sob. "Jessie." Pushing Art aside he came to her side, touching her arm. "Jessie, I'm here to help you."

"Oh, Corbin!" She raised her head, trying valiantly to smile. "Sorry I missed our wedding."

He sank to his knees beside her, gathering her into his arms. "We'll make it another time. Archie, Bowlegs and the others went out and bought new duds just for the occasion. We can't disappoint them."

"No, we can't." She sighed. "Oh, Corbin, I didn't rob that coal company. You've gotta believe me."

"I do." He kissed the top of her head. "Its all some terrible mistake. And I'll stick by you."

She had expected scorn. Anger. Recriminations. Never in her wildest dreams had she expected him to be so understanding. She had never loved him more than she did at this moment.

He looked scathingly at Art. "I'll prove just how silly this thing about your being an outlaw really is." He didn't notice that she stiffened as he made that statement.

"Silly . . ." she repeated. Putting her hands on her knees she dug so fiercely at her own flesh that she winced. He believed in her, even with what had happened. Corbin was trusting and she the foulest sort of human being to so deceive him. Corbin was closing his eyes to the truth because of love. How that hurt her conscience now. If she loved him she would tell him the truth. "Corbin . . . I . . . I . . ." It was no use. Coward that she was, she couldn't form the words.

"I love you, Jessie. I nearly went out of my mind when you just upped and left like that." His fingers traced the soft curve of her cheek and tangled in her hair. "Where did you go and why?"

"I needed to see someone. I had to go, Corbin. It was very important." How could she tell him that she had ridden all that way to warn Wade? The truth would be incriminating. *Oh, what a tangled web we weave,/When first we practice to deceive!* she thought, recalling to mind a quote she once read by Sir Walter Scott on the subject.

"So important that you would go without even leaving me a note?" For the first time since he'd walked through the door he was voicing disapproval.

"I didn't have time." She reached out for his hand, squeezing tightly. "But I would have been back by Sunday. If I'd had to lasso a star and ride in on its tail I meant to be here to marry you." She clung to him, trying desperately not to cry. She'd been given a second chance and it meant the world to her, just as *he* did. "But now . . ."

"Hush. Everything is going to be all right." He scooped her up in his arms protectively, looking daggers again at the sheriff. "I'm going to see that the lawman here pays for his stupidity. I'll expose him before the whole town as a dunderhead."

"And are you also going to take on the citizens of Castle Gate as well?" Art asked sarcastically, not at all

364

moved by the touching scene of Jessie curled in Corbin's arms. "The men at the Pleasant Valley Coal Company are adamant in placing your . . . shall I say fiancée . . . at the scene of the robbery. There are at least four men who will testify that she was with the men who robbed them."

"Then they'd all had too much to drink . . . !"

"Sure, Corbin. Sure," Conners snorted. "Well, I can tell you one thing. They're about as mad as rabid dogs about the whole thing. Lost two weeks' worth of payroll. The miners were threatening a lynching when I rode into town to bring *her* back. Whole town is up in arms. Not having captured the outlaws who stole their money, they said she'd do just as well."

"Over my dead body!" Corbin touched the handle of his gun. "Anybody who comes anywhere near her with that in mind will find himself as full of holes as a sieve." His eyes sparked blue fire, warning that he meant every word.

"OK! OK. I get the idea." Art left him alone with Jessie in the cell, saying, "One minute more. That's all. Just one minute and then you've got to leave."

"Oh, Jessie! Jessie. Jessie." Whispering her name, Corbin gathered her to him, his voice breaking as he asked, "Why? Why did this have to happen when we had our whole world before us?" He buried his face against her neck.

It's my fault, Jessie thought. Tears dampened her cheeks. Her heart was constricted with pain. No matter what happened she should have kept her promise to herself to stay clear of any skulduggery. Instead she'd gone riding right into trouble. Now she would have to pay a fearsome price. That sheriff was hellbent on proving her guilty. If a man was that intent on something, he usually got his way. She forced back the agony that threatened to consume her, but she couldn't suppress a tortured groan. She clung to Corbin as if he were the only security in a rushing river, a haven of safety. She could hear the tick of his watch against her ear, tolling away the time they could be together.

When much too soon Conners came back to tell him his time for staying was up, Corbin squared his shoulders and said an emotional goodbye. "I'll be back, Jessie. Sooner than you can imagine. I promise."

Corbin paced in front of the sheriff's office for a hellishly long time. Though he wouldn't admit it to Jessie he was more than a bit apprehensive about what was going to happen now. If Conners was a skunk, and he knew that he was, he would find witnesses to make Jessie look as bad as Billy the Kid and Jesse James combined. Somehow he had to thwart him. But how?

Corbin walked around the town of Rye Grass Station deep in thought. Remembering the saloon where Jessie had beat him at billiards, he visited that establishment with the hope in mind of learning anything at all about Jessie that could be beneficial in her defense.

"Do you know a pert young woman by the name of Jessica Watson?" he asked a man chalking his cue.

"What's it to ye?" The man didn't even try to hide his disdain.

"I'm trying to help her and I need some information."

"Sure. Sure. Well, I don't know anyone by that name!" He dared Corbin to say differently. Seeing that he would get nowhere here, Corbin moved along.

He asked other people in the saloon about Jessie, about Wade, as well as other questions. His inquiries were met with hostile stares. The bartender, barmaids, and patrons were silent, refusing to give him any information. It was discouraging. Much more than that it piqued his suspicions. Just what was it these people were trying to hide? Disgruntled, he left, nodding briskly to a couple of cowboys who were just going in as he was going out.

Corbin visited just about every establishment he could think of where Jessie might have been known. Again and again he was met with silence or with comments that it "wasn't smart to get involved." It gave him an eerie feeling. Were they afraid of incurring Conners' wrath or was something else going on?

Corbin's steps took him to the boardinghouse. With relief he found that Marie Simmons was only too anxious to talk. "Pretty little thing she is. I took to her right away!" she said, leading him to a small drawing room on the first floor and indicating a bluevelveteen chair. "Then, when I saw the two of you together I knew it was real love. She was just as excited as a bumblebee about your courting her. I said to myself that it wouldn't be long until she'd be moving out of here for a home more permanent."

"We're going to be married, ma'am." Remembering his manners, Corbin took off his hat, balancing it on his knee.

"Imagine that! And she didn't say a thing to me about it." She giggled in delight. "I'm so glad. A woman as pretty as Jessie shouldn't be all alone. A woman needs a man."

"We were going to get married Sunday."

"Sunday? Then I'm stunned that she just upped and left the way she did."

"Do you know why she left?" Corbin couldn't hide the catch in his throat. "You said once before that she didn't tell you where she was going, but perhaps you know *whom* she was going to see." Corbin leaned forward

367

eagerly. "She might have mentioned it in conversation. Think." Any information might prove valuable, perhaps lead him to a witness who could vouch for Jessie's innocence.

"The only name I ever heard her speak was yours." The woman clasped her hands together. "Oh, she sets quite a store by you. It's always Corbin this and Corbin that. You know the young women who board here always seem to confide in me. And we have such a nice group of sweet young flowers." An seemingly unending stream of conversation followed about things that didn't interest Corbin in the least and about people he didn't even know. Then she stood up, leaving the room for a moment only to return with a cup of strong, hot black coffee. "Just between you and me I think your Jessie might be in some kind of trouble."

"Trouble?" Maybe now he would get someplace.

"I wasn't certain I should mention it, but you being her beau and all, well . . ." the sheriff came by the other day asking a parcel of questions." She looked at him quizzically over the rim of her glasses. "Do you know just why?"

A gut feeling told him to be cautious, lest this woman babble things that were better kept secret. "Just routine I'm sure."

"Routine?"

"Art Conners is the kind of man to notice pretty young women when they come to town. No doubt he was trying to make some time until she let it be known that she was taken."

Marie Simmons breathed a sigh of relief. "That's just what I thought. Oh, yes, she is the kind of young woman to please many an eye."

Corbin stood up and plopped his hat back on his

head, feeling disappointment in every nerve and sinew. He was getting nowhere. He'd have to think of another way to help Jessie. Thanking the woman for her time and hospitality he moved through the drawing room, opened the front door and walked quickly down the steps.

"Oh, young man, I forgot to tell you." Running down the steps Marie Simmons caught up with him before he was out of sight. "When you do see Jessie, tell her she should be more careful. You just never know what some folks are capable of."

"More careful? About what?" Now that Jessie was in jail was a fine time for the woman to be issuing a warning, he thought wryly.

She seemed to be debating with herself as to if she should continue, then blurted out, "About leaving all that money of hers around." Touching the cameo at her throat nervously she continued, don't like to have that much money just thrown around, as you please. Invites thievery and thievery gives my boardinghouse a bad name."

"Money?"

"She should put it in a bank," she whispered. "That's what they are for, after all!" She seemed to think it necessary to continue now that she had started. "Of course I found it by accident. She left the room in such a mess that I was only doing my job in cleaning up a bit, so that it would be pleasant when she came back. I was changing the bed linen when I noticed how lumpy the mattress was. And I just had it restuffed last year. Well! I put my hand underneath and it was then that I found all those bank notes and bills stuffed in a hole." Suddenly she seemed defensive. "It's all there, in my safe."

"In your safe? Money?" Corbin's blood ran cold as he

remembered Bob Meeks's accusation that Jessie had been involved in the train robbery and that she had been given a share in the proceeds. But no, there were other reasons she might have a lot of money. Her savings. That was what he preferred to believe and yet he found himself asking, "How much?"

"Eight thousand, nine hundred and ten dollars." The woman's face colored as she realized the implication of her answer. "I . . . I counted it so that I would have an accurate account for when Jessie came to retrieve it. I thought I'd better tell you, particularly since you're going to marry her and all." She smiled cheerily. "It will make a welcome nest egg for when you do have that wedding."

Corbin couldn't talk. His mind whirled as he tried to digest this new barrage of information from this woman. What was Jessie doing with so much money? There was only way to find out and that was to ask.

This time when Corbin's strides took him to the sheriff's office it was with the purpose of asking Jessie a pertinent question. Perhaps the most important question of his life.

Chapter Thirty-eight

Jessie knew the moment she looked into Corbin's eyes that something was terribly wrong. His walk, the set of his shoulders, reinforced that impression. Instantly she rolled from her cot and standing, crossed the small distance that separated them, clinging to the bars. "Corbin, what is it?"

"I want to speak to Jessie alone, Art," he said tersely to the sheriff who was standing behind him. When the sheriff hesitated Corbin said again, *"Alone!"* The door to her cell clanged shut as Corbin came inside. With a grumble Conners granted Corbin his request, leaving the room then slamming the door.

Tension hung heavy in the air. Jessie had the feeling that her world was just about to crumble. "What's wrong, Corbin?" She tried to wrap her arms around his waist, to seek the comfort of his warmth, but he held her from him so he could look into her face.

"I've spent the last few hours combing this town for some answers, trying to find out about you. Seems people are either afraid to speak or their trying to hide something. Which is it, Jessie?"

Jessie avoided his searching eyes as she answered, "I

371

don't know."

"Well I think they're trying to protect you. My question is, why?"

"B-b-because . . ." Even now she just couldn't find the nerve to tell him about her outlaw connections. "Because . . . they are my friends." She tried to make light of the situation. "Hell, they know the same as you that I'm being framed."

"And are you? Or is there something more to this situation than meets the eye?"

Pride stiffened her back and held her head erect. "I didn't rob the Pleasant Valley Coal Company if that is what you're asking," she shot back. Of that she *was* innocent.

"And that train I was on? What about that?" She ignored the question but a worried frown etched its way across her face. Corbin had hoped beyond all reason that she would be able to dispel his suspicions but her manner only reinforced the nagging at the back of his brain. "I visited the landlady at your boardinghouse, Jessie. Marie Simmons. She made a startling declaration."

"Mrs. Simmons?" In the batting of an eye Jessie scanned her memory for anything incriminating she might have said but couldn't think of anything at all. In truth she'd hardly spent any time at the boardinghouse at all. "And . . . ?" she asked cautiously.

"She told me she found something in your room." Corbin watched her closely, trying to gauge the effect this statement had on her. He couldn't miss the flicker of apprehension that darted its way into her eyes or fail to perceive a sudden, trembling catch at her lower lip. "More than eight thousand dollars, to be exact as to what." Even now he foolishly hoped that she could explain all his suspicions away.

Jessie thrust her hands into the pockets of her pants. Her heart was beating so frantically she thought for a moment she just might choke. A fearsome debate warred in her mind. She could make up some cock and bull story or she could tell him the truth. What was it going to be? "Oh, Corbin . . ." Breathing a deep sigh she opted for the truth. "All right, the money is mine. It wasn't cows or roping that brought me up to Wyoming that day I nursed you back to health."

Corbin looked at her for a long moment before he spoke. "What are you saying, Jessie?"

She opened her mouth to answer but it was as if she was suddenly struck with laryngitis. A stricken silence followed as they maintained a grotesque pose, their eyes locked in sadness. At last Jessie found her voice.

"Corbin, I'm . . . I'm not everything you thought me to be. Well . . . sometimes circumstances lead to a body doing things she hadn't outta do. And . . ."

"Spell it out, Jessie." Corbin's voice grew harsh as his impatience mounted. "Don't talk in riddles."

"OK, I will!" Her voice was dangerously close to breaking. "I was with the men who robbed that train you were on." There. At last she'd told him.

"Godamighty!" The word exploded from his lips.

Their gazes locked and held again. In his eyes she saw a flicker of affection mingled with a great sorrow that swiftly passed as he clenched his jaw. In its place was an icy glare that chilled her to the very bone. Struggling to break the hold his eyes had upon her, Jessie looked down at her hands, clasped tightly together.

"Please don't hate me for not telling you sooner."

"One of the Wild Bunch! You *are* an outlaw." His face was suffused with color as he clenched his hands into fists.

In all her life she'd never felt such anguish but, damn it, she thought, now was not the time to cry. Nevertheless the moisture of humiliation and sincere remorse welled behind her eyelids.

"Yes—at least I was." She grabbed at his arm, but as he pulled away from her she caught only his shirt. "When I saw you, lying on the ground with the blood staining your clothes, I nearly died. I loved you even then, Corbin. That's why I took you to one of those windbreaker shacks and watched over you. I was so sorry! So terribly sorry for what had happened to you. But I didn't know. . . ."

"Sorry. But you did take your share of the money!" His eyes were bright with shards of anger.

"Yes. It's a hard, cold, cruel world, Corbin. I needed it." Even as she spoke she knew what a pathetic excuse it was. She had been wrong and only knew that all too well now. This time in jail had given her time to really think. If only she could live her life all over again she'd do so many things differently. "But . . . but I'll give it back."

"An outlaw. Riding with those bastards!" He leaned his head against the bars. "And I am the biggest god-damned fool alive. I should have put two and two together and come up with four, not five. But I loved you. I didn't want to see the truth that was only an inch before my nose. And yet if I'd stopped to think about it . . ." He closed his eyes against the pain the truth was causing him. "You being there at just that moment. Coming from out of nowhere to be my *rescuer*. It all would have made sense if I only hadn't been so blind." So, Art Conners was right after all.

She started to go to him, then hung back. Dear Lord, she had never felt so helpless. What could she say? How could she make him understand? In hopes of securing at least a measure of his forgiveness she rattled off the whole story of her time with Butch and her other friends. "Wade, my adoptive pa, was accused of killing a man. But he didn't do it. He was going to hang, but Butch saved him from the rope. I lived with the outlaws since I was just a kid. It was the only life I knew."

He whirled around. "Thieving! Robbing trains! Evading the law!"

She shrugged. "Butch only stole from those who could afford it. At first it was just to sustain ourselves but later I think we were all motivated by the excitement."

"Excitement?"

"Well, it seemed exciting to me. All my life I wanted to be just like Butch and the others." She threw up her hands. "OK! So I was dead wrong. I didn't know that at the time. All I knew was that *I* wanted to be like *them*. One of the boys!"

"To steal!"

She hung her head in shame. "Yes."

He walked around in a circle, feeling at loose ends. Oh, how he wished he could just tear her out of his heart but he loved her even now. Even now knowing what she had done. *The Wild Bunch.* The words hammered in his head. The very same bastards who had so callously murdered his brother.

"To steal and to murder."

"No! Most of the members of the gang have never, ever hurt anyone at all. Not Butch. Not Wade. Not me. Never me." She stared up into his face, wishing with all her heart to see that cold, hard expression return to the loving look she'd seen only a few hours ago. "Oh, Corbin. Can't I have a second chance?"

"A second chance?" A bitter gleam lit his blue eyes, an angry flush stained his cheeks as he remembered that day when a bullet had struck him in the arm. The enormity of her betrayal in not telling him the truth hardened his heart.

"Oh, Corbin, I did so much thinking all that time we were apart. I told Wade I was giving up outlawing forever. *For you!* I wanted to be the kind of woman you deserved. And I would have been . . ." She couldn't help the tears now. They rolled freely down her cheeks.

"If you hadn't been caught." To Corbin's mind she had ridden off to join her outlaw friends in yet another robbery. Why else would she have left so suddenly without even a word?

"I can explain that." She grasped his hand, lifting her eyes in supplication. "Please, listen." In answer he tore his hand away as if her touch burned him. Jessie told the story anyway. "At the celebration at your ranch I saw one of the outlaws I used to know. He told me that my pa, that Wade was heading right into a trap. I had to warn him." Her voice was shrill as she tried to make him understand. "Corbin, I just couldn't do anything else. But I didn't take part in that robbery. I only went along to make certain Wade didn't get hurt."

"And you expect me to believe a word you would say now! Now, after I know how many falsehoods you've already told me." Corbin's voice climbed above his fury as he forced himself to speak calmly. "How can I believe you? How can I?"

"I love you, Corbin."

He could see the heaving of her breast as she sobbed out his name. For just a moment all he could think about was the sweet softness he'd felt brush against his chest when they had made love. Dear God, he wanted to take her in his arms and feel her warmth again.

"Those so-called friends of yours killed my brother!"

The words rose like a wall between them.

"Corbin. . . ."

He grasped her shoulders and looked down hard into her eyes. His features were chillingly devoid of expression, his lips clamped tightly together. So much so that lines showed on each side of his mouth. Then with one final look he turned his back.

"Sheriff! Sheriff, I'm ready to leave now." Without turning around he pushed through the open door. Closing her eyes, Jessie could hear the sound of his heels as they struck the hard wooden floor. Moving farther and farther away. The sound was replaced by a low, sobbing wail that came from her throat, a keening as she mourned the death of Corbin's love.

Chapter Thirty-nine

The cell door closed behind Jessie and she was all alone. She could cry freely now, without any thought to pride. Cry! It seemed the only thing left to do. Flinging herself down on the cot she let all her grief out in a flood. Tears came in an overwhelming flow, pouring from her eyes, rolling down her cheeks, drenching the pillow beneath her head. In an attempt to stop the torrent she put her fingers to her eyes and pressed hard.

All her troubles had been of her own making, she realized that now. Right from the first she should have told Corbin the truth. She should have trusted in his love. Perhaps if she had explained things to him then she wouldn't be in the mess she was in. He might have even helped her to convince Wade and Butch not to pull that damned fool robbery. Oh, why hadn't she opened up to him?

Because she'd been fearful of his reaction. And frightfully muddle-headed. The truth was she really hadn't been remorseful about what she'd done until now. Now she fully realized what her foolishness had cost her. *Corbin*. She'd lost him. What a ghastly punishment it was.

"Tears, dearie?" Bob Meeks's voice cut through the air

like a knife. "1 can hear you crying all the way over here."

"It's . . . it's none of your business," Jessie sobbed, feeling a heated resentment toward her jailmate.

"Oo-ee, ain't we acting like the princess! Well, I'll tell you this, bucko, you'll be friendly toward me all right when I escape this jug!"

"You'll never get out of here." Jessie sniffed through her tears. "That sheriff is watching us both like hawks."

"But if I did?"

"If you did? You won't!"

"I *will*. And if I do I'd be willing to take you with me. 'Course now there'd be a price. A crafty man doesn't do nothing without a reward." His low-throated chuckle gave an all-too-clear hint of just what he would expect from her were she to agree. Meeks had never been secretive about his lust for her, or for any woman most probably.

"I wouldn't go to a cockfight with you!" Jessie turned over, putting her hands behind her head to stare at the ceiling. That's just what she needed was a jail escape to nail the lid on her coffin. Then what would Corbin think? Strange, but suddenly renewing his faith and love for her was more important than her fate.

"Well, we'll see. You see I've got myself a little plan. That short, squat little deputy has puddin' for brains. A little smooth-talking and I should have him eating out of my hand. Enough so to get him to come close enough to bang him on the head. 'Course now, that's where you could sure help me. For you he'd probably come inside your cell if you was to ask. All you'd have to do is crash that wooden stool into his skull, grab his keys and you and me could walk right out of here before the sheriff makes *his* rounds. What do you say?"

"Drop dead!" She wouldn't get involved in such a dastardly scheme. No, her time of outlawing was definitely over. If she ever got out of here she'd never even touch a gun again. She'd be prim, proper, and respectable.

"Have it your way, you little bitch! But you'll be sorry when I'm out of here and you're awaitin' your trial. Believe me, that sheriff will see to it that you don't get any fair jury."

"I don't care. I would never leave with you." Not, with Bob Meeks, of all people. She would never be able to forget how cruelly he had shot Corbin without even a second thought. As a matter of fact, she hoped Meeks's escape attempt was thwarted if he made one. A man like that should be hanged.

Jessie returned to her misery, finding that at last she had no more tears to spare. Closing her eyes she sought the sweet oblivion of sleep only to be awakened by a voice telling her that breakfast was there.

"Black coffee. Thick with just a bit of sugar. Thought you might like it that way, miss. And eggs and potatoes. Sheriff wouldn't allow no bacon. I would have brung it to ya if he would've."

Jessie opened her swollen eyes and tried to focus on the person bending over her. The rotund shape and the man's voice told her it was the deputy. "Take it away, I'm not hungry."

"Are you sick?" There was a genuine note of worry in his voice. She couldn't fault him for his treatment of her. In truth he had been a pleasant man in spite of her circumstances. She found herself actually liking him.

"No, I'm not sick. Just tired. Drained. I cried myself to sleep."

"I'm sorry!" He sounded sincere. "But . . . but please. Try and take at least a few bites. You gotta keep up your strength."

"For what? My hanging?"

"Aw, shucks. They ain't a gonna hang you. If they did the whole town would have a fit. The last woman they hanged hereabouts caused a whole heap of trouble to come down on the sheriff's head. He's just bluffing. Tryin' to scare you some." He put his finger to his lips. "But don't say I told you so. OK?"

Jessie tried to smile. "OK. And . . . and I will try to eat a little bit."

"Good. Good!" Setting the tray down he left, taking one last look at her over his shoulder. "Sure seems a shame to cage up such a pretty little filly." He clucked his tongue as he walked down the hall toward Meeks's cell.

Jessie sat up on her cot. "I better watch carefully just to make certain that mangy outlaw doesn't implement his scurvy plan," she breathed. Only when the deputy had gone could she breath a sigh of relief.

Wide awake now, her brows drew together in a renewal of her sadness. Corbin! The thought of him brought a mist of tears to eyes she'd thought had been drained dry. With him she had been so happy. Now suddenly he was the source of her greatest despair. A desperate feeling of loneliness overcame her. A numbing sorrow possessed her. Corbin had gone out of her life without even one last kiss.

Chapter Forty

Corbin lay on his back in his bedroom, staring up at the ceiling. Nothing could alleviate the tight knot in his belly. Hard work wouldn't be able to help him this time. He'd worked himself into a sweat riding hard all day and it hadn't done a blasted thing. All the while his mind had been on Jessie. Even after hearing it from her own lips it was still hard for him to believe. Jessie, the woman he loved, an outlaw!

After leaving her cell, Corbin had frequented the saloon trying to drown his troubles and tortured heart in a bottle of whiskey but all he had gotten was a throbbing headache this morning. Even so, one pain didn't seem to cancel out the other.

He had listened to two of the sheriff's men talking about the two outlaws in jail. There was talk of Conners making an example of them. Using them as bait to lure the other members of the Wild Bunch into making an attempt to save them.

"Hang 'em, Art says."

"Naw. Won't hang a woman. Ole Art remembers the storm that erupted when they hanged Cattle Kate and her fella side by side. People had a fit at treating a woman that way. Naw. They'll hang Meeks but not that pretty little ole piece of fluff."

"Would be a waste if they did." The man had leered. "I was hoping Art would give me leave to be of aid in teaching her to mend her ways. What I wouldn't give if he would, if you know what I mean. I'd like to spend a few hours with her."

It was all Corbin could do to maintain his composure. All he had wanted to do when that man had talked about Jessie that way was ram his knuckles in his face. Instead he had taken his bottle and sat down at a small table across the room to sulk in soulful solitude. That he could look across the street and see the sheriff's office windows from that table hadn't entered his mind at first. Or had it? Certainly his eyes had been drawn to the windows time after time wondering what Jessie was doing at the moment. Was she crying?

"I don't care!" he said aloud, causing all the others in the room to turn their heads and stare for a moment. He'd tried to tell himself that over and over again, but it was nearly as big a lie as Jessie had told him when she'd said she broke horses and roped cows for a living.

Now in his bedroom he realized just how much he did care. No matter what she had done he couldn't stand by and let Jessie stay cooped up in that prison. Conners was out for blood, so to speak. There was no telling just what he might do in his attempt to lure the others into his cells. It was quite a feather in his hat, he thought, to have caught one of Butch Cassidy's gang and he was anxious to add to the number. The truth was that Jessie's capture hadn't made the townspeople happy at all. Just the opposite. Corbin had the feeling that there were more people in Rye Grass Station than he had at first realized who were secretly on Butch Cassidy's side.

Sitting up, he raked his hands through his hair, swearing softly. It bothered him having Jessie in that jail. She wasn't just *any* outlaw. Could he just sit by and watch as the snare was tightened? No. The truth was that he hadn't even told Conners about the money for fear of what it might mean to Jessie's fate. It was still at the boardinghouse in Marie Simmons' safe. So much for his being deputized! He'd kept it a secret. But once word got out of Jessie's being wanted, Marie Simmons would put two and two together and take that loot to the sheriff. It would be proof positive of Jessie's guilt.

He stood up angrily, lit a lamp by his bed and paced restlessly back and forth. Drawing the curtain aside he looked angrily out at the night. A shaft of moonlight reflected another sleepless soul. Archie. Corbin could guess why he wasn't sleeping. He'd taken the news almost as bad as Corbin.

What was Jessie doing now? It was well after midnight. Could she sleep after what had happened yesterday? Or was she, too, pacing about? Was she feeling guilty about the things she had done or was she laughing softly to herself about the fool who had believed her? Ah, yes, he was a fool all right. He'd been suckered in by her big green eyes and that wistful smile. Swearing beneath his breath he let the curtain drop into place. The knot in his stomach only seemed to be growing tighter. Walking over to the nightstand he poured himself a stiff shot of whiskey and gulped it down. He stared at the glass in his hand. For a man who never drank to excess he was sure swilling it down now. But then it was the only thing that seemed to dim the pain at the moment.

Corbin settled himself in a chair by the window. What would have happened if he hadn't found out about that money? What would have been his future with Jessie then? Would he have gone through with the marriage? Yes. It had been his plan. Even to marry Jessie in that jail cell if necessary, just to make her his wife. He had stupidly thought that perhaps that might have helped her chance of being acquitted of the charges against her. Now he knew that wasn't possible. He couldn't tie himself up with a woman like that—a gun-toting she-cat who robbed trains and heaven knew what else.

Corbin looked toward the half-empty bottle, wondering if he should have another drink. Did he really want to get drunk again tonight? No. He knew that if ever he needed a clear head it was now. What was he going to do about Jessie? That question had to be answered.

"Corbin . . ." Archie's voice. "I'd like to come in if I might." A light tapping at the door punctuated the sentence.

"Come on in . . ." He wasn't really in a mood for company right now but then perhaps talking to Archie might do him some good.

"I saw the light under your door when I came in. Well, I haven't had the time to tell you how sorry I am that things worked out the way that they did." Archie looked like a man with the load of the whole world on his shoulders. "I liked her. Really liked her."

Corbin laughed mockingly. "Yeah. So did I."

"And I still do. I don't care what she did; I think that deep down she's one hell of a fine woman." Picking up the bottle Archie put his lips to the rim and took a long draught.

"A fine little lady," Corbin said scathingly. "Make a fine little homemaker, that is, if she can find time to cook, clean, and raise the children between robberies." He sat back in the chair, leaned back and closed his eyes.

"Maybe she would have given up her scoundrel's ways,

Corbin. For you I think that she would have. I think she did."

"Yeah. That's just why she's in jail right now. Went all the way down to Castle Gate just to check on the scenery. For our honeymoon? Sure. Sure."

Oh, why couldn't he get her face out of his mind? Every time he thought of her something moved inside him, tore at him, gripped him so hard he couldn't let go. Why did this ache go all the way down to his groin? Why couldn't he push from his mind how perfect she felt in his arms? All he could think about was what it was like to be with her.

"Things ain't always how they seem, son." Archie seemed to be wrestling with some inner thought. At last he blurted it out. "I was accused of something I didn't do once."

"You, Archie?" Corbin laughed. Archie was the most honest man he'd ever known. "Of what? Spitting on the sidewalk?" Because of so many men chewing tobacco, spitting the juice on the boardwalk *was* a jail offense.

Archie's face paled as he made a startling confession. "It was said that I killed a man."

"Killed a man?" Corbin drew back as if he'd just been struck. "Not you."

"I didn't, of course. But the evidence against me was pretty stiff." Archie's fingers whitened as he gripped the neck of the bottle. "You see, when I was a young man and didn't have sense enough to pour spit out of a boot, I rode with Quantrill."

"Quantrill?" Corbin was shocked. He'd heard all about that Confederate guerrilla chieftain who had used excessive violence in his raids against the North. He'd even attacked a town in Kansas and massacred about a hundred and fifty people. Archie didn't seem the kind of man to follow after such a brutish leader.

"I've shocked you. I didn't mean to, son. It was only to make you see that all of us can find ourselves in a compromising situation." Archie walked back toward the door, taking the bottle with him. "You don't need any more of this." He put his hand on the knob, twisting it tensely.

"Archie?"

"Yeah?"

"How did it turn out? Your predicament, I mean."

"I ran away. Broke out of jail and left Kansas and all my family behind. I've been a loner ever since, having more time than I'd like to reflect on my misdeeds." He heaved a sigh. "What are you gonna do about that little gal?"

Corbin shook his head. "I don't know." He looked at Archie, his torment clearly written in his eyes. "What would you do?"

"First of all I'd get her out of that jail. Art Conners is a polecat. He'll use her to make himself look like a dad-blamed hero." He snorted his disdain. There was a long pause. "Then I suppose I'd just sort of let things take care of themselves. But I guess you'll have to be the one to decide, son." With that said he left Corbin to his own thoughts.

Get her out of jail, Corbin thought. Ha, that was about as probable as getting the sheriff to close the saloons on Friday night. Or to declare next Saturday "Wild Bunch Day." Conners was feeling cocky on the whole matter, strutting about the town boasting about what he was going to do. There wasn't any legal way to get Jessie free. And yet . . .

No! He had taken an oath to uphold the law, that when his services were needed he'd help in tracking down outlaws. It wasn't in his code to set anyone free who'd done wrong. But if he didn't set her free? Could he just stand by and let her come to harm? Let her be sent to some prison to wile away her life behind bars?

Corbin's gaze touched on the Winchester, the rifle Jessie had given him after their time together in that blessed little cabin. Her gun. She'd gifted him with the weapon to insure that he would be safe upon his journey back to Utah from Wyoming. Now he knew the reason she had been so cautious. He'd been riding through outlaw territory. Did that matter, however? The important thing was that she had cared enough to see to his safety. And the palomino, she'd given that to him too.

"Probably stolen," he muttered, remembering the man who'd shot at him and hurled accusations at his rapidly retreating form. Nevertheless, Corbin was going to repay that gesture now.

Chapter Forty-one

It was dark in the jail cell except for the flickering light of one lone lantern. Silence pervaded the room except for Meek's loud snoring. Well, at least she wouldn't have to listen to the outlaw's taunts, she thought but neither could she sleep. There was just too much on her mind.

Sitting on her cot Jessie stared into the lantern's flames. Strange how with just a few scattered memories one's whole life could pass before one's eyes. She'd been thinking of her childhood and how she'd tagged after Wade. She'd' wanted to make him proud of her. Early in life she'd decided not to burden him with a girl who wore frilly things and jumped at snakes and bugs. Perhaps when all was said and done she'd wanted to replace the son he had lost. Would she ever see Wade again? Not for a long, long while. And Corbin. Always he hovered in her mind's eye. Corbin had taught her that being a female wasn't so bad after all, that it could be wonderful. For him she'd wanted to be all woman.

The cell door behind her creaked open. Thinking it to be the chubby deputy she didn't even bother to turn around but just said softly, "Leave the tray by the door. I'll get it later when my appetite returns." Only when he didn't answer did she turn around. To her surprise it wasn't the deputy at all but Corbin.

"Hello, Jessie."

His eyes moved over her and she was instantly aware of how disheveled she was. Her eyes were red and swollen from weeping, her hair was a tangled mass that fell into her eyes, there were smudges on her face from where she'd tried to dry her tears. Her boots were scuffed and dirty from traveling all the way to Price and back. Even so, it was wonderful to see him again.

"Oh, Corbin!" She wanted to run to the refuge of his arms but held herself back. Just looking at his face was pleasure enough.

"Haven't you been eating, Jess?"

"No."

"Are you really as miserable as that?" There was a shadow of pain in his eyes. As the minutes ticked by the tension between them mellowed. She felt his mood change. A far different emotion infiltrated the icy barrier which he had erected around himself since he'd first learned of her guilt.

"I had to come," he said at last.

He did care for her. He did! Jessie's heart thundered so loudly she was just certain he could hear. Just his being near her made her incredibly happy. Gently she asked, "Are you still mad at me?"

"Not mad, just disappointed. I believed in you, Jessie, and you let me down. But no matter. . . ." In his hands he held her two carpetbags which he set down on the bed. "Here are your clothes and as many of your possessions as I could gather without arousing suspicion."

She was confused. "What will I need them for?"

390

"I'm going to get you out of here."

"Out?" She looked around for the sheriff. Only he had the authority to open that door. Art Conners, however, was nowhere in sight. Not a legal acquittal then, she thought warily.

"I'm going to set you free and let you get as far away from the sheriff as possible." He swung the cell door wide open. "I have your pinto saddled. Your Winchester is in the saddle holster and tied alongside is a week's ration of food in a leather sack. If you travel northwest I think you'll be safe, if you stick to the Outlaw Trail that is. Art Conners told me he's lost many a man when they've chosen those pathways."

"You're going to set me free?" His words should have given her reason to hope but instead they caused her throat to go dry. Swallowing hard she reached up to touch his face. "And so in the end I am to be given the harshest punishment of all. Exile."

"Not exile." She was making it so very hard for him to say goodbye. "Oh, God, Jessie!" Fearing to give vent to his anguish he turned his back, clutching at the handles of her bags. "I got the money from Marie Simmons, too. Just to keep it out of Conners' hands. I suppose by now you've guessed he came to the boardinghouse and ransacked your room to get his hands on this." He reached into one of the bags, grasping a fistful of the banknotes.

"It was the sheriff?" All this time she'd thought it was Billy.

"He wanted evidence. If I were as law abiding as I profess to be I'd give it to him but . . ." He let out his breath in a long, deep sigh. "But, I didn't want him to have it knowing he could place the blame squarely on you if he did." Corbin put the money back as if the very touch of it burned his fingers. "If you are really serious

391

about going straight, Jessie, you'll return it to the railroad when you can."

At the moment she didn't care a fig about the money. He could have set a match to it for all she was concerned. Truly money was the root of all evil. It had been her ruination. But if it would make him happy then she would oblige. "I'll give it back. You have my word."

Her heart hammered painfully in her breast. She could only stare at him mutely. He was going to set her free and yet in so doing he would be sending her far, far away from him. For just a moment she didn't want to go.

"I'll let you make the choice, knowing full well what is right and what is wrong." Corbin looked restlessly over his shoulder. "We'll have to hurry. We don't have much time. Mitch isn't always smart. I'm afraid I used his good nature to aid me in freeing you."

"How?" The thought of what Meeks had intended to do made her shudder. She wouldn't want to be the cause of the stout little deputy's pain.

"Remember, I've been deputized," As if to remind himself he touched his star. "It's not unknown for me to take my turn at guard once in awhile."

"They'll know you set me free and you'll have to pay the price. I couldn't bear that, Corbin." She'd made such a terrible muddle of things as it was.

He tried to put her mind at ease. "I'm not worried about it. Besides, I used subterfuge. Conners is home, safely tucked in bed, I presume. I followed him just to make certain." He held up a ring of keys. "As usual Mitch is in charge of the night watch. I told him that some drunken cowboys were threatening a gun fight and that I'd watch you until he came back." He tapped each key in turn. "He doesn't even know I have these." He laughed mirthlessly. "I'm afraid that I resorted to your ways, Jess. I took them from him without asking. Stole them!"

"But you'll get into serious trouble helping me." She shook her head. "I won't go. Not and have you punished for freeing me."

He shrugged recklessly. "I'll worry about that later and take the chance I can talk my way out of any serious reprisals. Oh, Jessie!" Her name melted on his lips.

With a groan Corbin captured her slender shoulders, staring down at her. It was as if in that brief instant he wanted to carve in his memory forever the features of the woman he thought he would never see again. With a mumured oath he bent his head and his hard mouth claimed hers with a savage intensity. His arms were strong and possessive as he crushed her against his chest. In that moment Corbin's resolve was nearly lost. The moment his lips touched hers his body exploded with a fierce surge of almost uncontrollable desire. Her mouth was achingly sweet against his. He nearly lost his head completely with his need to make love to Jessica the way his body prompted him to.

Jessie returned his kiss, craving his touch, longing to be in his arms like this forever. But forever was not to be. Not now. Even so she could cherish this moment. Her arms closed around his waist as she embraced him wanting more, so very much more. Her body was aflame with desire. She ached to be naked against him, to have him possess her as he had on that warm, starlit night at the ranch.

"I love you, Corbin. So much that it hurts." Her hands roamed over his shoulders, down his hips. She opened her mouth to him, parting her soft lips to his quest. He hadn't said he still loved her. Did he? For the moment it didn't matter. Just loving him was enough.

Reluctantly he lifted his mouth from hers. His voice was a whisper when they finally broke apart. "We've got to hurry, Jessie. Or all is lost. That good-natured fool will be coming back any moment."

"I don't care! I don't want to go. Corbin . . ."

He didn't give her any choice. Dropping the keys on the floor where Mitch could find them, he took her by the arm, practically dragging her out of the cell. Unfortunately the noise he made awakened Meeks. The sound of the outlaw's vile swearing, his plea to be set free too, his threats to tell what Corbin had done, accompanied their flight to the back door of the sheriff's office. There Corbin gave her one last kiss.

"Do you still love me, Corbin? Do you? I have to know." She drew a ragged breath as she waited for his answer.

"Yes! I can't sleep at night for want of you. I miss your laughter, your smile, the sparkle in those beautiful green eyes of yours." He'd never felt this gut-wrenching need for one particular woman before. Losing Jessie tore out his heart. She had come to mean so much to him. One last farewell kiss, that was all they had time for. With that thought in mind his mouth closed fiercely over hers one final time, urgent in his need. Her body fit so perfectly against his.

The sound of a door opening interrupted their embrace. "Someone's coming," Jessie breathed. She was halfway hoping that she would be caught, but Corbin was taking no chances.

"Go on. Get out of here!" he ordered, giving her a hard swat on her backside. "What we had is over, Jessie. If you are to go on living free, it has to be that way."

"No!" She didn't want to believe that and yet when she looked back at him his face appeared as if it had been chiseled in stone. Jessie raised her hand in a signal of goodbye. Then she was gone, leaving the only man she would ever love behind her.

Chapter Forty-two

Under the cloak of night Jessie rode at a furious pace away from Rye Grass Station. She bent close to the churning muscles of her horse, sought a firm grip on the reins as she guided Sagebrush onward. She couldn't allow herself to be caught. Not after the sacrifice Corbin had made involving himself in her escape. There was no doubt in her mind that Meeks would take great delight in telling the sheriff that Corbin had helped her escape. She damned him beneath her breath, all the while vowing that she would beat that coyote of a sheriff at his own game yet.

Jessie rode long and hard, until the first rays of the sun sparkled upon the horizon. She thought herself safe from pursuit until the sound of horses' hooves coming closer and closer echoed in her ears. Fearing that she was being followed she quickly headed for a small clump of trees to hide from the pursuing horses, but it was only a wagon thundering down the road.

Jessie was drenched in perspiration from the strain and exertion of her ride, Sagebrush's sides were heaving. It was time for a rest, she thought. Dismounting, she led Sagebrush behind the foliage and there allowed them both time to regain their strength.

For the first time since she had embarked on her strenuous ride Jessie had time to sort things out in her mind. After Corbin had opened the cell door and sent her on her way, Jessie couldn't help being a little jittery. The feeling of being totally alone swept over her once again. Every other time when the law had been after her there had been others she could rely on. Now she was completely on her own.

Where did she go from here? First and foremost her intent had been to get far away from Rye Grass Station, which she had done. Now what? She had to formulate a plan. She couldn't go south. That vigilante group of miners in Crystal City was undoubtedly still mad as hell about losing two weeks' pay in the robbery. She didn't want to be tarred and feathered or worse. If she were seen they would recognize her in a minute. Nor could she hang around this area very long. She could stay only long enough to get her second wind. Butch's hideout? No. It was too risky to ride all the way up to the Brown's Park hideaway when the hills were swarming with lawmen out looking for the Wild Bunch. Nor did she want to inadvertently lead anyone to their retreat. No, the time had come to make a clean break. To start all over again. To get as far away from Utah and the surrounding hills as she could.

Wyoming? No. The Wild Bunch was just as notorious there as here. Besides, all too often the posses of Utah and Wyoming cooperated with each other in chasing down those who were wanted. Corbin had talked a lot about Colorado when they were together in the windbreaker shack. It was the place he had left. She had been to a place called Windsor with Wade a time or two when she was younger. As she remembered it wasn't a bad little town.

It seemed logical to make a new beginning in a new state. Besides, the idea that Corbin had once lived there endeared her to the place.

Jessie's eyes touched for a moment on her carpetbags, tied firmly behind Sagebrush's saddle. It was a reminder that Corbin had collected all her belongings, *including* the stolen money from the train robbery.

"Damned money," she grumbled. What was she going to do with it? It was yet another problem to deal with.

For just a moment temptation teased her into wanting to keep it. It would be difficult enough to start over as it was but penniless? And yet Corbin had given the money to her, telling her to let her conscience be her guide. She had made a promise she didn't feel she should break. Not after all that had happened. By returning it then she would make amends as best she could for what she had done. Perhaps then Corbin wouldn't think so badly of her. She'd deposit the money in a bank along her route and then telegram the railroad as to where it was *after* she had passed on through the town. Perhaps Corbin could even forgive her if she kept just enough back to get her safely settled. Once she'd been able to earn a bit of a nest egg she'd return that, too.

Jessie still had the clothes she had ordered from the Sears Roebuck catalogue. With those clothes it shouldn't be difficult for her to get a job somewhere in Colorado and start a whole new life. She knew sums and reading, thanks to Wade's insistence that she go to school. Perhaps she might get a job as a teacher in a town somewhere. If she could instruct Butch and the others in reading and sums with their high-handed ways, she could educate just about anybody. And then again maybe she'd make her way working on a ranch. As of the moment she wasn't really sure just what her new life would bring—except that it would be a new life without Corbin! The very thought caused a physical ache in her heart.

She couldn't blame Corbin for the way he felt. He had been as understanding as any man could be. She couldn't have expected him to leave everything behind and come with her. He had at least admitted that he still loved her and that, at least, had soothed some of her pain.

Corbin was as fine a man as there could be, she thought. At least he had given her the benefit of the doubt and had listened to her explanation. He hadn't believed the sheriff's accusations until it had been proven without a doubt that she was an outlaw, until by her own words she had confessed her association with the Wild Bunch. How could she expect him to go on as if nothing had happened? He held Butch's gang responsible for his brother's death. That he could still have affection for her even after knowing what he did made him very special.

Oh, how she would miss him. Corbin was one man in a million. She would never find another man like him. Fact was she never wanted another man at all—not if she couldn't have him. Leaving him was the hardest part to bear.

Well, at least there was a slight glimmer of hope on the horizon. Maybe after a year or two away from Utah, things would die down just a mite. Who knew? Maybe she might be able to return someday and live a respectable life, see Wade and Aggie again. Wade and Aggie! Oh, but the temptation to run to Wade surged through her but doing so just might hinder his efforts to live a peaceful life with Aggie. If by some stroke of ill luck she was tracked down, it would implicate him in all that had happened.

She had gone through all of this in order to protect Wade in the first place. She couldn't point the law in his direction now or all would have been in vain. She had to be totally on her own and stick by her decision to move on to that area near Windsor.

Jessie was getting edgy. She waited until Sagebrush was well rested then climbed back into the saddle. It just wasn't safe to wait too long. Any time now her absence might be discovered and then before you could say "jack rabbit" there would be a posse after her. Right now she must get away from here and fast. She knew the country like the back of her hand. There was a route she was familiar with where no one could follow her.

With one final look toward Rye Grass Station, whispering Corbin's name in one last goodbye, she guided Sagebrush down the road that would take her in the direction of Colorado. The horse's hooves struck dull echoes in the silence of the early morning as its forefeet hit the ground in a steady gallop as she headed far, far away.

Forty-three

Corbin was completely exhausted by the time he got back to the ranch. The melancholy he felt over Jessie had drained him as much as the hard ride back. He was not prepared for the furor that awaited him as soon as his horse cleared the gate. Right away Archie ran up to him before he even had time to dismount.

"We've had some cattle stolen." His voice cracked, indicating the emotion of the situation.

It was the last thing Corbin wanted to hear. "Are you certain they haven't just strayed?" he asked, hoping it was that simple.

Archie looked taken aback. "The way I watch over them? At this time of night they were in their pens. Happened by my reckoning a little over an hour ago." He shook his head. "Naw, they've been stolen all right and by someone who doesn't have enough sense not to leave telltale tracks behind."

"How many rustled?"

"Quickly figurin' I'd say as many as ten but the worst news is that Stamash is among the missing."

"Damn." Corbin got off his horse, and followed Archie to where the tracks were.

"Look at the broken rails on his corral. They didn't even take time to open the gate. Must have been in one helluva hurry to get him out," Bowlegs exclaimed, hurrying to join them.

"Looks like two men done it," Archie said. "One had a perfect set of horseshoes but look here." Both men got down on their knees as Archie held the lantern high to illuminate the spot. "Just a little bit of metal is missing from the arc. There. See that little chip. That kind of flaw will make it quite distinctive for the sheriff to track."

"Not the sheriff. Us!"

"Us?" Archie shook his head. "Come on, son. I know you're upset about that Scottish bull and all—but hell, he's so distinctive no brand is gonna hide him for long and—"

"Whoever took him will be caught soon," Bowlegs declared. He blocked Corbin's way but stepped aside when he saw how intent he was to ride.

"Can't wait for that. Saddle up." Though he was bone-tired Corbin knew that if they gave the rustlers any time, they'd soon vanish into some hideaway or other. Then Stamash and the rest of the cattle would be forever lost.

Riding furiously over the rugged terrain, Corbin and his men came upon the remains of a campfire where it appeared the rustlers had stopped briefly to rebrand the stolen cattle with their running irons. Getting ready for a fast sale, Corbin thought angrily as he dismounted and searched through the ashes. Well, just as Archie said, Stamash would not be easy to hide. Unknowingly the rustlers had put a noose around their necks when they'd taken such a distinctive animal, though he doubted they had sense enough to know that.

"We're gonna get ourselves killed, that's what!" Archie grumbled as he pulled his horse alongside Corbin. Bowlegs and Tippett were of like mind but even so they obediently followed Corbin as he remounted his horse and rode out.

"Sure could use the sheriff's help." Bowlegs called out.

With a grimace Corbin remembered how smug he'd been about Conners being home safely in bed when he'd freed Jessie. Oh, how he could use his help right now. If it just wasn't such a long ride back into Rye Grass Station he might have gone along with Archie but emergency dictated a man's actions.

The trail was easy to follow. They were traveling over the least broken land in the area where the trail was smoother than any of the terrain they'd encountered so far. The soft dirt left as sure a trail as if the outlaws had purposefully marked the way. Curiously, however, the prints weren't headed toward the Brown's Park area where Butch Cassidy supposedly had a hideout, nor toward the direction of Hole-in-the-Wall, but south. Corbin and his men had one advantage. Four men on horseback could travel much faster than men driving stubborn cattle.

They raced across the barren prairie land for perhaps half an hour, Corbin watching the sky. A worried frown gathered on his face as the line of clouds moved toward them with increasing speed. That was just what they needed. A storm was coming over the horizon. If they didn't hurry the rain would wipe out the tracks and then all their efforts would be for naught.

"We've got to find them before the storm hits. Ride, men. Ride!" he ordered.

By around ten-thirty in the morning Corbin and the others seemed to be gaining ground. It was a rugged area through which the trail was taking them. Trees whose tips almost seemed to touch the sky grew thickly. The path they were following had a slight upward slant, a meandering course. It was a strange place to be bringing a tiny herd. Nevertheless the wind carried the distant sound of lowing cattle.

Riding to the steep mesa they looked down into the gully below where the trail veered to one side. The men were careful to avoid a steep slope or a short dropoff. At last they came to a place where they could look down below without being seen. Sure enough, two men with about a dozen cattle were down there.

"Look at those lazy-assed bastards. Moving as leisurely as you please. Even taking time to brew themselves a pot of coffee around a campfire for Chrissakes."

"Nearly as if they don't even fear being followed."

"Look, there's another man over there." Bowlegs pointed to a man striding toward the other two rustlers. It was three men, not two.

It was surprisingly easy for Corbin and his ranch hands to make their approach but they did so warily. No one ever knew what a cattle rustler might have up his sleeve. Splitting up, each closed in from a different direction. Corbin crouched behind foliage as he moved. Only when he was nearly upon one of them did Corbin catch sight of a star. The early morning light bounced off the silver emblem. In that moment he recognized Art Conners. So the sheriff was already out doing his job, Corbin thought, though he wondered how the sheriff had so quickly gotten word that Corbin's cattle had been rustled.

"Probably found out about my freeing Jessie from Mitch and rode out to offer his recriminations," Corbin whispered to himself. "Then he was told about the stolen cattle and knowing all the ins and outs of the area had insight into just where the outlaws were headed."

Taking his gun from its holster Corbin crept forward. From the looks of it the sheriff was alone. A foolhardy move on his part and a good way to get himself shot, Corbin mused. Well, now he would have four extra guns to come to his aid in taking these bastards back to stand trial. He was just about to let Conners know he was there when the sound of Art's angry voice urged him to caution. What was this? He was calling the rustler by name! Pausing for a moment, Corbin strained his ears to hear what was being said.

"Frank, you blithering fool! What in the hell did you think you were doing taking that goddamned hairy-headed bull?" It was Conners talking.

"You said take the ones who looked as if they'd fetch the best price. Me and Billy just took you at your word. He's one fine stud bull! Shoulders as wide as a gate. You should be thanking us, instead of being so damned mad."

"You dumb bastard! Just look at him. Take a good look. You think it isn't going to be as obvious as a pig in a chicken coop to have that one in our possession? There isn't another bull like that for miles and miles around here."

"We could use sheep shears to cut all that hair away," a high-pitched man's voice offered.

"Yeah, well, Billy, I'd suggest that you just start cutting. With your damned pocket knife if you have to."

Corbin froze in his tracks. Conners was one of them. As a matter of fact, from the way he was talking, he was their leader. Why, that dirty low-down scoundrel.

To think how that man had persecuted poor Jessie when he himself was going against the law. Suddenly everything seemed to fall into place. Conners was the most avowed spokesman against the Wild Bunch. And why? Because by fanning the sparks of discontent, by spouting off about how fearsome Butch Cassidy's gang was and how many cattle they stole, he had been taking the heat away from himself. No doubt some of the stolen cattle that had been assumed to have been Cassidy's doing had really been taken by the sheriff himself! Well, now he would be caught red-handed.

Corbin saw the three shadows of his men out of the corner of his eye. He had help nearby. With that thought in mind he worked his way toward the fire, slipping along on his belly while the outlaws' backs were away from the fire. Corbin had the intent of tackling Conners from behind but he was spotted. He found himself staring down the barrel of the sheriff's gun.

"Corbin! What in the hell are you doing . . ."

"Following the skunks that stole my cattle, Art. Don't suppose you know anything about it?"

"Been following them myself. Got two rustlers right over here," he pointed with his gun at one of the men who didn't look to be more than just a boy.

"Cut the crap, Art. I overheard what was going on. You've made quite a nice tidy little profit for yourself, I would wager. What's the matter? Doesn't the town of Rye Grass Station pay you enough?"

"As a matter of fact, they don't. A man has to do what he has to do if he wants to have anything in this life. But then a big cattle baron's son wouldn't understand that." His eyes closed to slits of hatred. "God, how I hated all the times Warren talked about his ranch. That dumb bastard took it so for granted while I would have given anything just for a chance to have anything half so fine. Now maybe I will have."

"With stolen cattle?"

"No one misses a steer here and there. Certainly you won't." He cocked the trigger. "Because you see now that you have created a little problem for me. I can't let you open your big mouth and ruin everything."

"You're going to kill me."

"Yes! It's a pity but the West is much like a jungle. Survival of the fittest."

Corbin realized that if Archie and the others didn't hurry, Conners just might make good on his threat. He had to stall the sheriff somehow. "Well, at least you could give a doomed man a last cup of coffee." Controlling his breathing, ignoring the pounding of his heart, he moved slowly forward as if there was nothing wrong.

"Coffee?" Conners looked at him as if he must be crazy. "Don't know why I should."

"Well . . ." slowly Corbin reached out for the coffeepot. "Warren was always telling me that you were a man who knew how to show hospitality." Grasping the handle he moved with the rapidity of a striking snake, flinging the scalding hot brew into Conners' face.

"Ahhhh!" As he put his hands to his eyes Conners fired a shot but it missed Corbin, striking a tree just a few inches from Corbin's head. That shot was a signal that brought the others running.

"All right, boys," Archie shouted, "you're covered! Hands up real quick like and we won't be so unfriendly as to shoot."

About that time one of the outlaws, the one named Frank, panicked and sent a shot through the air without even aiming. Bowlegs dove behind a fallen pine as a bullet whizzed through the air.

"Anybody hurt?" Corbin inquired quickly. Bowlegs was holding his arm.

"Just a flesh wound. That shot just grazed me but I'm a tough ole fart, boss." Angered, the ranch hand sent a response from his own Colt.

For just a moment the air ricocheted with gunfire but the shooting stopped as suddenly as it had begun. When it was ended Conners and the younger of the two rustlers were caught but the third had unfortunately escaped. Bowlegs had shot over his head trying to stop him but he had ridden off. Corbin shrugged his shoulders. It didn't matter. What was really important was that he'd gotten Stamash and the other cattle back. With the running irons as evidence he could prove the other cattle had been rebranded.

"Thanks, boys." Corbin exclaimed.

Archie beamed as if he had brought the rustlers to justice single-handed. "It wasn't nothing. All in a day's work, son."

They headed back toward the Rolling Q slowly, herding the stolen cattle and their two prisoners. The sheriff was handcuffed with his own irons. Billy's hands were tied behind his back.

"The jail is real cozy and the grub is fair to middling, as you know, Art. I'm sure you'll be familiar with your own accommodations." There was a circuit judge coming to try Jessie and Meeks. Now he would be useful in seeing Conners brought to justice.

Chapter Forty-four

The tiny courthouse was packed as tightly as a sardine can when word got out about the sheriff's trial. Following upon Meeks's hanging it made for an exciting time in Rye Grass Station, although it was a period of depression for Corbin. Only now did he fully realize how very dear Jessie had become to him. It was more than just loving her. Jessie was his heart and now she was gone. How ironic it was that the very same man who had accused her of being an outlaw was now standing trial on that very same charge.

Art Conners' trial was one that would be talked about for years to come, or so it seemed. Because he had once been a Pinkerton agent it caused a great deal of interest in areas outside Utah. Newspapermen came from all directions to cover the trial. Corbin could only hope that wherever Jessie was she would read the story and realize that the man who had hounded her was no longer powerful. It was his hope that then she might return to him and give him another chance at making her happy.

It took longer than a week to select a jury but in the end Corbin was satisfied that justice would be done. The trial itself lasted three and a half weeks, as little by little, more became known about Art Conners. Far from the law-abiding citizen he had played he was found to be guilty for a multitude of sins, the leader of a cartel that reached all the way from Price, Utah to Laramie, Wyoming and included as many as thirty-five or more men. In truth the man had swindled, stolen, and cheated his way to an amount of money that made Jessie's share of the train robbery look like chickenfeed.

Two of the men who had been in the posse with Warren, members of the outlaw cartel Conners had formed, were forced to testify that Conners had killed Warren MacQuarie. Shot him down one cold winter night when by accident Corbin's brother had stumbled unwittingly upon several branding irons and thereby come close to learning the truth. It was not Butch Cassidy and his gang who had killed his brother, Corbin was shocked to learn, but Art Conners who had blamed the Wild Bunch to cover his own guilt. At least of that crime Butch Cassidy's gang was vindicated.

By late June a verdict of *guilty* on all counts was handed down and Conners sent to the Utah State Prison. As for Corbin, he spent his days at the ranch and many of his nights in a saloon in town trying to forget his heartache in the arms of saloon girls. Not a single one of them could match up to Jessie—and in the end he had to admit that no woman ever would. Not where he was concerned.

"Where is she, Archie? Where could she possibly be?" he asked his foreman over and over as if he thought the kindly old man would know. God, what kind of a fool had he been to just let her ride out of his life? At the time he had thought he was doing what was right, and yet had he? Now he knew the answer to that question was no. No matter what Jessie had done, he loved her. Wasn't it just

410

possible in the back of his mind he had been ashamed to make an outlaw girl his wife? Now he realized that it wasn't important to him at all what Jessie had done in the past.

He realized that it wasn't always possible to have the power to choose what one did in life. Jessie had been a victim of her circumstances: orphaned at an early age, rejected by her only kin, and left abandoned in an unfamiliar town. Corbin had visited Billy in his jail cell and learned from the young outlaw's lips the details of the story. Just as Jessie had said, the only life she had known since childhood was roaming with Butch Cassidy and his gang. Corbin with puffed-up pride and a sense of morality had judged her when, in truth, had the same thing happened to him he might have done much the same.

Compassion. Forgiveness. He should have learned those qualities somewhere along the line, and yet he had been so quick to judge Jessie when she had disappointed him.

Spring turned into a blazing summer, a lonely time for Corbin. Although he had waited, hoping against hope that Jessie would return, she didn't and he had begun to despair of ever seeing his renegade angel again. Even so he had it in mind to try and had hired a Pinkerton agent to look for her. If he found her again he would never let her go.

"It's going to be like tracking a whisper in a windstorm," he said to Archie forlornly; but nevertheless, he had to try.

Part Three:
Gentle Surrender

Colorado and Utah
Summer 1897

Ah! a man's love is strong
When fain he comes a-mating.
But a woman's love is long
And grows when it is waiting.
—Laurence Housman, "The Two Loves"

Chapter Forty-five

The dingy hotel room seeped with desolation. The plaster was cracked and chipped, the bed was lumpy, the curtains were so faded it was nearly impossible to see that once they had been a shade of blue. Jessie fought hard to keep her spirits up as she sat on the sagging bed, agonizing over her predicament. Just as she had promised she had given back the money from the train robbery but now poverty and despair were her only reward. She had barely two coins to rub together and the hotel clerk raging about the pay for her room. For the first time in her life she knew the worry of finding enough money to pay for a decent meal.

Not that she hadn't found work. As she had slowly moved her way across the Wyoming and Colorado countryside she had made a little money doing odds and ends, but always there was the fear that if she stayed in one place too long, people might start asking questions. She was on the run and she knew it all too well.

Jessie had ridden Sagebrush much of the way, until her state of finances had forced her to sell the noble beast. Strangely it had almost been like selling her child. Wade had given her that pinto when she was just a child and

Sagebrush a foal and they had been together all those years. Still, dire circumstances often led a person to do things they didn't want to do. She told herself now it was all for the best. Sagebrush would be happy with the rancher who had purchased him. Besides, in her present state she would never have been able to afford the livery.

Hitching rides on wagons and stowing away on railroad freight cars had gotten Jessie the rest of the way to Windsor. At last she had reached the destination she had decided on. And yet even being in the straits she was in Jessie could proudly boast that she hadn't reverted to her old ways. Every penny she had made had been earned honestly. But being respectable just wasn't as easy as she had first thought. Not at all. Though there were plenty of jobs for men, all too many doors were shut to a woman and the jobs that there were just didn't pay a very good wage. Jessie had nearly reached the end of her rope.

I'm not going to give up, she thought. Life had to go on no matter how a person was hurting inside. And Jessie was hurting. Oh, it didn't show outwardly. She smiled and tried to be pleasant to people she came in contact with but the truth was she was keeping everything bottled up inside, her sadness, her mourning for a lost love. Although the sharp edge of her misery had dulled there were times in the quiet of the night that she still cried herself to sleep. Every day, however, when morning came she told herself to look ahead. One of these days she'd find her opportunity. Somewhere out there was a key to her future. Somewhere.

"Miss Olson!" A furious pounding startled her out of her thoughtful pondering. For just a moment she had to remember that *she* was Miss Olson. Bessie Olson. It was a name she used just in case she might have any Pinkerton agents or posses following her trail.

416

"Yes!" she shouted back. Her emotions were dangerously close to the breaking point. It was as if she was on the brink of flying into a million pieces. She knew all too well what he wanted.

"Unless you can come up with the money you owe me I will have to ask you to leave. This is a hotel, not a charitable institution. I have someone interested in your room," he called out. "Well, which is it?"

"I'll get you your money. Just give me a few hours. I promise." So far she had been good to her word. Pride had goaded her on. She'd sweep out a store or do something to get the money. Instead of a hot meal she would have to use any money she made this morning for her lodging.

Dressing in her plainest dress, Jessie hurried out the door and down the steps to the boardwalk. One by one she visited all the stores and businesses upon the town's Main Street asking the same question. Did they need any help? One by one she got the same answer. No. It was discouraging. Though she'd made a vow never to become a saloon girl she was close to breaking that promise as she veered in the direction of the town's saloon. Better to be pawed and leered at than to sleep out in the street and starve. With that thought in mind she tried one more time, inquiring at the local eatery if they needed their kitchen cleaned.

"No, but we need a cook. Our usual one has been struck down with a fever."

"A cook?" It was the one thing Jessie abhorred and yet as Wade had often told her, "Beggars could not very well be choosers." Agreeing to take on that job she followed the tall, skinny man to the kitchen.

"There's your apron. Make yourself right at home," he said, giving her a half smile. "Hope you make good biscuits. If you do, we just might keep you on, at least until our regular cook is back."

The kitchen smelled of onions, cooking grease, smoke and strong lye soap. A strange combination, Jessie thought, grabbing up her apron and tying it around her waist. Quickly she moved around the room, taking stock of the supplies. Opening cupboards, checking the pantry, she tried to remember all that Aggie had taught her during the winter months they'd been at Hole-in-the-Wall. Biscuits? Somehow she had to manage the task or she would find herself right back where she started.

Jessie stumbled about in the kitchen searching for the flour, salt, and baking powder. All the while she tried to remember Aggie's recipe, the one Butch and the boys had always savored. A pinch of this. Two pinches of that and a whole heap of flour. Sifting, measuring, spilling milk all over the floor, she soon had the kitchen in a mess. Even so, she knew she had been successful. Running her hands through her hair she heaved a sigh, then rolled out the dough, cut it into small circles and put those precious flat little balls on a sheet. Only when she put them in the oven, however, did she realize that it wasn't lit.

Damn! Some cook she was. Nevertheless she kept her calm, searching for and finding the matches in a box in the cupboard. Realizing the fastest way to start a fire was with newspaper she searched about the kitchen for yesterday's daily. Wadding pages of it she threw them into the stove, then struck a match and watched the flames take hold, setting fire to the wood. At last she stood back, basking in its warmth and breathing in the fragrant smell of baking dough. Then she set about the task of cleaning up the working area before that tall, skinny man came back.

Jessie swept the floor and taking a rag wiped the

counters clean. Picking up several of the pages of the newspaper that hadn't found their way into the fire she quickly scanned the paper for any listing of a job she might be able to fill. A barber was wanted for a new barber shop opening in town, a wagon driver was needed, a woman, experienced, was wanted to make hats. As usual most of the jobs listed were for men doing heavy work loads. Impatiently she let her index finger run down the column.

Wait! There it was. The answer to her hopes. *Governess needed,* the ad said. *Desire a respectable, educated, well-mannered lady to take care of three children on a ranch near Greeley, Colorado.* Greeley? That wasn't very far from where she was. And wasn't it where Corbin had once had a ranch, the M bar Q, or some such thing?

A governess, she thought. Could she manage such a job? She'd never been around children very much and yet she could read and add up numbers as well as just about anybody. How difficult could it be? A ranch. She wouldn't even have to worry about lodging.

Jessie's fingers trembled as she took the biscuit pan out of the oven, using the end of her apron to guard her hands against the heat of the pan. It was all she could do to keep her mind on her cooking as the morning wore on. Jessie fried countless slabs of ham, and scrambled and fried so many eggs she nearly ran out of supplies. And all the while her own stomach rumbled with hunger and her mind kept remembering that ad for a governess. At last when the breakfast crowd had left, the thin man came back, heaping praise upon her head.

"Your biscuits have gotten you the job," he said grinning from ear to ear. He rewarded her by letting her partake of her own culinary creations and Jessie tried not to gobble the food too quickly. Then at last, borrowing a

419

pen and piece of stationery she sat down at a table. Being careful to say just the right words, she wrote an answering letter to the ad, giving her hotel name in case there was a response. Then she mailed it, crossing her fingers and hoping against hope.

The waiting was horrible, testing her patience. And yet, when a week and a half had come and gone, she got her answer. She, *Bessie Kaye Olson,* had been given the job.

Chapter Forty-six

Jessica awakened in the morning with a feeling of anticipation. She had spent a long time lying awake last night feeling hope for the first time in a long while. Today was the day Charles Taylor would ride into Windsor to take her in his buggy to his ranch. Hurrying in her toilette, she was ready before the sun was up. She packed her bags, paid her hotel bill, and waited on the boardwalk. She was wearing a blue velvet skirt and fitted jacket and her best white blouse. Her auburn hair, which had grown long enough to arrange into a fashionable bun, held a small blue hat with three flowers stuck into the band. Very proper. It was just like how the most respectable women of the town dressed, even to being a bit spinsterish.

It was a long, tedious wait but then a deep voice called out her assumed name. "Miss Olson?" A tall, well-dressed man with graying brown hair took off his hat and made his introduction, putting his large, firm hand in her small, gloved one. "Buckboard is across the street."

Taking her by the elbow he led her in that direction, then helping her onto the carriage seat, he flicked at the reins and sent the buckboard bouncing along the road. Building after building seemed to speed by as the horses stirred up a choking dust. Hanging tightly onto the edge of her seat Jessie tried to maintain a cautious poise lest she unknowingly utter a swear word and ruin everything.

"You look rather young, Miss Olson." Charles Taylor said with an aloof coolness. "Have you had much experience?"

"Lots and lots," Jessie answered, forcing a smile. It wasn't really a lie. It had been tedious helping Billy with his studies. "And . . . and . . . I just love children."

"Mmm. Well, we will see." As a gust of wind came up he reached up to secure his hat. "My wife has been teaching them their numbers, reading, and such, but she is recovering from a recent bout of anemia which has, I'm afraid, left her too thin and frail to do much work or spend time with the children. Until she is recovered fully I'm afraid there will be many things I might ask of you." His tone was curt as he eyed her warily.

"I can cook if need be. I make darned fine biscuits." Jessie tried a bit of conversation to thaw him out. "I've never been to Greeley before. But I have heard it's lush and beautiful."

"Not where the ranch is. I'm afraid it's rather barren. The neighboring ranch across the Cache la Poudre River has all the trees, I'm afraid. Seems a shame the widow is hardly ever there to enjoy them."

"A widow?" Jessie clucked her tongue in sympathy. "Poor, poor woman. I'll have to do my best to comfort her. I've suffered my own loss, you know."

"You are widowed?"

"In a way." She didn't want to be asked to explain. "What's the widow's name?"

"MacQuarie."

Jessie's face went pale. "MacQuarie?" The thought that it had to be a relative of Corbin's hovered at the back of her mind.

"Henrietta MacQuarie." He looked at her with a worried quirk of his brow. "You look as if you are going to faint. I hope I don't have a sickly woman on my hands."

"It . . . it's just the heat." Jessie took off her hat and fanned her face. Dear God, MacQuarie, she thought. But then wasn't that what had really brought her here? It wasn't any coincidence, if she were really honest with herself. She'd remembered Corbin talking about this town and his ranch nearby. At the back of her mind all the time must have been the hope that perhaps if she came here she might see him someday. MacQuarie. That name brought back so many poignant memories. Quickly recovering her composure she asked, "What are your children's names?"

"Arthur, age ten; Jenny, six; and Nancy, age eight." As if her questions bothered him he remained tight-lipped and silent the rest of the way. Jessie was glad when at last the buckboard rumbled through the tall, wooden gate marked Circle K and up the road to a fine two-story red brick house with a large porch. Standing there, hanging on the railing, were three small cherubic forms that ran out to meet the buggy as it pulled up.

"Daddy! Daddy!" called out the youngest, running to meet him. The other two children followed close behind, eyeing Jessie up and down.

"Howdy, Miss Olson." Arthur was all smiles as he pushed his large-brimmed hat back from his freckled face. "We knew you was comin' today."

"Howdy, Miss Olson," Nancy skipped over and opened the gate, her blonde curls glistening in the sun's rays as she bounced up and down. "We're sure glad to see you. Seems we've been out here by the gate watchin' for a long time."

"Hello, Arthur, Nancy, Jenny." Jessica said nodding in the direction of each child as she spoke their name. "It is nice to meet you. What a lovely welcome you have given

423

me. I'm much obliged."

"I think she's pretty, Daddy." Arthur was quick to voice his opinion.

"So do I. I hope she's nice, too," Nancy added softly.

Jessie threw back her head and laughed, feeling relaxed for the very first time. "I promise I will be." Jumping from the buggy she lifted up her two carpetbags and carried them onto the porch.

"Good. Mama isn't always. Sometimes she yells at me."

"Nancy! Mind your manners. Your mother isn't feeling well. It means she isn't always of a mellow temperament." As if he were shooing a flock of chickens, he hurried the three children inside and Jessie followed, eyeing the front hallway as she stepped inside the door.

This would be a perfect place for her to live. It was clean and it was comfortable. Working at the Taylor ranch was just what she needed. It would give her time to ponder, test, and try her own strengths and to learn more about family life. Jessie had never really been around children much before and yet, the Taylor kids seemed to like her. Certainly she knew she already adored them.

The children ran through the house calling as they ran, "She's here. She's here. Miss Olson is here."

Charles Taylor swatted the youngest child on the behind. "Shhh. How many times must I tell you? Your mother might be sleeping . . ."

A soft, feminine voice from the drawing room interrupted him. "It's all right, Charles. I'm awake. We have company. Henrietta is here."

"Here, Arthur, take Miss Olson's things up to her room." The boy reached up for the largest carpetbag, staggering under its weight. Stubbornly, however, he managed. Jessie watched as he scurried up the stairs. "Come along, Miss Olson."

He talked to Jessie as if she, too, were one of his

children. She made the decision that she really didn't like him, that was until she saw the way he treated Mrs. Taylor. It was obvious to Jessie that Charles Taylor adored his wife. He hurried over to the woman's side, helped her plump up the pillows behind her head, and draped a knitted shawl over her shoulders.

Jessie could see that the blonde-haired woman, who she learned was named Mary Beth, had once been a great beauty. Her beauty still shone forth, in fact, despite the dark circles beneath her eyes, the paleness of her skin, and the thinness of her body. Her lips curved in a smile and her sunken eyes showed a slight sparkle as she looked toward Jessie.

"We are so glad to have you here, Miss Olson. It will be so good to have a woman to talk to again. Henrietta lives just far enough away that she often keeps herself a stranger. Now that I'm sick we don't see each other as often as we used to." She put her hand to her throat. "Oh, I'm sorry. Let me make the introductions. Miss Olson this is Henrietta MacQuarie."

Jessie smiled, holding out her hand to the most beautiful dark-haired woman she had ever seen. "It's a pleasure."

Henrietta MacQuarie, however, did not respond to her friendliness. Instead she looked down her nose at Jessie, much the same as if she were studying a new species of bug. "The *governess*." On her lips it sounded like an insult. "Did you get your credentials at a college?"

"College?" Jessie nodded quickly.

"Which one?"

Jessie thought quickly. "A small college in Wyoming. You probably wouldn't even recognize the name."

"Oh. . . . Well, I attended a college in the south myself." As if Jessie had suddenly disappeared she turned her attention back to Mary Beth Taylor. "As I was saying,

425

I have written letter after letter to my brother-in-law, telling him that I just can't manage the ranch alone, but he is just too stubborn to come back here. That's why I told him I'm thinking quite seriously about the idea of selling it. The only problem is that he won't agree and he, unfortunately, owns half the ranch."

"You want to live in Colorado Springs then?" Mary Beth sounded quite disappointed. "I will miss you, Henrietta. But tell me, is there a young man you've set your eye on? Is that why you want to move there so suddenly?"

Henrietta tightened her lips. "No! Most definitely not. If I ever remarry it will be to the man I should have married in the first place. Once he sees reason and comes back home where he belongs, then I'll make him realize that it makes sense."

"Then you really don't intend to part with the M bar Q?"

"Not if he comes with it." She laughed haughtily. "I'm quite certain my threatening, however, will make him think." As the clock in the hall struck nine she hastily put on her gloves. "I simply must be going now. I have to go into town to the telegraph office. I have a telegram to send." Henrietta thought how very clever she was. Corbin was a gentleman who always came to a lady's call of distress. How was he ever to know that she had set fire to the barn and some of the line shacks herself? "I'm pleading with him one last time." She nodded coldly in Jessie's direction. "I enjoyed meeting you, Miss Wilson."

"It's Watson. Jess . . ." Jessie's heart lurched as she realized her mistake. "Watson was my maiden name. Just call me Bessie. Bessie *Olson*." She watched the woman leave, thinking how true it was that a book couldn't be judged by its cover. Pretty is as pretty does, Aggie always said.

"Charles has been wonderful," Mary Beth was saying,

"but he's had so much to do that we haven't had much time to talk. Not only looking after the children but so many other chores have taken up most of his time. It does get lonely laying abed or sitting around doing nothing." She sat forward a little and looked directly into Jessie's eyes. "Time was when I could run circles around anybody here at the ranch, but not any more."

"I heard about your illness and I'm sorry." Jessie took an instant liking to the friendly, frail woman. It was a good feeling to be able to help someone who was so desperately in need of aid and companionship.

Mary Beth and Jessie talked for a long time just getting to know each other. Then Nancy came in to take her by the hand, wanting to show the new governess to her room. It was up the stairs and down the hall, close to the servants' quarters.

"This will be your room. Mine's right over there." Nancy pointed down three doors. "I wanted you near me so I can crawl in bed with you on nights when it thunders. Thunder scares me, Miss Olson." She giggled nervously. "Can I crawl in bed with you when I get scared? I used to go to Mama but I don't want to bother her now. She needs all the rest she can get. We all want her to hurry and get better."

Jessie couldn't help smiling. The child was so sincere and such an adorable little girl. "You can call on me anytime you'd like, whether you're scared or not," she said to reassure the child that she would be nearby. "That's part of my job here. To see that you, Jenny, and Arthur are well taken care of."

Nancy seemed thoughtful for just a moment. "I like you, Miss Olson. I really do. You're much nicer than that Henrietta."

"You can call me Bessie if you want to. Somehow I don't answer as promptly to Miss Olson. People have just called me Bessie all my life and Miss Olson sounds a little strange to me. I have to stop and think: hey, that's me."

They both laughed, then Nancy said, "Maybe you might want to dress up a little for supper tonight, Miss Ols . . . Bessie." Nancy corrected herself. "Daddy has invited Walt Willis to have supper with us. Well, the truth is that Walt sort of invited himself, but anyways he will be here and he sure is interested in you. Cook prepared a special dinner to welcome you to the Taylor Ranch. Mama's even going to sit at the table tonight. We want you to like it here so you will want to stay."

"Oh, Nancy. I like it here already." Jessie wasn't just trying to make the child feel good, she really did.

"Well, I gotta go. Papa wants to take you on a tour of the ranch and then you'll need to get all pretty-like. See you later, Miss . . . Ols . . . Bessie."

When she was alone in her bedroom, Jessie opened the small carpetbag and took out a change of clothes. Things had worked out so well that she nearly thought she should pinch herself to make certain she wasn't still abed at that ghastly hotel. For the first time as she looked around her, Jessie was filled with a sense of hope—yet it was tempered by the thought of Corbin, wondering how he was and hoping he was happy, and she couldn't help wondering about Henrietta MacQuarie. If she was related to Corbin, she certainly had designs on him and that didn't sit well with Jessie. Not at all.

Chapter Forty-seven

Corbin looked at the telegram and swore an oath. Certainly Henrietta was becoming a nuisance of late. Always it was the very same thing, "Come back to the M bar Q." As if he didn't have a ranch to run right here! And yet this time it did appear to be an emergency. There had been vandalism on the ranch they jointly owned. Some disgruntled ranch hand, who no doubt had suffered the barbs of Henrietta's sharp tongue. According to the telegram there had been a fire and the ranch had nearly burned down.

"Trouble, son?" Archie read his expression.

"A family matter. A sister-in-law who never ceases to be a source of irritation." A pain in the backside, he thought, but didn't say it.

"Warren's widow."

"Yes."

"Ever thought of marrying her?" Corbin would have been annoyed if it hadn't been so obvious that Archie was trying to help. "It wouldn't be the first time a widow and a man's brother tied the knot."

"Oh . . . no!" He shook his head violently. "If you had ever met Henrietta you'd know just what a bad idea that would be." He laughed. "Were she to come here she'd make Bowlegs shave off his three-day-old beard, have you wearing a tie, and put ribbons around all the cows' necks." He patted Archie on the back. "I guess I just might say that Henrietta is enough to turn a stallion into a gelding and a bull into a steer. Certainly she came close to doing that to Warren, God rest his soul."

Archie winced. "Then, by God, we don't want her here."

"Don't worry. I'm going *there* to see to a business matter. I want to keep my dear sister-in-law as far away from here as possible. You see, she's a troublemaker." Folding the telegram he put it in his pocket. "Come on, Arch. Let's go to the train station. I need to buy a ticket."

"You're going by *train?* After all that's happened to you?" Pulling his hat low over his ears as they walked along Archie gave warning. "Don't go getting shot again. If there's another train robbery don't go playin' hero."

Corbin smiled wryly. "You know, Archie, if being shot again would bring Jessie back into my life, I'd welcome the bullet."

"Still thinking about her?"

"Yes. Evening and morning, and morning and evening. She's like a familiar tune that I can't get out of my head. I loved that woman with all my heart, Archie. I really did."

"I know."

"And now I'll never see her again." Corbin tried to shake off his melancholy. "Well, we'd best get going if I plan to leave by Saturday." Corbin wanted to make the journey as quickly as possible. This time he'd go directly by train to Greeley without going by way of Denver first. This time he didn't need to visit the bank. The Rolling Q was becoming quite profitable.

"I'll go with you. I'm going to make certain it isn't a one-way ticket."

"Believe me, I'll be coming back," Corbin said adamantly. "On that you have my word."

Chapter Forty-eight

The warm morning sun teased at Jessie's eyelids until she was fully awake. Luxuriating in the feel of clean sheets and a feather mattress she stretched, sighed, and smiled. Yes siree, she thought, she was going to enjoy her stay with the Taylors. It had been relatively easy to fall into a routine. If she wasn't exactly happy because of her tortured memories of Corbin and what might have been, well, at least she was content. She hoped the job would go on for ever and ever, or at least until the children were fully grown.

With that wish in mind she was determined to succeed and so far, even Charles Taylor, who Jessie thought of as a "cold potato," had commended her. She felt a fierce burst of pride whenever she received a compliment from the icily reserved man.

The clock on the tiny table by her bed chimed six times. Stretching her arms, Jessie sat up. One thing about living in the Taylor home was that she had learned to be punctual. There was a time for this and a time for that and Charles Taylor expected everyone to be prompt.

Jessie had settled happily into what was expected of her. Up early for breakfast with the children, reading, writing and arithmetic, lunch with her wards, then an hour or so when the children were allowed to play. In the afternoon there was more study, a long walk with the children or a buggy ride, dinner and then time to do whatever she pleased before reading them a story and tucking them into bed.

Once in awhile she was called upon to do a few minor chores—setting the dinner table with silverware and napkins, or helping Mary Beth back and forth from the bedroom, but mainly her duties were the children. She was seeing to their needs so that their mother could have her rest.

Rising from the bed, she washed with water from a matching white pitcher and basin decorated with red roses. The Taylor home was a little bit like heaven, Jessie thought. All velvets, ruffles, and fresh clean linen. Everything matched, even all the cups and saucers—and not a one of them was chipped.

The Taylor home had a staff of servants to see to their every need. There was even a laundress to wash, iron, and mend. Jessie appreciated that woman's efforts now as she dressed in a crisp, starched white shirtwaist and brown twill skirt. Pulling her hair back into a dignified bun and securing it with hairpins she thought how practiced she was becoming in the art of being a lady. If only Corbin could see her now!

Jessie had only one concern: how to learn to play the piano. It was, Charles Taylor said, a skill he wanted most adamantly for his children to learn. *All* governesses knew such things, he said. He'd even sent back east for a piano which gave Jessie a bit of respite until it came to figuring how to play the dad-blamed thing. She had it in mind to spend some time on her day off going into town and seeing if one of the saloon piano players could teach her.

Taking a last look in the mirror, Jessie hurried out the door just as Nancy and Jenny came out of their bedrooms. With a giggle of greeting they each took one of her hands

432

as they walked down the stairs. Jessie really had grown to love the children. Jenny, Arthur and Nancy tugged at her heart. It was a vent for her emotions. They needed her, and most importantly, they liked her back.

When they entered the breakfast room the girls quickly took a seat beside Jessie before Arthur got the chance. It was always like that, the children clustering around her like bees to a flower.

"Ham and eggs again?" Arthur voiced his distaste.

"You will eat what is placed in front of you without disparaging comments, young man," his father scolded.

Jessie tried another approach, telling the little boy how handsome and strong he would be when he grew up if he ate what he should. Cocking his head as he thought about that, Arthur at last ate everything on his plate. Jessie suggested a buggy ride after their lessons as a reward.

"As a matter of fact, I was hoping that I could ask you to ride into town this morning," Charles said, dabbing at his mouth with a napkin. "There is a problem in the west field that I need to attend to, so I won't be able to go to the bank. The weekly payroll needs to be picked up. I'll impose on you to do so instead."

"Payroll?" The very word brought back unpleasant memories. "No, I . . . I just couldn't . . ." Things had been going so well that she just didn't want to go anywhere near the town — much less the bank, of all places.

"Why?" The word was snapped at her. Charles Taylor was not used to being thwarted.

"The . . . the children . . . and . . . and our reading . . ."

"Forget that, at least for the present." He looked at each of the children in turn. "Besides, they'll accompany you and maybe you can do a bit of studying on the way. How about it, children?"

"Yes!"

"I want to go!"

"So do I."

What else could Jessie say? Taking a letter from Mr. Taylor, which vouched for her authority to get the payroll, Jessie followed the children to the buggy.

Offering her hand first to Nancy, then to Arthur, and lastly to Jenny, she helped them climb onto the buggy seat alongside her. "Well, at least I will have some very pleasant company on the journey," she said, putting her arm around their shoulders and giving each a gentle hug. Giving the reins a not-so-gentle flick, she started the buggy off down the road.

Looking back over his shoulder, Arthur could see Walter Willis leaning on his pitchfork and gazing at them from across the creek.

"See that man back there, Miss Olson?"

Jessie glanced back, recognizing the man who had come to dinner at the Taylors' the day she'd arrived. Walt Willis was a heavy-set man with dark hair, graying at the temples, a full, dark brown mustache and close-cropped chin whiskers. He was the foreman of the neighboring ranch. "Yes, I see him. What about him, Arthur?"

"He's been askin' a lot of questions about you. Where you come from, if you are married, if you have a family. Walt-the-Watcher they call him."

The news of his asking questions about her made Jessie nervous. All she needed now that things were going so well was for someone to spill the beans. Then, remembering how obvious it had been that a bit of matchmaking had been playing the night he was their guest, she told herself that Walt was just interested in finding himself a wife. Even so, it made her more than a bit jittery on the ride into town. What would ever happen to her here if the past caught up with her?

Chapter Forty-nine

The train was excessively behind schedule, arriving at the station a full hour and a half late. At least it had arrived, however, Corbin thought as he looked out the window. It had been a long journey over mountain passes at spiraling heights, over bridges, through valleys and past boom towns, giving him a renewed look at the land he'd left behind. Now he was back, but for only as long as it took to get things flowing smoothly at the M bar Q again. He owed his brother and his parents at least that much. For love of their memory he didn't want the ranch to fail.

The crowd on the platform was thick, with people milling about as they waited to greet loved ones arriving. At first he couldn't see Henrietta and thought for a moment she hadn't come to greet him. Then he spotted her. She was dressed elaborately as usual in a large-brimmed hat with ostrich feathers, and a high-necked dress of green with a row of tiny pearl buttons from the throat to the narrow-corseted waist. Though it was not an excessively hot day she carried a fan that she tapped anxiously against her hand. Her head was held at a lofty angle as she looked this way and that for sight of Corbin.

He could tell by the expression on Henrietta's face when she saw him step off the train that there was going to be trouble. Her smile, the way she moved, the look in her eyes, the practiced way she touched at her hair all told him exactly why she had wanted him to come here. It had nothing to do with barns, burned or otherwise.

"Corbin!" She waved slightly, then catching up the hem of her dress, moved forward. Rising up on tiptoe she pressed herself against him as she kissed his cheek in greeting. "It's so good to see you, darling."

"Good to see you too, Henrietta," he answered dutifully. Corbin decided to get right to the point lest she misconstrue his coming so quickly to her call for help. "I can only stay a day or two. It's a busy time at the ranch."

"A day or two?" She was clearly disappointed and obviously a bit miffed. "Well, then that's the way it must be." She took his arm as they walked down the boardwalk. "Really, Corbin, I just can't understand why you insist on keeping that shabby little cattle ranch in Utah when you could be here seeing to the ranch your father built."

"The Rolling Q is the ranch that *I* have made prosper," he answered. "Though the M bar Q means a great deal to me, too. That's why I've come."

"I see." She sniffed disdainfully, leading him to the area where the baggage was being distributed.

"I didn't bring any baggage. Just this small carpetbag," Corbin responded, holding it up. "Now, just what is all this about sabotage? Who would have reason to want to destroy the ranch? How much damage was done and have you done anything about getting it repaired?"

She pursed her lips in annoyance. "Must we talk about that now, Corbin? I haven't seen you in quite a few months and all you can talk about is the silly old ranch."

"Silly old ranch?" Corbin's blood heated to a slow boil. "Well you didn't seem to think it was so *silly* when you wrote that telegram pleading with me to come here."

"Corbin, don't raise your voice. Everyone is staring."

436

"Let them stare." Seeing the tears that sparkled on her lashes, he quieted. Not that he was taken in by her feigned show of sorrow, no, it was just that like she he didn't want to create a scene. He did wish, however, that he had taken Archie up on his suggestion that he come with him. And yet, as gruff as Archie could pretend to be, he too would undoubtedly have come under Henrietta's spell. "All right. All right." Corbin forced a smile. "Let's declare a truce for the moment."

The tears were gone and in their place was a smile that was nearly as dazzling as the sunshine. "I had my driver bring the carriage but I had him park it quite a ways away. So you and I could be alone with our conversation." She fit her gloved hand in his to lead the way, turning for just a moment to say, "Welcome home, Corbin."

There were so many things that Corbin wanted to say to her but they died on his lips. What was the point? There was just no reasoning with Henrietta. No, the only thing to do was to see to a new barn and whatever other damage had been done and then get the hell away from her. Why was it that whenever he was anywhere near her he felt as if he were drowning, as if she would drag him down?

It seemed to be an unusually busy day in Greeley. Carriages, buggies and wagons seemed to be everywhere, congesting the road. Corbin immediately found himself longing for Rye Grass Station. Even its busiest day didn't compare with this. What made it even worse was that everyone seemed to be in such a hurry. Manners seemed to be at a premium here. Dust got into Corbin's eyes, up his nose and made him sneeze. Even so he found himself obediently following after Henrietta as she weaved back and forth in an effort to dodge each vehicle, at last crossing the road.

"There he is."

Corbin started to cross when suddenly a young woman

in a buggy caught his eye. The auburn hair, he supposed. So much like Jessie's. Then suddenly the young woman turned around to talk to the child beside her and Corbin's heart stopped for an instant and then seemed to spin. It was Jessie! The very sight of her made him lose his head. Forgetting everything but the need to catch up with her, he ran after the buggy.

"Jessie! Jessie!" He might have thought it to be a case of mistaken identity had she not reacted to the sound of her name. For just a moment their eyes met, then she looked away.

"Corbin! Really. What do you think you are doing?" Henrietta was in a huff. "Chasing after some woman that way." Her eyes narrowed to jealous slits. "She's only a governess, I dare say."

"Governess?"

"Mary Beth Taylor has taken ill and has hired that young woman to aid her with the children. Bonnie Wilson, or Bessie Wilson, or Olson—or something like that is her name. Though I heard you call her Jessie."

Corbin was wary. "For a moment I thought I knew her." Chasing him had upended her hat and now she paused to straighten it. "You remember Mary Beth, don't you?"

"Mary Beth? Yes. I was at her wedding. The oddest match of the decade and yet it seems to have lasted." How he spoke coherently, Corbin didn't know. All he could think was that Jessie was here! Here, where he had least expected to find her. It was like the answer to a prayer and he found his eyes traveling up to the sky. Tonight, as soon as he was settled in at the ranch, he was going to make a little call.

Chapter Fifty

It wasn't like Jessie to go to bed so early, without first reading a story to the children, but after seeing Corbin in town this morning she had needed her solitude. Corbin was here! His name sang in her heart. Corbin. Corbin. He was Henrietta MacQuarie's brother-in-law. The one thing that she had hoped for, longed for, had come to pass. Corbin had come, though for what reason she didn't really know.

"Corbin. . . ." she whispered, feeling a sinking feeling in the pit of her stomach. A twinge of jealousy intruded on her happiness. He had been with *that* woman. That haughty, strutting woman. Just the thought of it caused Jessie pain.

She remembered again Henrietta's comment to Mary Beth, that she wanted to marry the man she "should have married in the first place." All too painfully Jessie realized she was right, that the man Henrietta had been talking about was Corbin. Oh, dear God, was that why he was here? To marry his brother's widow? That thought pained her so much she could hardly breathe.

If only that woman hadn't been so very beautiful. A perfect lady who looked as if she never even sneezed. What chance did Jessie have against her wiles? She would bet her bottom dollar that Henrietta MacQuarie didn't have a price on her head. And yet perhaps there was still a chance that he still cared for her, Jessie thought. Hell, she wouldn't give up without a fight. That just wasn't her way. She wouldn't give him to that uppity snob!

"Miss Olson. Miss Olson." Nancy's voice was accompanied by a soft knocking. "Are you feeling better?"

"A little. I'm just tired, dear. It has been such a long day." A long day, Jessie thought. That was an understatement. At that moment when she'd looked into Corbin's eyes she had feared that she would faint. She'd wanted to throw herself into his arms and might have had it not been for the dark-haired woman accompanying him.

"A man in a gray pinstriped suit was here to see you, Miss Olson, but Papa sent him away."

Nancy's words worked their way through the fog in Jessie's brain. What was she saying? "Here?"

"He was asking for Jessie. Papa said he must have made a mistake . . ."

"And he sent him away?" Corbin was here and now he was gone. She bounded out of bed, dressing as quickly as she could in a brown skirt, blouse and jacket, pulling on boots. She had to catch up with him. Dear God, Corbin had been here!

Like a bolt of lightning Jessie was out of the door, running down the stairs so quickly she nearly tripped and fell head over heels. Regaining her balance she nearly flew to the front door.

"Nancy, I'm going to borrow a horse from the stables," she called over her shoulder.

She ran frantically to the stables, harnessing the first horse she came to, swearing as her hands shook while she cinched the saddle. At last in a burst of impatience she pulled the saddle off and climbed upon the mare to ride bareback.

She nudged the sorrel mare out of the stables, moving down the pathway toward the MacQuarie side of the river. If she remembered correctly there was a bridge right beyond those trees.

A full moon looked like a bright, shiny coin balanced on the horizon, lighting Jessie's way. Passing over the bridge she headed for the ranch house, yet when she got there she was suddenly shy. For a long moment she just sat there staring at the glow of lamplight coming from the windows. Then such a sudden urge to touch Corbin, to be in his arms, spurred her on. Gathering up her courage she dismounted, tied the sorrel's reins to a tree and walked up the steps of the porch. Raising her hand she knocked, but instead of Corbin answering the door it was Henrietta.

"Yes?"

"I want to see Corbin, please."

The woman's face hardened into a mask. "Corbin isn't here."

For just a moment Jessie thought that she was lying until she spotted him walking up the path, his masculine form haloed by the moonlight. Calling out his name, Jessie ran forward and into his arms.

"Jessie! Oh, Jessie, it is you." His hands tangled in her hair as he kissed her deeply, drinking in her sweetness. He murmured her name over and over again as he wrapped his arms around her.

"Are you glad to see me?"

"Glad? It's like the answer to my dreams." Seeing Henrietta in the doorway and wanting privacy in their reunion, Corbin took Jessie's hand and headed toward the stables. Jessie walked beside him, listening to the frantic clamor of her heart. Then they were alone.

"Jessie. . . ." He leaned against the heavy timbers of an empty stall taking her with him. "Right now all I want to do is to kiss you and kiss you and. . . ." He made good on

441

his word, kissing her with a hunger that made her tingle all the way down to her toes. Snuggling in the warmth of his arms she felt his heart beating as wildly as her own.

"I thought maybe you came all the way to Colorado just to see that widow," Jessie said softly. "Did you, Corbin?"

He growled low in his throat and purposefully tickled her ear with his warm breath. "What do you think?"

"I think you didn't. But why are you here?"

"Business. Someone burned down the barn and Henrietta begged me to come and see to the ranch. You see, Jessie, perhaps I haven't been quite honest with you. I know how you resent those who you call 'cattle barons.' Well, I'm such a man. My father founded this ranch and when he died he left it to me and to my brother. That makes Henrietta and me partners now that Warren is dead."

She stroked his hair. "A cattle baron, huh?" She laughed. "I don't care. I love you even if you are rich." Her breasts touched his chest as she moved closer.

"Oh, God, but am I glad I did come. Otherwise I might never have seen you again, Jess." He buried his face in the fragrance of her hair. At least for that he could be thankful to Henrietta. "Jessie, I should never have blamed you in any way for my brother's death. I was a fool, blinded by my prejudice. The truth is Art Conners was a cattle rustler, blaming his misdeeds on your friend Butch's gang. He . . . he killed my brother."

"The sheriff? After what he did to me, putting me in jail that way?" She was outraged. "Why that dirty, low-down polecat."

"I found out in town when I got my tickets at the train station that you had given back the money from that train robbery. I'm proud of you, Jess."

"I guess I just don't make a very good *outlaw* now that I've found you, Corbin." She smiled against his lips, but the very mention of it was a painful memory.

"Marry me, Jessie! Jessie Watson, I want you for my wife."

She shook her head. "How can I, Corbin, when I'm still wanted for that Pleasant Valley Coal Company robbery? Who is going to believe I didn't do it?"

"We'll work it all out. I just want to be at your side. Please, Jessie. Please!" He placed one hand against the wooden wall beside her shoulder. With the other he let his fingers run through her hair with a stroking motion that was pure delight. "Marry me!" His voice was soft and persuasive, as if she needed any prodding.

"Yes! Oh, yes!" Suddenly the future seemed bright again as he swept her into his arms.

They didn't see Henrietta standing in the doorway, her face frozen in outraged anger. Why, he's in love with that little nobody, she thought, the gorge rising in her throat to choke her. An outlaw, or so they both had said. Jessie Watson. Jessie Watson. She must remember that name.

"We'll have the wedding we should have had before, Jessie. I'll invite people from miles around just to show them you're my girl forever. . . ." Corbin was saying.

Wedding? Henrietta shook her head. Not if she had her way. First thing in the morning she'd ride into town for the marshal and then just see what happened after that.

Chapter Fifty-one

It should have been the happiest moment in Jessie's life but what followed was a nightmare beginning the very next morning after seeing Corbin. She had no sooner revealed to the Taylors that she was getting married then a loud pounding shook the door.

"What in the world . . . ?" With an indignant huff, Charles Taylor opened the door. Three men with glittering badges pushed their way into the room past him.

"We're looking for a woman named Jessica Watson," one man said.

"There isn't anyone here by that name," Nancy called out, peeking from around the corner.

"Jessie . . . Bessie . . . the same thing." Striding into the room he caught sight of Jessie and something in her expression gave her away. "Yeh, this one's her. I remember seeing a wanted poster. They call her the 'renegade angel.' "

From that moment on it seemed as if Jessie were walking through the mists of a bad dream. She had been reunited with Corbin but at a treacherous price. Having escaped from prison only added to the list of crimes she was said to have committed. Shackled to the marshal and his deputy at the train station, it didn't take her long to realize who was responsible. Henrietta MacQuarie's self-congratulating smile as she stood on the platform gave her away. Jessie realized she was going to pay very dearly for Corbin's love yet even so she would not have traded even one of his kisses for her freedom.

What made hurt her heart ache, however, was that she didn't even have time to say goodbye before she went journeying by train from Greeley to Price, where she was to be incarcerated and the trial was to take place.

"I won't let anything happen to you, Jessie," Corbin promised. She almost believed him.

The trial was short and sweet. What touched Jessica's heart most of all was that Corbin stepped forward as a witness in her defense, telling about her rescue of him, her tender care. He even confessed to having been the one to let her out of Art Conners' prison in spite of what it might have cost him. He brought with him Charles Taylor, who gave testimony of how he had sent her on an errand to retrieve his payroll and that she had returned with every penny. Those were hardly the actions of a thief.

"She could have run away with that payroll," he said, "and lived quite well for a long, long time; and yet I don't believe she was even tempted. A thief? No. I consider myself a good judge of character and I believe her to be a fine young woman."

Archie stood up in her behalf, and Bowlegs, indeed, all the friends she'd made at the Rolling Q ranch. Most importantly, however, was the stationmaster's testimony that Jessie had given back some money. "From a train robbery," he stated.

Several people Jessie had met along the way to Colorado all spoke highly of her, told of how hard she had worked and of her honesty. Even the man at whose eatery she had made biscuits spoke out on her side. But it was Butch's testimony that saved the day. Dictated to his lawyer, it declared in bold words that Jessie Watson was innocent of the coal company payroll robbery. She had, as it said, merely come along to preach to the others about the error of their ways. The deposition was signed in Butch's sprawling hand.

The jury debated for less than ten minutes, and when they returned, a verdict of not guilty was read. *Not guilty.* At last Jessie knew she was really free. What might have ended in a great sadness now ended in a triumph.

She looked up to see Corbin coming toward her. Then he was in front of her, his face a mixture of worry and of love. Then wordlessly he gathered her into his arms. "I do love you so, Jess," he said at last. "More than anything in the world I want you to be my wife."

How could she say anything but yes? She kissed him and caressed him and murured over again how much she loved him. "Mrs. Corbin MacQuarie," she whispered. As they left the courtroom, Jessica viewed a sunset. A tentative smile touched her lips as hope sparked within her. A chapter of her life was ending — but a new one was just beginning.